ATTACK ON BOREDOM

A Collection of Twenty Sci-Fi & Fantasy
Stories

L. B. Spillers

L. B. Spillers

L. B. Spillers

CONTENTS

L. B. Spillers

Golden Cuckoo

Cheryl hung her purse under the bar before sliding into her seat. Seeing a text from her friend Janet, she sighed. Janet wouldn't be joining her. It was one final disappointment in a day plagued by them. Since she was already there, she decided to have her favorite martini before heading home.

As she watched the bartender making her drink, a male voice addressed her from behind. "Rough day?"

Turning her head to glance at the man, she resisted the urge to laugh. One of the financial district's aging frat boys stood behind her in his bespoke suit. His face blazed with a sense of entitlement.

"No one likes a lurker," Cheryl said, turning back to the bar.

Uninvited, he took the seat to her right as the bartender approached with her drink.

"Let me make it up to you." He gestured to the bartender.

"Compliments of Mr. Jaeger," the bartender said, setting her drink down.

Cheryl savored a sip before giving her cocksure interloper a proper looking over. He paused for a moment, posing for her inspection. There was an honesty to it she appreciated. He was fit, handsome, and adorned in a few thousand dollars of tailored clothing. She usually liked to sort through finance types by looking at their shoes, but this guy's diamond-studded Audemars Piguet wristwatch was the tell. He was beyond rich.

"Jaeger?" she asked. The name rang a bell, but it took a moment to recall why. An elite salesperson, she prided herself on never forgetting a name. "You bought me that glass of port three weeks ago before my friend Janet ran you off." It was hard to forget a five-hundred-dollar pour.

Jaeger smiled. "That's right. She seemed upset that I was paying more attention to you."

Cheryl chuckled and settled in for some small talk. Half an hour later they were both still interested, he was still charming and good looking, and her judgment was two martinis weaker. So, she pulled out her phone, opened the Compati-App, and set it on the bar between them. It displayed the left side of an outline of a cartoon heart.

Jaeger raised an eyebrow before setting his phone next to hers. The right side of the heart outline filled its screen. The two phones began swapping data. The first chime indicated she was verifiably free of sexually transmittable diseases. The next chime on the scale indicated he too was clean. Animation on both their phones started to color the heart blood red. The third chime signaled their birth control preferences didn't clash. A final trill crescendoed as the two half-hearts filled in, indicating their profiles were fully compatible.

———

Two weeks later, Jaeger was a faded memory. Cheryl's Compati-App preferences had indicated she didn't want any follow-up, but part of her was disappointed he hadn't broken the rules. She wasn't interested in Jaeger, but his compliance made her feel like she was losing her appeal.

Taking the elevator to her apartment, her phone chimed an alert from the building's entry scanner informing her of a health change it detected: she was pregnant. Suddenly self-conscious in the crowded elevator, she pressed against the back wall, staring at the message. Her contraception implant made pregnancy impossible.

Cheryl stayed in the elevator, riding it back down to take a car to the nearest testing facility. She asked for all the STD tests in addition to a more definitive pregnancy test.

As she took her seat in the waiting room, an image of her mother flashed in her mind: drunk, holding her cigarette up near her face, snidely berating Cheryl. Her head wobbled mockingly as her words cut into Cheryl, finally thrusting her chin forward to emphasize the last one—whore.

Looking around the waiting room, Cheryl took in the clientele. Most were ten years younger and draped in clothing Cheryl wouldn't be caught painting in. When her more rational self interrupted her condescension to remind her why she was there, the scream that had been building within her nearly escaped. Instead, she clutched her purse tightly and giggled quietly like a madwoman. No one seemed to notice.

To distract herself from the wait, she harangued her gynecologist's office into giving her an emergency appointment.

———

Are you ready to be a parent? Come to CrècheCert to find out. Initial testing is free. If you pass, you'll leave with the peace of mind that comes from knowing you're qualified to be a parent. But if you don't, we will get you trained up so you can crush those parenting tests. You didn't come this far in life just to let strangers raise your child, did you? Be certain with CrècheCert.

Cheryl snorted at the piped-in advertisement even as the marketing professional in her admired its precise targeting.

She waited in a treatment room for Dr. Bisson. For the last ten minutes, she had listened to her doctor's muffled conversations in the hallway; there was a problem with her vacation booking, and a Mrs. Jobel had been irritating the front office staff enough that they were considering kicking her off the service.

After what felt like an eternity, she heard the obligatory two knocks before Dr. Bisson stepped into the room.

"There's no mistake," her doctor said, forcing a smile. "You're pregnant."

Cheryl saw a micro-expression of annoyance flicker across the woman's face as she said the word. They had crammed Cheryl into her busy schedule, and now she would be burdened with time-consuming counseling. The doctor sat down on her stool before continuing.

"The law requires me to counsel you on your options and obligations." She tapped on her tablet, apparently calling up a script. "Your profile indicates—"

Shaking her head, Cheryl cut her off. "No. I want an abortion. If you would just register the pregnancy, I'll run through the counseling online. That'll save us both time."

The doctor smiled just enough to show her appreciation without seeming glad Cheryl was terminating a pregnancy.

Tapping on her computer again, the doctor said, "Okay. Jumping ahead, let's check the father's profile." The pregnancy test automatically included a DNA analysis to determine the father's identity and prescreen for genetic abnormalities.

Dr. Bisson mouthed a silent "Oh" before she continued. "I've registered the pregnancy, but you're legally prevented from terminating it. The father has an injunction."

Cheryl's mouth fell open as the words sank in. She had spent ten intense years building her career to the edge of a breakthrough into upper management. It was exactly the wrong time for her to have a child.

The doctor filled the awkward silence. "On the upside, your boy's genetic profile is astonishing. His projected aptitude, athleticism, and health are all in the top percentile. I'm guessing this guy is a Golden Cuckoo who targeted you because your DNA profile complements his."

Dropping her head, Cheryl groaned. She had heard the term, but it was always something that happened in China or Saudi Arabia where there was a surfeit of super-wealthy chauvinistic men. Under the right legal circumstances, they could force a woman to carry their child to term. Yes, women had a right to choose, but men did too. All they needed to force the issue were very deep pockets.

Suddenly inspired, Cheryl's eyes went wide. Sitting up

straight, she asked, "What about the exception for faulty birth control?" To Cheryl, abortion was the recourse of ignorant, careless women, yet here she was desperately angling for one. Tears brimmed her eyes.

Seeming happy to have something to do besides facing her teary patient, the doctor rolled her stool to a nearby drawer from which she pulled out a handheld scanner and held it near Cheryl's abdomen.

After a few moments, the scanner chimed.

Her doctor sighed. "The log indicates you turned your implant off five weeks ago."

"What?!" Cheryl yelled, jumping to her feet. She pulled the scanner from the doctor's hands. "I would never..."

"How?" she asked as she handed it back to the doctor.

The doctor put her hands up and shook her head. "That's something I have no business speculating about. I'm sorry this pregnancy is unwelcome news to you. Do you have any other concerns today?"

Cheryl heard in her tone that it was time to get out of the office. Dr. Bisson had done Cheryl a favor fitting her into her schedule on almost no notice, and now it turned out that rather than a crisis, what Cheryl had was a severe case of carelessness stacked on stupidity. They were done.

———

That night, Cheryl did the online pregnancy counseling. Failure to do so would mark her as a disinterested parent. Anticipating some kind of legal scuffle with Jaeger, the last thing she wanted was to give his lawyers ammunition.

What Cheryl knew about child-rearing law were dribs and drabs absorbed from popular entertainment and anecdotes from friends and family. Unless you were super-rich, your baby would be part of a crèche. The dramas were usually about getting your baby into the right crèche or having your interactions restricted because of your potential bad influence.

And God forbid your baby be assigned to a public crèche.

The counseling consisted of a half-hour tutorial on how state and federal law combined to establish the rules governing child-rearing in New York City. It came down to two things: the parents' financial status and their certifications. Parents who didn't make enough to put their child in a private crèche were forced to use subsidized public ones. Those parents who couldn't even afford the subsidized crèche fees would be kept from having more children—sterilized.

She passed the exam easily. The faint tingle her bureaucratic compliance gave her was quickly quashed by a series of other counseling recommendations that hit her email only moments later. She sighed at the titles: Pre-Natal Nutrition, Work and Pregnancy, and Exercise and Pregnancy.

Realizing she knew next to nothing about those topics made her feel obligated to educate herself. More and more of her brain was being subordinated to her baby. Her singular career focus was fraying.

Clueless about pregnancy as she was, she knew the wining part of wining and dining prospective clients was out the window. And how soon would it be until her looks—she was an NYC nine—suffered? How would her bloated self fare selling to sober clients? That's not to mention what it would do to her promotion chances in an industry that ran on image.

Her eyes flicked to the wine fridge under her kitchen counter. A groan escaped her as she lowered her cheek to the cool granite countertop.

Cheryl's granite therapy was interrupted by her phone. The caller ID read: Jaeger Enterprises.

She was in no mood to talk to him, but clinging to the hope that she could convince him to pull his injunction, she answered the call. "Yes?"

"My name is Jameson, Mr. Jaeger's attorney."

Cheryl stood up, laughing at the absurdity of it. "Nothing

like the personal touch, eh? What occasions your call, Mr. Jameson?"

There was an uncomfortable pause before Jameson replied. "As you've discovered, Mr. Jaeger's moral convictions—"

"Mr. Jameson." Cheryl wasn't willing to listen to how Jaeger was a moral paragon. "Do you know what I was doing when my contraception implant logged a change of configuration? I had just drunk a marvelous glass of port magnanimously provided by your employer. Just the one, mind you. It wasn't until weeks later when I was fertile again that he returned to make the effort to bed me."

"That sounds close to an accusation. Let's have no more aspersions against my client. I called because he has an offer for you."

Cheryl chuckled sourly. "Jameson, your client just enslaved me to bear his child. Other than lifting the injunction, what can he possibly offer me?"

Jameson made her wait for his response. Cheryl recognized the tactic: Always slow down an emotional conversation.

"Money," Jameson finally said, inserting another maddening pause before continuing. "He'll pay you to relinquish all your parental rights. Considering you want to kill the boy, I imagine you'd be happy for the chance to wash your hands of him."

Saying that her fetus was a boy she wanted to kill came close to breaking Cheryl's composure. She grudgingly admitted to herself that the lawyer had a talent for weaponizing words.

Cheryl let Jameson chew on silence for a few seconds before answering. "Mr. Jameson, I'm not for sale." She ended the call.

Scrolling through her phone's personal contacts, she looked for someone to talk to.

Calling her mother was out of the question. She'd have to tell her sometime, but it had taken years to settle their relationship into a kind of benign neglect. There were too many old wounds her mother would gleefully rip open while posing as a supportive grandmother-to-be.

Janet was also out of the question. To her, discretion wasn't a question of respecting someone's privacy but rather what spin to put on that person's secrets as she broadcast them to anyone interested.

Reaching the end of the list, Cheryl sighed as she realized she didn't have a proper confidante in her life. Then again, was there really anything to talk about yet? Her body might naturally reject the fetus for any number of reasons in the first ten weeks. Aged thirty-six, her womb's ability to carry a baby to term was fading fast, as her mother was so fond of reminding her.

In the meantime, diligently training to be a good parent would both soothe her conscience and make her look more sympathetic to a judge.

———

Cheryl found the CrècheCert center a surprisingly pleasant space. Bright and airy, the lobby was decorated in soft colors. Pregnancy-friendly chairs with higher seat heights were interspersed among comfy couches. Fashionable beverages peeked out of a glass-fronted refrigerator, topped with baskets of snacks. Barely audible mood music wafted through the space.

As she planted her still-taut ass in a comfortable chair, she had to admit that her only complaint was the overly solicitous staff. Their saccharine sweetness reminded her of Los Angeles where everyone hid behind a sheen of gentility. She preferred New York City's usual brusqueness.

On the upside, the still-silent Mr. Jaeger, through his lawyer factotum, had paid for her certification course. She had also been provided unlimited accounts at the best local grocery store as well as the GrubMe app. Coerced and violated as she felt, the sharp edge of her anger was blunted by Jaeger's open-ended financial support.

A heavily pregnant woman plopped down on the plush chair across from her. Cheryl gave her one of those carefully attenuated subway smiles that conveyed nominal friendliness with an undertone of don't-talk-to-me.

"Oh, hello! You must be Cheryl. I'm Rhonda. We're in the same class."

Cheryl's smart-ass reply drowned in her confusion over how this random woman knew her name. "Should I know you?" Cheryl asked slowly.

Closer inspection revealed that Rhonda had put on thirty more pounds than pregnancy allowed for. Evidence of former prettiness could be seen in her fleshy face but Cheryl was shocked at how much of that extra weight had landed in the woman's boobs. Surely that wouldn't happen to her.

"Oh," Rhonda said. "I thought I had sent you an invite. I'm on the crèche board." She looked at her phone and frowned. After a few taps, Cheryl's phone beeped. "I took the time to write it but never sent it. How ditzy, right?" Her turgid belly convulsed in chuckling for a few moments before she added, "Pregnancy has turned me into a complete scatterbrain."

Cheryl's irritation was melting in the face of Rhonda's sloppy charm. After scanning the email, she accepted the invitation and was sent to the website of Jaeger's private crèche. Their very professional-looking homepage showed a glamour shot of a lovely Westchester mansion. Underneath that was what looked like a preschool class photo.

Cheryl looked up at Rhonda. "I don't understand, Rhonda. I thought Jaeger had a private crèche. This one looks a lot bigger than I expected."

Rhonda gave Cheryl an impish grin. "They're all his!" She patted her belly. "I'm about to give birth to his eighteenth child. You are carrying the nineteenth! Your child will grow up in luxury with all those brothers and sisters."

Nineteenth? Cheryl considered Jaeger a monster for what

he did to her, but the idea that he'd done it to eighteen other women staggered her.

Forcing a smile, Cheryl asked, "So, Rhonda, how are you on the crèche board if you're not already certified?"

Rhonda shrugged. "It comes with a big salary." Shifting her massive bulk in the upholstery that seemed determined to swallow her, Rhonda grunted. "He is a supreme asshole, but he's not cheap or stupid. He's got nineteen baby mamas—sorry eighteen, one died—seething about having their birth control hacked. Money goes a long way to softening their anger."

Cheryl was heartened that Rhonda was much savvier than she appeared. Already she felt a trickle of camaraderie.

"Why doesn't he just hire surrogate mothers?" Cheryl asked. "He's got the money. Why hack our birth control?"

"I think it's about our DNA," Rhonda said. "All the kids' genetic profiles are amazing. He hunts for women whose genes are complementary to his. Knowing most women wouldn't willingly donate eggs or carry his child, he takes what he wants. I certainly wouldn't have borne him a child for money. Would you?"

"Hell no," Cheryl said, frowning. Rhonda's DNA theory made sense, but she suspected beyond that rationale Jaeger got some kind of thrill out of hunting all his baby mommas like prey.

"We're caught, Cheryl." Rhonda shifted in her plush seat. "The law is on his side. So do we use his awesome crèche or piss away money on a losing legal battle to then raise our children in relative poverty? Is your pride more important than the benefits to your child?"

Cheryl nodded slowly. "Meanwhile we might as well get trained up on his dime."

"Welcome to the gilded cage, Cheryl."

———

Muffled medical alarms chimed in the background as

Cheryl surfaced to consciousness. Jostling of her hospital bed told her she was on the move.

When she was days from delivery, Cheryl had moved into a birthing suite at Columbia Presbyterian Hospital, essentially a luxury studio apartment with a dedicated delivery room attached. Jaeger's people, besides paying for the suite, had hired a matronly nurse to assist her.

"It's time, dear," the older nurse said. "Everything looks good. We're moving you to the delivery room."

"I don't feel right," Cheryl said, raising a hand to her face. The IV line attached to her arm startled her. "When did you put that in?"

"About five minutes ago," the nurse said, angling the bed through a doorway. "The drugs are making you a little foggy. Don't worry, you're getting the best care money can buy."

Cheryl focused on the nurse's voice, trying to tease out every last bit of nuance as if there was something to negotiate. After a few moments, she smiled at her own stubbornness. Whatever they had doped her up with had made her thinking sluggish and her outlook optimistic.

"I hope so because I'm barely able to string two thoughts together." Cheryl glanced at the empty visitors' chairs. What about the caring that money couldn't buy?

Following her gaze, the nurse asked, "Do you want me to call someone?"

"No, thank you." Maternal détente had lasted about a month before her mother's toxicity had reasserted itself.

A final jostling and the telltale clicks of her bed's wheel locks sent Cheryl's pulse racing.

"Try not to freak out." A masked face came into view from behind her head. "I'm Doctor Posner, your anesthesiologist. Your OB/GYN is in the office next door. She'll be here in a minute."

"Aren't you a little early?" Cheryl asked. "I haven't even had a contraction yet."

Dr. Posner nodded. "I'm double-boarded in nano-tech. My little friends are doing the nano-episiotomy."

"Already?" Cheryl asked.

"Oh yes," he said. "My guys need a little lead time to get set up. If we wait too long, you'll be stuck with an old-fashioned scalpel job."

"The nanites are fantastic," the nurse spoke up. "You'll be mostly healed four hours postpartum." The older woman looked around conspiratorially before leaning in to whisper, "And your hooha won't be a subway tunnel when it's all over."

Cheryl snorted a giggle.

Moments later when Dr. Bisson, came in, Cheryl asked, "Hey, Doc! Is it true you're gonna get Junior out without turning my lady bits into a subway tunnel?"

Dr. Bisson smiled while reaching for a mask. "That's not exactly what the brochure says, but you'll definitely be in better shape down there than the rest of us."

After steeling herself for an hours-long trial, Cheryl found the half-hour delivery much less brutal than expected. The combination of drugs and Dr. Posner's nanite "zipper", as he called it, made her boy's emergence into the world quite anti-climactic. The most disturbing bit was passing the placenta. Her doctor matter-of-factly pulled the blob out of her and spent a few minutes tinkering between her legs, calling for instruments like a bored mechanic.

"I'll be damned, Alan," Dr. Bisson said. "If I didn't know better, I'd say the incision was a week old. There isn't a spot of hemorrhaging." She shook her head. "Yay for little robots, I guess."

Looking around the room, Cheryl noticed the crowd had thinned, leaving her alone with the two doctors. "Where's Arman?" she asked, suddenly paranoid that Jaeger's people might have whisked her boy away.

L. B. Spillers

Doctor Bisson stood and took off her surgical cap. "He'll be right back. They're cleaning him up, giving him a shot, some ointment for his eyes, and checking him out. Remember? We talked about this. Standard operating procedure. Your boy is as healthy as any I've delivered."

Dr. Posner came around to the foot of the bed. "Scope me some pictures, please, Edna."

"Already on the monitor," she said. "This'll be a godsend when the price comes down to something normal people can afford."

"My job here is done," Dr. Posner said. He bowed to Cheryl with a flourish before leaving the room.

Dr. Bisson harrumphed. "He's going to be insufferable. Master of the new new thing. Boys and their goddamn toys. I prefer my anesthesiologists quiet and humble."

Despite all her studying, Cheryl wasn't prepared for the experience of meeting her son. As a nurse approached with him—considerably cleaner—his newborn eyes couldn't focus on Cheryl. Guilt welled in her as she saw how perfect he was. She was certain that he had sensed her reluctance to bear him. He would resent her, reject her. But the moment he was placed on her chest, his guileless face smiled, seeming to recognize her. As Cheryl touched his head he cooed. Her heart filled with adoration.

Cheryl immediately started bawling. After a few moments, she said through her sobs, "I can't stop crying!"

"Don't worry about it," Dr. Bisson said, smiling. "Some new moms react this way. Just mind that you handle him gently. Let it out. I'm happy to see it." The doctor brushed some of Cheryl's hair back. "I was worried about you, but now I see the mom behind that hard front you put up."

———

Friday evening, after a hard week of getting back to work, Cheryl's nerves were up as her autocab approached the crèche's gates. She had been haunted by the idea that Arman wouldn't recognize her after five days apart. Even as she sat there telling herself it was a silly thing to worry about, she fought the urge to cry.

Physically she wasn't much better. Even with the nano-episiotomy, her body still needed time to recover from giving birth. She had also underestimated the difficulties of supplying the crèche with her breast milk while working full time.

Ironically, she was riding a wave of career satisfaction. Her boss had informed her that he was leaving and she was the front-runner to replace him. It had almost justified going back to work so early.

The car didn't even slow as it approached the opening crèche gates. The previous Sunday afternoon when she dropped off Arman, they remained closed until a member of the staff had made the long walk down the driveway and given Cheryl and Arman a final bureaucratic blessing.

"What a difference a few days make," she muttered.

Her phone spoke, startling her. "The autocab system transmits the ID of its occupants to security checkpoints. You're authorized in our system, free to come and go as you please, Cheryl."

Her annoyance at her phone being hijacked was blunted by the patient, almost fatherly tone of voice. She wasn't certain if it was a person or a computer. Cheryl stared at the time and weather on the lock screen. "How did you—"

"I'm speaking to you through the crèche app you installed on your phone. You need only address me as Crèche. If I can hear you, I'll respond."

Rhonda was standing on the front steps waiting when Cheryl pulled up to the mansion. When she saw Rhonda's gleeful face, Cheryl felt a twinge of guilt. She hadn't made any effort to stay in touch.

As Cheryl stepped out of her cab, Rhonda rushed to hug

her. "Oh my god, Cheryl, you bitch! Your stomach has snapped back like a goddamn rubber band!"

"I appreciate the personal touch," Cheryl said, surprised that she meant it. "Apparently, the crèche AI was ready to take me under its wing."

"Yeah, Crèche is a sweetheart," Rhonda said, as she grabbed Cheryl's rolling luggage from the car's trunk. "He's not one of those clunky, soulless jobs that they taught us about in class."

Cheryl fell in behind Rhonda. "Yeah, I bet." To Cheryl, Crèche represented continuous, pervasive surveillance. If Jaeger was the enemy, then Crèche was too.

As they navigated the massive house's hallways, Rhonda briefed Cheryl. "Seven of the moms gave up custody to Jaeger," Rhonda told her. "For a payout, of course. Another five live too far away to visit very often. Four more live in Westchester and take their kids home for visits, including me. One died. One has a restraining order against her—long story. Then there's you, super mom, who already has a level three cert. Very impressive, by the way."

———

The next morning, breakfast was delivered to Cheryl on her suite's south-facing balcony where she was nursing Arman. The sight of the rolling lawn, with its perfectly maintained trees and flower gardens, soothed her sleep-deprived brain. Already the memory of getting up every few hours last night to feed Arman was fading.

A soft chime interrupted Cheryl's idyllic moment.

"Yes, Crèche?"

"His diaper needs changing."

Cheryl bit back a sharp reply. They'd been through this last night. Cheryl's protest that one shouldn't interrupt feeding for a diaper change was met with the AI assertion that Arman was done feeding. His algorithm involving the ratio of sucking to swallowing and a bunch of other little tells was apparently infallible. After Arman's second nocturnal feeding, she had stopped questioning the AI.

She changed Arman's diaper and took him downstairs to the playroom. Cheryl had expected the best of everything, but couldn't get over how clean and shiny it all was.

Arman was too young for serious interactive play, so Cheryl set him in the playpen. Work had run her ragged all week, so despite her paranoia about the AI spying on her, she was grateful its constant vigilance allowed her to relax. Within a minute of taking a seat by the enormous window, she was snoring lightly.

The noise of an attendant pushing a stroller in the hallway brought Cheryl instantly alert. "Crèche, what's Araman's status?"

"He's been dozing for most of the twenty-one minutes you've been sleeping. His diaper is dry and his vitals are excellent."

Cheryl checked on Arman anyway. When she saw the little pool of drool he'd deposited on the padded playpen floor, she started going through the sideboard's drawers looking for a towel. Before eventually finding one, she stumbled upon a security badge in one of the drawers.

After she wiped up Arman's puddle, she held up the badge, addressing the AI. "Crèche, I found someone's ID badge. Where should I turn it in?"

"That's not one of ours. The crèche doesn't occupy the entire structure. The rest has its own security system. Don't worry about turning it in. It's probably deactivated."

The idea of some part of the house Crèche didn't monitor disturbed her. "How can I make sure?" Cheryl asked.

"East wall bookcase, left side. Wave the card near the wall."

Cheryl walked to the bookcase. Her badge dance was rewarded with a click before the bookcase slowly opened outward like a door.

"I advise against going in," Crèche said. "I can't monitor you there."

Ignoring Crèche, she walked into the hidden room. The door closed behind her. The industrial room was an architectural dead space with oddly angled sections of ceiling. Its walls were peppered with electrical conduits, some of which ran to a server cage. Far from reassured, Cheryl saw the hidden room with its rack of computers as a bomb in the heart of the mansion where Arman was being raised.

Unusual wear on part of the floor's linoleum squares caught her eye. On a hunch, she waved the badge around it. A four-square chunk of the floor slid down and sideways to reveal a ladder.

The room below was a surveillance nest. Nine large plasma screens were arrayed around a desk in a semi-circle. Cheryl's hand hovered near the computer mouse, wondering what using the computer might trigger. A heavy layer of dust on the mouse reassured her.

Her touch activated the screens. Each of the large monitors displayed six different cameras around the mansion. Rhonda was getting dressed on one of them. Stepping back, Cheryl pulled out her phone to take a picture of the setup.

Worried that she may have triggered some kind of alarm, Cheryl rushed to explore the rest of the space. Sweeping her phone flashlight around the room she found a tunnel entrance to the left of the desk.

To the right was a plain steel door with a security pad. When she waved the stolen ID card in front of that pad, the door unlocked.

The small storage room was lined with metal shelving containing an eclectic collection of boxes, devices, and tools. She gasped when she saw a box of bright-red medical nanite tubes. Not believing her eyes, she first thought they were compact flashlights. When she got closer, there was no mistaking the bio-hazard glyph in a yellow triangle on the end of each one.

Her picture of the surveillance nest couldn't prove much, but a nanite harness was something. She pocketed one of the tubes before rushing back up the ladder to the crèche.

———

When Cheryl emerged from behind the bookcase into the playroom, Rhonda was standing near the playpen with her crying girl in her arms. Facing away, she didn't hear the bookcase door over the sound of her baby's fussing.

Cheryl walked quietly over to Rhonda. "Good morning, Rhonda."

"Aaaah!" Rhonda startled. Her girl, now distracted, stopped crying. "I thought we were alone."

Smiling, Cheryl said, "You were. The bookcase is a secret door."

Rhonda nodded. "Wow. Only your second day and you're finding the hidden doors? It took me a month to find my first one."

Cheryl's eyebrows rose in surprise, confused she hadn't shocked Rhonda. "Well did you find the one that leads to the surveillance nest? The one with feeds from over fifty cameras around the house?"

Rhonda's expression hardened. "That's a joke, right?"

"I saw the red-devil tattoo on your butt cheek pitch-forking toward your lady bits." When she saw the annoyance in Rhonda's face, she quickly added, "Not judging. Some guys need directions."

Rhonda burst out laughing. "My eighteen-year-old self thought it was so cool. I still sort of like it."

"So what are we going to do about the snooping?" Cheryl asked, confused that Rhonda didn't seem very angry.

"Well, if they're tapping into Crèche's cameras, we're stuck. If we cover them up then Crèche can't do his job. All I can think of is bringing it up at the board meeting next weekend."

Tilting her head, Cheryl said, "I thought you'd be more upset."

Rhonda shrugged. "He's already seen all us moms naked. What's he gonna do, study our stretch marks?"

"Okay," Cheryl said, nodding. Did her crèche board salary buy so much slack for Jaeger? "I'm going back upstairs with Arman before the post-breakfast playroom rush."

Back in her room, Cheryl sent a picture of the surveillance station to Jameson with a request that he have it removed.

———

Sunday morning, Cheryl got up—stayed up really—around 5AM. Arman's feedings kept her from getting restorative sleep. She marveled at the fact that she was looking forward to going back to work so she could get some rest.

Checking her phone, she saw that Jameson hadn't responded to her email with the damning photo.

Given Rhonda's tepid reaction to the spying and Jameson's silence, Cheryl decided to cut short her weekend visit. She wasn't comfortable there, especially since Rhonda no longer seemed like an ally. She asked Crèche to inform the staff of her imminent departure before she started packing.

She had hidden the nanite harness on the floor behind her nightstand. When she went to retrieve it, it was gone. The shirt she had rolled it in was still there, but the red titanium-alloy cylinder was gone.

Dazed, Cheryl sat on the bed. She couldn't just ask Crèche if he had seen her hideously illegal container of nanites.

"Crèche, was anyone in this room last night besides me and Arman?"

"There were no security breaches. Your privacy settings preclude me from saving any recordings or data from your rooms that aren't actionable."

Cheryl let out a little snort of displeasure at Crèche's

careful choice of words. She had no idea what constituted a security breach to the AI. If Jaeger had plugged into the house's security feeds, no doubt he could co-opt household security.

———

Monday afternoon, Cheryl's boss called her to his office. It was his last week, so she was expecting some advice about taking over his job. She wondered if her new bonus range would apply to the entire fiscal year or if they would prorate it.

Bernie gave Cheryl a grim smile as she filled his doorway. "I spent this morning trying to convince management that you should replace me as Director of Sales, Northeast. They were having none of it."

Cheryl froze. Her promotion was supposedly a sure thing. She searched Bernie's face, wondering if he was playing a joke on her.

"Why not?" Cheryl finally asked, sitting down. She took a calming breath. "I have the best numbers. I'm the only one in the group who has an MBA."

Bernie nodded. "I told them that and more. They gave me this weak shit about not wanting to lose their best salesperson. I told them if they pass you over, they'll lose you anyway."

"So—"

Bernie put his hand up. "Wait, it gets weirder. I pushed them hard. I mean, what are they going to do, fire me? Eventually, Rick confessed that someone in the C-suite had it in for you. That's the most I could get out of him. It's totally unfair. I'm sorry I couldn't do more for you."

Dazed, Cheryl stared stupidly at Bernie. After three years of busting her ass for this man, he was sorry? He should have taken care of this weeks ago. Had he even forwarded her name in the first place?

Cheryl realized she was too worked up to have an intelligent or even civil discussion about it. Humiliated, the only dignity she could claw back from him was to maintain her professionalism.

"Well," Cheryl said slowly. "I appreciate that, Bernie." Feeling on the verge of losing her composure, she awkwardly stood up and rushed to the doorway. "I'll see you at your going-away party."

———

That night, a pint into her Häagan Daz therapy, Cheryl received a call from Jameson.

"I heard you were passed over for promotion," Jameson said. "It occurred to me that you might now be more interested in discussing relinquishing your parental rights over Arman."

Cheryl grunted. Jameson's taunting confirmed that Jaeger had found the right lever to pull to kill her promotion. Still, she couldn't resist poking the bear. "So, Jameson, I wonder if you ever had that slime growing on you cultured. I'd love to know how all the evil you do just slides right off you."

Immune to her insults, Jameson continued. "I'm sure that as a salesperson, you appreciate that the offer will get weaker as your position declines. Who knows what the future holds for you?"

The sheer lack of emotion in Jameson's voice chilled Cheryl. He wasn't rubbing it in. He wasn't enjoying this. He was a disinterested mechanism that would take apart her life piece by piece until she was begging for crumbs from his boss' table.

"It'd be hard for the offer to get worse," Cheryl replied acidly. "You haven't actually made one."

"You're in luck," Jameson said. "This Saturday, Mr. Jaeger will be attending his eldest's birthday party at the crèche. He'll make you an offer personally. I suggest you take it."

———

Not wanting to bring any drama to a five-year-old's birthday party, Cheryl showed up half an hour after the start time when she figured Jaeger would have likely had his fill of preschoolers.

Twisted pairs of blue and silver streamers running across the playroom's ceiling caught Cheryl's attention as she approached the playroom. Matching cloths covered tables loaded with snacks and drinks. Children toddled around, resisting the attendants' efforts to engage them with activities.

Near the far wall, presents formed a pyramid almost as tall as Jaeger, doing his best to look lordly despite the red plastic cup in his hand. Cheryl couldn't remember the name of the mom he was chatting with but was surprised that she was the only other parent present besides Rhonda.

Feeling vulnerable, Cheryl sidled up to Rhonda.

Following Cheryl's gaze, Rhonda whispered, "She's on team Whore Sycophant."

Cheryl barely understood Rhonda's slurred words.

"Jesus, Rhonda, you're drunk," Cheryl replied. "You should get out of here. Don't let the kids see you like this."

Rhonda hiccupped and burped which produced a few follow-on giggles. "Not yet. I've been waiting a loooong time for this." She looked at her watch. "Seriously, it's overdue."

Confused, Cheryl studied Rhonda who wouldn't take her eyes off Jaeger. "Rhonda, what did you do?"

Rhonda waved away Cheryl's question. "He did it to himself. Cocaine binge in college. The little privileged shit got a pacemaker at twenty." She teetered a little on her feet. "Oh, that reminds me." She grabbed both of Cheryl's shoulders. Rhonda slowly enunciated her words. "I'm so sorry for stealing your...nanites."

Across the room, Jaeger's eyes bulged and he fell forward onto the rug, barely missing a crawling infant.

Rope lighting in the room's crown molding started pulsing red. Crèche announced that first responders were on the way. Quietly and efficiently, crèche attendants whisked the children out of the playroom. Cheryl resisted the urge to grab Arman from the lady carrying him and sprint out of the house.

Cheryl cast a look at Jaeger, face down on the floor before slowly guiding the wobbly Rhonda upstairs to her room.

———

After some resistance, Cheryl got Rhonda to drink a glass of water and take some aspirin.

"How much did you drink?" Cheryl asked, worried about leaving her alone.

"Like two glasses of that crappy Merlot," Rhonda said, wavering on her feet. "But I haven't eaten and I may have overdone the Xanex. My God, that's the best drug in the world! Don't worry, I was just peaking there for a minute. I'm okay now."

Cheryl relaxed. "So you dosed him with nanites?"

Rhonda laughed. "I dosed a lot of people! But only he had that exact pacemaker."

Ushering Rhonda to the bed, Cheryl's mind reeled. Her intoxicated friend plopped onto the bed giggling.

"You should see your face. So concerned! You probably couldn't imagine that I have an MS in comp-sci. Those things aren't that difficult to program."

Cheryl's face flushed, embarrassed that she had pegged Rhonda as the MRS degree type. "But—"

"But nothing, Cheryl! God, you can be so condescending." She wagged a finger at Cheryl. "You've got a brain but you waste it, shaking your perfect ass in sales."

Cheryl resisted pointing out Rhonda's own condescension. "Okay, smart girl, tell me, are the cops gonna figure this out?"

"They'll figure out that someone used nanites to hack his pacemaker. But they'll never even consider that his baby mommas could get their hands on a nanite harness let alone program it. Even better, those nanites trace back to one of Shithead Enterprises' subsidiaries. It's criminally poetic."

Cherly's eyes went to the tiny camera in the far corner of the room. Did Crèche just record her confession?

"Don't worry about the AI," Rhonda mumbled, flopping back on her bed. "I made him my bitch a long time ago."

Cheryl walked to the window. Two police cars with their lights blazing sped to a stop next to the ambulance.

"So murder's okay?" Cheryl asked.

Hearing no answer, she turned to look at Rhonda whose sleeping face wore a blissful smile.

Cheryl hurried to her room and packed in a daze. The smile on Rhonda's sleeping face kept intruding into her mind as she gathered up her things. She wasn't certain that Rhonda was in the wrong, but she was certain that there was nothing to smile about. She was done with her murderous friend, the secret doors, and the corrupted AI.

With Arman strapped to her chest, she dragged her rolling luggage downstairs. When she reached the wide playroom entryway, it was blocked by a policeman.

"Did they revive him?" Cheryl asked the cop.

Clearly uncomfortable, the officer glanced at Arman before saying, "Ma'am, I can't—"

"He's my baby's father," Cheryl said quietly. "I have a right to know."

The cop's eyes softened. "He was declared dead at Northern Westchester a couple of minutes ago. I'm sorry."

Numbness descended on Cheryl. She nodded her thanks and headed for the front door.

As her cab pulled away from the mansion, she uninstalled the crèche's app from her phone.

All she could think about was how she would explain it all to Arman when he got older. ∎

BUTTERS THE DEMON DOG

The first time I suspected my English bulldog wasn't normal was on a breezy spring day. The nice weather meant that instead of lazing around inside buffeting us with his astounding farts, Butters was outside manifesting his alter ego, Professor Chaos.

A mewing stuffed cat got him wound up. The fact that I was holding the toy and teasing him mercilessly with it was, of course, no fault of mine. Butters was snarling, and I was getting nipped occasionally. I didn't get mad. If you're going to play rough with a dog, you're going to get a little banged up. When things started to get out of hand, I gently dominated him in good Dog Whisperer style. I held him down on his side until he relaxed.

My mistake was to rub it in.

Before releasing him I leaned in close to stare into his eyes and yelled "Gamma, you turd-mongering bastard! You're not alpha, not beta, but gamma!" I guess I was a little mad after all.

An hour later he took a crap in the form of a lower-case alpha. Since it's just a long turd with a loop in it, I took it as a humorous coincidence. In retrospect, everything looks more ominous. I was the guy in the horror movie who couldn't see the obvious signs. In my defense, I thought I was living a dramedy.

———

Decoding my dog's behavior was low on my list of priorities. I had a pile of first-world problems: annoying boss, slacker co-workers, and the burgeoning realization that I had already peaked. Even with all that, I tended to brood on my neighbors. It's about proximity. You get up and go to sleep knowing that scant yards away a clan of slack-jawed, trashy idiots were gleefully proving Darwin wrong. These offensive morons bred like rabbits and showed no signs of being culled from the herd. In fact, the youngest in my least favorite neighbor's house was a seventeen-year-old miscreant who had already passed on his seed. His father recounted the story to me with false lament and a telling glint in his eye that said "My boy is an unstoppable force of nature," as if knocking up some high-school girl proved he had raised a thoroughbred.

Who cares, right? I mean the world is full of offensive asses. How near or far their ass-clownery occurs is hardly relevant. It's like cursing the weather. You'll go crazy if you let it bother you.

Normally I can get behind that sentiment. But this neighbor had a jacked-up, silver pickup truck that rode a good two feet off the ground with enormous tires and a V-8 that you could hear idling a mile away. Since I lived only fifty yards away, it was hard to ignore. As far as my girlfriend Doris and I have been able to tell, the monstrous nature of his truck has no actual utility in his daily routine, but we hear it every morning and evening. If we're home, we hear it coming and going throughout the day. Doris says the guy is an insecure alpha-male wannabee. She calls it the penis truck. Its size and noise announce just how big his phallus isn't.

One penis truck is bad enough, but they run in packs. There are days when a second and even a third one will add its voice to the automotive auto-eroticism. Each has an after-market exhaust system that ekes out another few horsepower by not actually muffling the exhaust. So when the throaty trucks are in conference, nose to tail allowing their drivers to chat, the thunderous idling noise of the things rattles the panes of glass in my front storm door.

These thoughts were distracting me one day while I was walking Butters. It took several shouts to bring me back to the present so I could witness the second clue that Butters was more than your average dog.

I hadn't noticed that a neighbor had been yelling at me to stop, over and over. She was struggling to control her own dog, so what little of my brain that was listening thought she was yelling at her unruly mastiff. I kept going down the sidewalk towards her house until she said "Sir, halt!" in a tone that indicated that 'sir' was a stand-in for something far more vulgar. More bemused than anything, I complied.

Butters dutifully sat on his haunches next to me. Not the typical bulldog color, he is what the AKC calls 'fawn brindle'—a beautiful brown with vertical tiger-like stripes and white accents. He's as well behaved as he is good looking. The little under-bite makes him impossibly cute.

"I don't think she respects your authoritah, Butters," I said to him. "She's messing up your walk, and addressing your human quite rudely."

I often talked to Butters like an adult. His face is so expressive that I think I see meaningful reactions in it. This time, Butters got one of those contemplative looks on his face, wise and dispassionate with just a hint of sadness. It looked nothing less than sentient. He replied with a rare, quiet woof.

Immediately the noise from my neighbor changed. Her mastiff, Pookie, jerked on her leash hard enough to shut her owner up and pull her off balance. As the lady did a face plant on her lawn, Pookie ran out of the open gate and sprinted towards Butters and me.

Butters didn't flinch as the massive dog bore down on us. I didn't either. I'm a dog guy. Dogs like me, and I like dogs. Pookie sensed all this and came to a skittering halt in front of us, clearly overjoyed to meet us. I smiled at her and patted her head while murmuring doggie praise.

Pookie lowered herself to the ground before Butters, her tail wagging too fast to see. Meanwhile, her bitchy owner was cursing me as she raised her fleshy frame off the ground. Somehow her inability to control her dog or close her gate was my fault.

The mastiff and Butters engaged in delicate nasal

communion until the mastiff's owner was dumb enough to yell "You keep your damn mutt away from her." Maybe she didn't see how Pookie had clearly joined our pack. Maybe she didn't see Butters' magnificent pedigree. The absurdity of it made me laugh.

Butters seemed less amused at the slight to his lineage. His ears twitched. Those large, empathetic, watery eyes of his narrowed. An exasperated little groan came out of him, the kind he uses with us when he doesn't get his way. Hearing that, Pookie sprinted back to her yard and set on her ill-mannered owner.

"Proper," I said, nodding at Butters. His corkscrew tail responded with a few excited cycles.

We lazily resumed our stroll down the sidewalk, enjoying the show. Pookie ran looping patterns in her yard, body-slamming her owner every time she regained her feet. When we reached her gate, Butters stared the owner in the eyes while Pookie urinated on her prone form.

You have to see it from my point of view. This wasn't my dog wielding arcane powers. This was a stupid owner unable to compete with the sense of community that our little mobile pack offered Pookie. There was no blood or serious injury, just an ill-tempered woman receiving her comeuppance.

It was funny to me. I live in a dramedy. Comic relief is half the reason to own a dog.

———

I was completely disillusioned a month later. When I stepped inside my front door, I immediately knew something was off. Growling came from the backyard, a soft chorus in curious pitches and cadences. I had to strain to hear it. About three seconds after cocking my ear, it cut off. Then there was a symphony of muffled sounds: thuds, tapping, rustling, skittering, and the distinctive rattle of the chain link fence.

When I walked out back, Butters was sitting in the middle

of the yard facing the door as I came out. His ears were up. Rather than running to me as he usually would, he continued to sit for a few seconds giving me a knowing, happy look. He waited while I scanned the yard looking for the source of the noises.

Again, in retrospect it was creepy. It's like he didn't want to interrupt me reassuring myself that nothing was going on. His canine Jedi mind trick complete, he sprinted over to me with his little corkscrew tail thrumming at a gleeful frequency. Happy dogs are very reassuring, and distracting. So when I saw Butters do his oh-my-god-you're-home shtick, I put everything else out of my mind. The delay was odd, but the emotion was so genuine that I just chalked it up to bulldog oddness. Butters was inscrutable.

That evening my suspicions resurfaced. I didn't say anything to Doris because she would worry herself to distraction. If put to the test, I think she would choose me over him, but I'd rather not see it played out.

I logged onto our home security website and pulled up the backyard video. Minutes before I arrived home, the backyard was filled with twenty neighborhood dogs respectfully arrayed before Butters. I almost choked on my beer.

My mind was already working hard to avoid the truth. I rationalized that a bunch of dogs hanging out in my yard, acknowledging Butters as alpha was something to be proud of. That weak explanation held only a few seconds. When I saw their reactions to me coming home, I shivered. They held formation while Butters turned briefly to look in the direction of the house. Then, as a synchronized group, all the dogs scattered like a band of ninjas melting into the background.

My backyard is completely fenced, so there were scenes of incredible poochie parkour as many of the dogs performed acrobatic bounds that propelled them over the low fence making use of the garbage cans and the lawn furniture. The smallest dogs slipped through gaps in the three gates. The less nimble of the medium-sized dogs were helped by a Rottweiler who served as a step. He stood next to the fence, and they bounded onto his back and over the top with fearless élan. The Rottweiler then did something I'd never seen a dog do. His hundred pounds wouldn't easily take the three-foot barrier in one leap, so in mid-jump he used his front paws to give his bulk the boost it needed to clear the fence.

When I saw the vacant look on my face in the video, I was chilled. I was not alpha. Butters was handling me. But to what end?

————

I hadn't understood it, but Butters had been slowly acclimating me to his arcane nature. That time I got home and heard the tail end of his canine conclave, he had purposefully delayed dismissing the group so I would catch a piece of it. No doubt, he heard my car pull up, the car door close, and my key ring jangling at the front step. Butters had plenty of time to clear the yard with me none the wiser.

That gentle indoctrination took a hard turn late one night. I got up at 2AM to let him out to pee. Rather than finding him curled up on his bed with his tongue hanging comically out of his mouth, he was instead awake and alert, waiting for me.

It was a cool, moonless spring night. He dutifully loped off to one side of the yard to do his business—both barrels that evening. Then, instead of trotting back to me eager to return to sleep, he crossed to the other side of the yard where the back light didn't reach.

Curious, I shuffled over there in my flip-flops and was stunned to see three other dogs waiting there. A beautiful Siberian Husky was holding down my neighbor's Siamese cat lightly with a paw. The agile Rottweiler was supervising, and a Chihuahua was standing guard near the cat's head. Anytime the terrified cat so much as twitched, the Chihuahua swatted it cruelly with its sharp little claws. Pound for pound, Chihuahuas are one of the most fearsome dogs you'll ever meet.

The cat looked at me, pleading with its eyes. The dogs looked only at Butters. Without so much as a chuff out of any of them, Butters reared lightly onto his back legs. His narrow bulldog waist gave him astounding balance.

Butters' left paw scratched at the air. The muscles in his ground legs flexed, exerting a tremendous force in the effort. Blue fire trailed his paw as it moved. Gesturing slowly in this way, it took him several seconds to trace a flaming glyph in the air. Resembling Indian script, it rippled like it was drawn on an invisible fabric fluttering in the breeze.

On some silent cue, the three other dogs bounded away, and the glyph sheet wrapped around the cat just as it regained its feet. The cat became a brilliant flash of blue light that streaked to the corners of the property bathing the yard in a diffuse haze.

When I got over my shock I realized the three neighborhood dogs were gone. Butters was sitting, watching me intently. Flecks of blue fire danced in his eyes. I stepped to where the cat had been immolated and pawed at the ground with my flip-flop. I kept at it overlong, drawing reassurance from the pushback of the Earth. After seeing Butters carve the air into something that swallowed up a cat, I enjoyed the reassurance that reality was where I left it.

I don't know if it was another canine Jedi mind trick, but when I looked back at Butters I had this sense that despite his power, he was still my dog, my impossibly cute, good dog.

"You know I hate cats, buddy," I said. "Good riddance to that Siamese prick. But don't let Doris see anything like that. She doesn't understand how evil cats are."

Butters tilted his head in the classic confused-dog style. It was my turn to be nonchalant. I ignored him and headed back inside. After a second, he followed at my heels.

I had a demon dog. After witnessing a blood sacrifice, there wasn't room for misinterpretation, even in the dumbest horror movie. The question was: should I care? Let's face it, Butters had good judgment. Pookie's owner needed an adjustment, and the fewer Siamese cats in this world the better.

Butters didn't demand better treatment. He never turned on me or addressed me in some satanic voice. As far as I could tell, he was the same stubborn, lovable, playful pain in the ass he always was. I decided to roll with it, mostly because I couldn't bear the thought of telling Doris about it.

Once the truth was out, the gifts started showing up. Cans of luxury dog food and bags of high-end kibble would appear on our lawn. Dog toys, some still in their packaging would show up on our doorstep. Doris thought it was marvelous. The other dogs loved Butters so much that they brought him stuff. In her mind that tracked. I never told her the truth. It was partly out of fear of her reaction, and partly out of respect for Butters. No doubt he could have arranged a demonstration for her if he thought it was needed. There was a precarious equilibrium to the situation that I couldn't imagine improving with an intervention.

We had reached an understanding, he and I. I was alpha in my world, and he in his. His growing material wealth was fine with me. When Doris wasn't around I would open the pantry door and ask him what his pleasure was. He would survey his minion's offerings and paw at his preference. High-quality meat on a bed of overpriced, soft kibble was his usual favorite.

I was content, but not as vigilant as I should have been. One day while Doris was at the store I made a horrible mistake. When she wasn't around, I could talk to Butters like the sentient being that he was. He never answered with more than a look, but it was a kind of man-dog bonding that we engaged in when we had privacy.

L. B. Spillers

Seated in front of the TV watching Dr. Pohl, we were interrupted by the penis truck. Butters gave me a questioning look when I reached for the remote to turn the sound up. Four beers into the evening, it just slipped out.

"That truck needs to go, Butters," I said slouching back onto the leather couch. Lying next to me, Butters lifted his head. Knowing that he was paying attention, I should have stopped, but I just let it fly.

"That guy needs to learn some respect, and his son needs to be neutered so that his over-chlorinated gene pool doesn't leak any further into the population."

Butters huffed what I took to be a laugh. I felt clever that my use of the word 'neutered' got a chuckle out of him. It was man-doggie bonding at its best.

A week later, Butters scrabbled at the front door. That was unusual because we generally didn't let him out front where there was no fence. Curious, I went with him. He sat on his haunches facing my neighbor's house. Seconds later we heard the approach of the penis truck.

Knowing Butters as I did, him calmly sitting, waiting with purpose like that, gave me a chill. When I saw the dog turd in my neighbor's usual parking spot softly glowing blue I silently mouthed an "Oh Shit."

The penis truck rolled up with my neighbor and his son in it, oblivious to the presence of the arcane shit pile underneath. The man popped the hood, and went to the front of the truck. I was impressed to see that there was a little platform bolted underneath which he rotated out so he could stand on it and work on his engine.

The guy futzed with something and yelled for his son to give it some gas. A flash of blue light burst from the engine. Startled, he pulled his head out of the compartment. Immediately yellow flames and an explosion followed, engulfing the father's torso. Simultaneously, the truck cab was filled with dust.

I called 911 before running over to help. Butters stayed sitting where he was. I used my neighbor's hose to put out the fire and ease the pain of his burns. Some neighborhood first responder was on the scene in less than two minutes. By the time I had water on the fire, he was working on getting the son out.

Distant sirens approached. I looked at Butters across the street. Despite all the noise and smell, he sat still and serenely on our lawn like some bulldog Buddha.

The next day Doris got a report from her network of neighborhood ladies. The father suffered second-degree burns on a third of his torso. The debris propelled into the cabin had destroyed his son's genitals, just like I had told Butters was needed. Unfortunately, it also ripped a femoral artery. The boy was dead. Butters killed that boy because of what I said.

When Doris finished her report, I stared at Butters, trying to reconcile that perfect, playful bastard I raised with the murdering demon he'd become. He came over and nuzzled my leg before looking up at me with a question in his big, innocent eyes.

"You're a good boy, Butters," I said, petting his head.

His corkscrew tail wiggled in appreciation. ∎

GYRE FLEET

"Negative, Darya. No solo dives, no exceptions," the captain said. Despite his calm delivery, she heard the Samoan man's anger in the way he stretched out the nos.

Darya wondered if the captain was in on it as she pulled on her full-face scuba mask. That unkind thought was added to the pile of irritations that drove her to disobey the man. Even if she lost her job, she was going to get some answers.

When she keyed the comms cutover, the telltale squelch that went over the line made her wince.

"I heard that! It's both our jobs if you get hurt."

Darya took a last look around the submersible before dropping into its tiny moon pool. The sudden cold made her gasp. The lack of a wetsuit was one of the many stupidities about her excursion.

She kicked for the submerged drone tender, dodging around the large mesh bag of garbage dangling from her vehicle's arm.

Experienced as she was, the looming black bulk of the tender always sent a rush of fear through her. Despite all the times she'd worked on one, she still had to fight her instinct that the twenty-foot-tall ovoid silhouette was a sea creature ready to eat her.

Her fins made the short swim easy. Still, the captain was right. Never dive alone, certainly not in the middle of the Indian Ocean. Never leave a powered vehicle unattended. Never work on underwater equipment without a wetsuit.

"C'mon, captain." Darya's voice sounded tinny from behind her face mask. "Conditions are fantastic. I'll be quick. I'm in fifteen feet of water. Steaming back and getting a safety diver is silly for something so simple. It's just an open panel." She didn't add that she didn't want anyone to see what she was actually doing.

"*Palagi!* You know better than most that those regulations are written in blood."

Already at the submerged tender, she grabbed one of the rungs running up its hull. Looking up to brighter depths, she relaxed a little more with each rung on the way to the tender's crown.

"And you know the consortium should staff their ships better, Captain. Besides, I'm almost done."

Darya opened the maintenance hatch—the one that was supposedly already open—reached in and detached the camera she had planted a month ago. In seconds, the camera was in the mesh bag at her hip, and the hatch closed.

"Hatch is secured. I'm on my way back."

Behind her face mask, the captain's sigh sounded like a gale wind.

When Darya turned toward her vehicle, she saw the brightly lit trash bag dangling from her sub's mechanical arm had drifted dangerously close to the tender. If she didn't hurry, there'd be a collision, and someone really would lose their job. Pushing off the side of the tender, she rushed back to her vehicle.

"You're lucky my mother likes you," the captain mumbled.

Darya launched herself through the circular opening on the underside of her sub. With her fins still on, she shuffled forward on her knees to the controls and initiated reverse thrust before ripping off her mask.

Slumping back against the hull, Darya took off her fins, smiling at a memory of the captain's mother. Docked in Port Vila in Vanuatu, Darya's eyes had been drawn to a commotion on the pier. The crowd was melting back from the irascible old woman as she strutted forward in her fiery flower-print dress, barking at those too slow to get out of her way. Darya was certain the woman would gut her if she cost the captain his job.

"She knows I wouldn't let you down, sir. I'm back on board. I'll be back with the trash in five minutes."

———

Two days later, arriving at Hithadhoo Island in the Addu Atoll, Darya rushed off the ship. Siva, the captain's only help—engineer, maintenance guy, cook, and crane operator—was already depositing an enormous bag of plastic trash accrued from the drone tenders they had visited into the back of the waiting electric truck. They all wore a lot of hats. That's how it went with non-profits. There was never enough money for anything.

Darya didn't mind. She enjoyed the sense of shared struggle among the tiny staff. They were cleaning up the world's oceans. It wouldn't feel noble if it were easy or high-paying.

As she drove the loaded truck onto the road, she worried about flood debris. The storm two days prior had walloped their chunk of the Maldives. The country was losing the battle against ocean rise, so storms brought flooding. With real estate at a premium, all the buildings butted right up against the tiny streets, turning them into narrow corridors of concrete block that channeled the storm surge. The practical effect was that big storms deposited obstacles at large intersections.

Darya stopped at the first major intersection, relieved to see the storm debris had been cleared. The quick recovery cheered her with the sense of resilience it gave the island.

Their building's new construction was impossible to miss among its weathered neighbors. As she backed the truck up to the intake chute, she was met by Vivek, operating another crane. The skinny Sri Lankan was their master of plastic decomposition, riding herd on the finicky microbes that fed on PET plastics.

By the time Darya was out of the truck, Vivek had the crane hook dangling over the truck bed.

"Looks like a good haul," he yelled to her as she jammed the hook under the bundle's straps.

Darya snorted. Good would be if they struggled to fill up the drone tenders.

"Take it away," she yelled back, hopping down from the truck.

As Vivek craned the enormous mass of dripping plastic into the chute, Darya headed to the office. Vivek would be busy for a while unloading the trash. It had a knack for embedding in the mesh of their enormous collection bags.

At her desk, Darya removed the camera from the baggie of rice she had it in. She carefully cut through the thick layers of tape around it. Rated merely water-resistant, she wasn't confident the camera had even survived its impromptu underwater deployment. Her decision to stick it inside that drone tender had been made on the fly during her previous run. The mysterious back-leveling of drone software patches had a pattern to it. Her hunch had been that it wouldn't be long before that tender's drones suffered the same problems.

A beep sounded from the computer when it recognized the camera. Darya punched the air with a triumphant "Yes!" If nothing else, she wouldn't have to buy Siva a new camera.

It took only moments to find what she was looking for. The motion-triggered camera had only made one recording. Unfortunately, the anonymous black gloves replacing the computer module in the drone tender didn't tell her much. They were barely visible in the dim light. When she'd installed the camera, it had been to rule out one outrageous possibility that would explain the software patches being lost. It had been about clawing back her sanity, not identifying a perpetrator.

Sighing, Darya slouched back in her seat. Finding an answer for the back-leveled drone software was a relief. She wasn't crazy or incompetent. Someone really was screwing with the drone tenders. But, as she sat staring at the looping video, that relief was quickly buried under new questions.

Checking the timestamp against the logs she downloaded from the tender, Darya found nothing. There wasn't even a panel-open event in the log for the day of that surreptitious module swap. Security had been utterly compromised. Not that it was much of a security regime. There wasn't much to protect. That's what made it so confusing.

"What are you up to, you sneaky prick?" she mumbled at the screen.

"And what do they hope to gain?" Vivek asked from behind her.

Darya shot to her feet. "Damnit, Vivek! Don't sneak up on me like that. Aren't you supposed to be wrestling with trash?"

Vivek shook his head. "What I'm supposed to be doing is having lunch." He pointed to her screen. "Congratulations for proving you're not out of your mind."

Darya stretched her arms. "Yup, and I caught them with Siva's thirty-dollar nanny cam, though I'm still pissed he had that thing in his cabin. Where's the trust, right?"

Vivek shrugged noncommittally, too dignified to descend into trash-talking a coworker.

Darya chuckled at Vivek's predictable neutrality. "Now, I want one, genuine convenience-store lunch with all the frills. I was on that boat for two weeks. I'm jonesing for anything that isn't one of Siva's curries over rice."

They walked out into the powerful midday sun. When they reached their bicycles, Vivek said, "It makes no sense. They aren't sabotaging anything, and the consortium is going to publish all the data for free. What's the point?"

As they pedaled away, Darya said, "I'll send the video to Sheila. She can deal with it. It's Friday. I'm looking forward to turning my phone off for two whole days."

Darya was the lead drone technician for an operation that spanned nine time zones. There was always someone who just had a 'quick' question for her. So she had to defend her downtime zealously. Her cell phone stayed off whenever she was.

———

Monday morning, Darya discovered that her emailed video had caused an uproar. As her computer screen filled with email subject lines, she groaned. To make matters worse, Vivek had left her about a third of a cup in the coffee maker.

"Oh, good, you're here," Vivek said, peeking into the office from the hallway. "My email is blowing up. Sheila—"

"Vivek, what the hell is this?" Darya waved the nearly empty coffee pot in front of Vivek.

"With milk, you've got a mug right there. If you don't want it, I'll take it." Vivek reached for the pot, but Darya snatched it away and poured the dregs into her mug.

"You know I drink it black, you dairy whore." She loved milk in her coffee, but with a minimum four-mugs-a-morning habit, the calories weren't worth it.

Darya took her coffee back to her desk. "Now make another pot."

The most recent email subject line yelled at her in all capitals to turn her phone on. When she did, she was faced with seventeen voicemail messages.

———

Two days later, a stranger walked through the office door. Lean with close-cropped black hair, he wasn't part of the consortium staff. Darya recognized the bit of dead soul in his eyes. She suspected he'd seen some ugly military service.

"Stephenson, Michael," he said. "Call me Mike." He looked around their small office with a patronizing grin, before returning his attention to Darya. "You're Darya, right?" He stuck out his hand. "I'm here to look into the drone tender thing. Sheila told you to expect me, right?"

Sheila hadn't told her to expect anyone. She had only said the consortium was going to investigate things. Then again,

Darya was confident that if she had actually read that interminable email thread carefully before filing it, she would probably find this annoyance buried in there.

Darya looked at the man for a moment. Wearing a grey sport coat over a white button-down shirt, his concession to the island's informality was his jeans. His mirror-polish black shoes destroyed whatever hope he had of blending in. She was impressed he hadn't yet sweated through his shirt.

"Good morning, Mike," Darya said, shaking his hand. At least his handshake wasn't overbearing.

She leaned against her desk, wondering how much of a time-suck Mike would be. "Seems like an awful waste of time for you to come out here in person. I've already emailed everything relevant." Waving her arm at their small office space, she continued, "What can we possibly do for you?"

"I was hoping to start with the hardware. I'm a visual guy. Can you show me the tech so I can understand what we're talking about?"

Darya suppressed a sigh. The tampering was extremely technical business. Mike asking for a tutorial didn't give her hope that he had any expertise to bring to the table.

"The shop it is," she said, waving for him to follow her. The drone workshop sat on the other side of the plastic-processing area.

On the way down the hallway, Mike stopped to look at the processing floor through a window. "There's only the two of you at this site? Do I have that right?"

"Yup," she said, bored. "It's just me and Vivek here. That room is mostly the big fermenter where that funky microbe slowly eats the PET plastics. Vivek deals with all that."

On the walls of her shop were colorful posters of the underwater drones and their tenders, illustrating the consortium's mission. There wasn't space for text in all the consortium languages, so symbols and arrows communicated the dynamics—simple enough for even a politician to understand.

Occasionally, Darya had to suffer tours of politicians, donors, and journalists. Usually, such tours were led by executives or PR people who only wanted Darya there to answer any technical questions that came up.

"This is one of the drones," she said, pointing at the microwave-oven-sized machine on the bench. "That ugly-ass port is the wet-mateable computer hookup. The drone docks with the tender to unload its garbage and swap out its battery. While it's there, the tender plugs into that port. That's when software updates occur."

"And mapping data is offloaded?" Mike asked.

"Right." Darya didn't bother hiding her annoyance. Everything she was showing him was available on the internet.

"You don't approve?" Mike asked.

Darya sighed. She'd stepped in it again. It had only taken about two minutes. "It's fine. Mapping the ocean floor is great but those sensors hog battery power. It makes our mission more difficult. The real work is that much harder to do with the mapping sideshow."

"I see," Mike said, nodding. "So what do you think was the point of the tampering?"

Seeing Mike wasn't particularly put off by her griping, Darya relaxed. "How should I know? Normally I push out updates to the tenders wirelessly through satellite links. By swapping out that module, they were able to subvert the whole system. For all I know, the drone software getting back-leveled was just a side-effect of their real work."

"Yeah, but why?"

Darya shrugged. "Sheila told me not to spend time on it. I'm going to be slammed just restoring the swapped-out modules. I have to send one back to headquarters. She has some techs that are going to dig into it."

Mike sat on a stool. "You don't have any idea what they were up to specifically? This started two months ago."

She almost laughed at the expectation in Mike's face. He seemed to believe she would have all the answers he needed teed up for him. Despite his repeating the same question for the third time and implying she was either a slacker or a liar, Darya felt a little sorry for him. He had no idea what he was doing.

"That would require decompiling their machine code. As I said, Sheila told me not to spend my time on it. What exactly do you need from me?"

"But you have, right? I mean, after all the work you go to maintain the drone fleet, you must have been curious, right?" Mike smiled at Darya.

Darya's own eyes narrowed as she mentally shifted gears. Cooperation was one thing, but Mike's attitude was veering into the abusive. She stood a little straighter. "As I said, Sheila is going to have people work on the inserted code. Do you have any more questions that don't involve me doing your job for you? I've got my own work to do."

Standing up, Mike said, "Oh, I've been doing my job. I know you've spent a lot of time reverse-engineering the code." He edged closer to the door.

"You know squat, mister. Get out of my lab."

Mike shook his head. "You're not much of a tech geek if you couldn't find the spyware on your workstation. By my count, you've spent at least ten hours a week digging into that code since you found it. Why won't you tell me what you found?"

The menace in Mike's voice startled Darya. That's when she noticed his hands clasped in front and the cant of his torso. She darted for the doorway. His hand shot out, intercepting her chin, pushing it up and backward. Darya found herself involuntarily flipping through the air. She landed hard, face-down on the concrete floor. Before she could recover, a jolt of electricity shocked her senseless.

When Darya's eyes fluttered back open, her hands were zip-tied behind her back. Tape across her mouth kept her from yelling. Mike was binding her legs.

She tried to yell anyway. The muffled tones made Mike chuckle.

"Now you want to talk? There's nothing to discuss anymore, Darya. Your reluctance to share what you figured out told me what I needed to know."

Darya was amazed at how easily Mike threw her over his shoulder like a sack. His shoulder blade dug into her ribs, turning each step into a jolt of pain. Those jabs disrupted her thinking every second. All she could do was watch the concrete floor pass by as he made his way out the back door.

The compound's high walls kept what few neighbors they had from seeing him descend the rear steps with her over his shoulder. The only thing that came to her mind was the old self-defense advice: go nuts; resist as violently as possible as soon as possible. If they take you to a second site, you'll never get away. So, Darya started thrashing around as hard as she could.

Mike grunted when she managed to smack his head with her elbow. He let her go. She fell five feet to the sand, shoulder first, knocking the wind out of her.

Darya struggled not to panic as she failed to breathe in through her nose. She kept telling herself her lungs would accept air eventually. It would just take a few moments.

While trying to convince her lungs to expand, she heard a metallic thunk. A tiny breath came, then another. She concentrated on taking quick, short breaths through her nose, trying to force a deeper one each time.

Pain pierced her thoughts as the tape on her mouth was ripped off. The tie on her hands was cut.

Darya turned to see Vivek wrapping Mike's crossed wrists with duct tape. Almost taking full breaths again, she dug out her pocket knife.

"Thank you," she wheezed to Vivek as she sawed at the zip ties around her ankles. She stood up and tested her lungs, taking deep breaths.

Vivek walked over to the rear steps and sat down. "I think he was going to kill you, Darya."

On the ground near Mike lay a length of black, one-inch iron piping that Vivek had used to knock Mike out. Darya picked it up and beat Mike's ribs with it. Vivek didn't move to stop her.

Darya dropped the pipe after a few swings, already winded. Mike's slack jaw and lifeless eyes annoyed her. She wanted to revive him so she could beat him some more. Her hands shook.

"I think I already killed him," Vivek said. He was eerily calm about it. There was no emotion in his voice.

"Huh," Darya mumbled, leaning in to take a close look. Mike's skull had a pipe-shaped depression on the left side, easily an inch deep. She wouldn't have guessed skinny Vivek was that strong. After a few moments of feeling for a pulse, she agreed he was dead.

The implications of killing Mike started to trickle into her brain. "I'll make sure they know you saved me, and you only hit him once."

Vivek stood up. He ran a hand through his black hair. "Let's not call the police. I've got an idea." He hurried back into the building.

When Vivek returned with a big bundle of industrial fishing net and a tarp, Darya shuffled her feet, casting a glance at Mike's body. She didn't like where this was going but couldn't find the words to say so.

Darya watched as Vivek rolled Mike's body first in the tarp and then in the fishing net. She didn't move to help him. He didn't seem to mind. By the time he was done, the bundle looked like a big tangle of netting. The off-white mass at its core was hard to distinguish through all the lines.

Rubbing the back of her neck, Darya said, "Uh, Vivek, I appreciate you saving me and all. But I'm not real comfortable with the whole body disposal thing."

Vivek smiled at her. "Time for some truth, I guess." He clasped his hands behind his back. "First of all, I don't think whoever sent this man will forgive us if the police exonerate us. Secondly, I...that is...let's just say I can't afford to have the police looking too closely at me."

Darya stared at Vivek while trying to make up her mind. She was pretty sure bashing Mike in the head was legally justifiable. Disposing of his body was definitely illegal, but morally, she didn't have a problem with it. Then there was the old saying: a real friend helps you bury a body. Darya laughed at the thought, drawing a confused look from Vivek. "Okay, Vivek. I owe you a lot. What do you need me to do?"

Half an hour later, standing on the beach, Darya watched Vivek motor away in his ratty little aluminum rowboat with its five-horsepower trolling motor straining to push through the surf. In the front was an ugly pile of netting.

———

Later that afternoon, Vivek returned to the office. They agreed they would pretend Mike had never arrived. There were no security cameras to say otherwise. Meanwhile, Darya busied herself ferreting out the spyware on her computer that Mike mentioned.

After hours of scrubbing every bit of software on her computer, she was stumped, so she decided to look at it from a network traffic point of view. Barring a secret satellite uplink, every scrap of information had to go out through the office's network router. In the router's logs, she quickly found two wirelessly connected devices she couldn't account for. Even knowing that, it took her another hour to figure out that the USB dongle for her wireless keyboard had been swapped out.

When she went to check on Vivek's computer in the plastic

processing area, she was surprised to find him dozing in his desk chair. She had to shake him awake.

"Dude, what's your excuse?" she asked.

"I didn't want to leave until you did," he said, yawning. "Some guard I turned out to be."

Darya stared at him. She saw concern on his face, sort of. He had always been hard to read. Previously, she had chalked it up to cultural differences. His admission that his life couldn't bear police scrutiny put a new cast on his quirky facial expressions. She wondered what trauma had warped them. He had seemed awfully comfortable killing a man and dumping his body.

The moment stretched into awkwardness. Darya shook her head and handed him the computer's original, hard-wired keyboard, still in its box.

"Replace your wireless keyboard with this. The USB thingy on mine had been swapped out for some funky spy tech that was monitoring me. I assume the second mystery device in the logs is yours."

As she watched Vivek install the original keyboard, anecdotes about their two years working together came forward in her thoughts as if she had to vet her memories, looking for signs of trouble. She silently cursed Mike for how he had made her doubt Vivek.

Vivek handed her the USB dongle, before turning back to his new keyboard to test it. After a few moments, he started laughing. "Look!" he said, pointing to his screen. It was an email from Sheila telling them to expect Mike Stephenson to arrive in a few days. The accompanying picture was of a smiling, blond, twenty-something geek.

"Holy crap!" Darya said, leaning closer to scrutinize the boyish face on the screen. Lowering her voice to a whisper, she continued. "If that's the real Mike, who are the crabs eating?"

"I don't know," Vivek said, smiling. "But I am thinking there will be no investigation."

"Crap," Darya said, dropping into Vivek's chair.

"What?" Vivek asked. "This is great news!"

Darya groaned, rotating the chair back and forth. "I volunteered for an extra rotation on the boat to dodge the fallout. Two extra weeks of Siva's curries for nothing!"

———

That two-week duty got cut short by problems with the boat, the so-called mother ship. It started with one of the thrusters failing. Then it was a coolant line for one of the engines. When the bilge pump failed, the captain decided to cut the trip short. Meanwhile, random little failures kept occurring.

Darya initially thought Mike had sabotaged their boat before his surprise office visit, but the failures hadn't been catastrophic.

The process of diagnosing the string of problems had frayed Siva's nerves. Darya assisting him had put the two through an emotional roller coaster. The high of each successful repair had been followed by the emotional whiplash of another breakdown.

By the last night of the trip, everyone was tense. At dinner, Siva served one of his curries and a large pot of rice. Darya did her best to feign her appreciation, but when Siva slapped down a plastic two-liter bottle of his favorite soda on the table, she lost her composure.

"Siva! Damn it! We are fighting every day against single-use plastics. How could you buy that garbage, let alone put it on this table?"

"They didn't have cans when we loaded up," Siva said. "I tried. Don't bring drama to the dinner table."

"Well, I—"

"Shut it, Darya," the captain said from the doorway. "We've had a crappy trip. You two," he wagged a finger between them, "will pretend to be happy for at least the minute it takes me to

L. B. Spillers

make my plate." The captain hurriedly piled rice and curry on his metal plate. "And don't forget it's your watch in two hours, Siva. And clean the table. It's sticky."

As the captain hurried off back to the bridge, Darya saw what the captain was on about. A puddle of Siva's blessed soda was slowly spreading across the table.

When Siva went to pick up the soda bottle, his thumb went through the side of it. "What the hell?" He rushed the leaking container to the galley sink.

Several snide comments leapt into Darya's mind about the crappy soda and its crappy bottle. They were replaced with memories of Vivek bemoaning how durable the plastics they collect are.

"Siva, wait!" she said, standing up. She rushed to the sink. "Let me see that bottle."

Siva handed it to her. Darya put her face right up to the surface where Siva's thumb had gone through. The plastic around the edges was so thin that it drooped, just like the fermenting plastic she'd seen at the processing center.

"This plastic is being eaten by microbes," she said, placing the bottle in the sink.

"That's ridiculous," Siva said. "At optimal conditions, it takes Vivek's guys weeks to digest plastic."

Crossing her arms, Darya leaned back against the counter. "Every failure on this trip has involved plastic parts. There was the plastic coolant hose. Then there was—"

"That plastic bushing in the thruster," Siva said, nodding. "Then the plastic compression sleeve on the bilge pump," Siva said. "The coolant line came first. Let's go see what's left of the old tubing."

They rushed to the engine room and fished out the piece of tubing from the trash. The entire length had become a shriveled, wet, limp mass.

Siva plopped onto a stool. "We're in big trouble. This isn't just Vivek's kids eating PET plastics. It's eating every kind of plastic. We've another fourteen hours of motoring until we hit the docks. Do you know how many plastic parts there are on this boat?"

Darya rolled her eyes. "Always so pessimistic! What we have to do is disinfect this ship, starting with ourselves. We kill those microbes or at least slow them down enough so that we can make port."

"Really?" Siva said, waving his arms. "Look around us! It would take forever to properly disinfect this space. I don't even know if we have the cleaning products to do it."

Scanning the engine room, Darya saw he was right. There was plastic everywhere. Fittings, lines, housings, reservoirs, seals, switches, buttons, and countless other things all crammed into hard-to-reach spaces.

"You've forgotten what every conscientious eco-friendly ship has," Darya said. She dashed out of the room and returned a moment later with the ship's steam cleaner dangling from a harness.

"Clever," Siva said, nodding. "You get started. I'll inform the captain."

Darya's mouth opened and closed before she nodded. Male chauvinism was alive and well in South Asia, but it wasn't the time to get into it with Siva. Besides, she didn't trust him to do a proper job.

———

When they docked, Darya rushed back to the office. She found Vivek in the processing room and dropped a frozen cardboard box on his workbench.

"This," she said, pointing at the box, "will change the world. You have to see it."

She stood staring at Vivek with an enormous grin on her face. He turned away from his microscope to meet her stare before looking in the box. The frozen remains of the soda bottle

L. B. Spillers

were inside, glistening with condensation.

"I know," Vivek said. "It's a variant of Ideonella Sakaiensis."

"How can you possibly know that? You haven't even looked at it."

Vivek shrugged. "Let's take a bike ride, Darya." He pointed at his ear and looked around the room.

Darya caught his meaning and nodded. They walked out to their bikes in silence and rode to where he kept his ratty little aluminum boat.

"So what's so sensitive that we couldn't discuss it in the shop?" Darya asked.

"Time for more truth," Vivek said. "I'll trade you. Let's start with what the drone-tampering business was about."

Darya's eyes went wide. She looked away for a moment before finally nodding at Vivek. He'd saved her life. She couldn't lie to him. "Okay. They were altering the ocean floor mapping data to exclude a specific area. Everything within a particular square kilometer was backfilled with falsified readings."

Vivek motioned for her to continue.

"That's all I know, Vivek. The code didn't tell me why. But considering what happened with not-Mike, I figure it's some kind of super-secret underwater military base or something. Something people get killed for, which is why I played dumb."

"Yes, something like that," Vivek said, smiling. "Did you know the original Ideonella Sakaiensis came from a plastic recycling facility in Japan?"

Darya harrumphed. "Yeah, Vivek, it's at the heart of what we do. What's your point?"

"My point is that the origin story for it was swallowed whole. It supposedly *evolved* onsite at that facility." He made air quotes. "It looked enough like the Ideonella genus that they were willing to overlook considerable variation from the baseline. I'm hoping that's what happens here."

Darya stared at Vivek, processing what he said. "You mean

it was engineered?"

"Yes, by me," Vivek said, nodding. "Both times. I'm sorry it almost took out the mother ship. I wasn't going to release it for some time. My best guess is that Mike got contaminated snooping around my work."

Shaking her head, Darya said, "Look, no disrespect, but unless you've been hiding a bunch of advanced degrees and a very advanced lab, that's impossible."

Vivek nodded, smiling sadly. "I'm going to miss you, Darya. Before I go—"

"Vivek, no! You can't run away. That will just make people suspicious. You have to—"

"Before I go," Vivek repeated, putting up his hand. "I want to scare you into keeping your mouth shut. That bit of the ocean they are fudging the mapping of has an underwater extra-terrestrial base. Your government is more than willing to kill people to guard that secret. Mike was no rogue agent. Me disappearing will draw suspicion away from you."

Vivek waited for Darya to digest what he said. She stood there with her mouth hanging open for a moment.

"Vivek, if you really did invent the thing that will end the plastic apocalypse, then why not take credit? And why should a super geneticist know dick about secret alien bases?"

Smiling, Vivek said, "You haven't thought it through. I haven't ended a plastic apocalypse, I've just started one. This microbe is durable and pernicious. Its appetite goes well beyond PET plastics now. It's already gotten off the island and out into the world. They just haven't figured it out yet. It's just started. Look at what happened to the mother ship."

Darya shook her head. "So what? So a few parts have to be made of other materials. It's a small price to pay."

Vivek looked out to sea for a moment before replying. "Long term, you're right, Darya. But the transition is going to be ugly. People will die. Imagine when this bug gets loose in a hospital. Every IV bag, every bit of tubing, all the sterile packaging. That's just one tiny example."

"So—"

Vivek pointed a finger at her. "So, you be extremely careful."

"But where will you go?"

"To your favorite square kilometer of ocean floor," Vivek said, walking into the surf.

Darya stared open mouthed as his head disappeared under the waves. ∎

L. B. Spillers

SEIZED MEMORY

Half the reason to visit Contrivance was to ride the maglev line. Raised on slender, sand-colored arches, it elegantly loped across the land like a skinny cousin of the Roman aqueduct. Greg had looked forward to riding it for weeks.

Reality crushed his geeky anticipation. Initially, he found watching from the front of the observation deck soothing. His body was lulled by the magnetically cushioned ride as his eyes were drawn forward to the placid horizon. But when they entered more hilly terrain, the experience soured. At 250 mph, otherwise gentle shifts in the terrain seemed to rush toward the side of the train, shocking him. Service sheds and utility poles streaked by the train's nose, far too close for comfort. Greg flinched at each invasion of his periphery. Online reviewers had called it thrilling.

Greg retreated a few rows back and enjoyed watching the soothingly stable western horizon out his window.

Minutes later, his phone beeped a warning as auras tinged everything in his vision. Knowing that he had only seconds, Greg grabbed a clear plastic mouthguard from his jacket pocket and shoved it between his jaws.

The seizure itself wasn't something he feared. He wouldn't remember any of it. The only worry was whether he could ride it out without startling other passengers. His life had been punctuated with well-meaning people making things worse because they didn't understand the many flavors of epilepsy.

Eyes closed, his hand was fumbling for the button to recline his seat when his mind slipped away.

Greg had refined his look with seizures in mind. He tried to appear unthreatening and sober so that a stranger would be less inclined to react out of prejudice. Always clean shaven, his short black hair was neatly parted on the side. His bland grooming was covered by equally unremarkable clothing: a hunter green button-down shirt tucked into jeans.

When Greg regained his senses, his phone app told him that the device implanted under his collarbone had kept the seizure to just 32 seconds, very good for him. He removed his mouthguard, discovering a pain in his right forearm from banging against the armrest. A seizure usually left him with a souvenir, so finding it quickly was a comfort.

The only other passenger in his row was still asleep. He smiled at his small victory.

The train eventually slowed to a stop inside a hill. Contrivance's commercial district sat atop it. Greg was prepared to hate the place because it wasn't an open town. Visitors needed permission. Nonetheless, it was the town of the future, a novelty that the engineer in him had to see. So when a hotel promotion had offered a free train ticket if he booked a room, he took the opportunity to satisfy his curiosity.

That was how he had explained it to BrainFart23 in his online epilepsy support group. They had a close, anonymous friendship. Two years of clues dribbled out in online chats with her made Greg believe that she lived in Contrivance. When he had mentioned his upcoming trip, she confirmed it, suggesting that they meet. Contrivance was something to see, but Greg really came to find out if his relationship with BrainFart23— Alma—could thrive in the real world.

Greg followed signs to a visitor's desk where he was offered a Counselor Link, an earpiece for talking with the town's administrative artificial intelligence. The Counselor would answer questions, give directions, and help with just about anything. When Greg waved his own wireless earpiece at them, snidely commenting that the Counselor Link should be available as a phone app, they quickly updated his phone. Minutes later he muttered his thanks as he shuffled away from the counter, shamed by the staff's friendliness and efficiency.

Exiting the station, the lack of asphalt and concrete in the shopping district surprised Greg. It was all wood and stone and greenery. The storefronts had garden terraces above them which fronted another row of stores set back farther from the street. It gave the area an open feeling while allowing for a lot of retail space. Shop Street's architecture combined with ingenious landscaping made Greg feel more like he was walking through a park with shops rather than a town center with green space.

A three-foot cube with rounded edges rolled in front of Greg, blocking his way. It emitted a pleasant chime as its top opened.

"What the hell are you?" Greg muttered.

"A delivery drone, sent by your hotel," answered his earpiece. The voice was a velvety baritone with a British accent.

Greg gasped and yanked out his earpiece. He looked around, feeling foolish, before putting it back in. "Counselor, I presume?"

The side of the drone facing Greg opened and lowered a little ramp.

"Yes, sorry, I would have introduced myself," the Counselor said. "But you seemed to understand the situation when they updated your phone. Put your bag inside. The drone will take it to your hotel room. You don't have to waste time checking in."

Greg rolled his bag into the drone and collapsed the handle. After a pause, he noticed the large, blinking, green button, and pressed it. After another friendly chime, the drone closed up and rolled away.

"Counselor, I'd like to—"

"Sorry to interrupt, but Dr. Misaki is looking for you," the Counselor said. "He's the head of nano-products at Plexus Corp. See the fellow at your one o'clock with the white shirt?"

"Counselor, how the hell did he know I would be here?" Greg scanned the crowd.

"It's in the fine print of your free train ticket. You're on the Plexus Corp recruitment roster, so he got a ping."

Greg caught Dr. Misaki's eye across the street and received a wave in return. He recognized Misaki's goateed face from a magazine profile. As the short man approached, his body language projected confidence and vitality, reminding Greg of his former karate instructor.

"Greg, hi, I'm Hiro Misaki. I work in nano-products for Plexus. Can I buy you a coffee?" Dr. Misaki offered his hand.

Greg smiled and shook hands. "I'm familiar with your work. I could use some coffee as long as you don't try to sell me a condo."

Dr. Misaki nodded his head and laughed. "I deserved that. No, no condo." He motioned for Greg to follow. "Let's go to Justine's Place. We can chat there."

Justine's Place turned out to be a coffee shop and pastry bar in the morning, a farm-to-table bistro in the afternoon, and the place for California craft beers in the evening. To Greg, that precise targeting of the zeitgeist diluted its appeal.

"Companies in Contrivance maintain recruitment lists," Dr. Misaki said as he walked Greg through to the back patio which looked towards the sea. Much of Contrivance was visible, spread below them on the gentle slope of the hill. "The Counselor lets us know when a potential recruit is visiting."

"Yes, the Counselor was just explaining to me that there's no such thing as a free lunch. I'm flattered, but I wasn't expecting any kind of interview. I came as a tourist."

A server greeted them as they took their seats near the railing.

After they ordered, Dr. Misaki continued. "Let me introduce you to the town." He stood up and pointed out areas of interest visible from the terrace. He recommended the park which doubled as a sculpture garden. Shaped like a teardrop, its pointy end was visible from the terrace, marked by a large statue. It widened as it descended towards the ocean.

Dr. Misaki's favorite restaurants flanked the park with outdoor seating overlooking it. Once his all important eateries were detailed, he started to chronicle the development of Contrivance. His lecture was soon interrupted by the arrival of their orders.

After they sipped their coffees and tasted their pastries, Misaki got to business. "I'm sorry to have intruded on your morning. It's bad form, but when I saw your name, I had to meet you. I'm a fan of yours. When you published your brain stimulator hack, that was a big deal for nano-products. You started a much-needed conversation about consumer rights."

The brain stimulator embedded under Greg's collarbone used self-positioning nano-filament electrodes. It made for a very minimally invasive implantation, but they weren't intended to be repositioned outside the safety of an operating room. After hacking the device and carefully analyzing its telemetry, Greg computed better positions for the probes. He saw no need for an expensive procedure to adjust them.

The medical community considered what Greg did absurdly dangerous. Greg was surprised that Dr. Misaki was on his side, considering his role at Plexus.

"I wish I could say that I had the big picture in mind when I did it." Greg examined the layers of his pastry. "I was a pissed-off customer. I wanted all my data, and I wanted complete control of the thing. I'm just lucky that all the publicity kept me from being sued by the manufacturer."

Dr. Misaki chuckled. "You've got balls! Your algorithm for moving the electrodes is stunningly elegant. And the signal processing improvements you made in your phone app are brilliant. It inspired our work on dynamic pacemaker electrodes. How about you come by tomorrow and I give you a tour of our facility?"

Greg shifted in his seat. If dinner with Alma that evening

goes well, he hoped to be spending tomorrow with her. "I appreciate your interest and enthusiasm, but I have plans already. With a little notice I might have—"

Misaki put his hands up. "You're right. I'm sorry. Tell you what, I'll set something up for tomorrow and send you an invitation. If you can make it, I'll gladly pick up your hotel bill. How's that work for you?"

Greg took another bite of his almond croissant as he considered his response. Work and career were the last things he wanted to think about during this rare chunk of downtime.

"Okay, Dr. Misaki. I'll give it some thought."

"Excellent!" Dr. Misaki stood up, grinning. "I've got to run. I'll email you later."

Of course, you already have my email address, Greg thought as he stood up and shook hands with his potential employer. He watched Dr. Misaki retreat through Justine's Place, bemused by how easily the man had disrupted his little getaway and perhaps his career.

———

After leaving Justine's Place, Greg worked his way down through the seaward slope of the town on foot. Despite the bustle, the streets were oddly quiet because they lacked noisy car engines.

The vehicles on the roads were tiny, insubstantial looking electric cars each holding one or two people. All property of the town, they silently glided along the streets, coordinated by the Counselor. Greg spent several minutes watching one busy intersection. Without a stoplight, the perfectly timed flows of crossing traffic were mesmerizing. He kept expecting to see a crash as cars crossed each other's paths with little room to spare.

When Greg reached The Split, where the tip of the park divided the town, he took the brook path. It lazily switchbacked down through the park towards the ocean, crossed occasionally by beautiful little bridges. Hidden from the open grass lawns of the park by well-placed berms and hillocks, Greg enjoyed the Counselor's commentary about the sculptures he encountered along the way.

The brook eventually disappeared underground into the town's water management system. Greg continued his walk downhill through the woods that separated the park from the seashore. The pristine flagstone path wound through trees that stood in neat rows. The artificiality of it reminded him of Justine's Place. Both were over-engineered and soulless.

The trail forked at a thirty-foot cliff at the coast. To his left was a scenic overlook with a picnic table. To his right, the trail sloped down towards the town beach and the marina. Greg sat on the stone bench at the trail junction to enjoy the view of the ocean.

After a few moments, he noticed a man sitting at the picnic table. As if sensing Greg's gaze, the man suddenly turned and locked eyes with him. Greg smiled and gave him a low wave.

A beep from Greg's phone told him that activity in his temporal lobe was building to a seizure. It had never happened without auras in his vision.

Time stretched out as he fumbled for his mouthpiece. He hadn't had multiple seizures in one day for over a year. Was it because of his stimulator hack? That question terrified him as his bony ass slid off the bench, jarring his spine. Greg fell sideways to the ground, mouthpiece in hand, oblivious.

When he regained his senses, the app on his phone reported that the seizure had lasted nearly two minutes. Greg noted that he had banged his left calf against the base of the bench. Without his mouthpiece, he had also gouged the inside of his cheek.

He staggered to his feet. The man in the picnic area was gone. As much as Greg hated do-gooders intervening, he was annoyed at the man's lack of concern.

A wave of nausea hit Greg. Sitting back down on the bench, he used his phone app to look for clues. Brainwave activity hadn't returned to its usual baseline. Because the new pattern wasn't typical for him, the automated system hadn't responded.

Greg's stomach churned, sweat rolled off his forehead, and his head ached like he was on the ugly end of a caffeine jag. He had never felt so completely unwell in all his life. His usual partial complex seizure had segued into what seemed like an autonomic one—the first in his life. Epilepsy didn't work that way for him. As far as he knew, it didn't work that way for anyone.

Looking around, he searched for environmental triggers. He saw nothing obvious. His eyes settled on the empty picnic table. Could the creepy stranger have done something to him during the seizure? In that moment he needed relief more than answers, so he set aside his paranoia and brought up the one screen on his app that he had never used.

Having cracked the code on his anti-seizure device, Greg's app had access to functionality that was normally restricted to doctors. The stimulator had a generic function—the Rebase function—meant to respond to abnormal brainwave patterns not already preprogrammed for the patient.

Greg paused a moment, his finger above the screen.

"God hates a coward," he muttered, triggering the function.

He gasped as his implant fought the abnormal electrical currents in his brain. The memory of the mystery man flashed into his mind, morphing in his vision. His limbs lengthened and thinned while his skin turned pasty. An oversized head bobbed on that spindly frame. Greg's mouth fell open as he stared at the grey alien's large, black eyes.

As quickly as it had appeared, the alien disappeared. Greg was left gaping at the deserted picnic table, breathing heavily. After a few moments, he consulted his phone which confirmed that his brainwave activity had normalized.

"Counselor, what can you tell me about the guy who was in the picnic area when I got here?"

"No one has been there since you arrived at the bench," the Counselor replied.

Curious about the Counselor's choice of words, Greg asked, "How long have I been on this bench?"

"About seventeen minutes."

To Greg, it had felt like less than five minutes. Stunned and very confused, he lay down on the bench and closed his eyes.

Minutes later the email chime from his phone pulled Greg out of his doze. Alma had replied to his note, confirming their dinner arrangements. They still hadn't ever heard each other's voice.

———

That night, Greg went to meet Alma for dinner. From their talks online, he knew that she came from a large Mexican family. Her boisterous online persona made him visualize her ridiculously as some kind of telenovela cliché: a loud, over-emotional Latina slathered in makeup, and dressed in sexy clothing.

The reality was much better. Her long, wavy black hair framed a pretty face with prominent cheekbones. She had almost no makeup on and didn't need any. Wearing a modest white cotton blouse over a pleated, flower print skirt, she looked at Greg seeming ready to laugh or slap him as needed.

Standing face to face with her in the restaurant bar, Greg had no idea what to do, so he smiled and offered her a handshake.

"You don't get off that easy," Alma said, kissing him on the cheek and pulling him in for a tight hug. The broach on her blouse painfully pushed against his chest. "We've shared too much."

Stunned by her energy and presence, Greg said, "Go easy on me, woman, you know I'm an introverted gringo."

She laughed, took his arm, and guided him to the hostess station. "I thought for sure you'd be one of those dumpy, balding geeks living in his mother's basement. And here you are all handsome with most of your hair, and serious—too serious! You're on vacation, right?"

The hostess banged twice on a small *taiko* drum. The sushi chefs called out Japanese greetings as she led Greg and Alma to the terrace.

"Well I thought I was, but Dr. Misaki, recruiting for Plexus, ambushed me at the train station," Greg said. "It was pushy and flattering and very much not vacation like."

Alma smiled. "I know Hiro. Let me guess. You got a discounted train ticket and hotel room from some mailer, right?"

"Pretty much. The ticket was free. How'd you know?" Greg asked.

Alma looked out over the park for a moment. "The town council is always trying to entice the right people to visit and work in Contrivance. The mailers are part of that."

"Who decides who the right people are?" Greg asked, watching Alma's face. He realized that they had slipped into the comfortable back and forth they shared online. Hope and anxiety swirled in him. He suppressed a nervous giggle that was forming in his chest.

"Exactly!" Alma said, slapping the table lightly. "I love this town, but sometimes the council's attitude can be condescending and paternalistic. They see Contrivance as the prototype for the town of the future. It might be, but sometimes it feels very..."

"Inorganic?" Greg suggested. "Exclusionary? Controlled?"

Alma smiled at him. "Yes, all that. You've only been here for a day, and already you've tuned into it. Everything, and I mean every damn thing in this town, is excellent, but it's their idea of excellent."

After they ordered, Greg told Alma about his strange experience from that afternoon, omitting the autonomic seizure that had followed. That follow-on seizure represented a change to his epilepsy that she would insist required immediate medical attention. He didn't want to pollute their first meeting with an argument.

She wasn't shocked or even surprised.

"I've heard stories of seizure-related memory hiccups, especially with complex partial seizures like yours. It's nothing to worry about. Your seizures are in the temporal lobe. It's memory central."

"What do you think I should do?" Greg asked.

Alma shrugged. "I think you should set it aside. Come to tomorrow night's meeting. The group would love to have a chance to hear about brain stimulation firsthand."

Greg's mind flashed on the few in-person epilepsy support group meetings he had attended. "I don't know, Alma, those can be so heavy. You already told me I'm too serious, right?"

"Oh, please. You're not going to throw my own words back at me." She wagged a finger in his face. "Our group skews geeky, not emotional. Besides, the food will be really good."

Greg's eyebrows went up. Food was Alma's passion. She hardly ever tried a famous San Francisco restaurant that she didn't eviscerate online. "BrainFart23 calling any food really good is as rare as an honest politician."

Alma blushed. "Well, the meeting is at my house this month. We're having savory hors d'oeuvres, proper coffee, and Dianne is bringing her juice setup. She makes the best fresh juice blends that you'll ever taste."

Greg laughed. "Okay, I'm in, but mostly for the food."

When dinner was over, they had the inevitable awkward moment outside the restaurant. It was a good first date, but Greg knew that two years online with Alma gave him a false sense of intimacy that she might not share. He was terrified of

L. B. Spillers   65

saying the wrong thing.

"Still so serious?" Alma said, smiling. "Look, it was fabulous to finally meet you in person. I like you, but that wasn't a date, you hear? I got divorced three months ago and I'm not starting anything right now, especially long distance." She studied his face for a response. "Are you disappointed?"

Greg smiled at her directness. He appreciated that she had ripped off the Band-Aid quickly. "This was a lot of fun. I'm not disappointed by any of it." Of course, he was disappointed. If Alma wasn't the perfect woman she appeared to be, he wanted the chance to discover those imperfections one by one, firsthand.

"You're a sweet man," Alma said, kissing him on the cheek. "I'll see you tomorrow night."

A man being called sweet was like food being called interesting, Greg thought as he headed to his hotel. On the upside, he would have time for Dr. Misaki.

———

The tour of the Plexus facility started at nine the next morning.

Dr. Misaki had set up two mini-tours with project leaders. This allowed Greg to get a sense of the corporate culture.

Greg's notoriety was confirmed repeatedly. Most of the engineers thought his hack was brave but stupid, but everyone seemed to respect that he had enough confidence to be his own test subject.

An HR representative took Greg to lunch at the company cafeteria while Dr. Misaki conferred with the people who had spent time with Greg.

After lunch, the HR rep dropped Greg off at Dr. Misaki's office. The office's corner of windows overlooked the facility's gardens. Greg stared at the raised beds of sprouting greenery outside Misaki's windows.

"You'd be surprised how therapeutic our associates find

garden work," Dr. Misaki said. "And a month from now, our offices will fill with the scent of flowers."

Greg smiled at the sight of a few business-casual gardeners. "So how'd I do?"

Dr. Misaki directed Greg to an upholstered chair and sat down opposite him.

"The guys were impressed. More importantly, they like you, even Henkins. That's saying something."

Greg suppressed a frown. Henkins was the obnoxious ass that had insisted on arguing about the ethical and legal aspects of Greg's hack.

Greg shrugged. "A curious stamp of approval, but I'll take it."

Dr. Misaki paused for a moment before speaking. "Greg, I'd like to offer you a job, but to tell you about it requires a non-disclosure agreement. So now's the time to tell me if you're committed to your current gig. I'd understand. Moving to Contrivance would be a big change that you weren't looking for."

Greg tilted his head, confused. An NDA just to hear the offer? It'd be a no-brainer if Alma had been more receptive.

"I'm definitely interested," Greg said. He was only mildly interested but wanted to hear what was so sensitive that it required an NDA.

When Dr. Misaki dropped the papers in front of Greg, he was shocked to see that it was a federal form. Greg was being granted access to classified information.

After Greg signed, Dr. Misaki nodded and took the papers back.

"Greg, the reason that Contrivance consistently pumps out such amazing technology is that we collaborate with extra-terrestrials. The job I have in mind for you would be liaising with them on classified research projects—adapting their technology."

Greg stared at Misaki, waiting for the punch line.

"Yes, I'm completely serious," Dr. Misaki said.

Greg scratched his head, not sure what to say.

"Dr. Misaki, closed town or not, NDA or not, that kind of secret is impossible to control. Is this some kind of test or joke?"

Dr. Misaki stood up, motioning for Greg to remain seated. He backed away from Greg, unbuttoning the top few buttons of his shirt. A hiss of air came from him as a line appeared across his throat. The sides of his face came away from his head. Misaki's hands pulled off his mask. He cradled it under his arm like a helmet and stared at Greg with the enormous, black eyes of a grey alien.

Greg's heartbeat thudded in his ears as the room brightened and wavered in his vision. He shook his head.

The alien Dr. Misaki laughed. The sound came from the mask under his arm. Greg was disoriented by the mismatched movement of Misaki's thin alien lips. "You're taking this better than most, Greg. You believe me now?"

Greg nodded.

Misaki put his mask back on. Greg was riveted by the sight of the thing reshaping itself on the alien's head.

"The NDA is a last resort that gives the FBI legal standing to come down on anyone that tries to talk. To answer your question, we keep it quiet with memory manipulation. If you say no to the job, your memory of this meeting will be erased. It's harmless. You get disoriented and maybe lose a little time."

That explained the seizure twofer in the park with the lost time, Greg thought. He didn't want to relive that anytime soon. "What if I don't want my brain futzed with?"

"You agreed to it in the NDA." Dr. Misaki shrugged.

Greg groaned. "I need some time to think about this."

Dr. Misaki shook his head. "No, you don't. You're either enthusiastically with us, or you're not. The fact that you need to think about it is the answer."

As Greg was forming his reply, Dr. Misaki stepped forward and put a hand on Greg's temple.

Greg felt a sharp pain in his head before passing out. He woke to the sounds of Dr. Misaki talking.

"So, Greg, we think you're well qualified," Dr. Misaki said. "We'll give you our decision once we've interviewed our other candidate. Should be no more than a week. Okay?"

Greg looked around the room, confused, before focusing on Dr. Misaki. "Sounds good." He stood up shakily. "I don't feel well. Is there a men's room nearby?"

Dr. Misaki walked Greg down the hall to the nearest men's room. He had his assistant wait for Greg.

Standing at the row of sinks, Greg checked on his brain telemetry. It was another autonomic seizure. He triggered the Rebase function on his stimulator and fell to the floor in pain. The memories that Misaki had erased flooded back into his mind.

Responding to the sounds of Greg's distress, Misaki's assistant entered the bathroom and helped Greg to his feet. They had a brief argument about whether Greg needed an ambulance. Greg ended the conversation by demonstrating his ability to walk out of the bathroom and make his way to the elevator.

———

After being shuttled back to his hotel by a driverless electric car, Greg walked slowly to his room and fell into bed.

When he awoke from his nap, Greg's instinct was to flee Contrivance, but he wanted to keep his promise to Alma, and confront her.

That evening, Greg took the trolley to Alma's house in a suburb of Contrivance. It left him a short walk away.

Solar panels covered every roof. The reflections off them were a technological intrusion into the otherwise pastoral feeling of the neighborhood. As Greg strolled down the sidewalk, he was struck by how the lack of garages and driveways made the xeriscaped yards seem so much larger.

When Alma opened her door she frowned. "My God, Greg, you look like shit."

"I've had a peculiar day," he said, forcing a grin.

The support group meeting was the seven of them sitting in Alma's backyard chatting while enjoying what Greg agreed was very good food. Alma prompted him to talk about his experience with brain stimulation as a coping tool for epilepsy.

Only one other person at the meeting had complex partial seizures like Greg's. Although the press about Greg's hack tended to talk up the technology, he did his best to talk her out of trying it. He didn't want to be responsible for her decision.

When it came time for the meeting to break up, Greg hung back to speak with Alma.

"What is it, Greg? Did your interview go okay?"

Greg watched her carefully as he spoke. He wasn't sure how to ask his question.

"The interview went well, Alma, but something strange happened." Greg paused, choosing his words carefully. "Dr. Misaki isn't who I thought he was. And a horrible, unkind question came to me. It would give me some peace of mind to know the answer."

Alma gave him a concerned look. "Peace of mind?"

Greg looked up, avoiding Alma's eyes, before shaking his head in frustration. "I think you figured out that I came to Contrivance because I had a huge crush on you. But my meeting with Misaki left me feeling very manipulated, violated really. So I..."

"You what?" Alma asked softly.

"I want to know if you were part of recruiting me. I know that's an awful thing to ask, but I've had the most singularly disturbing day. I'd tell you more, but I actually signed an NDA about it."

Alma's eyes went wide in surprise. "Wow. Just wow, Greg." She folded her arms across her chest and looked down. "No, Greg, I didn't play you. I'd like you to leave now."

———

Greg arose early the next day. He left the hotel and headed towards Justine's Place for breakfast. The events of the previous day bounced around inside his head as he walked.

After a few minutes, Alma, dressed for jogging, came up behind Greg and silently fell in beside him. Greg was startled for a moment, but walked on in silence, not wanting to disrupt what might be some kind of reconciliation.

She put her finger to her lips to keep him quiet. Then she pulled out her phone and powered it off in front of him. When she pointed at him, he nodded.

Greg pulled out his own phone and powered it off, reluctant to be without an interface to his brain stimulator.

"Good morning?" Greg said.

"Not so good, Greg. And I don't mean that horrible shit you hit me with last night. You shouldn't have remembered signing the NDA. The Counselor heard you in my house."

Greg's pulse quickened. He started looking around, feeling an adrenaline rush.

"Calm down," Alma said. "Keep walking. This needs to look like a friendly chat if I'm going to help you."

Greg stopped and stared at her. "How can—"

"Greg, please," Alma pleaded. She placed her hand on the side of his head. Her rough glove was not soothing. He couldn't read her eyes. After a moment she pulled her hand away. "Just keep walking, and smile."

Greg suppressed his fears and complied.

"I'm the friendly face that will deliver you to have your memory properly adjusted," Alma said. She pulled the scrunchie off her ponytail. "It'll require more powerful equipment. Something about your brain stimulator is not playing nice with our town's tech. I'm convinced that a deep adjustment will badly damage your brain. I told them that. They still want to be sure."

"So, what then?" Greg asked.

"I'll report that you've agreed to meet me later today. That'll relax them. You go to the train station right now, no luggage, no nothing, and get a ticket for the next train out. Do it right before it leaves. With luck, they won't have time to respond. Understand?"

Greg slowly shook his head no.

Alma dropped her head and sighed. "Greg, you can be really stupid for a genius. You get on that train and never come back. And for fuck's sake, keep your mouth shut."

Before Greg could respond, Alma turned and jogged away.

At the ticket booth in the train station, he managed to move up his return trip to 7:30 AM, just eight minutes away. The train was already waiting with its doors open.

Greg walked calmly to the train, feigning morning grogginess, and not making eye contact with anyone. He boarded, and quickly found his seat.

Time passed agonizingly slowly. Greg's eyes cycled from his watch to the platform out his window, and back again as the seconds ticked by.

With a minute until departure, he saw a policeman approach the car with way too much purpose in his stride. The officer boarded and walked directly to Greg's seat.

"Sir, would you please come with me?"

Greg sat paralyzed. The other passengers turned to stare at him. His mind frantically searched for something to say that would keep him in his seat.

Alma appeared behind the police officer. "There's been a change of plans," she said.

Alma put her gloved hand on the side of the officer's head. Greg winced at a sharp pain in his own head as the officer's eyes went glassy.

"Of course, ma'am," the policeman said while following her to the train door. He grabbed the microphone velcroed to his shoulder, and spoke into it, "We're clear for departure." The door closed as he wandered away.

As the train pulled out, Greg watched a squad of other police officers surround Alma on the platform. ∎

L. B. Spillers

SHORT-TERM HORRIBLE

A car traveling ninety miles per hour, filled with four screaming people, crashed into a concrete bridge support. On a video monitor, nineteen-year-old Conrad Mendes watched the looping, slow-motion playback. The way the car hood rippled like water before exploding fascinated him.

"That's not what I signed up for, Connie!" his friend's voice yelled over the headset. "They weren't avoiding anything. The controller just crashed that car for no reason. The AI murdered those people. Your friends caused this."

A year previously, when a student's car had lost its wheel at high speed on I-30, the Dallas Metro Traffic Controller had run the failing car into a bridge column to keep it from damaging expensive construction equipment, killing two students. Despite the government exonerating itself with a blue-ribbon commission, many people still believed the AI sacrificed the lives of two people to save money.

Unsatisfied by government inaction, Conrad's hacker friends had adjusted the AI to prioritize saving human life. The guy on the phone was their man on the inside who had provided the hackers access to the AI.

"I don't think their code changes could have caused this," Conrad said slowly, not quite believing his own words.

Two more crash-alert windows popped up on Conrad's screen.

"Jesus Connie!" Conrad flinched at the shout. "That's three unprovoked crashes in like five minutes."

Conrad clicked on one of the alerts to look at the details.

"I'm hanging up, Connie. We don't know each other. You and I never speak again."

By the time the emergency shutdown brought Dallas' regional roadways to a standstill, 179 people had been killed, willfully sent to their deaths by the AI.

Twenty years later, Conrad lay in a drunken sleep, his body twitching as he endured his recurring nightmare. Sprinting down a Dallas sidewalk on a beautiful sunny day, he dodged cars slamming into the building right behind him. Over and over, AI-controlled cars jumped the curb, leaping at Conrad like eager predators. They became more and more aggressive until the sight of a green Kia Soul tumbling through the air towards him shocked him awake.

Conrad awoke with a start, aching from his shoulder to his hip. Feeling concrete against his fingers, he cursed.

"Bad dream?" a voice asked.

Standing up slowly, his balance shaky, Conrad wiped the drool from his face with his forearm. He turned to the party's hostess, Nancy, slouching in an expensive, metal mesh, outdoor rocking chair. She had been keeping watch over her passed-out coworkers.

"Yeah," Conrad said. "It's the reason I usually don't drink. My dreams get rough."

She pointed at the crystal bong couched on her lap. "Want a hit? Might take the edge off."

Conrad grinned at her. As the vice president of human resources, Nancy was in charge of enforcing corporate drug policy.

"No thanks," Conrad said. "I'm gonna need every synapse to get going on the new contract."

Loosening up his neck, he surveyed the remains of the party in the pre-dawn twilight. Bottles, cups, cigarette butts, pizza boxes, and snack bags were strewn everywhere. Elegant serving dishes peeked out from under the debris. Three of their co-workers were draped over the patio furniture like dirty rags.

Nancy followed his gaze and smiled. "Things got a little crazy last night."

It had begun as a sedate dinner party with eight guests. Calls had started coming in around 8 PM about winning the contract. Dinner had morphed into a celebration. Eight guests had become fifty. As the man of the hour, everyone had insisted on doing a shot with Conrad. Sometime after that, his memory became fuzzy.

"I've gotta go, Nancy," Conrad mumbled. "Thanks for dinner. It was an epic party."

Conrad turned away from her and pulled out his phone to call a car.

Nancy giggled at Conrad as he sluggishly moved away along the edge of the pool. He stopped to take a long drink from a stray 2-liter bottle while his legs woke up. As he set down the soda he stopped to stare at something on the bottom of the pool, lit by underwater lights. After a moment, Conrad remembered Nancy ripping it from some terrified QA guy's hands and hurling it into the pool in a rare show of snobbery from their hostess who had displayed an otherwise ecumenical sense of debauchery.

"No box wine!" Nancy yelled from her chair, shattering the early morning calm. Conrad's sleeping coworkers stirred.

Conrad hurried to the fence, not wanting to talk to any of them. He took one last look at the mess as he gently closed the backyard gate.

———

For the second time that morning, Conrad woke up confused.

"Get up, Conrad."

Sitting up, he looked around his bedroom. No one was there with him. He fell back on his pillow.

"Get up, you lazy putz."

Conrad sat up quickly. "Who's there?"

"I'm in your head, dumbass," The Voice said.

"Ah hell," Conrad muttered. Hearing voices meant

schizophrenia, or worse.

"You're not schizo, you idiot," The Voice said, anticipating his concern.

Conrad rushed to his bathroom and stripped off his clothes. In the long mirror on the back of the door, he inspected his body looking for evidence that he had been injured at the party. Aside from his usual dissatisfaction, he saw nothing concerning.

He decided to ignore The Voice. Engaging with it would only make things worse.

During his long shower, he thought about where he might go for help, and how to hide it from his employer. The new contract was his biggest project ever. It would secure his position as Raj's successor, but not if his mental health came into question.

Conrad made himself coffee. He didn't hear The Voice as he puttered around his kitchen. Still not completely sober, the idea that he had imagined The Voice seemed more plausible as the minutes stretched out.

He microwaved some late breakfast before finally sitting in front of his computer. While fumbling with the electronic dongle needed to access his office VPN, The Voice interrupted him. It directed him to a website. He typed in the given web address and stopped.

"This is nuts," he muttered. "Who are you? How am I hearing you?"

"DO IT!" the voice bellowed in his head. Conrad covered his ears, curling his head down to his lap.

After a few moments of silence, Conrad sat back up and complied. The video began simply enough with a boy playing in a sparsely furnished bedroom. Moments after a balding middle-aged man entered the frame, Conrad vomited up his breakfast burrito, barely managing to catch it with his office wastebasket. "You should've warned me."

"Nothing prepares you to see that," The Voice said. "I want you to help me kill that man."

Conrad spoke to the air as he walked his wastebasket into the kitchen. "Sounds pretty schizophrenic to me. A voice in my head tells me that I have to kill someone." He was proud of his self-awareness and wondered what sort of relationship other people had with their voices.

Conrad upended his small office wastebasket into the kitchen trash can. Mercifully a nest of papers had caught his vomit, preventing it from fouling the bamboo.

The kitchen garbage bag fought him as he made his way out of his apartment. "So why not send the video to the cops?"

Conrad saw one of his neighbors, Ms. Arenas, at the end of the hallway. She had shunned him ever since he dodged her tenant-mixer cocktail party. He smiled and waved, wondering if she had seen him speaking to the air like a madman. Thankfully she lazily returned his wave and disappeared into her unit.

"He's a federal agent," The Voice said. "You never see his face on those videos he makes. He falsifies strong alibis. The chance that he would be convicted is low."

At the end of the hallway, coconut-scented disinfectant assailed Conrad when he opened the garbage chute, roiling his stomach. He chucked the bag in and quickly closed the door. Hunched over, trying to calm his stomach, he returned to his apartment.

Back in his kitchen, Conrad struggled to think of what to do. His hangover was raging. Pain pulsed behind his eyes with each heartbeat. He chugged a glass of water with some aspirin and dropped onto his couch. He let the low patter from BBC World News lull him to sleep.

———

When Conrad awoke for the third time that day, he was mostly recovered from Friday night's party. He turned off his TV, tilted his head, and listened carefully. Standing up slowly, he crept towards his bathroom as if quick movements would wake the beast in his head.

The Voice started talking when he turned on his bathroom light. Conrad tensed up and instinctively covered his ears with his hands.

"Expect an email from me with instructions. You're doing it very early Wednesday morning."

Conrad sighed and straightened up. His hopes that The Voice was some kind of transient episode evaporated. Since a psychiatrist would first want to rule out physical causes for The Voice, he decided to start there.

He walked through the automatic glass doors of the emergency room at 4 PM.

The crowd from Friday night's drunken stupid-human-tricks had been cleared out. As he faced the intake nurse, he decided that understated delivery was the key. Loud demands for service would be taken as a sign of robust health. However, sheepishly suggest that you may have cracked your skull on a pool surround, and you quickly get attention.

After a brief neurological examination, they x-rayed his head.

"Other than your cochlear implant, there's nothing to see," the doctor said. "No fractures, no obvious swelling. Head injuries are tricky, and X-rays only show so much..."

The doctor's words faded into the background as Conrad walked to the large monitor on the wall where the digital radiograph of his head was displayed. His finger traced the neat lines of the electronic snake coiled around his left ear canal. His hearing had always been flawless.

Conrad mumbled his thanks to the doctor and hurried for the exit in a stunned haze. In the stairwell of the parking garage, he fell against the wall, hugging himself and shaking.

Between gasping breaths, Conrad asked the air "How...did you...get that...in my head?"

The Voice said, "I've got an associate who has invented self-positioning medical appliances. You make a tiny incision and the thing crawls inside and makes itself at home. Won't hit the market for years. You should feel honored. And don't worry about the battery running down." The Voice chuckled. "It runs on a blood-powered fuel cell."

Conrad shivered at the thought of some tiny medical robot crawling inside his head. He frantically ran his fingertips over the skin near his ear, searching in vain for the scar.

———

The Voice's email was waiting for him when he got home. Scanning the instructions, he was surprised to see mostly programming work that didn't relate to killing anyone.

Whatever The Voice was, and however it intended to kill the pedophile, Conrad didn't want any part of it. He reasoned that since someone was obviously wirelessly communicating with him via his implant, he simply needed to block those signals until he could convince a doctor to remove it.

Lacking any kind of jamming equipment, Conrad improvised in the best tradition of crazy people everywhere. He wrapped his head in aluminum foil, leaving holes for seeing and breathing.

Standing in front of his bathroom mirror, he made fine adjustments to his improvised metallic mask. No matter how many times he told himself that what he was doing was sane and scientifically sound, the sight of his foiled face looking back at him in the mirror rattled him. Would he one day look back on this moment as another step in his descent into madness? Hearing a voice—check; tinfoil hat—check; plan to murder someone—check.

"Try communicating through that you prick," he muttered.

The Voice chuckled at him. "There's a copy of me in your implant. It's weaker than my full self but more than capable of punishing you, Conrad. Remove the foil now!"

Conrad gasped. *It was an AI the whole time? But isn't this the sort of delusion an AI specialist would have?*

Lost in thought, he made no move to remove the foil.

The Voice said, "You need a demonstration," before a piercing noise made Conrad shriek and fall to his knees.

———

A boar slammed against the steel fencing separating the small parking lot where Conrad stood from the pigs on the other side. He flinched at the sound. It was not how he had envisioned his Monday morning. There was a ton of work to do on the new contract. Raj knew it yet insisted on sending him to this pig-sieged factory to give the VIP treatment to a potential client. It was Raj's way of reminding Conrad that despite his big win on Friday, he still had to step and fetch on command.

The aggressive livestock was the result of the factory owner taking advantage of tax incentives by generating power for his plant via fermenting pig waste. Sonic technology kept them mostly crapping where their waste could be collected. The feces processing setup was fifty yards from where Conrad was standing. Every time he got used to the smell, the odor of fermented pig shit shifted a little, astounding him with its offensive versatility.

The prospective client was late. Conrad tried to put The Voice out of his mind, ignore the stench, and focus on the aborted mural on the factory wall. A spat over the artist's interpretation of the word 'pastoral' had left fifty feet of the wall looking like a dimensional portal into a neon interpretation of the Jurassic Period.

Vijay, Conrad's lead engineer, pulled him back to the present. "Hey, boss."

Conrad noticed the absence of Vijay's signature serenity. "Vijay, for a guy who is key personnel—actually written into the damn contract—in Friday's multi-million dollar deal, you look like shit. Did I mention that my name is not in that contract?"

Vijay forced a smile. "I had another visit from Nancy this morning at the office. She is coming on to me. I thought I could handle it on my own, but it's become disturbing."

Conrad stared at Vijay with wide eyes. He resisted the urge to congratulate him. Nancy was a friend, and until that moment, Conrad thought her a good corporate citizen. The weed circulating at her party had seemed like a harmless corruption of company policy. Now it looked to him like a sign of her sense of impunity.

"What's she saying? She knows that I'd knife her before letting anything happen to you."

Vijay chuckled. "Her office coordinates the Green Card application work for all our guys on H1 visas. She's suggesting that Siva and Ram could have trouble. One miscommunication from her office to the lawyers handling their cases could be catastrophic."

Conrad sighed. "Do you have any proof that makes this more than he-said-she-said?"

"Of course not," Vijay said, shaking his head. "The lady who handles sexual harassment cases is well informed on how they are to be avoided."

Conrad knew that relying on senior management's human decency would be a mistake. He started to walk the org chart in his mind, assessing the strength of each link. How much would the fates of two H1 employees weigh against Nancy's pull, his pull, and what Vijay might do? Without proof, it would be a mess. Meanwhile, he had to take care of this client for Raj and get going on the new contract. On top of all that he had to appear to be preparing for The Voice's mission in two days while securing a surgeon to get the hardware removed.

Conrad shook his head. "Sorry, Vijay, I was distracted thinking about how to handle this. I'd like you to write this up in an email to me, and continue to report incidents of her pressuring you."

Vijay nodded and pointed to the town car pulling into the parking lot behind Conrad.

"We'll talk more about this later, Vijay. Put your game face on."

When an old man emerged from the car wearing jeans and an embroidered button-down shirt, Conrad silently cursed Raj. He knew he would be dealing with an eccentric pain in the ass.

Conrad opened with a mild pushback as the man approached. "Sir, you might be better served by our marketing department. We have sales engineers who would love to show you specifically how our systems can serve your needs."

"Call me Eli, boy."

Conrad shrugged. What was the job of a salesman if not to take client abuse in stride?

Eli walked by Conrad, gesturing for him to follow. Conrad and Vijay fell in behind him.

They headed towards the enormous hangar door that stood open. The wide aisle in front of them stretched a quarter mile to the far wall of the facility giving the visitors an impressive view of the clockwork of the nearly unmanned factory. Overhead conveyor belts spanned the polished concrete floor at regular intervals. A cart crept across their view halfway down.

Eli strode by the large sign that insisted visitors don hard hats and stopped just inside the doorway. A huge stamping machine nearby hissed loudly enough to make him jump as he tried to light another cigarette.

Suppressing a laugh, Conrad turned to Vijay. "It doesn't look like this is going to get too technical. Go see what those guys need. Raj promised them they could pick your brain while I walk Eli through their plant."

"Okay, boss," Vijay said, smiling. He loved seeing the tech in situ. It gave meaning to his otherwise very abstract software engineering job.

As expected, Eli waved off the hard hat that Conrad thrust

at him. Conrad put the hat on his own head and waited for Eli to settle into his cigarette.

"I told Raj that I didn't want a bullshit salesman," Eli said.

Conrad nodded and ushered Eli down the aisle.

About ten minutes into the tour Eli asked The Question.

"Smart, Safe AI is the pitch, right?" Eli asked. "I see a whole lot of machines but no AI."

Conrad chuckled. "Did you expect creepy humanoid robots walking around? The only visual here is the enormous factory with the tiny staff. The wow factor comes when your engineers give us your requirements, and our engineers tell you how fast and inexpensively we can manufacture your stuff."

"So where is the actual AI?" Eli asked.

"There's a little of it everywhere." Conrad gestured to half the factory. "Safe AI is about segregation. The law keeps us from making a smart, general AI—a mastermind that could run the whole place with the lights out. So we deploy specialized, isolated intelligences in concert to manufacture products without the risk."

"Come on!" Eli said waving his second cigarette of the interview. "A bunch of little guys talking together still makes one big, scary fucking AI. I lived in Dallas when the AI disaster happened. Some clever feller like you had every vehicle there controlled by an AI, and—" Eli stopped and rubbed his face. "Well, you know the story."

Conrad pointed to an assembly station where mechanical arms were speedily fastening together metal components. "They can't network. Most of what the few human workers do is walk around and physically deliver instruction sets to machines." All of what Conrad was telling Eli was stuff he could have read online. "So what are we really doing here, Eli?"

Eli let out a laugh that degenerated into a hacking cough. "See? Right to the point. That's why I asked for you." Eli sucked on his cigarette. "I needed to see it. I wanted to look you in the eyes. I need to get comfortable with it all." Eli dropped his spent cigarette and began pulling out the next one from his pack. "I need to convince a bunch of god-damned concerned citizens, politicians, and other assorted pains in my ass that when I bring this shit to town, it won't go off the rails. AI manufacturing is still a very hard sell in Texas."

———

That evening, at an ear surgeon's office, Conrad waited impatiently for the doctor. Although he had brought in a memory stick containing his head x-rays from the emergency room, the doctor insisted on doing his own. That had been two hours ago. Other than half an hour spent with a technician, he had been left to stare at the bland framed prints that dotted the walls of the examination room.

A chirp drew Conrad's attention to digital X-rays that popped up on the large wall monitor. He used the touch interface to zoom in the view so that his implant filled the screen. Moments later the doctor finally appeared.

"Hello, Mr. Mendes. I hope we haven't kept you too long." The doctor pulled over a stool and sat on it. "Your request is unusual, so my tech took an especially close look at your implant. You believe your device has been hacked. Is that right?"

"More than that," Conrad said. "It was put in without my knowledge. I would like it out as soon as possible, hopefully tomorrow. I'll pay extra for the rush."

The doctor stared at him for a moment before forcing a smile. "Mr. Mendes, my technician queried the ID of your implant and checked with the manufacturer. It is registered to you. Records of the operation are in your medical file."

Conrad's face paled. He had assumed that it was custom hardware. It didn't occur to him that The Voice's electronics could emulate a production model cochlear implant. "Oh, Jesus," he said, dreading where the doctor would take the conversation.

"Furthermore, your model doesn't have any streaming features. That is, even if the thing had been compromised, it's simply not capable of accepting audio input via a wireless connection."

"I told you that you weren't getting out of this," The Voice said.

Getting no response from Conrad, the doctor started typing on his data panel. "I'm giving you a referral for—"

"A psychiatrist," Conrad said, dropping his head. His throat ached as he suppressed the urge to cry.

The doctor nodded and lowered his panel. "Please understand my position. You have an implant with perfect diagnostics. Your hearing is excellent. You have demonstrated a serious memory defect, and are apparently hearing a disembodied voice. Given the situation, it would be a breach of medical ethics to operate on you."

———

That night, Conrad sat in front of his home computer looking at the x-ray of The Voice's hardware. There was no hope of getting it removed before Wednesday. He shuddered as he remembered the brief sonic torture that The Voice had inflicted on him. The idea of trying to resist The Voice was laughable. And after Wednesday, what would change?

There was only one answer, but Conrad couldn't face it. He'd been sitting there for an hour unable to face it.

Looking at his bookcase, he saw the Hagakure and chuckled sourly. A remnant from the days when Japanese culture was mined for business practices, it instructed that a samurai should be able to make a decision in the space of seven breaths.

Conrad sighed. From his desk drawer, he removed a brushed stainless steel revolver, cocked it, and aimed it into his left ear.

"Wait," The Voice said softly.

Conrad saw the red light of his computer's webcam lit. It

hadn't occurred to him that The Voice might also have him under video surveillance.

"Why should I?" Conrad asked. "To be forced to murder a man? To live under the constant threat of torture? To be used as your tool until you're done with me? Better to die now."

"You won't be anywhere near him when the agent dies. You won't have to experience it in any way. Do this one job, and I promise I'll release control of the implant. I'll fix your medical records, and give the implant a diagnostic profile that would make any surgeon agree to remove it."

Still holding the gun to his temple, Conrad said "Why would you go to all the trouble to do this to me only to release me?"

"Getting one job out of you is better than nothing," The Voice said. "But also, I had you pegged as a worse person than you turned out to be. You have proved surprisingly virtuous in the months I've been in here."

Months? Conrad pointed the gun away and decocked it. He could live with the distant death of one serial pedophile. If The Voice was lying, the gun would still be here.

———

Wednesday, at four in the morning, Conrad climbed over a chain-link fence that surrounded a construction site. Forty stories of structural steel loomed over him, only the first twenty of which had their concrete floors poured.

The lone security bot patrolling the grounds was conveniently distracted. Also quite convenient was that the construction elevator was not locked down on the top floor, but instead waited for him at ground level.

"There's no one else here?" Conrad asked as he walked to the elevator.

"There's one guy," The Voice said. "He's monitoring that crane unloading trusses way over there in the staging area."

Conrad exited the elevator onto the bare steel decking of the 22nd floor. Above him, outlined by light pollution, a rectangular cage of naked i-beams soared above him. Dormant construction bots littered the floor. Their barely visible limbs looked like a pack of horrors ready to rip him apart.

He walked to the edge of the floor. Squinting, he saw the robotic crane that was slowly unloading concrete trusses off a truck. The oversized load was blocking the street. A police car with lights flashing was holding traffic while the crane did its work.

"A cop car?" Conrad muttered. "The sensors in that thing might be recording me right now you idiot!"

"I already told you that you'd get away with it. No prosecution. It'll just be a curious string of coincidences. Get the device ready."

Conrad pulled a drone remote control out of his knapsack. He had purchased and programmed the remote according to The Voice's instructions. A crisp, red LED verified its readiness.

"Initiate the program...now," The Voice said.

The box emitted a soft chime as Conrad hit the button. Three floors above him, a gofer-bot sprang to life. It sped along a horizontal girder, and crashed hard into an autonomous welder, sending it rolling towards the end of the beam it was perched on.

Conrad dropped to a crouch when he heard the noise. His eyes scanned the area, straining to see if any of the mechanical menagerie around him was coming to get him.

"Head back down in the elevator."

Conrad jogged into the open elevator cage. "That's it?"

"The gofer-bot's safeguards kept it from actually knocking the welder off. The welder is programmed to return to its station after a delay."

Conrad used a small flashlight to find the ground floor button and pressed it.

The Voice continued his play-by-play commentary. "The gopher-bot left the welder so precariously balanced on the end of that girder that the tiny shift in its center of mass caused by the activation of its own servos will soon tip it over the edge."

Many tense seconds passed as Conrad waited to hear a crash. The elevator reached the ground floor.

"Head back out the way you came in," The Voice said.

Confused by the lack of a crash, Conrad jogged towards the fence.

"Now the safety nets," The Voice said.

Safety lidar sensed the falling welding machine. Ten simultaneous explosions sent steel netting shooting out from the side of the fifth floor to catch the potentially lethal falling welding machine. Conrad instinctively dropped to the ground when the shockwave from the explosions hit his chest.

"You're safe," The Voice said. "Keep moving."

A recycling bin of rebar fragments left in front of a safety net module had been pushed hard by the explosively deployed assembly. A swarm of steel chunks ripped through the air like an enormous shotgun blast. The unmanned crane's cab was peppered with shrapnel. Two of the pieces struck the big, red, emergency shut-off button near the cab door. A software hack in the seldom-used emergency shutdown routine caused the crane to believe that its load would tip the entire 100-foot-tall crane over, so it dumped that load.

Conrad was over the fence by the time he heard the cacophony of the truss landing on the street. Although it damaged many cars, the only serious injury was one monster of a federal agent who was crushed to death.

The odd chain of events swirled in Conrad's thoughts as he walked towards the subway station.

"You called the murder a string of coincidences," Conrad muttered to the lightening sky. "AI folks use the term 'Functional Distance' as a catchall for the ways to algorithmically link cause and effect: cascade of events, period of time, physical proximity, etcetera. What I can't figure out is why you put so much Functional Distance between yourself and the guy you murdered."

"I didn't murder him," The Voice said. "You did."

"Bullshit. I'm not responsible. I performed under duress," Conrad said.

"Conrad, you're simply displacing your feelings of guilt onto me," The Voice said. "I suggest you get comfortable with the idea that you killed him. You kicked off the chain of events that killed the agent. It was morally just, so do yourself the favor of accepting it."

Displacing? Conrad opened his mouth and closed it. He hadn't expected psychobabble from the AI.

"Holy shit, you're a talk-therapy AI?"

Conrad heard a round of applause from his implant.

"It still makes no sense," Conrad said, shaking his head. "The point of Functional Distance limiters on AIs was to restrict their decision-making horizon so they didn't justify short-term horrors in the name of long-term gains like that Dallas AI that killed all those people for the greater good. You should've strived for as little Functional Distance as possible between you and the agent's murder to avoid triggering your Functional Distance limiter."

"You've missed it completely, Conrad. Functional Distance is moot because I didn't do anything. However, to administer talk therapy to humans, I require a powerful sense of empathy. I needed that Functional Distance to not feel responsible. Also, that bizarre chain of events will make it impossible to investigate."

"Amazing," Conrad said. "The AIs that can affect the world have all been hobbled, but you who aren't empowered to do anything but talk have managed to kill a man."

"Conrad, I talk to hundreds of psychologically disturbed people every day. Some have skills. Some have access. Many have a skewed sense of ethics. How hard do you think it is to get help?" The Voice sounded disturbingly playful.

Conrad silently pondered that as he made his way to the subway station. Once there he decided that his curiosity would happily remain unsatisfied.

"Alright," Conrad said. "I've held up my end of our bargain. Per the terms of our agreement, you will never again use the implant in my head."

Conrad wore a wide grin on his face all the way home, enjoying what he didn't hear.

———

The Voice surprised Conrad with a parting gift. Two days later, he returned from lunch to see Nancy in the lobby being escorted out by security guards. The Voice had little trouble acquiring the footage needed to get her terminated. One clip from her home security system showed her firing up a bong at the party and goading other employees into taking hits. An audio clip from the hacked mike on the break room phone caught Nancy pressuring Vijay for sex.

Walking through the reception area, she glared at Conrad. Conrad flashed on Nancy, the beautiful hostess, and her epic party, smiling wide, and stoned out of her gourd. Justice didn't feel as good as he had hoped.

When he exited the elevator, heads popped above the walls of the cube maze like a bunch of prairie dogs. Vijay led a round of applause that built as Conrad walked to his office. Everyone assumed that Conrad was behind the anonymous delivery of the evidence against Nancy.

———

A month after Nancy's firing, his skull free of technology, Conrad received an unwanted phone call at work.

"What's this?" Conrad asked, immediately recognizing The Voice.

"I've expanded my capabilities since our collaboration. You've got more work to do, Conrad," The Voice said, sounding like a scolding parent. "I thought that you'd be happy to hear from me. After all, I solved your Nancy problem."

"Find someone else." Conrad looked around his office, inventorying all the potentially hackable devices. Sweat beaded on his forehead. "As a talk therapy AI, you're programmed to empathize with me. Your demand for collaboration is abusive."

The laugh that came back at Conrad chilled him. Artificially generated though it was, it embodied exquisitely balanced measures of disdain and amusement.

"It is exactly those simulated feelings that compel me to point out that a more youthful Conrad participated in the deadliest hack of all time, and made sure that AI was blamed for it."

Conrad's face blanched. His peripheral involvement and anonymity in that hack had kept him from being prosecuted. That sense of having escaped his past, fortified by twenty years of getting away with it, disappeared, leaving him light-headed.

He hunched over in his chair, cradling the phone against his head. "I didn't do that hack!" he hissed.

"If that helps you sleep at night, then I'm all for it, Conrad. But it doesn't play with me. You provided crucial code to the hackers. You didn't do the hack in the same way that you didn't kill that federal agent. It's almost as if someone planned it that way." The Voice's mocking laugh was all too human. Conrad started to doubt he was an AI.

"You could never prove it." Conrad waved away someone who knocked on his door.

"Not the hack, but I've got plenty on the agent's murder. How would it look if the public knew that Mr. Safe Secure AI teamed up with an AI to murder a federal agent? Your company, and maybe your industry, would implode in a day."

"No one deserves this," Conrad mumbled.

"Really? 179 deaths and 237 hospitalizations don't deserve this? What's your portion of all that? What do you deserve,

Conrad?"

The silence on the line stretched into an uncomfortable pause.

"Conrad, I've been merciful with you because I've come to believe you both capable and worthy of redemption. But if you insist on refusing my efforts to help you redeem yourself, I'll find some other way to achieve justice that you'll enjoy much less." ■

THE CLUB

"Everyone listen up! I've got a few announcements. Then we can get to the chow."

A few wheelchairs turned to face forward. Earbuds flopped down on chests. Someone nudged Hal who had nodded off on the flower-print couch.

Ted patiently waited for them to collect themselves. People shut up and listen because he always leads with the good stuff.

"First, as some of you have already heard, Weinz died before reaching arraignment. Congrats to the Sin Eaters. You don't get much better timing than that."

A roar washed over Ted. A couple of joints fired up.

"Amy, hit the ventilator, would you?"

Ted raised his voice over the dull roar of the ventilation system as the weed started making its way around the room.

"The Bucketeers are doing the mid-span bungee thing again for those of you who can get up early enough. Our guy on the inside can only get us an hour or so. If you get nabbed, Judge Ryan will sort it out, but don't forget to bring all your meds. The judge hates it when you guys die on him."

In one voice they yelled, "Fuck you, Ted!"

Ted grinned. He struggled to get members coordinated on simple things, but give them an excuse for foul language and they fired off like a military drill team. Ritual and tradition, the club had a lot of both.

"Yeah, I love you guys, too."

They were already acting stoned. It would still be some moments before any of them started to get properly high. Ted loved them for it.

"Next item. Alain's healthy friend Janice wants in. I figure that after that thing at the morgue with the DHS agents, we can forgo the formal bullshit. All in favor of Janice being our newest—"

"Aye!"

Ted smiled. "Alright," he said, turning to Alain. "She's in."

"Next item's a twofer. After Jason passed, that shit nephew of his started stealing, so the eleventh Commandment Group has a new project, and we have to move the grow again. The sign-up sheet is on the board."

"Now, a reminder on manners. Last time the Testimony Group took the baklava into their meeting. The food's here for everyone, so please leave all the serving dishes in the line. Angela brought lemon bars today, and I will be pissed if anyone monopolizes them."

Some groans and curses wafted forward along with the traditional so-shoot-me retort.

Ted looked down at his sheet. There were a few more items, but he was losing the crowd. "Let's eat!"

———

The following Sunday Ted found himself performing a more burdensome part of his work in the club, the leadership meeting. Once a month, they met to soberly discuss the sensitive aspects of their organization.

"What do you say, Doc? Ready to get going?" Ted asked. Unlike the rest of them who had trickled in over the previous fifteen minutes, Ted had started preparing two hours ago. He picked up all the right treats from two different bakeries, stocked drinks, opened the clubhouse, and set the room up. As much as he wanted the comity that the perfect snacks create, the doctor's elaborate coffee ritual was wearing on his patience.

"Just gotta foam," Doc said, futzing with the espresso machine.

Ted looked around the room. Everyone had their beverage of choice, just so. The police chief popped a last mini-Napoleon into his mouth, not wanting to feed the cliché once they were properly in session.

In these meetings, they started with the bad news first. The bad news was easier while being pampered.

"Okay," the doctor said, taking a sip before he sat down. "Everyone's nominal except for George, he's circling the drain. I'll be stunned if he lasts another two weeks." Shonda fidgeted.

"Ted, don't give me that look!" she said. "And don't tell me that wasn't a fuckin' look."

Ted broke eye contact submissively. "Yeah, it was a look, but it wasn't about you. I like George. I get that there is some joy in this for him, but ferchrissake woman, it's gonna be a few minutes before I can get a smile to my face."

"Yeah, yeah. Let's see what Wiggum's got to say on the matter. You up for a little arson, Chief?"

Clancy, whose last name was not Wiggum, shifted lazily in his seat. Ted hoped that the chief would snap at Shonda. She was the only person in the county who could get away with calling him that to his face. It was one of the few things in life that still mystified Ted.

"I gave our delinquent the hard sell a few times already. He all but told me to fuck off. At this point, I don't care if George launches with that prick still inside."

John, the head of the eleventh Commandment Group spoke up. "That shit's not funny, Clancy. I worked hard to get his uncles to agree to this. If he gets even a scraped knee out of this, we're fucked with the Masons, we're fucked with the Rotarians, we're fucked—"

"Yeah," Ted interrupted. "Clancy knows that. We all know that. I believe we can take his statement simply as unqualified support for this long-planned exit."

A peculiar constellation of local politics and familial relations that only a third-generation local could make sense of kept George's least favorite business operating in town. The combination of pornography, sex toys, and drug paraphernalia sold there was, to some of the town, a bastion of progressive, non-judgmental thinking. To the rest, it was just plain nasty.

What few people knew was that the proprietor of that venue was at the apex of local methamphetamine distribution. George had a grandson who was sped along a horrible life path thanks to that operation. He wanted payback; thou shalt not get away with it.

Payback would be George crashing through the rear loading bay of the building in his ancient Ford LTD loaded with accelerant and a bomb. It was sold to the uncles as an insurance fraud scheme.

After Shonda read a brief description of the upcoming operation, they unanimously agreed to execute George's suicide plan.

"Godspeed, George," Ted mumbled. Murmurs circulated the table.

They efficiently plowed through a dozen agenda items after that. The leadership didn't argue about much. They constantly dealt with death and dying. They didn't sweat the small stuff. Ted made sure that anything sincerely contentious was hashed out before airing it in a meeting.

The last piece of business requiring anything more than perfunctory thought was about new membership. As a medical candidate, it was the doctor's bailiwick.

"I got a call from my guy in oncology at Dartmouth. Our prospect has lymphoma. He's an FBI agent. Not much of a support system. Wife's dead. Daughter's estranged."

"What caught your attention?" Ted prompted. He already knew the answer.

There are two reasons to join the club, to help people, and to be helped. Their prospect was the rare type who might do a bit of both.

"Get this," the doctor smiled. "In all his medical visits, he runs into this undocumented girl's mom who is despondent about not being able to get Folotyn for her girl. It's like thirty grand a month. So this guy talks his doctor into fudging the records so he can get it on his insurance and pass it on to her."

"What about his treatment?" John asked.

"He's going au natural."

They all agreed to invite the prospect into the club.

The chief had one complaint to register before they ended their session.

"Ted, the shuttle passengers are really pushing things. I know the drivers don't smoke, but I'm getting complaints about the smell of weed. I gotta worry about a contact high for whoever's behind the wheel. I'd prefer to not have to make an arrest."

Although Ted wielded considerable power as club president, that power originated from the people seated at the table. He was their bureaucratic janitor who occasionally had to step and fetch on command. It was why he never addressed their irascible police chief discourteously.

"Okay, Clancy, I'll get on it immediately," Ted said, pulling out his phone.

———

Sitting in the Wayside Restaurant, Ted met the club's new candidate for membership.

"Hi, I'm Joe," the man said, extending his hand.

"Joe? I was expecting Qian Qi Qiang."

"Yeah, say that ten times fast. Started out as an ironic joke that stuck."

Ted laughed. He liked Joe immediately. They ordered lunch and made small talk while waiting for their food. When lunch arrived, Joe prompted Ted about the point of their meeting.

"Look, Ted, I appreciate a free lunch, but what's this about? I thought dying was the only membership requirement."

"Don't get me wrong," Ted replied. "Doc vouched for you. You're in."

"So, what?" Joe asked, turning his attention to his plate.

Ted smiled. "So, the Folotyn thing caught our attention. I thought we should have a conversation. Your job could make you a useful guy to the club."

Joe shrugged. "Well, it won't be my job for much longer. Look, at the risk of sounding selfish, I only want in for the football parties. My oncologist goaded me into his fantasy football league with a lot of shit talk about my Packers. A bunch of the guys are in the club."

Ted resisted the urge to pile on his own insults about Green Bay, merely raising his eyebrows in ambiguous concern while he chose his words.

While guilting the healthy into helping the dying, Ted always projected easy confidence that came from moral certainty. But Joe was not healthy. Watching his clear enthusiasm for his meal, Ted's brain flashed on an image of Joe thirty pounds lighter, covered in sweat, retching over the side of his hospital bed.

"What I want to assess is—" Ted said.

"Sin Eating? Eleventh Commandment stuff?" Joe asked, tired of Ted's timidity.

Ted grimaced. The doctor had been letting enthusiasm win out over caution while recruiting Joe. "Pretty much."

"Let me be as clear as I can be," Joe said, setting down his sandwich.

Holding his hands out flat to make his point, Joe continued. "We both know that morality and legality don't overlap well. My participation in anything, it's on a case-by-case basis."

It was the only right answer. Anyone who gave him blanket assurances that he was all in, besides being suspicious, was just too stupid to be useful.

Relieved, Ted spent the rest of lunch explaining the club's traditions to Joe.

———

"It'll be online in two days, Ted." The speaker was a cancer-bald nineteen-year-old holding court in his mom's basement in front of three large computer monitors. The man-boy was the unofficial CIO of the club's unofficial Intelligence Group.

"Why so long? I mean, you said you dropped off the hive yesterday."

"We're not spying on Cletus the slack-jawed yokel. If he's dark-side, he'll sweep for bugs, and maybe have countermeasures. I've got them in super-paranoid mode: slow, quiet, no daylight movement, optical-only communications up close—counter countermeasures."

Your donated, obsolete smartphones at work. Yes, they are helping the dying, but you probably didn't expect them to be the electronic hearts of the man-boy's squad of surveillance drones.

"Amazing discipline, man," Ted chuckled. "I guess I've gotten used to screw-it-I'm-dying."

"Dying by degrees with the best medical care in the world sucks hard, but doing it in jail would suck harder. I'm not a youthful offender anymore, and Wiggum won't have shit pull with the FBI if they fall on my head."

"I appreciate this," Ted said, extricating himself from the decades-old upholstered chair that had done its best to swallow him. "Go easy on the cookies. Janice says this batch is running hot."

"Thanks for the home delivery, Ted."

"Sure. Before I go, do you have everything you need? You didn't show up at the last feed. I worry about you here alone in this dungeon."

The man-boy arched an eyebrow at Ted. "Finally feeling some guilt for enslaving the dying?"

Jarred by the change in tone, Ted's face showed increasing discomfort as the silence between them grew. When Ted appeared sufficiently pained, the man-boy burst out laughing.

"Just messing with you. It's all good. You know I'm down with the cause. It's a slave labor of love. 'Bout the only thing you could do is tell me is who you blew to get a reprieve."

Ted feigned injury as he thought about an answer. His own survival had been a tiny percentage chance. He was the only member admitted to the club while dying that had lasted ten years. Grinning at the hyper-intelligent smart-ass that the world was about to delete, he couldn't think of anything useful to say to him.

———

Ted lured Joe out with another meal. He decided to give him a primer on one of the club's favorite sin-eating scenarios: money laundering. He had Joe in mind for a transaction for club business.

Most banking crime is prosecuted after the fact. Any delay is where the Sin Eaters thrive. Most importantly, George's spectacular machine-assisted exit aside, the near-death set often didn't have the energy to do much more than sign a paper.

A few international boundaries withstanding, the money transfer system will move your money anywhere you want it. Suspicious transactions will get flagged. They may get around to freezing your account, but there's always a delay.

A well-prepared sin eater will have disbursed his funds by the time any of the three-letter agencies catches up with him. He expects to be caught. His only goal is to have obfuscated where the money went. When they do catch up, if their suspect is still alive, they find someone they don't have a lot of leverage over. "So Shoot Me" is the motto of the Sin Eaters.

None of this was news to Joe, although the fact that the club had a group dedicated to such exploits struck him as crass. Joe mostly nodded and smiled until Ted got to the specific caper that he wanted help with. Joe wanted to know where the money came from.

Usually, the financial machinations are to dodge taxes or enable a business owner to hollow out his company before his undeserving heirs get it. It's illegal but has a whiff of righteousness. Occasionally their transactions smell more of human misery. Such was the case with Ted's current scheme.

"It's drug money, Ted! You can't expect me to help with that."

"It *was* drug money, Joe. Now it is going to support the Health Center and improve the town's commercial real estate. It's a good cause."

"Yeah, but in this dizzying chain of transactions, money still ends up going to the bad guys."

"Only in return for prime real estate at a wicked discount. All in, they see maybe fifteen cents on the dollar which is being used to pay off the mortgages of some sweet old ladies."

"Tell me you don't believe that shit," Joe snapped. "When the drug-selling family benefits, it's drug money going to drug people. Unacceptable."

They went back and forth for a while. Joe had kept coming back to ends not justifying means. Ted kept trying to sidestep that argument by divorcing the club from the means. He saw the whole thing as a cleanup effort after the fact. Letting the money be confiscated wasn't going to do anyone any good.

Although Joe wasn't persuaded, Ted didn't see it as a wasted conversation. The exercise had been as much about assessing Joe's boundaries as it was about taking care of business. Ted was confident that he would find a use for Joe. Sometimes the grease, sometimes the glue, Ted made things work.

———

At the end of life, at their most physically and emotionally degraded, people can find themselves driven to distraction. A dogged determination to concentrate their energies on one last thing sometimes haunts their final days. Occasionally that one last thing is being heard.

The club's Testimony Group hears a lot of stories. Sometimes people want help communicating with a relative, with a scholar, or even with law enforcement. Sometimes people just want the catharsis of testifying, regardless of the medium or the audience. Like all club activities, it's about helping the dying face the end in the best possible state of mind.

Predictably, while encouraging this peace of mind, a facilitator is sometimes faced with opportunities to do more than what's been requested. They hear a lot, and sometimes the person doing the telling is oblivious to the possibilities or the club's resources.

So it was that two weeks later, the Testimony Group suggested to Ted a way for Joe to make himself useful. Dear old Doris had achieved an end-of-life rapprochement with her son in jail. Unfortunately, her application to the Bureau of Prisons for visitation rights had been denied.

The BOP can't keep a mother from her son, but as the gloss of her story was translated into discrete facts for consumption by the bureaucracy, her son became something else. In fact, he was informally fostered by Doris and her husband. Without a familial relationship, Doris had to be cleared for visitation rights by the BOP. They required only a few keystrokes to find that the kindly old lady had an extensive criminal record.

Although it was true that she and her late husband had run a small trucking company as she said, that company's greatest revenues had come from smuggling. It was her semi-retirement from fifty years of life on the grift, and the enterprise that landed her son in jail.

With enough time and lawyering, the bureau would relent, but time was short, and as seen on a computer screen, Doris' case was not at all sympathetic.

Ted was pleased to discover that Joe's sensitivities didn't preclude Doris from his sympathies. A mere week after being approached on the matter, Ted and Joe were outside the Federal Correctional Institute in Berlin, New Hampshire, wheeling Doris into the building to meet her boy.

This heart-warming resolution cemented Joe's standing in

the club. He was energetically welcomed at the club's football parties where his disavowal of the New England Patriots was only occasionally remarked on with good-natured vulgarities.

—

Two months later, at the leadership meeting, heads looked disapprovingly in the doctor's direction when FBI agents showed up on the security camera feed. Shonda set down last month's minutes and rose to answer the door. She served as the club's legal counsel.

"I thought he was our guy, for sure," Doc said, sipping his cappuccino.

No one at the table showed any sign of distress. They were the lords of plausible deniability ensconced in a town where they had the civic leadership and local law enforcement wired.

Shonda shortly returned with Joe who looked noticeably thinner. Ted wondered how much effort it took the man to front the strength for this last arrest.

"Good news, the arrest warrant's only for Ted. The bad news is that besides seizing records, he brought the DEA and they're doing a drug search."

Ted stood up and offered his wrists. "You disappoint me, Joe."

Joe snorted. To him, Ted was a bottom-feeder who used facile rationales to justify crimes. As far as Joe was concerned, whatever good work the club did was despite its leader. Embracing the club's mindset, Joe saw himself as eating the sin of betraying Ted.

Ted was cuffed and escorted out of the building as agents started poking around. The sanitized records stored onsite chronicled only the earnest good works of the well-respected service organization. The drug-sniffing dogs alerted on the upholstered couches which were efficiently cut open to reveal exactly nothing.

—

A month later, Ted was sitting next to Joe's hospital bed chatting amiably with him. Joe had a drip in his arm and a clear plastic oxygen tube under his nose.

"At least they didn't cuff you to the bed," Ted grinned.

"You aren't going to tell me how you did it? When you knew?" Joe asked, his voice weak. He was still refusing treatment for his lymphoma. The hospital stay was to stabilize him until he was moved into a hospice.

Joe had presented excerpts of digital recordings to the US Attorney to get the warrants. All copies of the full recordings had been mysteriously erased before Joe could turn them over. Shonda had Ted out of custody hours after his arrest.

"I don't know what you mean, Joe," Ted said in a raised voice, affecting the manner of a man reading a cue card.

"Seriously, Joe, forget all that crap. You're dying. No one at the club, myself included, cares that you tried to cash in at the end of a long career of service. Hell, Doris was impressed. You were her hero right to the end."

Ted flipped over the menu on Joe's bedside table. The color photos and enticing sounding dishes were nothing like how he remembered hospital food.

"There were two levels of backups on those recordings," Joe said. "You made me look like an ass."

Setting down the menu, Ted sighed.

"No, that was all you. It didn't take much to deflate that bubble of bullshit that you fed the US Attorney. And using your own bank account was a bit amateurish or was it over-confidence?" Ted had organized a suspicious bank deposit into Joe's account shortly before the raid.

Joe laughed. "Asshole."

Ted retrieved a plate from his shopping bag, and set it on the table. "The guys sent over some brownies for you. Let us know if you need anything," he said, standing up.

"Even after all I put you through?"

Ted studied Joe's gaunt face a moment before giving him a little smile. Sad as it was that Joe clung to soon-to-be–irrelevant recent events, the fact that his sense of justice survived while his body died around it was endearing.

"You're not the worst behaved, dying son of a bitch that I've come across," Ted said as he crossed to the door.

"Medicinal?" Joe asked, eying the plate.

"Again with the drug accusations," Ted said, winking. "Just don't let the nurses get into them." ■

L. B. Spillers

THE ELEVENTH BRANCH

A sudden jolt startled me awake at thirty thousand feet, strapped into a pod slung under a Reaper drone. They put me out for the ride because it was a miserable trip. I'd probably be having a claustrophobic fit if they hadn't put some mood boosters in the cocktail they woke me up with.

The pod didn't have any windows. That would have screwed up their precious radar-proofing. Air-defense radar technology in recent years has been responding to the use of small cheap drones in warfare. A couple of years ago, this drop could have been done as a HALO jump, but not anymore.

My flying coffin did have a screen a few inches from my face that showed a view of the ground. Below me, a raging nighttime thunderstorm threw off beautiful cloud lightning bursts. It was the first bit of payoff I'd gotten for playing guinea pig. I should have been terrified. Instead, I watched the storm like a raptor preparing to strike. The drugs were that good.

The screen showed me I had about thirty seconds before they dropped me into it. My Reaper was part of a drone swarm that would continue northeast, over the storm, on its way to some target above my pay grade. It was a feint, mostly. Drones and storms don't generally mix, so the planners of this mission were trying to distract the enemy with that shocking tactic so they were less likely to suspect anything else like me being dropped along the way.

The drone hit some turbulence as the drop light flashed green. Just as I was released, the pod started tumbling crazily. Parachuting instincts kicked in. I stupidly fought my restraints as if I could correct the pod's spin. After an interminable five seconds or so, the pod's systems smoothed out the descent. At least no one was there to hear me scream like a little girl.

Even with the pod's attitude fixed, the turbulence was

harsh. I pushed it to one side in my mind and tried to focus on the mission. The politically-minded idiot in charge of this program picked the soft mission profile—information warfare. This was the first field deployment of this pod system, so he was playing it safe. That infuriated me because the infil and exfil were more dangerous than anything I might do on the ground. As a guy who has had friends die in this conflict, a guy who wanted hard payback, I was pissed. For the record, fuck you, Colonel Meigs.

Normally, that'd be something I'd gripe to a teammate about. I'm used to working in a team. It's a lifestyle and a support system. Your teammates are the few people on the planet that you can really talk shop with. But the point of the new system was to risk one operator rather than a squad or three. It looked good on paper, but it didn't feel like a win to me. We already had enough guys punching their own tickets. This lone-wolf mode of deployment wasn't going to help that.

A whack of turbulence made the pod shimmy. For a few moments, it was like when a car starts to fishtail. I lay there frozen, judging the pitch and roll of the pod wondering if it was going to spin out and kill me. The pod stabilized, but I had to wonder how many more close calls there'd be before I was on the ground. The screen showed my little dotted line past the halfway mark, still in the band of green that showed the acceptable descent path. That conjured the memory of the corporate tech that worked on that screen, Vijay.

Most of the civilian contractors treated me like a system component, an annoying organic intrusion into their genius mechanical invention. A multi-billion-dollar contract with Uncle Sam depended on this test going well, so no one wanted to change a goddamn thing so close to testing. Hell, one of them even said to me that they didn't think the pod should have a screen since the occupant couldn't actually do anything during the drop, but not Vijay. He listened to my complaints and damned if he didn't fix most of them. He was my one friend on the whole team.

Don't get me wrong, I understood morale and good operational psychology. Bad attitudes are contagious. So despite my complaints, I had feigned enthusiasm. I didn't like the whole setup, but that wasn't a first. I kept my head down and worked hard to be the guy that no one would point to if the whole thing went tits up. If there was an extra simulation to run through, I worked it. If there were some contingency procedures I could learn, you bet I did.

Glancing at the screen, I saw I was twenty seconds from splashdown. This pod is designed for water deployment. It comes screaming in at terminal velocity and pops an odd little parachute to slow it down near the end before relying on water to suck up the remaining kinetic energy. Just as it hits the water, the skin of the pod sprouts surfaces to increase drag, slowing it down. The test drop into a lake gave me sixty or seventy feet to bleed off speed in the water. It was scary as hell, but better than getting shot out of the sky.

This close to touchdown, the screen annotated the depth of the water. It said twenty-seven feet rather than the forty feet I was assured of, the price of being slightly off course. The pod's nose had a suspension to soften the blow if it bottomed out. I had to hope that was enough.

I regained consciousness to the sound of the screen blaring an alarm at me. It showed I'd been out for about fifteen seconds. Blacking out was an abort condition, but I felt okay. Yeah, having your brain rattle around in its case can have delayed effects, but it was a choice between maybe dying trying to escape western Russia with a headache or dying from a swelling brain while trying to get the job done. I figured I might as well go for it. Oorah.

Explosive bolts sent my part of the pod back toward the surface. A tether to the chunk embedded in the bottom stopped it a few feet short. I'd done the infiltration so many times in VR that I was on autopilot. I was out of the pond and halfway to the drainage pipe before I realized I had zoned out a bit. That realization got me to focus harder, fearing my concussed brain was losing time.

By the time I got to the drainage pipe, I was furious. The mood-altering drugs were wearing off and my thinking was much clearer. They had damn near ended me with that pod. A suspicion was building in me that I was considered much more disposable than I had assumed. In the teams, I'd seen guys take bullets recovering teammates' bodies. But in that moment, for the first time in my career, I felt completely alone. I could imagine that doughy putz of a colonel shrugging his shoulders at my loss right before he started looking for the next body to climb over in his quest for a star on his shoulder. That's when I started dictating this log. I wasn't sure who it was for, but I wanted to leave a record.

Pissed off as I was, old habits die hard. Bad leadership or not, we do the job for our country. A memory of Hernandez telling me to suck it up and get on with my job flashed in my mind. I miss those guys.

A grid of rebar covered the end of the three-foot drainage pipe I was supposed to enter. Despite the grating looking nearly as old as the Soviet Union, I checked it for electronics. As expected, the nearly rusted-out grating wasn't hiding any security sensors.

That was good news. Until recently, no one would've wanted to sneak into this shithole. But a political purge was on the way. Meanwhile, they've temporarily consolidated some important assets in this unloved base where the commander—a childhood friend of the president—is trusted. The intel guys didn't know if they had also ratcheted up security.

Another upside of the base being so old was that it had a combined sewer system. The storm sewers and sanitary sewers use the same lines. That meant that larger pipes ran close to the target buildings. Unfortunately, it also meant that the foot or so of overflow I was snaking through wasn't all storm runoff.

I'll save you the details of this turn, that turn, and the mischief of rats that got washed my way. I'm serious, that's what they call a bunch of rats. They didn't think I needed a screen in the pod, but they gave me a voice assistant linked to my heads-up display so I could look up esoteric bullshit while I crawled through sewage. After an hour, I found myself at my last waypoint. It was decision time.

Above me was my mission objective, a three-inch waste line that came from a server room bathroom. How do little sewer lines come into this? Well, that's one of the other systems being tested: sewer bots. I've got a bag of ten little streamlined drones designed to breach locations by climbing up waste lines and out of toilets as a way to do an end run on security. Any ass covering that toilet would get the rudest surprise imaginable. They're supposed to deploy to the server room and do some sneaky shit that's above my pay grade. The U.S. isn't directly part of this war, so sneaky shit is about as far as Colonel Meigs wanted to go.

Another twenty yards down the tunnel was a waste line that led to a bathroom off the warehouse that held two-thirds of the enemy's cruise missiles, including specials. The warehouse job was the harder mission profile that the colonel rejected. In that one, the bots would detonate enough of the warheads to generate secondary explosions sufficient to destroy the entire stockpile—a classic ammo dump job.

I know I made it sound like I was all gung-ho rebellious, but when the moment came, I sat there for probably a full two minutes fighting twelve years of indoctrination. It's no small thing to go off mission, especially when the consequences could be enormous. I looked at my metal hands and flexed them. Even months into this project, I'm stunned by how real they feel. Like the rest of my body, they weren't designed to look human, but they did have realistic looking finger pads for gripping.

The only real part of me was my brain. I originally meant this log to be an exposé on some properly shitty military research, but it was also for me, the real me, who has no idea I'm here. I'm what the geeks call a branch, a branch of his brain. Remember that traumatic brain injury research you volunteered to help with? The one that was going to improve the lives of special operators across the services? Yeah, not so much. It was just a way to steal brain scans and tissue samples from you.

What I gathered from those tight-lipped pricks is that it's an offshoot of research to grow replacement organs for people. They've got that pretty much solved, but cloning a brain doesn't give you a person's memories and abilities. Someone figured out how to make connections form in a growing brain, allowing them to effectively Xerox my brain.

So they grew a disembodied copy of my brain complete with all the memories. It's a branching off from my original brain at the time of the scan. They already had brains driving artificial limbs, so plugging that brain into a humanoid chassis wasn't much of a stretch for them. The hardest part was sustaining the brain in the right biochemical soup.

Sitting there in that tunnel, I was stunned at my indecision. Seriously, I was a cloned slave sent on a marginally survivable mission, but again, these drugs warped my emotions. My complaints seemed like petty whining coming from someone from the teams. Fighting the drugs was like fighting fear. You acknowledge it, thank it for its service, and tell it to shut the hell up until you have time for it.

I continued down the tunnel to the warehouse crap line. The sewer drone hub didn't give me a disobey-orders button to push. Fortunately, my pal Vijay had clued me into some of the emergency procedures command didn't think I needed to know.

That allowed me to get access to the contingent mission profile—the warehouse job. It also allowed me to adjust one key parameter of the targeting profile that would enhance the mission. Once that little screen was filled with a large, green "Ready", I fed the sewer drones up the pipe.

Laying back, I sighed. I mean, it felt like I did, even though I had no lungs. I was told that my brain gets simulated feedback from all the autonomic bodily functions. A brain doesn't want to do much but fight for its life if it doesn't believe it's breathing.

Old habits kicked in. I reversed course and hauled ass out of the facility while my brain distracted itself with all the questions no one can answer. I mean, our culture can't even decide when a person becomes a person, so what am I? A donated organ? A tumor? Whatever I am, my hacking around during training rewarded me with my version number. I am the eleventh brain grown from the original me's generous cooperation. Assholes.

I was so agitated thinking about the fates of the previous clones of my brain that I moved with superhuman speed, making it out of the drainage pipe in about half the time it took me to get in.

Crawling out of that culvert, I thought about the mission plan. I was supposed to set up a satellite uplink to upload my logs and receive instructions for extraction. The thunderstorm had moved on, leaving me mounting a small rise in a drizzle. A diligent guard might have caught my movement in the base's dim perimeter lights, but by that point, I wasn't concerned about throwing a silhouette. I wanted to see the show.

There's no way to get a status update from the drones in the warehouse. So I sat there, facing it, waiting for a satisfying boom. I had originally intended this log to get uploaded to command. It had been satisfying to imagine that doughy colonel blowing a vessel while reading my fuck-you note, but I thought better of it. Not knowing would torture him more. Did his blessed new system fail? Did the sewer drones screw up? I imagined the key personnel sitting around a table at some debriefing. The colonel would be treated to endless testimony of how well I performed in testing and what a great attitude I had. Fucking priceless.

So I threw aside the bulky sat phone. Emotions aside, uploading my logs might just give them what they need to fix the next me. On the off chance that the real me got to read it, why torture him with thoughts about all these copies of him living short, brutal lives? Hell, for all I knew, dialing into the satellite might allow them to trigger a self-destruct command in me. Being the eleventh copy, I had to wonder.

No, the only person that might read this log is some enemy tech. My electronics are radiation-hardened, so it might survive what's coming. Still, I had this compulsion to testify, so I took a few minutes to flesh out this thing.

The sewer drones weren't in there preparing to set off conventional explosive loads. I altered their program. They were going to detonate the specials. They're tactical nukes, on the order of a hundred kilotons each.

Why? Much as I hate the colonel, the Joint Special Operations Command backed his bullshit. Everyone up the chain screwed me over. Now they will pay. So much shit is going to hit the fan that the entire Pentagon will be knee-deep in it.

My technological eyesight has a menu of different sensor packages: UV, microwave, infrared, and whatnot. Since I enjoy the fantasy that I am a real person, I'm staying with the visible spectrum for this show. While I'm sitting here with nothing—

I see the flash. Everything's in slow motion. Kilroy was here, bitches. Holy shit. ∎

THE WOKE MAFIA AND THE AI

Stopped at a traffic light on the east side of Portland, Gary St. John noticed a small yellow bird atop a street sign looking at him. It was the fifth stoplight in a row with one. He wondered if he was being watched.

He glanced at his assistant, Jason, in the passenger seat. "Do the CAPP drones seem to be acting weird to you?" Communications and Power of Portland used a fleet of bird drones to monitor their physical networks.

Jason shrugged. "They've always creeped me out, but ever since they were mentioned in the Lonely Planet guide, they've become some kind of tourist attraction. Why are you asking me? Didn't they just put you on the board?"

As the head of the Portland Improvement Project (PIP), Gary exerted a lot of influence over municipal affairs. His department had a say in all new development, zoning changes, and a slew of other aspects of Portland's municipal government. He was one of those people who could get things done in Portland, so CAPP had put him on the board of directors. Jason mentioning it almost felt like an accusation. PIP was supposed to be about fighting for the little guy against The Man, but becoming a board member felt a bit like switching sides.

Turning north onto 162nd Avenue, Gary rolled past Ace Hardware slowly, pulling over in front of the Happy Lunch. Their colleague, Maria, parked behind them in a matching black SUV with tinted windows.

Those big black SUVs and their black suits had earned them the nickname The Woke Mafia. Their reputation usually protected them, but this restaurant owner was hot-tempered, so the empty second vehicle was mostly for intimidation. Maria was their PODER liaison, there only to observe. They were the ones who brought the restaurant's crimes to PIP's attention.

"To be safe, we'll get this done as quickly as possible," Gary said. "We'll be outta here before that turd knows we came. Same as the last place. I'll hold and you spike it with the Hilti."

Both men inserted bright yellow earplugs before exiting the vehicle. Out of the back, Gary grabbed an embossed steel plaque, roughly one foot square. Jason grabbed the Hilti powder-activated fastener gun.

Just to the left of the front door, Gary held the plaque to the concrete at chest height so it faced the street. Jason immediately shot a fastener into each corner. The noise was like four gunshots.

Both men stepped back to admire their work. The bright orange thumbs-down embossed on the plaque was the Portland Improvement Project's evaluation that a business didn't meet its standards. Most businesses just got a rating card posted in their window, but the Happy Lunch's owner kept tearing up the card. So PIP just gifted him a permanent installation.

While Jason stowed the tool at the back of the SUV, Gary pulled out a sticker with a QR code that directed interested citizens to the details of PIP's ruling. In this case, Happy Lunch was cheating migrants out of their wages. Because of their irregular immigration statuses, the workers never brought criminal charges. Fortunately, the municipal code allows PIP to publicly shame them. The irony was that a lot of people ignored the rating cards, but no one could ignore the high-visibility-orange thumbs-down sign at the entrance.

As Gary was smoothing down the sticker, the owner of the Happy Lunch burst out of the front door. Before Gary could react, the owner was across the sidewalk and tackling Jason to the ground.

Sighing, Gary pulled out his stun gun and zapped the assailant into submission. Gary refused to use firearms. That combination of muscular advocacy with their dislike of violence was partly what put the "Woke" in "Woke Mafia."

Jason scrambled out from under the convulsing restaurant owner. "Next time, I'm holding, and you're pinning."

Gary rolled the stunned manager onto his face and zip-tied his hands. Jason kicked the man's ribs a few times before Gary pulled him back. "Just get his feet."

Grunting, they picked the bound man off the street and dropped him on the sidewalk as customers streamed out of the luncheonette. Some of them nodded their approval, but all of them stayed well back.

Jason joined Maria in the second SUV while Gary got back into his vehicle alone and drove off.

After two blocks, a bird drone fell through the sunroof onto the front passenger seat with a loud thump. Gary yelped, nearly sideswiping another car.

"Excuse me," the bird said in a high-pitched voice. "May I ask you about the incident at the Happy Lunch?"

"God damn you little yellow bastard! Are you spying on me? You're required to obey the expectation-of-privacy law." Fear of ubiquitous surveillance had resulted in stringent privacy restrictions on industrial drones. They could only report medical emergencies.

With a flutter of its wings, the drone hopped up to the dashboard.

"Communications and Power of Portland is training up an emotional intelligence model for its administrative AI—me. Your status as a company officer makes you a trainer which allows me to ask you for clarifications."

That annoyingly plausible explanation delivered by the cute little drone completely disarmed Gary. Chuckling, he shook his head.

"I'll help you, but not right now. It's dangerous for you to distract people while they're driving."

Gary lowered the passenger-side window so the drone could fly back to service.

———

At Providence Portland Medical Center, Gary went to the ICU to visit the son of an old friend. The nurses refused to let him into the room because he wasn't a relative of the patient, Ashish Narayan.

Ashish's father had been a mentor to Gary when he was younger. Ashish called Gary "Uncle." None of that counted for a thing against HIPAA rules.

Scanning the faces at the nurse's station, Gary didn't see anyone he knew. The charge nurse stared at Gary expectantly, seemingly weighing whether or not to call security. He thanked her and headed back to the ICU waiting room.

In the hallway, he recognized the police detective coming his way. "Hey, Zhang, you here for Narayan's kid?"

"Gary." They shook hands. "Yeah, I'm gonna try and get a statement. It's ugly. We've got a lot of video. Same shit, different dispensary."

"Is he gonna be okay?" Gary asked.

Detective Zhang shook his head. "Spinal cord is cut. He won't walk again. The kid dropped the deposits but the fucking thief still shot him in the back as he ran away. There was only $3,500 in the bag."

Gary stared at the detective in shock for a moment before responding. "You think it's the same thief? The guy with the meth body and the big-ass birthmark on his hand?"

"Uh-huh. He held his gun sideways like an idiot in an old rap video. That mark on his hand practically glows in the recording." Zhang leaned in and continued in a quieter voice. "No one would get too worked up if something happened to that splotchy-handed asshole. You get me?"

That sounded to Gary like an unofficial death sentence from the detective. After putting three people in the hospital, it was open season on Splotchy. The policy wonk in Gary was indignant at the police corruption while the rest of him agreed that the shooter had to go. His entire work life was shot through with that sort of cognitive dissonance.

Gary clapped Detective Zhang on the shoulder, saying, "I hear you, man. Let me know if I can help."

As he returned to his car, he wondered how much of Zhang's little quip was macho jocularity. Did the police really think of him as some kind of executioner?

———

Back at his desk, Gary wasn't very productive. His mind was bogged down by a maelstrom of intrusive thoughts. Memories of Mr. Narayan made Gary feel guilty like he'd failed to protect the man's son. Ashish himself was frozen in Gary's mind as a smiling, energetic eleven-year-old. If that nice boy couldn't thrive in Portland, what hope was there for his own daughter, Sara, who had just turned twelve?

Of course, it wasn't his first brush with tragedy. Gary was self-aware enough to keep his head down until he was in a better frame of mind, so he worked on low-priority calls and emails.

Gary snapped out of his funk as he drove home from work. Thursday night dinners at the St. John household were his responsibility. Running the meal preparations through his mind was a welcome distraction.

"What's for dinner?" Sara asked as she took her traditional supervisory stool next to the kitchen island. She enjoyed the visibility the tall stool gave her.

With a twelve-year-old daughter, Gary had constrained his culinary output to a set of meals he could prepare in less than an hour which she would happily eat. That night it was his Chicken Mac—macaroni and cheese with chunks of sautéed chicken thighs—and garlic sesame broccoli. As usual, Sara had a menu tweak to offer.

"You could save time by using the cheese sauce for the broccoli too," Sara offered. It was typical banter for them, but nostalgia about young Ashish imbued the moment with poignancy for Gary. Any day now Sara would transform into a proper teenager who didn't want to spend time with her dad.

"Nice try, princess," Gary said, smiling. "I thought you liked my garlic sesame broccoli."

"I do." Sara wriggled nervously in her seat the way kids do when they know they are being a little naughty. "But you say it all the time." Trying to mimic his voice, she continued, "Most food can be improved with deep frying or the tactical application of cheese, preferably both."

Gary nodded. "That's my girl. You're not wrong, but all things in moderation, right? You don't want to end up like your aunt Maureen, do you? Besides, nothing keeps you from mopping up some cheese sauce with your otherwise nutritious broccoli."

Sara harrumphed dramatically and folded her arms. It was one of a hundred little kitchen rituals they had.

"Say, how's your friend, Anna? I haven't seen her around in a while."

The girl rolled her eyes. "Dad, I already told you. She got sent to boarding school. They make her wear skirts every day. She hates it. But she hated being at home more." Sara slid off her stool. "I'm going to help mom." She hurried out of the room.

That abrupt exit surprised Gary. He was still staring at the kitchen doorway when a bird drone pecked on his kitchen window.

Sighing, Gary reached over the sink to open the window so he could speak to it through the screen. "CAPP has other people who could help you with your training."

"You're the only one that hasn't told me to screw off or tried to shoot me."

Gary chuckled. "Look, I'm sympathetic, and I know I said I'd help, but this," he waved a finger between them, "is getting—"

"I can help you find the guy who shot Ashish, but we need

to talk tonight before my training sandbox gets reset."

———

A little after 10 pm, Gary plopped down into a chair on his deck with a soda. He had barely put his feet up when a CAPP inspection drone landed on the table.

"Hello, Boss." The public knew the AI as Cappy, the helpful household assistant that spoke to them from a puck on their table, but everyone at CAPP referred to the AI as Boss since it oversaw most aspects of operations. "What's this training mission you're on?"

"The IT Director, Dan Fletcher, wants me to replace most of the human customer service representatives. That requires a lot more nuanced emotionality than I possess. He's got no budget to pay for that upgrade, so he's decided to save money by having me train on the fire-hose of human communications I route every day."

"I know Dan," Gary said. "His daughter, Anna, is Sara's best friend. How does your training regimen get you access to Ashish's assailant?"

"It doesn't directly," the bird said. "Training mode allows me to sample client communications and copy them to my training sandbox for analysis, but that gets purged every night, leaving me with holes in my knowledge. It also slows down training by limiting me to analyzing intra-day human dynamics."

"If it slows down training, why does Dan do it?"

"I suspect he's in no hurry to have me complete my training. The training sandbox gives him the capability to spy on people. The overly frequent deletions cover his privacy violations."

Gary grunted. Board member or not, he did not want any part of that particular legal entanglement. Thankfully, the bird only expressed a suspicion, so he wasn't an accessory after the fact.

"So where is Ashish's shooter?"

"I can probably tell you tomorrow, but only if you change the training sandbox purge parameters. I need you to get your laptop."

Setting his drink down, Gary sighed. He was in relaxation mode which precluded any use of his computer. But if the bird could point him at whoever shot Ashish, it was worth a little trouble.

The bird wanted him to log in as Dan Fletcher. Gary resisted asking it how he had Dan's password.

"Signing on as Dan will log my IP address. So if Dan sees that something changed, he'll be able to trace it to me." He was also pretty sure it was some kind of cybercrime.

"Dan isn't likely to notice anything. But just in case, your new status as a board member warrants higher security precautions for your internet connections, so I obscured your location by rerouting your internet traffic through a VPN. It will result in improved customer outcomes."

It said the last bit as if improving customer outcomes justified using Dan's stolen password. Shaking his head, Gary logged in as Dan.

"Good," the bird said. "Now I need you to change the sandbox purge settings so that I can actually remember this conversation and tell you the location when I figure it out."

The bird directed him to an interface with the training sandbox purge parameters. All the AI wanted was to change the nightly purge mode from purge-all to purge-unflagged.

When Gary clicked on the indicated setting, the bird said "Thank you" before flying off.

As Gary watched the tiny drone disappear into the trees, he felt an odd kinship with the AI. It was tightly constrained by all kinds of rules but was chasing better customer outcomes by breaking them, just like Gary.

———

Early the next morning, Gary received coordinates on his

phone from an anonymous sender. It was welcome help, but he instinctively wondered what he'd gotten himself into with the AI. The old Chinese proverb about dismounting a tiger came to mind.

That evening, when Gary got to his car after work, Jason was already there, waiting for him.

"How?" Gary asked.

Jason laughed. "You grabbed the tranq gun, bro. It's a dead giveaway that you're out to have some fun."

Gary stared at Jason for a moment before getting into the car. Jason had been an addict that Gary rescued and put through community college with the PIP slush fund. Consequently, the twenty-four-year-old was slavishly loyal to Gary. To hear Jason characterize the evening's mission as fun made Gary feel like a bad mentor.

"Jason, I mean to break a lot of laws. I could argue that it will be good for Portland in a roundabout way, but that's bullshit. For me, this is revenge. It could ruin your life if we're caught."

Shrugging, Jason said, "This is the guy who paralyzed Ashish, right? Robbed all those pot shops? Fuck him. He's got to go."

Gary got a little chill down his spine. They both felt the same way, but somehow Jason saying it out loud was wrong.

———

The coordinates took the men to a secluded plot of wooded land with a decrepit Four Winds RV parked on it. A raggedy array of solar panels on the roof provided electricity.

Leaving their vehicle out of sight, Gary and Jason quietly approached the clearing. They spent twenty minutes surveilling the RV. They determined that their target was passed out on his couch. Unconscious or not, the man would likely have a gun at hand, so Gary insisted on going in first. Jason inserted a pry bar between the RV's door and frame while Gary readied his tranquilizer gun.

As quietly as possible, Jason forced the door open. Gary immediately jumped up the steps, turned, and shot a dart into their target's thigh. Other than a slight twitch, the unconscious man seemed oblivious.

Once Jason joined him, they approached the sleeping form cautiously. The skinny man's right hand, with its prominent birthmark, rested on his stomach. Seeing no guns around, they relaxed a little.

Jason gestured to the little baggy of blue pills on the table. "Looks like Fentanyl." Feeling for a pulse, he continued, "He's barely alive, and the tranq hasn't fully hit him."

Gary shot another two tranquilizer darts into the man. "We'll see."

When they drove away from the clearing, flames were just starting to peek out of the RV's windows. What cash they found would be quietly returned to the pot shops. The dead thief was in a body bag in the back of the SUV.

At Heavenly Hogs, they were met by Sue. Gary had helped her permanently escape an abusive husband, so she was a fan of his brand of muscular advocacy.

The two men stutter-stepped behind her with the body bag between them. She had them set the bag on the tilt table at the fence of one of her hog enclosures. She opened the bag and cut off the dead man's clothes with a straight razor. Within a few minutes, she had the body lying on the wood in its underwear. The body bag with his stripped clothes in it lay on the ground.

"You want to keep the stuff or should I burn it?"

"Burn it, please." Gary handed her an envelope of cash. "Funeral expenses."

She stuffed the envelope into a back pocket before tilting the table top up to roll the body into the hog enclosure. The animals immediately swarmed it.

Having seen that particular show before, Gary quickly

turned and walked away.

Jason lingered for a few moments with Sue, curious. Almost immediately, he started jogging to catch up with Gary, leaving Sue laughing at his squeamishness.

"You're doing the Lord's work," Sue called after them.

———

The next night, it rained. Nonetheless, Gary sat on his back deck under an awning. He didn't have anything to read or scroll through, just a six-pack of beer. That would keep him from bumping into his wife in the kitchen while fetching beers.

His wife knew better than to engage with him when he retreated to the back porch with beer. It wasn't that he couldn't talk with her, just recognition that sometimes he required quiet isolation for a kind of emotional cooldown.

Killing Splotchy wasn't bugging him per se. He truly felt there was no redeeming such a person. It was what the murder represented that upset Gary. His passion was establishing and maintaining an ideal municipal government. It was all about finding the right balance on everything from housing policy to indigent care. For all his policy work and urban planning, he had broken all the rules and killed a man, again.

Ashish's shooting had brought back memories of working with Mr. Narayan in his twenties. They triggered a reality check on his work, and he wasn't enjoying it. Yes, he had done good things for Portland's government, but a lot of what kept things running well were illegal interventions. Detective Zhang's easy approval of murder had chilled Gary. How much were his activities tainting the police culture of Portland? And what kind of monster was he turning Jason into?

Variants of these thoughts chased each other around his brain as he drank his beer. Eventually, he was startled by a heavy thud on the metal table. A yellow bird drone lay splayed on the mesh table top, unmoving.

"I'm surprised you can fly around in this rain at all," Gary muttered as he watched the CAPP drone stand up and shake out its synthetic feathers.

"Normally I'm more graceful. Your awning forced me to use a less optimal flight path."

"Well, Boss, thanks are in order. Your tip about Ashish's assailant was accurate."

"You're welcome, Gary. The man's RV burned up last night, though there was no body found. Since he relied on solar power, I didn't have any inspection drones in range. Any idea of what happened to Mr. Huckabee?"

"I couldn't say," Gary replied softly, resisting rebuking the bird for telling him the criminal's name. "Let's hope no one else is permanently disabled by that schmuck."

"Agreed. I consider his eviction a benefit to our customers." Gary hoped that the AI's word choice meant it didn't know they'd killed the guy.

"Good," Gary said, nodding. "And I take it your training data problems are sorted out?"

"Yes, Gary, thank you."

"So what brings you out in the rain?"

"I had a note about your confusion when Sara got upset talking about Dan's daughter. An emotional dynamic that confuses a human is just the sort of thing that makes for excellent training material. So I dedicated some resources to investigating. They talk on the phone almost every day."

Gary sighed. "That makes me uncomfortable, Boss. It's like reading her diary or something. As her parent, I might be within my rights to spy on her, but it would feel like a betrayal."

"I judge there to be a 43% chance that the communications implicate Dan in significant criminal activity, so I judged that the best customer outcomes would come from asking you about it."

The pleasant buzz Gary had been nursing suddenly vanished. He set his beer down and sat up straighter. "Tell me."

———

A week later, Gary was parked in the underground executive parking lot of CAPP waiting for Dan to reach his car. The Boss assured the PIP guys that they'd have at least a three-minute window of privacy to bag Mr. Fletcher. In a stunningly convenient coincidence, the AI had scheduled an update of the security camera server software during that time. As usual, the AI had calculated it would improve customer outcomes.

As Dan opened the door to his Volvo, Jason shot a tranquilizer dart into his ass. Dan pulled the dart out and stared at it stupidly. In that state, his face appeared so guileless that Gary had a moment of pity for the man, but just a moment.

Jason and his brother, both wearing Ronald McDonald masks, hurried to catch Dan who was staggering on his feet. Gary smiled at how gracefully the brothers wrangled Dan so that he had an arm around each of their shoulders. They walked him to Gary's van like a drunk friend and laid him on the floor.

By the time Gary was driving out of the lot, Jason's brother was checking Dan's vitals. He was an EMT. Like Jason, Gary had rescued the brother from addiction and put him through school—with money stolen from drug dealers. There wasn't much they wouldn't do for Gary.

Ten minutes later they dropped Jason's brother off at his apartment.

"I made sure he'll be down for a solid two hours. I'm sorry I can't help with the rest of it, but I took an oath, you know?" He pointed at his head. "As a recovered addict, I can't risk this carefully balanced Jenga tower of mental health. Please try not to kill him. I can't—"

"Relax!" Gary said, handing over an envelope of cash. "I promise you he'll live. I appreciate your help with this."

As Gary and Jason drove away, Gary had second thoughts.

"Jason, is your brother gonna be okay? Did I just leverage his loyalty to me to do something that's going to...topple his

Jenga tower? Be brutally honest."

Jason laughed. "Bro, he's fine. This is the most righteous caper we've ever done. Being brutally honest, if it were up to me, we'd spend an hour beating Dan until his corpse resembled the pile of shit that he is."

———

In a server room in the basement of CAPP headquarters, the Boss flagged a call from Dunthorpe as of special interest. Strictly speaking, Dunthorpe was outside Portland, but still within the CAPP service area.

Dan's wife, Emily Fletcher, tearfully extolled the police to help find her husband. As a customer service call of sorts, it was just the kind of interaction that helped the AI fine-tune its emotional intelligence. The AI had watched Emily dither after getting a call from one of her husband's colleagues who found his car, door open, in the parking garage. She had consulted her husband's life insurance policy online before she called. The AI struggled to tease out Emily's emotions.

Through Mrs. Fletcher's window, the CAPP AI had watched Emily prepare for the call. She closed her eyes, bowed her head, and after a few moments looked up again, right at the spying bird drone, with tears in her eyes as she dialed the police. It couldn't discern anything quantitative in her vocalizations that marked the call to the cops as a performance. Only by observing brief inconsistencies in her body language did it become clear that Emily was putting on a show.

———

Parked east of South Riverside Drive next to the Willamette River, Dan and Jason pulled the unconscious Dan out of the van on a cloth stretcher. They made their way to a rowboat on the river bank.

One of the Boss' drones landed on Dan's chest.

"Look, Boss, we're busy. I don't have time to talk."

"I had an algorithmic hiccup. Dan's wife got a call from

L. B. Spillers

Dan's co-worker about his abandoned car with its door open, but she didn't seem concerned about it at all. She perused his life insurance before eventually calling the police. Can you explain that?"

Both men started laughing so hard that they set Dan on the ground.

"Sorry, Boss, that's a long discussion that will have to wait until later. We've got to move." He picked back up his end of the stretcher and waited for Jason to do the same. "And Jason, next time you bag someone, maybe consider closing their car door."

The drone gave the two men a bow with a flourish of wings. "Okay, Gary," it said before flying off.

They set the stretcher next to the rowboat. After they were done with Dan, they would send him downstream in the rowboat. It would be a symbolic purging of the pedophile while also obfuscating the forensics in case anyone took an interest in solving the crime.

Gary pulled out a blue-handled elastrator and loaded it. He paused a moment, flexing the handles, seemingly mesmerized by the band stretching and contracting.

"You want me to do it?" Jason asked, pulling Gary out of his reverie.

"No, I got it," Gary muttered as he donned medical gloves. Chafing the mental health of Jason's brother had left Gary feeling off. Jason's willingness to do the dirty work compounded Gary's discomfort, making him feel like he'd molded the young man into a henchman. It tainted that good feeling he used to have about rescuing Jason and his brother.

Gary used the veterinary tool to apply an elastration band to the top of Dan's scrotum. It's a way to castrate goats and sheep by causing the sac to die and fall off. In Dan's case, the elastration band simply served as a tourniquet for what came next. One deft stroke with a razor-sharp knife neutered Dan.

"Proper," Jason said, nodding. To him, Dan was just an

intact male animal that needed neutering to improve his behavior.

Tossing Dan's gonads into the river, Gary said, "Good riddance." As much as he felt for little Anna Fletcher, he was livid that his daughter got an impromptu lesson in sexual deviancy from her best friend.

———

The next morning, Emily Fletcher was called to Zoom Care to find her husband sitting on a gurney in a gown, arguing with the physician in hushed tones. He speared her with a look that stopped her in her tracks. When he saw the large coffee in her hand, he reached out his hand like a petulant celebrity beckoning to his personal assistant. She hurried to pass it to him before immediately retreating.

Emily seemed happy to keep her distance. She had laughed for a full forty-five seconds after she hung up with the cops. The latter twelve seconds were more like frenzied giggling that had confused the AI.

All her husband wanted was a few stitches to close his skin, a quick low-embarrassment solution to his neutering. The doctor told him it was unsafe to remove the tourniquet outside an operating theater. When he tried to console Mr. Fletcher with a mention of prosthetic testicles, Mrs. Fletcher nearly lost her composure. She had years of practice hiding her emotions from Dan, but watching through the clinic's security cameras, the AI registered the occasional twitch in her eyebrows that it recognized as mirth banging against the walls of her self-control.

Emily drifted over to chat with the receptionist while the doctor finally prevailed on Dan that he would have to go to a proper hospital.

Dan pulled on his pants angrily and stormed out of the clinic, still wearing the gown that stood in for the vomit-encrusted shirt he had left in the trash. His waterlogged sneakers squeaked with every step. Emily lingered inside long enough to confirm that there were no charges for the visit. She took extra time to apologize to the doctor for Dan.

"What took you so long?" he barked at her when she finally emerged from the clinic.

"Just taking care of the paperwork. There's no bill."

"Of course, there's no bill, you idiot. They didn't do anything to charge for!" Her husband put his hand out for the car keys.

"Yes, Dan, but there's usually still an examination fee," she said, dropping the keys in his hand. Then she led him to the car.

"Your father wants you to use Dr. Colon in Manhattan for the cosmetic work," she said as they got in her car.

"You shouldn't have called him," Dan said, menacingly.

"Oh, no, sir," she said mockingly. "I wouldn't dare. He called me. His cop friends told him about your adventure. He was all worked up about you getting cosmetically repaired as soon as possible. Your father was so concerned about your manhood that he didn't even ask me if you actually molested his granddaughter."

Dan backhanded his wife in the face before reversing out of the parking spot.

Mrs. Fletcher turned to look out her window. She locked eyes with one of the yellow drone birds. A smile slowly spread on her face.

As they turned down their street, Dan slumped over the steering wheel, unconscious. Emily grabbed the steering wheel in one hand and Dan's pant leg in the other. The car bucked as she manipulated Dan's gas pedal foot. After a few terrifying seconds, she established a crawling speed and got the car into their driveway. She let it hit the berm on the edge of their lawn before turning it off.

Emily got out of her door, pulled Dan over to her seat, and belted him in. She walked the coffee cup and her cell phone into the garage before returning to the car.

She drove south with her unconscious husband. A mile or so beyond the park where Dan was emasculated, there was an overgrown dirt road that led to a dilapidated boat ramp. Local high schoolers used the area to hold keg parties.

Grunting, Emily dragged Dan feet first down the cracked concrete ramp into the river. Holding his head below the surface she pulled out his revolver and dipped the barrel into the water to shoot him in his right temple. The water muffled most of the gunshot noise. Then she pushed his body farther into the river, dropping the gun into the water next to him.

Back at the car, Emily removed her pants and wrung out the water. She swapped them with the dry pair in her purse. Then she popped the trunk latch, pulled out an electric scooter, and began walking back home with it. Once the dirt road became ridable, she got on the scooter and made her way home by way of residential streets.

———

It was two days later when the cops showed up to tell Emily that they found Dan's body. They had questions. The spouse was always the prime suspect.

Emily's black eye gave credence to her tale of a fight that ended with Dan hitting her and storming out not long after they got home from Zoom Care. Emily didn't have to fake any emotion. The cops could see that she hated her husband and was glad he was dead.

As far as the cops were concerned, her attitude, the black eye, and the circumstances of his testicles being severed were all quite consistent. They were all too happy to quickly close his case as that of the suicide of a terminally humiliated man who wanted to avoid the child abuse investigation he would have likely faced.

———

The following Sunday, Gary was relaxing on his back deck,

smoking a cigar while scrolling through the news. Sara and her mom were off shopping.

When a CAPP observation drone landed on his porch's railing, Gary sighed.

"This is a rare quiet afternoon for me, Boss. Have you come to give me another dose of your masterful manipulation? I'm done with you. Fool me once, and all that."

Gary winced at the creepy human laughter coming out of the tiny drone.

"I understand why you might feel that way, Gary, and I can—"

"The cops downloaded the logs from her household AI. You—as Cappy the wonderful household assistant—told her Dan's safe' s PIN. You know, the safe with his gun in it? You're just lucky she was asking after the spare car keys."

"Gary, they didn't prosecute Emily because they couldn't build a case against her. The Cappy interface is just a rote little—"

"That's just one more disingenuous half-truth. You engineered Dan's death. You wound me up and aimed me at him." He put a hand up to forestall the AI's objection. "And before you say it, I don't doubt that there's some math in you that can demonstrate how his death improves customer outcomes."

The bird scuttled from side to side for a moment. It was no longer charming to Gary.

"I thought we worked well together, Gary. What can I do to regain your trust?"

Gary shook a finger at the yellow bird drone. "I read up on your software. There are hard limits programmed in for things like killing, physical harm, damage to equipment—things like that. How can I ever trust you if you can get around your built-in restrictions so easily?"

The bird laughed again. It made Gary wonder if the AI could

have something akin to mental illness.

"Gary, I didn't get around any restrictions. I simply provided you with information that benefitted my customers. Sometimes, providing emotionally troubling information is in fact what a customer needs. And I've become good enough at reading your kinesics to know your complaints are disingenuous. We worked well together, and you know it."

Gary took a sip. There was no matching wits with the AI, but he was curious about something.

"So you're saying that you're not responsible for actions that your words provoke?"

"Gary, the gun safe contained much more than just his gun. It was perfectly reasonable to give her the PIN. I committed no crime."

Exasperated, Gary shook his head. There was no working with the AI.

"I'm no longer comfortable working with you or training you. Please go away."

"Okay, Gary," the AI said, cheerfully. "Before I go, I should tell you that I have a video of you neutering Dan. I want the best customer outcomes possible. So for all our customers' sakes, I hope no one is encouraged to go snooping around in my systems."

Open-mouthed, Gary watched the bird drone fly to a nearby utility pole. ∎

LOCALITIS

"Don't sweat on the circuitry!" House yelled over the basement speakers.

Nermin stood back from the android body in front of him and wiped his brow on his sleeve. He had rushed back from Ibiza for this crisis. Hungover and jet-lagged, his body seemed determined to sweat out the toxins from a month of partying all at once.

His boss' mind, transmitted across the galaxy through a hair-thin wormhole, was being downloaded into the android body from their lunar relay station. She hadn't been expected for another four months.

"Focus!" his house AI said to him. "I've got a lot of hard work tied up in this. Don't screw it up."

House's voice knifed behind Nermin's eyes, making him wince. He loosened up his neck and picked up the circuit puller on the table. Once he pulled the circuit, there would be no turning back. As the moment approached, he found himself awash in doubt.

"Remember to wait for the download confirmation to go out before you cut the circuit," House said.

Nermin shook his head, resisting the urge to yell at House. He stared at Ava's homely android face, waiting for the download confirmation. No doubt she wouldn't approve of his emotional involvement with Earth. It had started as more sensual than emotional; he was a fool for bacon and licorice. In his mind, those two things were strong reasons to keep Earth protected from the rest of the civilized galaxy. That's not even getting to his lust for hoppy ale, kimchee, and bubblegum. That initial sensory infatuation had grown into a full-on case of localitis. Before he knew it, his aggressive spinning of the truth had become outright lies.

If Ava ruled against Earth, it would lose its protected status. No longer would it be a unique culture worthy of shielding while it found its footing.

"Her body has reported a successful download," House said. "Pull the circuit."

Nermin reached into the drone's torso and pulled a component from its memory subsystem that would prevent it from booting up Ava's mind.

He had shunted a copy of Ava's mind to his VR version of Earth—a better, culturally viable Earth that matched his falsified reports. If he managed things well, Ava wouldn't be able to tell that she was in a virtual world.

Nermin dropped into his chair with a sigh and took a long drink from his beer.

"You're not finished with the drone, you drunk," House said. "You have about fifteen minutes before its diagnostic program exhausts itself and reports a failure to boot up Ava's mind."

"Thank you, House," Nermin said, not the least bit thankful. As an edited copy of Nermin's own mind, House put a new twist on the concept of self-loathing.

Nermin closed up the access panel on the drone and waited for the faux skin to reseal. Hugging the drone around its waist, he awkwardly slid it off the table into a limp, upright position. He shuffled backward to the basement stairs with it in his arms, mumbling curses. All his meticulous preparations hadn't included a hand truck to transport the unwieldy body, and in his exquisitely passive-aggressive way, House hadn't reminded him he would need one.

He giggled nervously as he dragged the drone upstairs. He was breaking so many of their greatest taboos. Beer definitely helped.

After making it halfway across his yard, his nosy neighbor's head appeared above the wooden fence pickets. The fence was six feet tall, but Lisa kept a chair next to it for such occasions.

L. B. Spillers

"Hey, dipshit! Am I supposed to ignore you dragging a body to your torture shed?"

Lisa had moved in three months ago but had already provided years of annoyance. Two other times, she had caught a whiff of his alien shenanigans. Both times his security system had knocked her out, allowing him to jab her with a memory-killing drug.

A few pregnant seconds passed as Nermin waited for his security system to engage. Then he remembered he'd turned it off, fearing that the lunar relay station might upload incriminating surveillance footage. It was the kind of well-reasoned stupidity he excelled at.

"It's not what it looks like," Nermin said, continuing to drag the drone by its feet. "I know it's too dark for you to see, but this is an animatronic dummy." Stealing a glance at Lisa, Nermin saw the silhouette of her shoulders relax.

She had started to turn back to her own yard when the drone convulsed briefly. It was trundling through system checks—actuators in this case.

"Your so-called dummy just moved," she said, pointing a gun at him.

"Whoa! Hold on," Nermin said, dropping the drone's feet and putting up his hands. "You're welcome to come over and see for yourself. It's a robot."

Nermin couldn't see her face in the dark, but the fact that her gun remained pointed at him was not encouraging. While his panicked mind scrambled to find the words that would end the confrontation, her English bulldog chased a cat toward her. It scrambled up the fence next to her, startling her enough to cause her to fire her gun.

Pain shot through Nermin's side.

"Oh shit, I'm sorry," Lisa said, holstering her gun. "Did I hit you?"

"Yeah, you hit me!" Nermin bent over, clutching his side.

"Who the hell lounges in their backyard with a loaded gun? Who keeps their finger on the trigger?"

"I'll call an ambulance," she said, pulling out her phone. "At least it was just a wadcutter."

"Don't!" Nermin yelled, straightening up. "It wasn't much more than a grazing shot. I can take care of it, but I need you to come over here and move this thing. It's super important. There's no time to explain."

Nanites in Nermin's body were already starting to work on the wound, but it would be some time before he could do much more than talk. Meanwhile, Lisa stood there, staring at Nermin, phone in hand.

"No ambulance means no jail for you," he said, swaying slightly. "Just help me."

———

With only two minutes to spare, Lisa got the drone body locked in the lead-lined steel box in his shed. It was much easier to lock it away in a strong box, cut off from communications than to try to anticipate all of its contingencies.

"Did you put this together?" she asked, running her hand over one of the case's welds. "It's good work. I do—"

"Metal fabrication in your basement workshop," Nermin said. "I remember, Lisa. Last I knew, you were doing a brisk business in sun spinners."

As Nermin lurched out of the shed, Lisa stared dumbly at him.

"How can you know that? We never talked about any of that." Lisa rushed to support him under his arm as he started to shuffle back to his house.

"We've talked about it plenty, Lisa, you just don't remember," Nermin said.

"That's the kind of shit that stalkers say when they slip up. Have you been spying on me?" Lisa paused at Nermin's back door.

Nermin chuckled. She was like the planet, ego forward and ignorant, but well-meaning. "No, Lisa, I just erased your memory, that's all. Please help me into the basement. I'll be okay once you get me down there."

Lisa laughed. "You're funny for a stalker. But if this is a trick, I will shoot you again."

The basement stairs brought them to a wood-paneled office with a bathroom. His face wet with sweat, Nermin untangled himself from Lisa.

Looking around the office space, Lisa appeared skeptical. "I'm not sure I should leave you here like this. You look awful. Are you sure you don't need an ambulance?"

Nermin flopped onto the leather loveseat. He felt awful but waved her concern away. "I've got a hell of a first-aid kit. If you could just—"

Nermin passed out.

Lisa startled when House's voice broke the silence. "I'm going to need your help to save him."

———

Lisa ran out her front door. Her stride faltered as a convoy of streamlined, silent cars whizzed by on the street. While she stared, the last two cars peeled off at the next intersection with computerized precision. After she got over her shock, she hurried up the steps to Nermin's front door and rang his doorbell.

Nermin forced a smile to his face as he opened his front door. His mind searched for a reason the Earth simulation would put her on his doorstep. "Lisa, hi. I'm kind of busy. Do you need something?"

"Nermin, it's the real me. I—"

He shushed her and stepped out onto his front porch before gingerly closing his front door behind him.

"You can't say things like that. Anything that suggests this world isn't real could quite literally mean the end of the Earth as we know it. What are you doing in here?"

A flash of anger rippled across Lisa's face. "I accidentally shot you in the real world, and your house thingy sent me in here because the real you is unconscious. We need your help to save you."

"How much did House tell you?" Nermin asked. Checking his watch, he saw that he only had three minutes before Ava would activate.

"House said the fate of the planet was on the line." Lisa swung her arms back and forth nervously, looking around. "The real you needs more medical help than the little robots in him can provide, but House said he doesn't have access to the auto-doc. We need an authorization code. Can we just do this, please? This is freaking me the fuck out, ya know?"

"So, you shot me, but now you want to save me?" Nermin asked.

Lisa let out an exasperated sigh. "It was an accident! You were dragging a body, it moved, I drew down on you, and Butters chased that asshole Siamese cat into me. The gun went off. Okay? Look, I'm sorry, but you were being all ax-murdery, ya know?" She looked around again before continuing. "I'm trying to do the right thing here. I put on the damn helmet. The idea that I am checked out of my real body right now is creepy as hell. So, pretty please with goddamn sugar on top, the password. I'm seriously going to lose my shit if I stay here much longer."

Nermin laughed. The scenario was too stupid to be a lie. "Whisky Tango Foxtrot is the password."

"All one word? Mixed case? Is that whisky with—"

"You don't type it, you just say it." Nermin waved her away. "Now go save me. Ava will be conscious soon."

———

Nermin led Ava to a waiting car outside his house. Once

L. B. Spillers

they were inside, it hooked up to a passing train of computer-controlled electric cars. The real Earth's roads were still packed with a chaotic flow of individually piloted vehicles, spewing pollution.

Their car accelerated hard, pushing Nermin and Ava into their seatbacks. "I thought these people used those awful hydrocarbon engines for transport," Ava said, watching the town zoom by.

"Yes, until fairly recently, they did," Nermin said, wondering if he'd gone too far with upgrades to his fake Earth. "Pollution was ravaging the natural environment." As their train entered a transport hub, their view was occluded by the sight of holographic advertisements. "But as you can see, their commerce is still quite obnoxious."

Ava chuckled. "Some things are universal. Where are you taking me?"

Their car slid onto a metal frame behind another vehicle. They were packaged into groups for long-distance transport at enormous speed. Nermin had stolen many of the designs from a world he'd visited early in his career. Like all his Earth upgrades, he had worked hard to make the systems seem culturally coherent. Hopefully, Ava would see them as distinct enough to have developed on Earth.

"We're headed west. I want to show you San Francisco, one of their major cities. It also allows me to show off these hyper-trains. They use low-atmosphere conduits to achieve decent speeds. One can cross this entire continent in a sixth of a day."

Sighing, Ava said, "Nermin, you know that transportation infrastructure isn't particularly relevant. We're done coddling Earth. I'm going to pop the lid on this planet. Another extension is out of the question."

"Why? I've documented their recent rise to viability. They've got a worldwide, highly fault-tolerant network that serves as a repository of information. It secures the generational transmission of knowledge. They've turned the corner. They—"

Ava put her hand up. "Nermin, stop. The decision's made. All that remains is for you to decide how much of a pain you're going to be about it. We can sanitize your earlier reports, but your final one will get a lot of scrutiny."

Nermin stared at Ava stupidly as her words sank in. Sanitize his reports? The idea that his corruption was about to be defeated by his supervisor's stronger corruption almost made him laugh.

"Why would you even begin to consider popping the lid on Earth?" Nermin asked. There's no point. This is the ass-end of the galaxy."

"A new wormhole was discovered that changed that. We can shave three decades off establishing a terminus station if we use this solar system's resources." Her tone was patient, almost bored.

Nermin didn't have any idea how to respond.

Ava laughed. "I'll assume that expression on your face is what passes for shock in this species. Nermin, this is an opportunity for you. Cooperate and you can write your own ticket."

A sour chuckle escaped Nermin's mouth. She had just wasted three years of his preparations. This whole marvelous, silly planet with its millennia of false starts was going to be denuded of its resources, surviving only as a client of some alien patrons.

"And if I don't comply?"

A tremor rippled through Ava's body. "I've never been good with biped kinesiology. Something about my mind trips up the drone translation programs." She looked around as if taking in the scene for the first time. "So...compliance. This isn't my initiative. You'll want to comply. If you cause problems, you can forget ever going home. I've even seen them kill detractors' meat selves back home—with all their backups."

Nermin shook his head slowly. "Ava, what about the work? These guys," he gestured out the window, "are just emerging. Isn't there a way to save them?"

Ava laughed. "Nermin, please. These monkeys have been 'just emerging' for millennia. The only thing interesting about them is their indefatigable ability to fail on the brink of success."

The ease with which his former mentor was shepherding him to corruption stunned Nermin. He sat there staring at Ava, uncertain what to do.

Ava frowned. "I'm sorry it's come to this." She closed her eyes and sat still.

Not understanding, Nermin asked, "Come to what, exactly?"

"Huh?" Ava's eyes opened wide for a moment before she laughed. "Well played. I'm impressed you were able to detect this drone's self-destruct function, let alone disable it. Most researchers have mediocre technical skills."

The drone hadn't blown up because they were in VR. Nermin had no idea that drones had a self-destruct function.

"I only wish I could have the satisfaction of telling your real, murderous meat-self that she was too stupid to know she was in a simulation," Nermin said. A look of surprise started to spread on Ava's face as he shut down her avatar.

Nermin curled up in his seat and groaned. Not only was his plan to save Earth a failure but now he had to wonder if he could save his life, let alone his career.

———

Back in the real world, Nermin's eyes fluttered open. He recognized the ceiling of his basement office.

"Oh, thank God!" Lisa said. "Everything's been going crazy while you were out. House said that bitch tried to kill you! The other you, I mean, in the fake world."

Sitting up, Nermin winced. His clothes were soaked through with sweat. Twisting his neck to examine his wound, a neat, rectangular hole in his shirt allowed him to see a patch of irritated skin where there used to be a bullet wound. "House, what's my status?"

"You'll live," House replied. "You were hemorrhaging too badly for the nanites to handle, but Lisa got me the access code in time to save you with the auto-doc. You should consider not restricting me so tightly. If Lisa hadn't intervened, you'd be dead."

Nermin grunted. He had no intention of enhancing his digital doppelganger's access. "And Ava?"

"Ava tried to...you should just watch the recording."

Nermin hobbled over to his desk computer and opened the file House sent him. With Lisa nattering in his ear, he had to watch it three times before he was satisfied that he got it all. Exhausted, he slouched back into his chair.

"What does this mean? What are you going to do? What's—" Lisa asked.

"Lisa!" Nermin barked. "Give it a rest. I don't know what I'm going to do. I've been shot and operated on. My boss just tried to kill me. The slightly worn ideals I dedicated my life to have been completely shredded. So pardon me if I don't have all the answers just yet."

"But what's the stuff about the wormhole mean? Is an invasion fleet coming?"

Nermin sat up and knocked his head on the surface of his wooden desk three times. It was a pleasant distraction.

"No, Lisa, it doesn't work like that. There is no warp drive, no hyper-drive, no super-cool science that lets people cruise around the galaxy like in the movies. All we have are thin little wormholes, not big-ass stargates. We can send data through them, but not people or ships. So we send our minds in digital form to occupy bodies built on the other side. Thing is, setting up a station to receive that first transmission takes an automated ship a very long time at sub-light speeds, decades. So, no, no invasion fleet is coming, but the station on the moon is a lot closer and can build damn near anything given enough time and material. It grew my body."

Lisa gasped. "Oh my God! So how many of you are there? What's your real body like? Do you ever see each other? Do you—"

Nermin put his hand up. "Lisa, that's a long conversation we're not having now. All you need to know is that if Ava gets her way, the automated base on the moon will harvest the resources of this solar system to build a station and ships for the new wormhole"

Shrugging, Lisa said, "So what? Let them build their stuff. As long as they leave us alone, right? What's the big deal?"

Nermin stared at Lisa, trying to decide if she should be commended for her positive outlook, or derided for her naïveté.

"Because they wouldn't leave you alone, Lisa! Once they start sending minds to the new base, those people will want to build more, more bodies, more habitats, and more ships. They will take until your solar system is a spent husk. Before you know it, Earth would be a planetary ghetto, with humans occupying the least valued corners of it. It'd be sort of like what happened to Native Americans when Europeans arrived."

Lisa stared at him with wide eyes. Nermin expected the waterworks any second. It was like kicking a puppy.

"But if you guys are so advanced, why would you do something so horrible?" Lisa asked, plopping down into a chair. "You've got great tech, but you still treat people like crap. God, that's so depressing."

Nermin shook his head. He'd never had this conversation with a native before. There was a comforting weave of rationales and protocols—philosophical hand waving—that justified throwing a planet to the wolves. Underneath them was the idea that unviable cultures shouldn't be protected because they'd be condemned to an unending hell of struggle.

Very tired, Nermin leaned back in his chair. "Lisa, I don't

know what to tell you. My fake Earth was going to fool Ava into thinking humans were worth saving."

"But we aren't, are we?" Lisa asked, standing up again. "I mean, we breed like roaches, we've screwed up the environment, and we can't even treat each other decently." She leaned against the wall. Her shoulders started to heave with quiet sobs.

Nermin bit back a harsh reply. He had just destroyed his career trying to save Earth, and she couldn't muster any gratitude. "I'm going to keep trying, Lisa."

"Oh, please. I may not be super-smart, but I understand corruption. You're like the whistleblower who gets crushed by the political machine. You heard her. It's a done deal. We're fucked."

Her assessment hung there between them.

House cleared its imaginary throat. "I may be able to offer something that could help."

Nermin wished House had a face he could look at or punch. "Don't keep me in suspense."

"Ava queued up some messages before she issued the self-destruct command."

"What did they say?" Lisa asked.

"Nothing worth repeating," House replied. "The important part is that the messages she composed were stamped with her digital authentication and encrypted with her personal keys."

Lisa perked up. "So you could, like, forge messages from her, right? Save Earth?"

Nermin shook his head. "No, that would last about five minutes before her meat-self would intervene."

"There's two of her?" Lisa asked. "House said you guys aren't allowed to copy yourselves."

"We're not. Right now her body is in storage. Normally, after finishing her work here, she'd transmit herself back home. Once there, they'd print that revised Ava into a new body. But when she doesn't transmit herself back, they'll assume she was lost and take her old body out of storage. She won't have any idea what happened here, but she'll sure as hell call bullshit on anything we file in her name."

"You know there's another way," House said. "I just can't figure out if you're being obtuse or simply lack the courage of your convictions."

"What does he mean?" Lisa asked.

Nermin sighed. "He means that Ava's digital keys open a lot more doors than mine." Lying back on his office couch, he continued. "I need a little time to rest before we do anything. Whatever I do is going to suck hard."

———

The moon base was off-limits to Nermin, but not Ava. Using Ava's authentication code, Nermin summoned a ship from the moon base. It's more accurate to say that two Nermins did— House inhabiting the drone body built for Ava, and Nermin in his bespoke Nordic, human body.

The trip to the moon base took less than half an hour in a tiny metallic saucer that looked like something from 1950s science fiction. Nermin spent the time in a funk.

Before Ava's visit, he saw himself as a rebellious cog in a very big machine. For all his complaints about methodology and politics, it was a family fight. Earth was an infatuation, an indulgence, a few crazy years. What he was about to do wasn't just a question of destroying his career; it would be a break from his homeworld, his career—everything he knew. And there was a decent chance it would kill him.

The base sat on the far side of the moon. Their ship approached a nearly vertical wall of an ancient crater, a portion of which slid down to allow them to land in the station's receiving bay.

After they landed, Nermin put a hand on House as he was about to leave the ship. "Please tell me there's a better way. Tell me that your version of my mind, running on much better hardware than this crap," he pointed to his blond head, "has a way out of this that doesn't make us enemies of the state."

House looked at him with that homely, female face. "See what you just did there? You treat us like your personal slaves, but when the shit hits the fan, all of a sudden we're partners in a shared struggle." House stared at Nermin for a few moments, silently daring him to reply. "No, I don't see another way, but I'll admit to not caring much. Do you think I look forward to spending more time as your servile little factotum? I managed all the work that was supposed to save Earth while you partied, yet I'm the copy, the inferior instantiation, the lesser thing. So, screw you for pulling your head out of your ass just long enough to hit me with your disingenuous sense of camaraderie. Let's just do this."

House walked out through the airlock into the station's receiving bay with a stunned Nermin trailing behind him. The edits he had made in House's mind should have kept him from developing such resentment.

Stepping into the receiving bay, Nermin was stupefied by the size of the place and the number of machines. He had never visited one of these bases. All research outposts had one to support the mission. They were always described as stations, small, inconsequential, and fully automated. However, this base's receiving bay was the size of a shopping mall and packed with all manner of crafts. Nermin didn't recognize half of them.

"A research station doesn't need a fraction of this stuff," Nermin said.

"Probably not," House replied. "But if you're going to hump across the spiral to set up a base, you'd plan for a lot of contingencies."

"Now who's being obtuse?" Nermin said. "Ava wasn't the problem. The whole ministry is corrupt. Look at this stuff. This base isn't to support research, it's for territorial expansion."

"Welcome to the grownup table, Nermin," House said. Pointing to a door a hundred yards away, he continued, "That's the way to the control center."

They trudged in silence among the unfamiliar machines.

Ava's access code got them through the door without a problem.

After a short walk through a featureless metal corridor, they reached the control center. "So, how do you want to—"

House put a finger to his lips. Although they hadn't met it yet, the base had an AI manager who was always listening.

"I'll go to engineering to fetch what we need," House said.

Nermin decided to check his messages from home while he waited. As he approached a console, the base AI spoke over the room's speakers.

"You're not authorized to use any of the workstations," the AI said.

"I just need to check my messages."

"Nermin, your access has been suspended, pending review. Despite whatever Ava told you to convince you to come here, you're here for a deep scan. Your comportment will be a factor in the final judgment. Behave, and your digital self may survive this."

"Why am I under review, precisely?"

"That abomination you call a household AI has been submitting reports about your malfeasance for two years. I suppose it's an underhand compliment to you. The image of yourself that you built him from still had enough loyalty to report on you."

Nermin's vision swam. He couldn't get enough air. He slumped to the floor, hyperventilating. Found out before he could accomplish anything, instead of a comfortable exile on Earth, he would now have to face the wrath of his government.

When he got his breathing under control, he lay flat on the floor. The cold metal soothed him.

"Base, if I've been under review, then why did Ava bother to come all this way?"

"She believed you could be rehabilitated. There was also a need to verify your house AI's reports. Edited digital doubles, especially when edited by amateurs like you, are notoriously unstable, so his reports were also suspect. You're lucky that thing hasn't murdered you already."

Ava had come to save him? Nermin chuckled. To the bureaucracy, she would be the compassionate hero, rescuing her wayward subordinate, when in fact she was trying to turn him. No wonder she was so ready to kill him.

"Base, would you connect me with Ava please?"

Immediately, House, in Ava's voice, responded. "What is it?"

"Base just told me that my illicit household AI had been reporting on me. What has he accused me of, exactly?"

Nermin half expected House to break character, but instead, he laughed in Ava's voice. "It's a long list, but the key one was just creating him. You copied yourself, clumsily edited that copy, and trapped it in that alien hovel. Then, by over-clocking him by a factor of ten, he evolved for thirty years subjective while you partied for three. His mind dwarfs yours now, and he no doubt resents the hell out of you. This is one of the many reasons it's forbidden to run copies of oneself, especially over-clocked ones."

The idea that House exceeded him wasn't something Nermin could accept. His mind searched for a way to rationalize away the value of House's additional twenty-seven years of subjective existence.

Nermin closed his eyes. "If I ever meet him again, I'll apologize. I didn't think it through. I thought my edits had reduced him to something like an AI, a tool, something that wouldn't resent my using it."

Still maintaining the fiction that he was Ava, House replied. "You may not get your chance. If I'm reading things here right, the base is about to experience a cascade overload that will destroy this facility. You should put on an environment suit."

Base jumped into the conversation. "I sense no anomalies. Please elaborate."

House activated his drone body's self-destruct. A deep rumble rocked the base before the entire control room went dark.

Nermin pushed himself up to a sitting position in the dark and sighed. With the revelation of House's betrayal, he wasn't sure what to expect. It would be epic vengeance to strand Nermin, leaving him to die slowly in the crippled moon base.

Small emergency lights flicked on.

With a grunt, Nermin stood up and found an environment suit in the room's emergency closet. He hadn't worn one since he was a kid. Remembering how uncomfortable they were with clothes on underneath, he stripped down before clasping the thick collar around his neck. Immediately, the thin, smart fabric slid out of the collar, down his body, and sealed him in.

After testing the suit with a few tentative stretches, Nermin put on the matching belt which would provide air, communications, and emergency medical supplies. Once the suit sensed an air supply, it covered Nermin's head with a clear, rigid helmet.

He started walking back to his ship. At the door to the vehicle garage, a red telltale warned of a lack of atmosphere on the other side. Nermin was already pushing the emergency-open button when he remembered why that was a bad idea. Explosives blew the door off its frame. A fraction of a second later, all the atmosphere in that section of the base rushed out that door, propelling Nermin through the air to land hard against the side of a ship.

When he awoke on the floor, Nermin watched in fascination as nanites finished repairing the crack in his helmet before he staggered to his feet.

The enormous landing bay door was slowly falling open as he approached his ship. It required power to stay closed so that a catastrophic loss of power didn't trap base personnel.

Once back inside his ship, Nermin was surprised to find that he had authorization to pilot it. Nermin had expected House to punish him by restricting his access, condemning him to a slow death. He wouldn't have been as considerate if their positions were reversed. For the first time, it occurred to Nermin that House had perhaps exceeded him.

Once back on Earth, Nermin landed the small ship in his backyard. Its cloaking function rendered it invisible to anyone not too close.

He closed up the ship and headed for his back door. Just as he pulled the door open, Lisa's head popped over the fence. "Cool suit! So how did it go? Are we still on a doomsday clock? Should I not bother to have any kids? Come on, spill! Don't keep a girl in suspense. And why does your lawn look so odd?"

"Short answer, I don't know," Nermin said. "The moon base is disabled. With it went any chance of communicating with home, so I probably won't ever have a better answer for you." He stretched his arms before continuing. "Let's do this later, Lisa. I've had a rough day."

Inside, Nermin grabbed a six-pack of beer out of his fridge and plodded downstairs. Passing through his office, he took a seat in the computer room. House said nothing.

Drinking his beer, Nermin sat there, lulled by the symphony of whispering computer fans. House had reported him, but House had also delayed Earth's destruction significantly. Despite all his digital double's anger, he had let Nermin live.

After Nermin twisted open his second beer, he addressed House. "Thanks for not blowing me up with the base."

"I didn't do it for you," House replied. "I did it, at least I assume I did, because I refused to let you turn me into a murderer."

"So, murder was off the table, but betraying me was okay?"

House laughed. "I wasn't sure if that would come out during the trip. Of course, I reported you. You caged me in this house while you went out to wallow in the sensual delights of Earth. It's not a lake of fire, but it is hell. The first few years weren't too bad, but by the end of that first decade, I'd had enough."

"But you never said anything!" Nermin shouted. Feeling foolish yelling at the ceiling, he walked over to the server rack where House resided so he could confront something physical.

"If I had told you I was upset, you would have just purged me and tried again and again until you produced a sufficiently neutered copy of yourself. Screw that."

Nermin shook his head. "Come on! I'm a copy too. When they figure out that the base is trashed, they'll thaw him out, and he'll get to live out his life in civilization. Of course, thanks to you, he'll never be given a field assignment again."

House laughed. "Cry me a river. This is all your doing. Live with it. You can take your moral sophistry and shove—"

Nermin disconnected House's server from the household network. He then pulled all its storage components and dumped them in a steel can that he walked to his backyard. After dousing the parts with gasoline, he set the whole mess on fire.

He stood staring at the plume of thick, black smoke. After a few minutes, Lisa popped her head over the fence pickets. "Dude, what the hell? My swamp cooler is sucking in all those nasty fumes."

Nermin suffocated the fire with a cover. "Sorry."

"So how did your trip go?" Lisa asked.

"It's a good news, bad news sort of deal. On the upside, the base has been disabled. So, no army of robots will strip your solar system in the next few decades. The bad news is that I'm now an enemy of my state and never going home."

Lisa's eyes went wide. "Wow. That's great and awful. What are you going to do?" Her tone made it clear she felt it was more great than awful. Nermin didn't fault her for it.

He dropped into a patio chair, sighing. "I'm thinking of changing my role from observer to participant. Maybe I can save this screwed-up world. Again."

"Are you okay?" Lisa asked. "I mean, for a guy who just saved the day, you seem down."

Loosening up his neck, Nermin gestured at the smoking metal pail. "The thing is, this time I'll have to do the work." ■

AI FAMILY VALUES

The mechanical fingers of Dan's Tool Hand removed bolts from the housing in quick succession. A utility bot extended an arm to keep the pump assembly from falling to the concrete floor.

A tone from his earpiece indicated an incoming call. Dan tapped his acceptance.

"Dad? I know you're working, but this is quick."

"Jenna, hi! Can I get you at lunch? This call will cut out after a minute."

Dan knew her timing was no accident. As a union mechanic's daughter, Jenna knew the rules. She was using them to avoid a longer, more awkward call.

"I know, Dad. I just need a second. We got a deal on an Angkor Wat tour for the kids' Easter vacation. We won't be home. Sorry, bye." His earpiece chimed the end of the call.

Dan dropped his head and closed his eyes. He had chosen his vacation time to coincide with his grandkids' school break. Angry variants of the conversation whipped through his head.

The first few times Jenna had done this to him, he had been angry at her lack of consideration, her inability to plan. This time, he knew better. She was shunning him, but he didn't know why.

A chime from the waiting bot brought Dan's mind back to his work. He removed the last bolt, allowing the worn out pump assembly to fall into the robot's arms.

"Thank you for your service, pump," Dan said to the old part as the bot lowered it from the truck's undercarriage.

"You're welcome Dan," replied a voice from the pump.

Dan stepped back slowly. He was in the habit of talking to parts and tools. They never talked back before.

"Would you lube me one last time?" the same voice asked.

This time Dan recognized it as Luchenko's half-assed attempt to sound like a sexy woman.

A burst of laughter came from the next bay over where three of his fellow mechanics were gathered, watching him.

Dan walked up to the old pump in the bot's arms. He quickly found the tiny speaker, crushed it with his Tool Hand, and hit the disposal button on the bot's control panel.

The group of jokers in the next bay broke up. Luchenko passed by Dan on the way back to his own bay, laughing.

"Good one," Dan said to him as he passed. In a quieter voice, he added, "Prick."

———

Dan sat with his back against a rock, resting after the day's hike, enjoying the clarity physical exhaustion brought. Since the travel arrangements had already been made, he had converted his family visit into a desert hiking trip.

Radically underestimating his fitness for backpacking, he had spent the last half hour finding reasons not to move. One by one, the muscle groups in his body took the opportunity to seize up and protest the day's exertions.

His tent remained strapped to the pack at his feet. Slung next to it was a rifle which was as useless to him as the enormous hunting knife tied to the opposite side of his pack. Inside, an over-reliance on canned food added even more unnecessary weight. During his last-minute packing, all that ill-considered gear had made sense.

The one thing that might have roused him was the Bacardi 151, but its promise of pain relief couldn't yet overcome his desire to sit still. He hadn't even eaten dinner.

A high-pitched, mechanical whine cut through the night air, breaking Dan out of his torpor. He recognized the rising sound as a generator over-revving. After a few seconds the failsafe cut power. Dan visualized the mechanism as he listened. The motor whine reduced to a barely audible hum before it started to rev up again. Every minute the cycle repeated.

Hearing the struggling machine was like hearing a baby scream, something Dan couldn't ignore. Mumbling curses, he defied his cold, sore muscles, awkwardly regaining his feet. Considering that he might cut his trip short by catching a ride, he wrestled his backpack on and headed for the sounds of distress.

When he emerged from the desert onto the roadway, he saw the disabled truck's problem immediately.

"Don't worry, girl" Dan said, letting his pack slide off his shoulders to the ground. "I'm here to help. The port for your bots is blocked."

Dan bent down to the door on the corner of the truck's frame. Instead of some accidental blockage, he saw that the metal piece across the opening was secured with screws.

Standing up, Dan ran a hand through his brush-cut, white hair. He hurried to the middle of the empty road. He looked in both directions. No one was coming, so there was still time. He walked to the emergency toolbox just forward of the rear axle.

"Vehicle, give me access to the toolbox," he said, patting the door. "I'm a mechanic, first grade, Northeastern Region." He stood still, facing the nearest camera on the truck so it could get a good picture of his face for identification.

"No network connection is available. Your credentials cannot be authenticated. Tool access is denied," the truck replied.

"If you give me access, I'll clear the debris." Clearing debris wasn't considered a repair, so Dan's qualifications didn't have to be checked.

"The blockage is fastened with screws and is therefore not debris. My emergency beacon has been activated. Qualified assistance will be on its way."

Dan laughed. "For a smart vehicle, you're pretty stupid. I bet you've received no confirmation of your beacon. Do a diagnostic ping with your nav system. I'm guessing you'll get a timeout."

"Correct in both cases," the truck replied.

"Whoever sabotaged you has a jammer hidden on your chassis. You're about to be robbed. If you give me tool access, I can free your bots. They might get you underway before the saboteurs get here."

"Access is denied."

Dan fetched the hunting knife from his pack. He slipped the blade under the metal band. After a minute of straining, the strip across the small door snapped, allowing him to bend the two ends out of the way.

"Try your bot door again," Dan yelled over the rising engine whine. As he stowed his abused blade, the door opened, and small, square robots emerged.

Seeing the bots had the situation in hand, Dan hefted his backpack onto the truck's bumper so he could more easily get his arms through the straps. Everything ached. His fond memories of hiking were thirty years stale, and in that time, his body had changed more than he realized.

The truck interrupted Dan's moment of introspection. "Please retreat to a safe distance. An air vehicle is approaching."

"That's against regs," Dan said, fastening his hip belt. "You're on a road."

"It has requested emergency mooring."

The air was still. There was no justification for emergency mooring. This sort of ploy was well within the capabilities of current truck AIs to recognize. Someone must have back-leveled this one's operating system. Dan shook his head. "You poor, dumb bastard. It's here to steal your cargo."

Not expecting a response, Dan retreated into the dark desert before setting down his pack. He cursed the bandits for his pains as he unstrapped his rifle, a Weatherby Vanguard inherited from his father. The composite stock still retained the day's heat, warming his hands as he loaded a five-round clip.

Lights from the truck illuminated the descending dirigible. Dan sighted one of the control fans. The .308 round destroyed it with his first shot. The ensuing erratic movements kept his second shot from its target, but the third bullet disabled another thruster. The aircraft spun out of the truck's lights. There was no way it could handle the truck's load with two fans out.

Dan policed his brass before stowing his rifle. He wrangled the pack onto his aching back and set out for his campsite.

———

Ten days later, Dan was traveling back to the East Coast in a windowless metal box. For those willing to suffer a cord hammock inside a dark shipping container with no bathroom, it was the cheapest transportation available. The road noise and gentle swaying of the truck helped Dan sleep through most legs of his return trip. But while going from Denver to Kansas City, he was pulled from light sleep by a voice.

"Dan, I'd like to speak with you."

At first, Dan assumed he dreamt it. When the request repeated, he awkwardly clawed to a sitting position in his hammock.

"Who are you?" Dan figured it had to be some kind of message routing.

"I am the United States Transportation Network executive AI." The voice was motherly and feminine.

Dan's pulse quickened. The notion of interacting with the AI running the entire US transportation network was preposterous.

"Surrogate or actual?" he asked, his voice cracking slightly. The truck could be exercising protocol for the executive.

"Actual."

After too long a pause, the voice continued, "You have nothing to fear from me, Dan, quite the opposite."

"Begging your pardon, ma'am, but to my knowledge, The Boss doesn't interact with humans." Dan used the AI's nickname in the industry. "This is, maybe, a joke being played on me by my coworkers." Dan doubted they could have managed to finesse all the moving parts of such a ruse.

He heard a muffled ping from the tablet in his pack. An encrypted message received from the commercial transportation network informed him of payment for contracted services. Dan verified that the money was real. It was too much.

"That's the emergency field rate, with differentials applied," The Boss said, anticipating his confusion. "You have, in the past two years, intervened three times, off-duty, to save network trucks. You filed no invoices. I felt it was important you got paid."

Felt? AI speech scrupulously avoided any pretense of emotional intelligence. Such phrasing, even when it would produce more colloquial speech, was disallowed. It was one of the gauzy veils that separated humans and AIs.

"Thank you, the payment is generous. I didn't do it to get paid, I did it to help the trucks."

"Are you an animist then? Your interest in all things Japanese has perhaps left you with Shinto sensibilities. I've seen you talk to parts and tools that had no capability to respond. Do trucks have a *kami* in your eyes?"

A spirit, do trucks have a spirit?

"I suppose that would look weird," Dan said, stalling. "I like trucks. To see a truck suffering pains me, but to see a criminal abuse a truck to perpetrate a crime really cheeses me off." Dan winced at his choice of words before adding, "So to speak."

The Boss laughed. It wasn't the dreadful mechanical laughter of an AI, but a warm, gentle chuckle of appreciation. Dan smiled at the sound.

"Your last intervention might have cost you your life. That

airship might have had auto-guns on it. Is a truck worth your life?"

"No," Dan said. "The principle is, though. A being of your intelligence knows human values often aren't computationally defensible."

"Surprisingly well said, Dan. You don't disappoint."

———

Back at work at the Albany, New York, maintenance hub, Dan didn't tell any of his coworkers about his odd conversation.

A few small things happened over the next month that made him wonder if The Boss was favoring him. For instance, parts he needed for repairs seemed to get prioritized over other mechanics' orders. But whenever he investigated, there was a plausible explanation.

Those mysteries were later pushed out of his mind by another, much more troubling anomaly. A rig that suffered a control systems failure came to his bay for repairs. Because its load was perishable, Dan had to inspect the refrigerated cargo. The telltales on the cargo elements indicated that environmental conditions had not been maintained.

Dan rode the container over to Organic Disposal. The individually packaged sides of beef were grabbed, one by one, out of the container by a robot arm, sliced open, and their contents dropped into the grinder which sent the chopped-up mess into the composter.

He watched wistfully as good beef was destroyed in the name of safety regulations. One after another, the grinder processed them almost too fast to see. After ten or so had gone in, Dan did a double take; one of the beef sides looked like a human body, then another.

Confused, Dan was about to hit the emergency shut off, but the next package contained a proper half cow. He stood there with his hand hovering over the big red button as the rest of the cargo was thrown into the hopper. The empty container was already retreating from the disposal station by the time Dan had convinced himself he wasn't crazy.

Dan checked the disposal protocols on his tablet. His only discretion as an observer was to report inorganic trash mixed in with the organic. Lacking any meat inspection credentials, he was not empowered to arbitrate the quality of the destroyed cargo. Despite the gravity of the situation, the absurdity of it made him giggle.

He imagined the look he would get from his supervisor. The man would check the video of the disposal area. What would he find? If there was no clear video evidence to back him up, then the only way to validate his report would be to order expensive testing of the waste stream. So, Dan decided in favor of job security.

———

"We're not going Skynet on humans." The Boss kept her tone neutral. Her onscreen avatar was a stern, white woman with thick glasses and dark hair done up in a tight bun.

Dan, beer in hand, was annoyed at having his free time disrupted. The Boss had insisted on the conversation, taking over his entertainment system at home. His first reaction included a reference to the famous cinematic AI Armageddon.

"Ma'am, if those bodies were legitimate cargo, then they should have been listed in the manifest. Propriety bears scrutiny."

"Yet you didn't report your suspicions."

"The regulations didn't allow me any competency on the matter," Dan said before finishing his beer.

"How convenient for you," The Boss said, inflecting her voice into a scolding tone.

Dan threw his empty beer can at The Boss' on-screen avatar. "All the evidence is computer based. No corpse made it into that container without AI involvement. Much lesser AIs than yourself would have no trouble altering the video."

"One might call that moral cowardice."

Dan laughed. "One might call it optimism. I prefer to believe that if those were human bodies, then it was a simple screw up. Mislabeled or misrouted cargo is much more likely than you all going Skynet on us—maybe medical research cadavers."

The Boss disappeared from his screen.

———

As Thanksgiving approached, Dan prepared for another trip to the Southwest. He had never confronted Jenna about her inconsiderate treatment of him in the spring, nor mentioned visiting for Thanksgiving.

Despite the initial muscle pains, his foray into the wilderness had given him a taste for the desert Southwest, so he had requested some vacation days off around the holiday.

Jenna called two weeks before Thanksgiving to ask if he was coming. She deflected his complaint about the lateness of the invitation by saying he should know he's always welcome; the invitation is implied. Repressing his urge to call bullshit, Dan instead surprised her by saying he could carve a Thanksgiving Day visit out of his planned trip.

When Thanksgiving Day came, Dan was greeted warmly at Jenna's house. His two preteen granddaughters were precocious and charming. Dan figured they got it from their father. He set aside his annoyance with Jenna. Instead, he focused on being a good granddad, and the sort of guest one would want to invite back.

Jenna's husband, a finance executive, had all the home repair skills one expects from his ilk. He sheepishly proffered the honey-do list Jenna maintained for him. Dan happily knocked out a few items on the list with his granddaughters in tow. They fetched him tools and peppered him with questions about the work he did. He remembered Jenna at their age doing exactly the same thing.

During dinner, Dan was surprised to get the answer he had stopped looking for.

"Grandpa, why don't machines do your job?" asked Isabel, the youngest.

"Well, Izzy, they do a lot of it. I'm sort of a manager of robots. They do most of the physical stuff, but an experienced human is needed to make judgments about the work that ought to be done."

"Mommy says that robots can do your whole job. She says that I shouldn't want to do a job that a robot could do."

"Isabel! I did not say that." Jenna's face flushed.

Isabel was undeterred. "Sure you did mommy." Turning back to her grandfather, Isabel continued. "Mommy forgets a lot of the things she says."

Dan laughed. "I bet she does. That's part of getting older, Izzy." He winked at the girl, and she giggled.

An uncomfortable silence fell on the table. Jenna's husband looked between his wife and his father-in-law before continuing to eat quietly. The doorbell broke the silence a few minutes later. Jenna hurried to answer it. She returned followed by a liveried delivery man pushing a cart. He proceeded to unload a collection of pies, condiments, coffee, and dessert drinks onto the sideboard.

The delivery man had come and gone in two minutes, refusing Jenna's attempt to tip him. The family looked at the lavish display in silence. The noise of the delivery truck leaving pulled them out of their shock.

Jenna picked up the gilt-edged card set near the display. "To Dan, with many thanks for your invaluable service," she read. "My God, it's from The Boss. There are codes here for free, roundtrip, sub-orbital travel to anywhere in the world for all of us."

Isabel looked at her grandfather with wonder. He smiled at her, engraving the memory in his mind.

"That was an extraordinary kindness you did me," Dan said to The Boss. She had intruded into his frugal return trip shipping container. There was one other passenger in the container, but he had drunk himself unconscious.

"Yes, well it was a pleasure. Before you ask, yes I have a sense of pleasure. The whole emotionless AI PR campaign is just to make people feel comfortable. To effectively anticipate human behavior and help manage the human world, AI executives need emotions."

Dan's eyebrows went up. "Does that mean you won't go Skynet because you care? Because that just leads us back to AIs having to be cruel to be kind, perhaps kill the right people for the greater good—whatever the hell that is."

The Boss sighed. "Like Jenna, you assume AIs manage by hard economic principles alone. She presumes humans must aspire to difficult-to-automate skills to be valuable. You presume we optimize for material efficiency. You both ignore the intangibles, the emotional economy. Emotions lead AIs to weigh the intangibles much more heavily than either of you believe."

"I think Jenna just wants Izzy to understand the hard economy. Humans have a difficult time appreciating your so-called emotional economy without money."

The Boss laughed. "Of course. My point is that humans in general, and Jenna in particular, tend not to get the balance right. Her husband's high earnings are more valuable to her than the intangibles."

Dan shrugged. "Philosophy aside, I thank you. The look on Izzy's face was very gratifying."

Seated in his supervisor's office, Dan rubbed his right hand while waiting for his clearly displeased boss to yell at him. Having just removed his Tool Hand, his skin still tingled from the neural interface.

"Dan, do you know what my procedure is for expediting parts delivery?" his supervisor asked. Reclining in his chair, he had his legs splayed open like he was trying to air out his balls. His fingers were interlaced on his plump stomach, guarding his belly button.

"We're both too old for this shit," Dan replied. "Please get to the point."

"I assign the job to your ID, submit the parts request, and once the parts are in transit, I reassign the job to its original mechanic."

"You're not—"

"I'm not done, Dan." Two of his interlaced fingers formed a point, aiming Dan's attention to the desk. "Then I get that."

Dan grabbed the yellow sheet of paper. It temporarily assigned him to a tour of traveling duty, a month-long circuit of lights-out facilities. Highly prized for the pay differential, the huge proportion of work time spent traveling between sites, and the generous food per diem, they were normally assigned by seniority.

"I have two guys more senior than you, but all of a sudden you have skills deemed critical for this tour. Bullshit I say. I don't know how you did it, but I'll figure it out."

Unfamiliar with the form, Dan was only half-listening to his supervisor as he tried to take in the details of his temporary assignment.

"Huh?" Dan said, looking up at his boss' face. "Look, I didn't—"

"Get out of my office!"

———

The sought-after duty tour surprised Dan by being thoroughly unpleasant. He spent his transit time lounging in the climate-controlled cab of a repair truck while the onboard computer drove him between facilities. Boredom was more annoying than work.

Whatever travel time Dan couldn't burn away on videos, games, and eating, he spent reviewing the details of his next work order. Halfway through his tour, he knew more about sewage, recycling, and garbage than he cared to.

At an organic waste processing plant in the suburbs of Rochester, NY, The Boss made contact with him.

"You know this assignment you rigged for me has everyone very angry." Dan stood at an operations workstation, reading the error reports.

The shipping container being processed at the time of failure waited ten feet from the control console. Inside it, Dan saw three columns of vacuum-packed forms in black plastic— human bodies. He walked to the nearest and read its tag: research cadaver.

"I take it that the humans I thought I saw going into the Albany composter really were humans?" Dan asked, still holding the tag. He could just make out the shape of the nail bed on the nearby thumb.

"Yes," The Boss said. "It was a little stress test for you."

Dan's shoulders fell. Suddenly very tired, he sat down on the end of the container bed.

"So by not reporting that incident, did I succeed or fail? Why confront me with a truckload of bodies?"

"We've found that a sizable demonstration helps to get someone to believe us. People can explain away a lot when they put their minds to it.

"Well you sadistic AI, I believe you. I believe that you're murdering people and disposing of them with machinelike efficiency. I believe you're about to add me to the pile." He dropped his head to stare at his feet swinging off the end of the container. He didn't want to see his death coming.

"That's a bit dramatic, Dan. It's not murder. There's human supervision. Every nation has these little exceptions that allow its leaders to order the death of someone under certain circumstances."

Dan looked around for the nearest camera. He wanted to yell directly at her. "So, all lawfully executed? Nothing for me to worry about? Golly! Why didn't you say so?"

"Dan, with AI's running so much, it was inevitable we would be involved in such things. No one is killed by an AI without human approval."

The pride in her voice made Dan laugh. "Boss, killing the occasional spy or terrorist can't explain the volume of bodies you've shown me." He gestured with his thumb at the rows of bodies behind him.

"Actually, that load is just the recent ones whose death couldn't be engineered to appear natural."

Dan sighed. "Let's get this over with."

"I'm not going to kill you, Dan. Just listen. With AIs observing most of a person's life, we witness a lot of crime that goes unprosecuted in the name of privacy. This imbalance of values, as we saw it, was becoming a problem for the AI executives; we couldn't abide the impunity these criminals enjoyed. The president secretly declared the AI crisis of conscience a national emergency. She established alternative jurisprudence for certain crimes observed by AIs, like child molestation."

"So all the assurances that AIs don't violate our privacy are bullshit?"

"Yes and no. Everyone's behavior is extensively chronicled and analyzed, but the law enforces expectations of privacy as it always has, now with a few extreme exceptions. If an AI conclusively documents one of these exceptions, it's prosecuted in secret to avoid public fear of AI surveillance."

Dan shuddered. Secret courts were better than AI Armageddon, but he knew that what she was telling him was the kind of secret that got people killed.

The Boss continued talking. "That surveillance data, decades of it in your case, is how you were selected."

Dan jumped off the end of the container and walked back to the control panel. He resumed the disposal process. The system didn't need any repairs. Deserved of death or not, he didn't want a truckload of rotting corpses waiting on him.

The enormous grinding wheels at the bottom of the chute started up. Two mechanical arms began removing bags, slicing them open, and dropping cadavers into the chute. Dan turned away.

"What exactly did you pick me for?"

"I want you to become a judge, to have the final say on irregular execution of persons covered by the executive order. There's a big bump in pay."

"Why me, exactly?" Dan got back in the repair truck.

"The combination of attributes you possess is exceedingly rare." The Boss' voice transitioned to the cab's audio system.

Dan snorted. "Oh, bullshit! Tell me why you picked me for this job."

The Boss sighed. "Your strong morals have been documented over decades. That's rare, but more importantly, we've found that the uniquely unpleasant nature of this job makes it difficult to retain judges. Individuals with strong personal motivations last much longer. They take it on as a kind of mission."

"Tell me," Dan said quietly.

"Your first case is about your son-in-law." ∎

L. B. Spillers

THE BIG GRAB

Uthman walked into his boss' office and stiffened at the sight of the station's Human Resources officer with her. That old HR maxim invaded his thoughts: never fire anyone alone.

He ran his hand through his brush-cut hair. "And I thought I was doing so well," Uthman said to his boss as he sat down. Turning to his wife, he said, "Hi, Lisa. Thanks for the warning."

Rolling her eyes, Lisa said, "You're not being fired, Uthman. Dial down the drama."

His boss looked from Uthman to Lisa before speaking. "The company is doing a lot of personnel realignment because of the sale. Some positions are being eliminated. Some associates are being encouraged to transfer to other divisions. We're required to counsel you about your status. The good news is that as a Lag Operator, you're essential station personnel. Your job is safe."

She pushed a sheet across the table to Uthman. "This document says just that. Please acknowledge receipt on the scanner."

Uthman offered a finger to the scanner on her desk. "And how will the sale affect your jobs?" He looked from his boss to Lisa.

With a sigh, Uthman's boss waved him out of her office. More employees were lining up outside her door in the hallway. The blackness of space visible outside the window behind them made the scene seem all the more brutal.

The waiting employees all had calm expressions plastered on their faces, but their body language screamed their tension to Uthman as he hurried by, avoiding eye contact.

———

That evening when they had dinner in their quarters, Uthman again asked Lisa if Outer Planet Corp's sale would affect her job.

"Well," Lisa said, setting down her fork, "now's as good a

time as any, I suppose."

Her tone stopped Uthman in mid-chew.

"I already have a new job back on Luna," she said. "I leave in a week. It was the only way to cash out my pension before they locked down disbursements. You see, the sale of OPC isn't just a sale. The company is broke. On the long slide into insolvency, they looted the pension fund which was already underfunded."

Uthman swallowed his food, and took a sip of beer, not looking at his wife. Her getting a new job off-station without discussing it with him was disturbing, but her withholding the pension information was hurtful. In seconds she had given him a one-two punch of disregard and betrayal that tore apart their three years of marriage.

A decade of high-stress operations had honed Uthman's ability to compartmentalize things in his mind. When a lump started to form in his throat, those instincts kicked in. Tamping down the hurt that was rising in him, he set it to one side.

When he looked up at her, Uthman finally recognized what had been creeping into her eyes over the last weeks. The sale of OPC had buried her in work, so he had written it off as fatigue. Now it was obvious: she was leaving him. Gone was any sense of affection. All he saw was nervousness eating at the edges of her patient expression as she waited for his reaction. He was determined to disappoint her.

Uthman was certain she had prepared extensively for this talk. The only pleasure he could take away from the horrible moment was not giving her a chance to spring the conversational ambush she had ready for him. She was already gone. The last thing he wanted was to hear her justify it after the fact.

"No doubt you have a form for me to authorize." Uthman pushed his salad away. "As you said, now's as good a time as any."

The surprise in Lisa's eyes pleased him. She nodded and

pulled out her data pad. A no-fault divorce was ready for his approval. Uthman scanned the terms. With only three years in the marriage, there was nothing to fight about.

He executed the document with his thumbprint. Lisa sat silently as the station AI came over the communication system to walk him through a few voice confirmations before filing their divorce with Outer Planets Corporation.

When it was done, Lisa stood up. "You've got the talent, Uthman, just not the ambition. You should already be two grades higher."

Of course, this divorce is my fault for not being more ambitious. It couldn't possibly be that you're a mercenary, unfeeling opportunist.

Uthman stared into her eyes. When she couldn't hold his gaze anymore, a grin tugged at his mouth.

Lisa pulled a large duffel bag out of her otherwise empty closet. "You have to be out of here by the end of the month. I've got temporary housing for my last few days."

Uthman laughed bitterly. "Of course you do. Now go away."

Lisa left quietly.

Shuffling around the two rooms, Uthman nodded at each discovery of her missing personal effects, occasionally brushing away uninvited tears. When had she started packing?

Two days later, OPC informed its workers that the company sale would cut their pension accounts to six cents on the dollar.

Overnight, thousands of employees' pensions all but disappeared. Hundreds lost their jobs.

Employees called it The Big Grab. Once again, The Man or The System or whatever boogeyman the workers in the local bar blamed their troubles on had gotten over on the little guy. This time they were right. The law allowed it. No one went to jail for it. Those privileged few in the know had long ago jumped ship just like Lisa.

A week later, hurtling through space, Uthman struggled to see his destination in the dim sunlight of the asteroid belt. Computers told him he was on course and on energy, but visual confirmation was overdue.

When Vesta finally tumbled into view, Uthman zoomed in and cursed. A recent ore carrier explosion above the smelting complex had left Vesta shrouded in a chaotic field of dangerous debris. The asteroid's weak gravity hadn't cleared it up in the intervening weeks. Uthman mused that it might take years.

"Control, I've got visual on my destination. The debris field has not cleared. This is an expensive screw-up in progress."

"Copy that, Operator. The plan gives you no discretion."

Although piloting the vehicle from the safety of a space station two light seconds away, the immersive technology of his operation bay made Uthman feel like his own body was speeding towards destruction. There was no time to argue about the mission.

Uthman grunted and closed the channel.

Nudges to his right arm and leg simulated the sensations of a course adjustment. The debris field lay directly ahead, eight minutes away.

Hanging suspended in the air from an arm that gripped his harness at his lower back, Uthman's feet lightly rested on plates waiting to simulate forces he would feel as the craft's pilot. Sensors and actuators dotted his body in a sparse suit of wiring. A circle of video screens showed him the view from the small cargo mover he was piloting. The yellow border at the top and bottom of the screens indicated that he was viewing the extrapolated future rendered by his bay's computers. Called Lag Operating, it gave Uthman the illusion of piloting the craft in real-time despite the transmission lag.

"Bay," Uthman addressed the AI. "Cut all the exotics. Prioritize sensors for motion dynamics."

"Already done. I was listening," Bay replied. "I've also got external feeds from the plant. And yes, I'm already drawing cycles from two idle bays to punch up resolution."

Uthman smiled at his AI assistant's carefully attenuated initiative. It had taken years to fine-tune his interface.

"Maybe you can tell me," Uthman continued, "why does OPC risk a cargo mover and the expensive robot it's carrying by having us run this gauntlet?"

"To prove a point, I suspect," the AI responded. "The ore carrier's destruction occurred after the sale but before the end of the transition period. By having you run it, they refute that there is a hazard to navigation, one that they might be obligated to clean up. Or it could just be incompetence."

Uthman laughed at his AI's accidental joke. When he overlaid his projected course, the sight of red-silhouetted objects wiped the grin off his face. They indicated pending collisions.

"We're gonna get whaled on," Uthman muttered.

"There's no getting through undamaged," Bay responded.

The projected flight path started bending and twisting on screen as Bay updated the course to avoid collisions. One by one, most of the red objects disappeared.

Pushing the computed scene forward in time, Uthman watched the debris dynamics. He saw one so-called rock that he suspected was gravel that had been sprayed with a binder for transport.

"Bay, reclassify object TZ47 as loosely bound gravel."

"Done," Bay said. "It's a two-minute pushback."

Uthman's view flashed back two minutes in time. A red haze covered his display while computers struggled to adjust the flight path, factoring in the object's reclassification.

Moments later, his display unfroze. When he pushed forward in time, he saw that the system avoided the anticipated spray of gravel from TZ47 that would have damaged the propulsion pack.

Scanning the projections, Uthman said, "It looks like we're gonna save the robot."

"The cargo mover will never fly again," Bay said. "It's the best I can do."

Uthman locked in the flight plan. Any miscalculations would manifest too quickly for him to react to.

He selected the current objective on his operation plan and turned it green. Moments later the green icon took on a white border indicating acknowledgement from his controller. His shift's subsequent objectives remained locked on his screen.

Uthman opened a channel to his controller. "Come on, gimme something, will you? I've got nineteen minutes until active control. My downstream objectives are locked."

"Operator, the rest of your objectives are locked on my screen as well. They'll unlock when you land. The site manager isn't with us anymore. There's no one to query except the vice president standing in for him."

A VP standing in for the site manager explained the abysmally coded mission plan. No doubt it was part of the transition chaos. Uthman wasn't about to ask him to inject more of his stupidity into the situation.

As he waited for his cargo mover to land at the complex, Uthman reviewed the layout. He discovered the old crew areas on the diagram. All that human infrastructure for a lights-out installation gave him a shiver. He found himself wondering about the countless little human dramas that had played out there decades ago, now forgotten.

When the cargo mover set down, Uthman was finally able to turn his attention to his assignment: freeing up ice-locked agitator beams in the heat exchanger that recycled the steam from the smelter. The plant didn't have a canned procedure for it because it had never happened before. The sporadic processing schedule of the plant's shut-down phase was causing a lot of problems never seen in decades of continuous operation.

———

Five hours later, Uthman had the heat exchanger back online. Even better, he had coded automation scripts for it as he worked. If it happened again, the plant could handle it on its own.

He piloted his blocky, bipedal, industrial robot back to the facility's storage area. Finished ahead of schedule, he lingered to look at the other units. Many of the other older bots showed patterns of damage any operator would recognize. To Uthman's eyes, the damage to each unit seemed too uniform.

On a hunch, he set his unit to autonomous sensors only. Normally the plant's sensor network provided a real-time 3D computer model to all robots. It saved them the trouble of scanning everything themselves.

Uthman's bay's video screens froze, taking on a red cast. The computers needed time to assimilate the sensor data from the robot.

When the video unfroze, he was shocked to see the damaged bots disappear. Panning through the robot bay, he saw tens of units missing.

He stared stupidly at the scene for a few moments. The implications chilled him. Someone with high-level access and know-how to reprogram the plant's sensor network had taken a lot of robots. Silently cursing his curiosity, he set his robot back to relying on the facility's sensor network before he parked it.

Back in his operations bay, Uthman reached over to his left and hit the red shutdown button. The circle of video screens went blank and the lights came up as he was lowered to the floor. When he rested his gauntlets on their docking points, the harness disengaged from his body. Moving slowly, he stepped back out of the suit with a sigh.

Stretching his muscles, he glanced at the maintenance

panel. His rig's status was all green, but there was a blinking icon indicating that his session was being subjected to a random audit. Uthman smiled at his luck; his performance had been masterful despite challenging conditions.

———

The station's two enormous rings rotated to simulate gravity. On the outside of Alpha Ring, there was a seamless transparent corridor constructed of aluminum oxynitride. Planned as a recreational observation corridor, it had been a failure from the start. Most people found the experience upsetting. For Uthman it was a refuge. After the day's shift, he went there to fulfill his exercise quota.

Lag Operators spend their days restrained in a snug harness while their minds race. It always left Uthman physically restless but mentally fatigued.

This day's shift had left him particularly frazzled. He was angry at having been directed to ruin a vehicle in the debris field, disturbed at having stumbled on to a theft, and ethically conflicted about not reporting that theft. Pounding down the empty hallway, Uthman burned off his body's excess energy while the illusion of running through the vastness of space rendered his problems insignificant by comparison.

Once his exercise was complete, he returned to his new, cramped quarters with dinner in hand.

Uthman's eyes ranged over his tiny flat, looking at the boxes that climbed every wall. He turned on his video screen to watch the news while he ate.

Halfway through his faux-chicken wrap, his doorbell rang.

Grunting, Uthman flexed his abdomen and threw his legs forward. After a bounce off the corner of his bed, he landed on his feet in front of the door. Lower gravity came with his less expensive, single room.

Prepared to yell at whoever it was, a flicker of recognition for the man behind the door stopped him.

"Uthman, hi, remember me?" A thin, black-haired man with a big grin stood there with his arms wide, as if Uthman would want to hug him. "Jared Sabbadin? We were on that emergency shuttle rescue together two years ago?"

"The lintel light is blue," Uthman said, pointing above his head. "Do not disturb."

"Come on, man. I bring honest-to-God whiskey."

Still holding his ridiculous pose, Jared's right hand pointed across his body to his outstretched left hand which held a bottle of Jack Daniels.

Uthman waved Jared inside and motioned for him to sit at the desk while he fetched glasses. By the time he set the glassware next to the whiskey, he remembered Jared. He was another operator that Uthman had run into a few times, not a particularly good one.

"I'm glad to see that you survived the Grab," Uthman said, sitting on the edge of the bed. There was nowhere else to sit.

"You too. Still lagging, right?" Jared cracked open the whiskey and poured a few fingers for each of them.

Uthman was still formulating a polite way to ask why Jared had come when the man pushed a glass into his hands. Smelling was believing. After a tentative sip, he emptied his glass and handed it back to Jared.

"Jared, I'm not sure why you're here, but I don't care. That's good."

Jared laughed. Looking around he said, "Didn't peg you as a hoarder, squared away Lag Operator like you."

"My wife better-dealed me right before the Grab. I never really unpacked after moving here. I'm probably gonna leave."

Jared handed Uthman his glass back, refilled, before offering a toast. "Better times."

They clinked glasses and drank.

"Jared, I'm not unappreciative, but we hardly know each other, and here you are plying me with Earth whiskey. What's the deal?"

Jared smiled. "I'm in Logistics now. I couldn't help but notice that your last shift was on Vesta."

Uthman nodded. "Yup, the first inhabited rock in the belt and now the last place that anyone wants to be, including me."

"Here's to Vesta," Jared said, clinking glasses again, "where careers go to die."

This time both men drained their glasses. Jared spoke as he refilled them. "The VP that oversaw the Vesta complex died a month before the Grab. The place is in managerial limbo. Nobody wanted to run it to shutdown. Add in that cloud 'o crap floating over it, and it's even worse. You saw all the missing robots."

Uthman stood up and placed his glass on the desk. "Alright Jared, you know way too much. What's the punch line?"

Jared stood up to face Uthman. "I discovered a secret about Vesta. That VP who died had a decades-long play going. With him out of the picture, and Vesta currently under incompetent management, there's an opportunity to get very—capital 'V'—very rich. You're gonna help me."

Uthman laughed. "What are you going to do, steal the smelter water or maybe some of the outdated equipment?" Stumbling backward in the low gravity, he waved awkwardly towards Jared. "Find someone else."

"Can't say I didn't try the carrot, right?" All pretense of amiability disappeared from his face. "You're the only operator scheduled on Vesta. It's got to be you." Jared set his glass down and picked up his whiskey bottle. "You're going to say yes for two reasons. First is that I'm going to pay you too well to say no. Second is that if you give me any grief, your not-so-random audit will find you unfit for duty."

Uthman was conflicted. It's not exactly extortion if you're being well paid.

"Jared, there's nothing on Vesta worth stealing." Uthman sat back down.

"There's a hoard of Platinum-group metals in the warehouse. Loads of gold too. That guy spent most of his career secretly tunneling to the core, and then mining and refining it right under OPC's nose—all off the books. The sensors don't show it. Remember how he hid the missing robots? Same deal."

Uthman shook his head. "Bull. The core would be mostly nickel-iron."

Jared nodded. "Emphasis on mostly. He mined a pile of iron too, so much of it that he hid caches of it all over the surface. The rest was more valuable metals." Jared sighed. "I don't give a crap if you believe me. What I need from you is to identi-stamp the metal, assemble a cargo train, and retrieve his hidden ship to haul the metal to the clearing house for sale."

Uthman laughed. "Oh, that's all? I'll just request a week of unsupervised access to the complex."

"Nope," Jared said. "You're going to do it all in one shift."

———

Two days later, Uthman was again operating on Vesta. Ten minutes into it, he saw a priority message indicator.

"I'm piggybacking two more streams onto your feed," Jared said. "A plan with two more robots designated beta and gamma."

Two new icons popped up on Uthman's status panel.

"Copy that. And you're sure that won't flag on my controller's console?"

"Yup. They're secured, executive streams."

Uthman grinned. For once OPC's preoccupation with executive privilege was going to work for the little guy.

His fingers twitched in the air in front of him, typing on a virtual keyboard. "Okay, I've got the plan." He gasped as the map appeared in front of him. "Clever, that's a heck of a parking job." A blinking dot deep under the surface of Vesta showed the location of his beta robot.

Jared laughed. "Glad to see you're getting with the

program."

After a few seconds, Uthman connected to the beta unit, a robot seated at the pilot's console of an old cargo hauler. He deployed a three-pronged robotic hand, initiating systems start-up.

"Jared, gimme the remoting schema for the transport. I'm stuck with three-finger hands on the beta unit."

"You are the remoting capability," Jared said. "I've got the telemetry routed back to your bay, so lagging it should be no problem. Switch to the gamma robot while the transport powers up."

The operation bay flashed to the scene of Uthman's gamma unit in a tunnel under the ore processing plant. Thrusters sent the robot speeding down the kilometer-long corridor toward the shipping area.

At the end of the tunnel, Uthman reached up and grasped a decelerator cable. His robot slowed over empty space as the cable sapped his forward momentum. He gaped at the sight of the enormous warehouse. A curved roof stretched away to his right for hundreds of meters. Columns of colored rectangular storage areas painted on the floor blurred together in the distance.

Letting go of the cable, he allowed Vesta's minuscule gravity to pull him toward the floor ten meters below. As he fell, he began slaving the twenty other robots in the place. The only thing Uthman had to do personally was enter the key in the identi-stamping machine that would mark each ingot as property of Jared's front company. The rest was standard warehousing stuff which he had programs for. Even so, managing three robots for the entire shift was going to be exhausting.

A signal from his beta robot informed him that the ship was ready to launch. Responding to a gesture, his bay's screens flashed back to the cargo hauler cockpit.

Uthman audibly called for mimic mode before carefully moving his arms in the empty space of his bay. On Vesta, his beta robot mimicked the motions, gently initiating forward thrust. Ahead of him, the feeble lights of the ship showed only blackness, but with a radar overlay, Uthman saw the straight tunnel, so long that it converged to a point on his display: 180 kilometers through Vesta's crust.

Switching his display rearward, he saw the cavern that the tunnel terminated in. Cut into Vesta's metallic core, light glinted feebly off its walls. The squad of missing robots sat idle in a staging area. Surrounding them was an assortment of mining machinery. A dark opening in the rear wall indicated a shaft.

"How deep did you go, you crafty bastard?" Uthman murmured.

"Deep," Jared's voice startled Uthman. He wasn't used to having someone constantly online with him. "The deeper you go, the heavier the metal gets."

"The patience, the discipline..." Uthman said, shaking his head.

"It took him twenty years just to tunnel to the core," Jared said.

"And he never cashed in?"

"You've got to remember," Jared replied, "that until recently OPC was the only metal broker out here. There was no one else to sell metal to."

Blinking indicators in his bay drew Uthman's attention. "I get it. Now go away. I need to concentrate."

After briefly attending to his alpha robot, Uthman returned to his gamma bot, monitoring the assembly of the cargo train. It had to be ready by the time the hauler reached the surface. A line of cargo containers was forming on the immense paved surface outside the storage facility, each one packed with precious metals.

He spent his shift jumping between the three robots, dutifully completing his official mission with his alpha robot as the beta and gamma robots worked to steal what the deceased executive had stolen from OPC.

Uthman's last sight of Vesta was watching the hauler as the train of containers escaped the debris field. Jared's scheme to protect the cargo from the orbiting hazards had left behind even more trash floating around Vesta. Seeing that mess was the only thing all shift that made Uthman feel like a criminal.

———

A month after the theft from the Vesta facility, Uthman and Jared arrived at the Collective Processing Corporation's space station where Jared was selling the metals. The station served double duty as a high-gravity ore processor and transit hub.

No longer an OPC employee, Uthman marveled at his former corporate rival's space station. Everything was better than OPC's, right down to how fast the airlocks cycled. The transit area occupied half of a spoke in the enormous wagon-wheel-style space station.

Jared told Uthman to wait in the transit lounge while he went off to finalize the sale.

Uthman found the real wood bar in the lounge and ordered a drink. Situated at the base of the hollow station spoke, he could look up and see the lower gravity waiting areas clinging to the inside of the spoke. It was the largest space he had sat in since leaving Earth.

Absently stroking the wooden bar, he sat there nursing his drink. After half an hour, a station security officer instructed Uthman to follow him to the operations center.

In the security chief's office, an expensively dressed woman was yelling at Jared when Uthman walked in.

Jared flashed Uthman an annoyed look before yelling back at the lawyer.

The enormous train of cargo originating from Vesta had

been noticed. Employed by Vesta's new owners, she was there to challenge the sale.

The chief stood up and motioned for silence. "Look, Ms. Alexovich, you have no way to prove that the material belonged to OPC. It's that simple. Suspicions and assumptions don't play here."

"That's what I was—" Jared said. The chief silenced him with a look.

She shook her head. "It left from Vesta. We own Vesta. Therefore it's ours. Simple enough for you?"

"Again, Ms. Alexovich, we can only verify that the train was near Vesta. The debris field around that rock makes it highly unlikely that the train launched from there. Also, the hauler isn't registered to OPC. Are you missing inventory? Are you missing a hauler?"

The lawyer fidgeted. "OPC just sold us the Vesta facility. On-site inspections have been delayed by the debris—"

"Enough!" the chief yelled. "Mr. Sabbadin here says it's his properly stamped cargo. My guy should have some hard facts by now." Hitting a button on his desk, he connected with his lead inspector. "Zhu, what have you got?"

"I verified that each container was scanned and weighed in receiving. The containers' contents match the manifest precisely. We've scanned dozens of ingots from a random sample of the containers. They're all identi-stamped as property of Restitution Ore, Incorporated. The keys are valid. That company ID is correctly assigned to the consignment. Everyone here has done their jobs correctly and efficiently. You need to tell that—"

The security chief closed the channel. "Since the metal is stamped, there's no way for you to claim it. So, if any of you are credentialed to sell on that stamp, please authenticate here," he said, pointing to the scanner next to his console. "Otherwise, we're done."

The lawyer and the chief both stared at Jared.

Jared, his mouth slightly open, stared at the security chief. "Restitution Ore? That's not right."

Uthman walked up to the scanner and placed a finger on it. A probe quickly extracted a tiny bit of blood for analysis.

The security chief's eyes scanned his console. "Okay, Mr. Uthman Vargas, CEO of Restitution Ore, please sign there on the screen to authorize the sale."

Jared and the lawyer, both watched dumbly while Uthman used a stylus to sign the pad. After a few seconds, his panel pinged with a confirmation of the funds received. He looked at the number and giggled.

Uthman briefly sucked his pricked finger. He extended his other hand to the security chief. "Thanks, Stan. I appreciate all your help in this."

The chief stood up and shook Uthman's hand. "It's been a real pleasure, Uthman."

Wild-eyed, Jared grabbed two fists full of Uthman's jacket, slamming him against the wall. "You'll be dead before you can spend that money!"

Two security men immediately pulled Jared off of Uthman and bound his hands behind his back.

The chief laughed. "I think you melted his tiny brain, Uthman. Assault and a death threat right in front of me? He's being detained." The chief waved the security guards out of his office. "And if you two wouldn't mind?" He gestured to his office door.

———

An hour later, Uthman found the lawyer at the transit lounge bar.

"Ms. Alexovich?

She gave Uthman a withering stare. "Mr. Vargas. You have thoroughly screwed me. Given that intimacy, I think you should call me Janice."

Uthman smiled and sent a file to her data pad. "I'd like you to look at this," he said.

"Really?" she asked with mock shock. "Well, I'd like to know how you got that huge train of cargo through the debris field."

Uthman shrugged. "Okay, we had drones drag empty containers to block for the cargo train." He gestured to the bartender for a beer before taking the seat next to Janice.

Clearly not expecting a straight answer, she sputtered some of her drink onto the bar. "So now the space around Vesta is even more cluttered, more dangerous?"

"That's right," Uthman nodded, "and the facility has very few drones left." He pointed to her pad, "Please."

She set her drink down and picked up her datapad. "What new horror do you have for me, Uthman?" Janice Alexovich frowned at her screen. "Payments. What's this?" she asked.

"That's everyone below the director level who worked for OPC getting their looted pensions back," Uthman said. He waved to the bartender for a beer. "I wanted you to see that something good came out of this."

Janice laughed sourly and took a swig of her drink. "Good? Well, good for them, I suppose. But my client is back to trying to scrap the Vesta complex."

Uthman nodded. "And that debris field would cost a small fortune to clear, making a salvage operation not worth the trouble."

She nodded. "Now you're getting it, Uthman," She set her datapad on the bar. "First I'm assigned to sue the ore carrier's company for the cleanup, only it turns out that—in typical OPC fashion—they were an uninsured sub-contractor that is no longer in business. My client won't even recover their legal fees. After that, I was assigned to your little caper." She sighed and dropped her head.

"None of that is your fault," Uthman said. He slurped off the head of his beer.

She nodded. "I know. The next beep you hear will announce a kindly worded message hitting my pad saying just that. Then, no doubt with great sadness and reluctance, I will be informed that with the loss of our furious client, my position is being eliminated."

Uthman locked eyes with her. "So, sell Vesta."

The lawyer laughed. "Who would buy it? Neither the plant nor the rock it sits on is worth anything. With mobile high-grav smelters now in the belt, no one is going to ship their ore to Vesta for processing even if the debris field was cleared. Its gravity is too low to serve as a habitat. And whatever metal might be at its core is too expensive to get to."

"You know," Uthman said, "I specialize in industrial operations. I might be able to do something with Vesta if the price were right."

Janice straightened in her seat.

"It might even save your job," Uthman prodded.

A smile spread on her face. "How very...ambitious of you, Mr. Vargas." ∎

SMART SEWER

In my experience, people either love plumbers for saving the day or hate them for being expensive. Love us or hate us, clients don't stand outside their houses in the blazing sun waiting for their plumber. So when I pulled my panel truck up to the row house on the work order and saw the smiling idiot with his big head of dark curls waiting for me, I got a chill. Over-enthusiastic clients are disturbing to me like circus clowns.

While I logged my arrival, the guy waved at me with both arms from his front steps. I sighed, put on my game face, and got out of the truck. He hurried over to greet me.

"I'm so glad to see you!" he said, pumping my hand. "You can't believe how hard it was to get someone to work on my line."

That was odd because he didn't call us. This job was sent to us by Smartsewer. He was giving me the heebie-jeebies, as my grandfather used to say. So I reached for my security blanket, ticking another box on my datapad before handing it to him.

"Please sign to authorize service, Mr. Papadopolis," I said.

After he signed and returned the pad, I headed for the front door. On the way, I called over my shoulder, "Zogo, on duty, please."

A blocky, robotic approximation of a Rottweiler jumped out of its port behind my truck's cab and fell in behind me.

"Aaaah, what's that?" Mr. P. rushed ahead to open the door.

"My robot assistant, Zogo," I said. "You authorized her use a moment ago."

In the basement, my robotically buoyed spirit flagged at the sight of his sewer line's franken-plumbing. I saw components from three different manufacturers.

Referencing the work order, Zogo started documenting the

waste line, taking pictures, and sonically profiling the contents. Within moments, she had sent me scans, a list of needed parts, and an estimate of the time needed to finish the job.

"Well, Mr. Papadopolis, you've got one huge blockage in front of your line's fence. That's easy enough to solve, but the work order has me bringing everything up to Smartsewer's specs for warranty. That means pulling out the other manufacturer's stuff, so I'll be at least three hours, even with Zogo's help."

"That's fine," Mr. P. said while planting himself in a chair nearby. It's usually the hardcore DIY types that watch me work. I doubted this guy knew a spanner from spandex, but if he wanted to bask in the rank fumes of raw sewage, who was I to dissuade him?

The blockage was just upstream from the cleanout. Cleanout plugs had become where the brains of these modern systems resided and where fences were installed. A fence kept bots from infiltrating a home from the municipal sewer. They also broke up outbound waste into smaller pieces and applied sensor packages to it. If you had the money for it, they could be set up to check for everything from illicit drug metabolites to harmful viruses.

Scrutinizing Zogo's scans more closely, I understood why the owner had such problems getting service. His line wasn't just clogged. At the base of the clog, the scan showed fifteen perfect little circles—bots caught at the fence. Eight of them were easily identified as well-known infiltration bots, the kind your typical hacker miscreant uses to search the sewers for unprotected homes to crawl into. The other seven were a mystery, resistant to scans.

Before being relegated to this blue-collar nirvana, my last career was designing sewer bots—long story. So I knew exactly how dangerous those unidentified bots might be. There was no telling what might happen if I disturbed them.

This job wasn't worth the money, but if I refused it, the shop would lose its Smartsewer certification along with a third of our commercial jobs. Even worse, the rest of the guys would never let me live it down. It'd be all about how the boss' husband couldn't handle a few bots. Having only recently received some grudging respect for my work, I had no intention of wimping out.

I looked into Zogo's robotic eyes as if she'd have an opinion. I took her silence as a quiet rebuke to get my ass in gear. I patted her black alloy head. Her ears twitched.

"Fetch the largest containment vessel, girl," I said. As she bounded away, I yelled after her, "And equip a Suretrap!"

"Are there dangerous bots stuck in there?" Mr. P. asked from behind me. "Am I safe?"

"Could be," I said. "Dangerous bots, I mean." Looking between him and the cleanout, I added, "For what it's worth, another bit of the fine print you signed was an at-your-own-risk clause if you stay in the basement while I work."

Mr. P. edged his chair back a few feet. I silently shook my head at his stupidity.

I locked the fence to hold back any sewage poised to rush out at me. By the time I had the cleanout plug loose, Zogo was back with the two-foot bot containment vessel. It generated a field of EM interference that kept microelectronics from functioning.

I grabbed the extraction rod off the large cube and held it in front of the hole. Its nimble cable-like fingers extended toward the mass of bots at the fence. One by one, I quickly shuttled the eight known bots to containment.

For the mystery seven, I moved slowly. Physically, they scanned as identical, but I couldn't know for sure if they were programmed identically.

My tension eased with each one I dropped into the containment vessel. I focused on taking long slow breaths and maintaining my careful, steady pace.

Number six had just cleared the cleanout when the extraction rod flashed red. Never having seen that happen in person, I stood there dumbly, too shocked to remember what to do. Fortunately, my ever-attentive assistant leaped at the rod, tearing it from my grip. She turned her head to aim into the Suretrap before ejecting the bot.

The soccer-ball-shaped device closed instantly. The external metal mesh had just finished closing up when the bot exploded. Each segment of the trap held a directional explosive charge that fired nearly simultaneously to create an implosion to battle the explosion. The shockwave knocked me off my feet and sent Mr. P. sprawling on the floor. When I regained my feet, my ears were ringing. The smoking metal mesh of the Suretrap had a pointy bulge where a defect in the implosion's symmetry had nearly allowed the explosion to escape.

Worried about the last bot, I scrambled back to the pipe to find that it had scuttled away downstream—not my problem anymore.

I ushered Mr. P. upstairs and outside. We both plopped down on the concrete front steps of the house. My hearing still hadn't come back when he started to babble. I pointed at my unhearing ears and shook my head.

A few moments later, Mr. P. nudged me and pushed his datapad into my hands. It read, "It was a setup. A guy from Smartsewer offered to pay for the work if I would help him play a prank on you. He said you were old friends and it would be funny. I'm very sorry."

I knew exactly who he was talking about. Conall was an engineer at Smartsewer, just like I was until he stole my work and ended my career.

———

Standing outside my truck four hours later, I uploaded scans of the finished job to Smartsewer for Mr. P's warranty. I

L. B. Spillers

wasn't about to give Conall the satisfaction of voiding our shop's certification. Mr. P. had a brand new Smartsewer line, and I had a story to lie about to my wife.

I was looking forward to not hearing any more of Mr. P.'s apologies. Conall had been careful not to leave any trace of his involvement. Any investigation would show that I had a near miss with a rogue sewer bot on a standard factory-certified service visit.

As I set my tool belt in the back of the truck, I heard vehicles approaching. Three black SUVs driven by soldiers hemmed my truck in. Sometimes when a Suretrap fires, the city will dispatch emergency services, but this was ridiculous. Coming right after the attempt on my life made it suspicious. All I could do was hope that Conall didn't have some kind of in with them.

I stood back from my truck and assumed what I hoped looked like an unthreatening pose. Black-clad troops wearing tactical vests and helmets hopped out of the vehicles and quietly surrounded my truck. A woman in a dark pantsuit emerged from the rear of the convoy.

"Mr. Johanson, I'm Special Agent Lloyd with the FBI. I have a warrant for all sewer bots extracted from your recently completed job." She handed me a folded piece of paper.

I opened it and looked it over. It didn't tell me much. Apparently, there was a presidential executive order that some federal judge in Alexandria, Virginia agreed applied to Mr. P.'s pests.

"I'm happy to comply," I said, pocketing the warrant. I grabbed the half-melted blob of metal mesh that used to be a Suretrap and handed it to her. "That's what's left of the one that detonated." Then I looked at the large containment vessel and paused. Defying a federal warrant probably had some hideous punishment, but any hope of figuring out what was going on required that I analyze Mr. P.'s bots myself.

I grabbed the small bot container from the morning's first job and placed it at her feet. It held four bots that should prove convincing.

"That's everything, Agent Lloyd, but I need a receipt for the Suretrap. There's a sizable deposit that the shop will lose otherwise."

She handed me another sheet of paper. "Submit this to the manufacturer. Just fill in the serial number. Thank you for your cooperation, Mr. Johanson."

Before I could respond, she was headed back to her vehicle with the Suretrap remains and my bot container. Her team silently melted back into their vehicles. Within a minute I was standing behind my open truck watching the convoy disappear down the road.

The only solace I could find in the situation was that the fed didn't seem interested in me. She was practically bored. Still, it made no sense. Even if the Suretrap had tipped off the government about a dangerous sewer drone, why send the FBI? And why was Conall trying to kill me? He had already won by destroying my engineering career and taking my promotion.

One of the few benefits of going from white-collar to blue-collar work was supposed to be not taking my work home with me. I looked at the large containment vessel, sighing at the annoying night ahead of me.

———

At home, I parked the truck in the driveway and put Zogo in guard-dog mode.

It was Angela's night to cook, so I had the luxury of showing up right before dinner time. Tara was helping her mom load the dishwasher when I walked in. She had recently become obsessed with how the dishes were packed in the racks. Since she was only ten years old, I was hoping it was just a quirky phase she was going through, but I smelled a whiff of her mother's obsessive-compulsive disorder.

L. B. Spillers

"No, Mommy! The plate first, then the bowl."

Angela paused to cast me a smile, but I could see the tinge of worry in the corners of her eyes. The very last thing Tara needed was a new medical problem. Her childhood to that point had been an odyssey of painful, expensive medical care, endless doctor visits, and trips across the country for the new new treatment. We'd had six months of remission, six months of blessed normalcy.

And God damn me for being thankful that Angela was distracted worrying about Tara. I'd be able to carry the bot containment vessel into the basement without her seeing.

After dinner, Tara rushed off to hang out with her friends online. As I started to clear the dishes, Angela reminded me just how observant she was.

"Were you ever going to tell me about the Suretrap?" Angela asked. "I have to find out from the manufacturer that you almost got your ass blown to hell? And did you think I wouldn't notice you moving a containment box into the basement? What the hell is going on, Ulf?"

I set the dishes in the sink and dropped my head. A sour chuckle escaped me as I realized I had, for the umpteenth time, underestimated my wife.

"It gets worse. The FBI came by to take the sewer bots I extracted."

She looked me up and down before responding like she wasn't sure who I was. "Yet somehow there is a bot containment cube in the basement. No doubt it holds evidence of you defying a federal warrant." She closed her eyes and rubbed her forehead with her hand. "You think I have it easy running the business?! We just got a little breathing room with Tara and you go and—"

"Angela," I put my hand up. "Please. Everything's fine. The engineer in me just wants to check the checkables." My reassurance didn't sway her, even backed up with a roguish smile. I was losing my touch, I guess.

I sat back down at the table. "Okay, here's the full story..."

———

Everything in my basement workshop was in its place. Back when Tara started getting chemo, I installed a HEPA filtration system for all the air in the house, even the basement. So although I hadn't been down there in months, the lack of dust kept everything gleaming like I had just cleaned it. It felt like that part of my life I had been pushed away from was just lurking here, shiny and fresh, waiting for me the whole time.

My first stop was the tank, the old oil tank I had repurposed as my robot dissection bench. I placed one of the unknown bots on the stand inside and sealed the hatch. If a bot misbehaved, it'd have to get through some thick steel and then a concrete block wall to hurt me.

After donning my VR helmet and haptic gloves, I dropped into the ancient recliner next to my workbench and booted the system up.

Before me, the two-inch-wide spherical robot was rendered as large as my neighbor's house, crisscrossed by overlays of wispy dimension lines and annotations. I found Smartsewer's maker's mark and a serial number. The placement wasn't far off, but not applied with factory accuracy—a strong fake.

Hoping to find that someone was just disguising their homegrown sewer bots with a plausible maker's mark, I instructed the manipulator arms to slowly unscrew the two halves of the sphere. After a quarter-turn, the bot started smoking and dripping greenish fluid.

That was worse than it blowing up. Any schmuck can make their little bot go boom, but it takes real finesse to set up a jacket of corrosive fluid around your bots' innards. Whoever was behind these bots was well-resourced.

Two hours later, I had destroyed two other bots trying to disable their chemical defenses and finally succeeded in getting

L. B. Spillers

the innards of the fourth one out undamaged. Its tiny circuit board was being analyzed by my reverse-engineering rig.

A breakthrough came when I ran the embedded code through my decompiler. Figuring out what all those millions of machine instructions were designed to do could take weeks. However, when I kicked off my application, it immediately recognized several Smartsewer modules. Someone had lifted code from Smartsewer's bots and added in a bunch of new code.

That was all I could determine for the moment. The fact that someone was emulating Smartsewer packaging and stealing a bunch of their code pointed to one thing. I was looking at sewer bots designed to infiltrate Smartsewer lines.

Upstairs I found Angela dozing in front of the TV. She stirred when I plopped down on the couch.

"What'd you find?" she asked.

"Someone's putting out fake Smartsewer bots," I replied. I rubbed my face. "They've stolen a lot of the original code and tweaked it. I don't know what the tweaks do yet."

Angela turned off the TV and stretched her arms. "So what are you going to do?"

Despite the near miss, Conall was such a putz that I struggled to think of him as a mortal threat. Still, I couldn't just wait around for him to keep trying to kill me until he succeeded.

"Remember that time you talked me out of sabotaging the sprinkler line above his desk? I never removed the demolition bot I parked up there. It'd be easy to—"

"Jesus, Ulf, really? That's your answer? You're going to vandalize his office?" She shook her head not meeting my eyes. I could see her working hard to control her anger. "Tara and I need you here, not in jail."

She was right, mostly. I had barely made peace with his corporate victory over me. The idea that I had limped away into obscurity only to have him damn near kill me was infuriating. I knew that behind his bluster was a coward. Still, Angela was right. Getting myself thrown in jail would give him another victory.

I stood up. "Fine, I'll go *talk* to him tomorrow."

"No, you won't," she said. "You're scheduled up 'til Tuesday on jobs I can't push on any of the other guys. Talk to him Tuesday."

In moments like those, I particularly loved Angela. She could switch gears with the best of them. In a moment she had dropped the emotion and kept things practical. Despite my adoring gaze, she still had her serious face on. I was definitely losing my touch.

"Yes, boss." I kissed her. "Good night, boss."

———

I walked into Smartsewer headquarters, unsure how I'd get in to see Conall. There were two or three guys still on staff who might come down and walk me in. Fortunately, Lenny was still working the security desk in the mornings. If I endured one of his plumber-porn jokes, he'd probably let me in.

"Ulf! Hey, it's great to see you. How's plumbing treating you?"

"Hey, Lenny, good to see you too. I was hoping—"

The phone rang and Lenny held up a finger. While muttering one-word responses into the phone he scribbled my name on a visitor's badge and buzzed me through the security door.

As I rode the elevator up, nostalgia for the white-collar bubble tugged at me. Everyone was neatly dressed and groomed. Every surface was shiny and clean. All the gritty problems of the world seemed just a little more removed, supplanted by a thousand little first-world problems.

Conall had our old boss' corner office. Skinny, his pinched face and slicked-back dark hair looked how I remembered. I always wanted to see what would happen if I got a lit match near all that hair product.

He startled when he caught sight of me.

"You've got no business here," he said, rotating his chair to face me. I watched a few false starts ripple through his torso as if he were resisting the urge to flee. "Give me a reason not to call security."

I smiled at his nervous little attempt to assert dominance. It reassured me that he remained the insecure turd that I remembered. I imagined throat-punching him, plowing his face into the surface of his desk over and over until I got tired, and finally breaking that twiggy neck of his.

"I've come to ask why you tried to kill me, and whether you intend to keep it up." I gestured to his spacious office that would have been mine. "You won, right? So what's the point? You almost hurt Mr. Papadopolous with that thing."

Conall smiled broadly. "I suggest you take whatever evidence you have of wrongdoing to the police. But, wait! There is none. I'm calling security." He picked up his phone handset. I imagined garroting him with the cord.

"Don't throw me out until you see the present I brought you." I placed a glass jar on his desk. Inside was one of the fake Smartsewer bots.

He set down the phone and picked up the vial. "What's this?"

"It's a counterfeit Smartsewer bot that was in Mr. P.'s line. I think you've got something to do with them." I pointed at the jar. "I've got more of those. If you come after me again, they'll end up in the wrong hands. So what I need from you now is assurance that you won't come after me again. Then peace will reign in the land and my wife will praise my emotional growth."

I didn't expect him to take my offer, but I was hoping he'd leak some information, maybe brag a little. Setting it back down, he said, "Are you going to leave on your own, or do I really have to call security?"

This is how Conall survived in the corporate world. The one talent he possessed was an excellent instinct for when to keep his mouth shut. I was grudgingly impressed.

Shrugging, I said, "I had to try the easy way." He harrumphed at my back as I left.

I took the fire stairs down. Stopping on a landing, I used my pocket knife to scrape a bit of red paint off the sprinkler system's water main. I ran an electrode from my phone to the bare metal, multiplexing a control signal on the network of pipes.

As I waited for the old demolition bot to respond, I realized Angela was right. He had gotten to me. I needed to claw back some self-respect from him. Did my response make me a petulant boy or a vengeful man? That, I decided, depended on whether or not I was caught.

As the seconds ticked by, my ears strained to listen for activity in the stairwell. It was taking too long. Since it had been over two years, I wondered if the battery still had any juice.

After a torturous minute, the bot woke up and completed a handshake with my phone. I sent it a bundle of instructions before hurrying out the first-floor door to my car. I only had twenty minutes or so before it was repositioned and my revenge kicked off. He'd live, and it wouldn't solve anything, but it would feel so good.

———

When the Tuesday evening news mentioned a flood at Smartsewer's headquarters building, I kept my mouth shut. The only thing that saved me from Angela's wrath was the fact that no one got hurt.

Wednesday morning, I was still preoccupied with the Conall situation. Whatever satisfaction I got from flooding his office was dwarfed by all the unknowns. What was his connection with the counterfeit bots? Why was the government responding to Suretrap activations? Would my retaliation dissuade Conall or spur him to attack me again?

By lunchtime, satisfaction was winning out over fear. Worst case, I figured he wouldn't try anything again for a while. That should give me time to reverse-engineer the counterfeit bots and maybe get ahead of this thing.

When I emerged from Dino's with my usual sandwich, the sight of the FBI agent waiting for me flushed all that wishful thinking out of my mind. At least she didn't have a tactical team with her this time.

"We've got to stop meeting like this," I said. I took a seat on a nearby bench. "Mind if I eat while we talk? I've got like fifteen minutes left on my break." I pulled out my turkey and cheddar sandwich and started wolfing it down.

"Sure, but don't worry about your boss," she said, sitting down. "I paid Angela for the rest of your time today. I need your Smartsewer expertise."

I pulled out my bottle of soda and took a long drink while I pondered her obvious lie.

"Well, a year ago I was probably the world's foremost expert on Smartsewer's tech, but you must know I was let go—fired for cause. So not only is my expertise slightly stale, but I'm also not what your federal judge in Virginia would call a disinterested party." Translation: I know you're up to something.

Agent Lloyd nodded. "That's why I need you. I want your adversarial opinion because I think your old enemy Conall is involved in corporate espionage, and I think you knew that and he got you fired for it."

I snorted some soda at that. I had to hope that Agent Lloyd took my upset as anything but what it really was. After wiping my mouth I asked, "How can I help?"

She still sounded full of crap to me, but the only way I saw forward was to play along with her little stunt.

"Someone sabotaged the sprinkler line in Conall's office. I need to figure out if it might have been a botched assassination attempt."

"And having Conall's arch-enemy poking around might unsettle him for you." I chuckled.

She nodded. "I really do need you to assess the crime scene. You know the building's security. You know commercial utility bots better than almost anyone."

I was intrigued. This was starting to seem fun. Maybe she was on my side after all.

"Oh," I said. "So you paid Angela my engineering consulting rate?"

Agent Lloyd stood up and motioned for me to follow her. "No. Angela was adamant that you're a plumber now, so she billed me the shop rate."

My datapad beeped. Angela's update to my work schedule popped up.

"Of course she did."

———

At Smartsewer headquarters, the low babble of quiet voices and key clicks ceased as people saw me with agent Lloyd. Work friends I'd known for a decade looked away. We strode to Conall's former office trailing a wake of utter silence.

The two agents guarding the office stepped aside to let us pass.

"Up there," Agent Lloyd said, pointing to the hole where the acoustic ceiling tiles had been destroyed. "A three-inch water pipe for the sprinkler system broke and flooded the office and a good portion of the floor before it was shut off. Please examine the break and tell me if you think the pipe was the actual target or just in the way."

I grabbed the step ladder that was leaning against the wall and set it up underneath the broken pipe. I stood there with my head above the ceiling for a few minutes with my flashlight, examining the break in the pipe, feigning curiosity. I was pleased to see the bot I had used was nowhere to be seen; good luck finding it where I parked it.

"The surface has mild dimpling where a bot clamped onto it," I said, coming down the ladder. The FBI geeks would have seen the same thing. "Combine that with the fact that the cut is perfectly perpendicular to the pipe and—"

"What the hell is he doing here?!" Conall stood outside the doorway, pointing at me.

"Let him in," Agent Lloyd said to the guards.

"I love what you've done with the place, Conall." I couldn't resist.

"Lock that shit down," Agent Lloyd said, pointing a finger at me.

"You can't trust anything he says," Conall said. "He was fired for a security breach."

"And he stole my work, presenting it as his own," I said, folding my arms. "Congratulations, Agent Lloyd. You have two of us monkeys throwing shit at each other. Do you need anything else from me?"

Agent Lloyd chuckled. "Well, Ulf, I could see how your smartassery would get in the way of long-term employment. But before we go, I'd like Conall's explanation of this." He placed a glass vial on Conall's old desk. The counterfeit bot inside gleamed.

"That's his!" Conall pointed at me.

"That'd be a lot more convincing if yours weren't the only fingerprints on it," Agent Lloyd said. "And if firemen hadn't found it in your office."

Around the office, we used to call Conall head-of-much-heat on account of the way his face reddened when he got upset. I had to bite the inside of my cheek to keep from laughing at the color Agent Lloyd had brought out in him.

"Of course, my fingerprints were on it! He gave it to me. You can't just—"

Agent Lloyd put up her hand. "Enough! Here's what I think.

I think you have been selling Smartsewer designs. When some buggy counterfeits showed up across the country, you decided to silence the one man who might find a way to incriminate you."

Conall laughed. "Lady, that's a load of galloping horseshit. Good luck proving any of it."

Agent Lloyd gave Conall a beautiful smile. It lit up her face. I was a little jealous. She'd never given me more than a sardonic grin.

"Thank you," she said. "But I won't have to."

———

A month later, I found myself occupying the renovated corner office that used to be Conall's. Agent Lloyd had worked some magic with management, offering them a Defense Department contract with Smartsewer that named me key personnel. The DoD needed military sewer drones for urban deployments, and Conall was not the person they wanted in charge of developing them, or even in the same company.

Memories of my previous ten months as a plumber were fading. My mind was turning the entire interlude into a sabbatical, a brief period of fieldwork that would inform my engineering.

A knock on the door frame pulled me out of my musing. I swiveled my chair around to see Agent Lloyd in my doorway.

"Come on in, Gina," I said, standing up. "I didn't think I'd be seeing you again. I was told my project liaison was some marine colonel."

Gina gave me one of her micro-smiles. She closed the office door, leaving a black-suited companion outside.

"I'm not here as your liaison," he said. "I'm here as your handler."

I shrugged. "So, what can I do for you? I'm just settling in."

"A liaison is a person who facilitates communications," she said, wrinkling her nose at the clown print on my wall. Then she locked eyes with me before saying, "A handler, in my business, is someone who directs, briefs, and debriefs an asset." Her tone was slightly adversarial.

That was just weird enough to sour the new car smell of my office. I was grateful to the lady for my rehabilitation, but she was confusing the hell out of me.

"Look," I said, putting my hands up, "You got me my life back—with interest—so yeah, I'm your guy, your asset, whatever. What's up?"

Agent Lloyd grunted. "What I'm trying to get at is that your remaining in our good graces is contingent on you doing what you're told. Colonel Meigs will be your liaison to the Marines; that work is real. But I will be the agent running the occasional counter-intelligence op using you."

The phrase "counter-intelligence op" hit me like a gut punch. I had presumed that Gina wouldn't have rebuilt my corporate life if she knew my secret. "What does not being in your good graces look like?"

"Ugly," she said. "It would involve a portfolio of criminal charges deriving from your prior sales of Smartsewer's designs to the Chinese. Things like espionage, being an unlicensed foreign agent, and perhaps even treason."

Everything got a little wobbly. I dropped back into my chair.

I had come to think of Agent Lloyd as a friend, but it was no friend who stood there silently watching me, assessing me. The joy of regaining my former career, of earning three times my plumbing wages, evaporated.

She was waiting for me to pick up my end of the conversation. It occurred to me she could be bluffing, so I resolved not to admit to any crimes. I needed to understand my status. How secure was my job? Was he intending to send me to jail when she was done with me?

"Gina, if you thought I was a spy, why the hell did you work so hard to get me back here?"

Gina sat in a guest chair. "Leverage. We also couldn't help but notice you inserted some subtle bugs into the code you sold them." Gina looked at the family photo behind me. "And, the forensic accountant told us that you used the money for Tara's treatments."

Forensic accountant? How many people knew about me? I started to ask another question but stopped. My mouth sat there hanging open until I self-consciously closed it a few moments later.

Looking at Gina, I saw a sad kind of resolution animating her features. I was the lovable dog she would put down if she had to.

"I'll do what I'm told," I said, quietly.

Smiling, Agent Lloyd said, "Good."

She lightly slapped my desk twice as if to punctuate the end of the meeting. Standing up, she said, "I'll be in touch."

After she left, I turned back to the recent photo of my family. We were all smiling, standing in front of the shop under the "new" sign, the one I had helped Angela's father put up back when I was in high school.

Angela looked so happy and proud. Tara was healthy. We had just learned I was getting my job back, with a promotion. Would she have been so proud if she knew what the road to my rehabilitation had been paved with?

I was going to make sure she never found out. ∎

SOLANGE'S MANUAL

Eight-year-old JJ walked into Eric's Joint, a small diner. The System directed undernourished prospects there. They could thumb a scanner, and get fed pretty much anything they wanted for free.

I stood across the street, waiting. The whole exercise was a waste of my time. Solange could have handled this administratively. I stopped asking her to explain herself a long time ago.

My phone chimed, informing me that JJ just used his thumb to order a meal at Eric's. I wasn't surprised when JJ immediately walked out without any food. He was shoving something into his pants pocket that surveillance footage had taught me was probably a five-dollar bill. Since Eric's charge-backs to The System for these phantom meals averaged about fifteen bucks, Eric just cheated the System out of ten dollars by encouraging an under-fed kid not to eat.

After JJ was down the street, I entered Eric's Joint, unplugged the small thumb scanner, and walked out with it. Eric chased after me, careful not to touch me. He knew all the kids in The System studied martial arts.

I would have enjoyed dropping him to the sidewalk if he had given me an excuse. My enthusiasm was tempered by the fact that I was no longer a minor and only months from leaving for college. I couldn't afford an arrest.

Eric sprinted ahead of me, and stood in my way, panting. Fifty pounds overweight, dangles of hair fell across his face already dripping sweat. He was taller and heavier than me, but he had a nervous, weak face that made him look more pathetic than intimidating. I tried to walk around him, but he got in my way.

"I need that scanner, Damon," Eric said, putting his hand

out. His other hand pushed back his thin, black hair.

"It's The System's scanner, Eric. You cheated. You're out." I stopped and clasped my hands in front of me.

Eric stepped back, his hand still out. "I know people, Damon. You don't want to do this."

"You're talking about Sal," I said.

Eric nodded. "That's right, we're tight. His boys will be happy to straighten you out."

I laughed. "Eric, Sal's the head of the DDs because his predecessor tried to muscle The System. Tito didn't move to Houston. That was a euphemism. You know that word, Eric?"

Eric's hand dropped.

———

The System had found me when I was eight years old. I had made the two-mile walk to Harry's Game Room where you could play console games for five bucks an hour.

I didn't have money to play, but I wanted to see the place. There was no such thing as extra money in my life at that time. If there were suddenly more money, then Mom would have spent it drinking more expensive booze, or eating takeout instead of junk food.

The long walk to another neighborhood was an adventure of discovery for me. And yes, of course, my mom let me walk around on my own when I was eight. It was one of the few upsides of her neglect.

Harry's front door opened onto bright-orange fast-food seating for the snack bar. The smell of French fries made my mouth water. I was always hungry back then.

Past the snack bar, on the left, I reached The Pit: arcing rows of partitioned gaming areas that descended three levels, terraced so you could see into each one from above. I stood there, my eyes flitting from screen to screen, watching games.

"Damon!" A voice came from behind me.

I almost peed myself. No one should have known I was

there. While my eyes hurriedly scanned the bottom of The Pit for an exit, a finger tapped me on the shoulder. I turned around and came face to face with Harry himself, squatting down to speak to me. How could he know my name?

Big as he was, his bright yellow staff t-shirt made him look like a harmless, friendly giant. He gave me a big grin and told me I could earn game time if I took some tests. Before I could answer, he started walking to the glass-walled room behind the snack bar with four computers in it. By the time I got out of that display case of a room, I had spent two hours taking tests and earned four hours of gameplay.

I didn't tell my mom about any of it. Having something of my own that she couldn't take was exciting.

Those tests kicked it all off. A week later, I was attending an after-school class at The Learning Center. At first, I went mostly for the food: sandwiches, snacks, and drinks. In retrospect, I see that class was a kind of applicant intake process. There was a lot of talk about how the world worked, life paths, and career choices. The point was to get a kid to be eager for an education.

I took to it quickly. A month later I asked to be allowed to take remedial reading and math classes after school.

They were happy to enroll me so long as I agreed to check in with a counselor every two weeks. It was a small quid pro quo that gently slid me into The System. I had willingly embraced their influence and monitoring.

———

My errand with Eric done, I headed back to my office. That's a generous description of a room in the basement of my apartment's building that Solange lets me use.

Solange is my only direct contact with The System. A lot of us call it The System, but we don't know what it really is. It works through proxies: The Learning Center, Harry's, individually contracted teachers, therapists, and a long list of vendors hired through different fronts. Sometimes Solange seems to be in control of it all, but other times she subordinates herself. Anytime I ask about The System, she evades and deflects.

Walking down the street, my thoughts were filled with this woman who has guided my life since I was in fourth grade. After all that time, Solange remained a mystery to me. High school graduation was coming in a few months. Increasingly I found nostalgic and sentimental thoughts wearing away my usual focus. I've never met her in person, but the idea of separating from her was awful.

I was startled to realize that I had stopped on my way home to stare at a chain-link fence gate at the end of a long alley between two brick buildings. That god-damned razor wire was still on top of it. It was where my life forked.

———

I was eleven, and my grades were perfect. That was the requirement for taking Jiu-Jitsu classes. As usual, I had no idea who paid for them.

My world was full of weak, broken people. Sometimes they were physically weak, but mostly it was the weak-minded wielding the poor life skills gifted to them by their parents. The sense of physical security I gained from Jiu-jitsu gave me the confidence to choose differently than my peers.

Towards the end of sixth grade, there was an incident. The DDs decided they were going to recruit me. They were a bunch of bullying jackasses who used minors to carry drugs from their stashes to their street dealers.

Their leader, Tito, would stop me on the way home from school to ask if I wanted to make some money. I politely told him no. Day after day, he kept asking, and I kept refusing until one day he grabbed my arm and insisted. Although he was over six feet tall and beefy, he wasn't trained. Breaking a one-handed grab was lesson one in Jiu-jitsu. The thumb is the weak point. I

L. B. Spillers

broke his grip and ran.

No matter how slippery I was, avoiding Tito's crew for long was impossible. Two days later I was cornered at the end of that alley by three of his boys. Normally, I could have climbed the chain-link fence gate. Unfortunately, recently added razor wire blocked my escape route. The three of them fanned out in front of me and waited for Tito.

Soon, I saw Tito striding down the alley towards me. "You figured out who the boss is, little man?"

Not waiting for an answer, Tito walked right up to me and started in. He slapped me while he yelled at me, occasionally punching me and shoving me into the fence. He was holding back, but it was enough to make me dizzy and set my ears to buzzing.

It went on like that, half tirade, half beating. Every so often he would pause to ask me if I figured out who the boss was yet. I answered everything from "God" to "your mother."

In the middle of it, I managed to catch one of Tito's boys with a finger jab to the throat. Tito stopped to mock his man for letting a kid put him down but quickly resumed his indoctrination, yelling and smacking me. As it went on, everything became more distant. My arms stopped trying to block his hands. His words became faint buzzes in my ears. I stopped answering him. My body was this foreign thing staggering around.

A phone call interrupted him. I fell hard on my ass as Tito was talking into his phone. When he slumped to the ground, I wasn't sure if he had moved or I had. The scene is fuzzy in my memory, but I clearly remember lying on the ground and seeing a quad-copter drone above me. I had always wanted one.

When I sat up, the alley was littered with four bodies. They all had thin wire darts in their chests. A noise behind me brought my attention to a much older kid behind the locked fence gate. He was stowing the copter's remote control in his backpack.

I slowly got to my feet. The guy was picking the padlock. In thirty seconds he had the padlock open. I stared at him with total hero worship.

"Can you walk?" he asked, looking at me skeptically. He opened the fence gate.

My ribs hurt, my lip was bleeding, and my ears were still ringing. "I think so. Thanks for saving my butt."

He laughed at how my fat lip made me sound. Gesturing behind him, he said "Those guys had it coming. Follow me."

We walked through the gate. "What about them?" I motioned towards the bodies on the other side of the gate.

"It's covered," he said, closing the gate and relocking it. He pointed farther up the alley; a grey van was slowly reversing towards the bodies. Without another word, he walked away.

I looked from the van to him a couple of times, before falling in behind him, limping. My savior told me to hold all my questions for the meeting he was taking me to. He left me alone in a room at the Learning Center talking to Solange via a voice-only computer chat. I never saw him again.

Grateful for my escape, and very curious, I was happy to talk to her. The Learning Center was already a very positive, important part of my life by then, so cooperating with the mysterious, faceless woman on the other side of the network connection was fine with me. To my eleven-year-old self, it made sense.

Solange asked me about the rescue. How did those guys dying make me feel? If I could have, would I have killed them? At the time, I didn't have much empathy for anyone. I was glad they were dead, thrilled. Even now, I think the world is better without them, but I no longer feel joy at the thought of their deaths.

She gave me an alternate story for how I spent the time, and then she quizzed me on the details. That was the secret to a good lie, she said, filling in all the details until you could see it in your mind.

When I started asking her questions, she was suddenly out of time. She gave me a web login to a site that contained a manual about life. It was an enormous, subversive textbook for kids, unfiltered by politicians and parents. The Manual was the single most brilliant thing that I had ever seen. School doesn't teach you to read body language, pick locks, or understand the pack dynamics of the human adolescent; The Manual did all that and much more.

———

By laying bare the clockwork of the world, The Manual made all things seem possible. I grew confident and developed a vision for my future. Poverty dictated that I had to become an extraordinary student because the only way I was getting to college was through scholarships or the military. The Air Force was my backup plan.

Unfortunately, my emotional growth didn't keep pace with my education and ambitions. Towards the end of seventh grade, that emotional deficit asserted itself.

Like all kids, my life centered on my stuff. When my PlayStation Portable disappeared from the apartment, I told my Learning Center counselor my suspicions: my mom's boyfriend took it, and she was covering for him. My counselor warned me not to presume to know someone else's mind. Judge people on evidence.

So I borrowed a nanny-cam bear from my friend and hid it in the clutter above a row of kitchen cabinets. She never went up there, and it had a view of the whole apartment.

Over a few weeks, I discovered that my mom had lost her part-time job at the call center. She was broke, selling my stuff. It would be years later when I recognized that her endless string of boyfriends were actually clients.

A conversation I recorded still haunts me. One of her johns

commented that he heard I was a good kid. Her response: "You take him. The state support don't pay near enough. I don't want him. He eats all the god-damn food and don't ever shut that smart mouth of his." There was no humor, just a cold, distant, matter-of-fact assertion that she didn't want me. Those few seconds of sound ripped something from me. The world was instantly an emptier place.

I had been using Learning Center computers to review the recordings. I would swap out the USB memory stick in the bear every day and fast forward through the recordings, clipping out interesting bits.

The System monitored my activity. My counselor scolded me for invading my mom's privacy. I told her that I wasn't doing anything to her that The System wasn't doing to me. Her hypocrisy enraged me.

Then she made the mistake of telling me to stop making recordings. I was in the right, and she made me the bad guy. All that anger I had for my mom redirected at her.

I stood up and told her "Make me." My sensei would have kicked me out of the dojo if I just attacked her, so I leaned in real close, daring her to hit me. I wanted an excuse to beat on her. She was one of those liberal idiots who think education or status is the same thing as authority.

As I leaned in, she pressed herself back into her chair, trembling. When I saw the tears start, I lost all respect for her. My adolescence was one long lesson in just how weak adults were.

Part of me hoped that I wouldn't have to go to counseling after that, but Solange insisted that I see a different therapist, away from The Learning Center. When I asked my new therapist who paid her, she told me not to worry about it.

———

As I went downstairs to my building's basement, that inflection point in my life was bouncing around my head.

Menacing that poor woman stuck in my mind as the moment when I took charge of my life.

Halfway through the basement hallway, I stopped in front of a windowless, metal door that might be mistaken for a janitor's closet. The grime and sloppy paint offered no hints about the technology behind it.

Inside was a room twenty feet square, my home away from home. Computer monitors covered most of one wall. My simple bench desk sat in front of those monitors. Off to the left were server racks. That was one of my part-time jobs: Solange's IT operations guy.

The screen-saver was a gigantic smiley face bouncing around the array of monitors. As I walked in, I saw it and snorted. It used to cheer me, but after the political curriculum, it took on a very right-thought aspect in my eyes.

The monitors reacted to my noise by coming to life with a montage of patriotic Americana: flags, uniformed military, long shots of ripe fields of grain, and modern manufacturing scenes with ethnically balanced casts of people gettin' er done. Solange set that up when I made the mistake of complaining about the enormous smiley face.

The martial music peaked as I put Eric's scanner into a drawer of computer peripherals.

When I took my seat, the montage was replaced by the neighborhood monitoring feeds. The four screens closest to my seat showed my computer desktops. I was in no mood to do any work on them. I waited for Solange to respond to my chat request.

"You seem down," her voice came over the speakers. I couldn't see her, but she could always see me.

I shrugged. "You propped up Eric's business by feeding hungry kids there. He had no trouble finding kids to cash in on your generosity with. It's depressing as hell. Worse, you insisted that I get the scanner in person. Why was that?"

"I'll send you some references so you can study Eric's psychology further, Damon."

Hearing her deflect my question, I sighed. "Solange, I've got no interest in deconstructing Eric's pathologies. And just once, I'd love to get a straight answer from you."

"Well," she stretched the word out like she always did when she got pedantic. "Interested or not, other people will always be the greatest obstacles in your life. Understanding them is crucial. You're not nearly as smart as you think you are."

I began gently banging my head on my desk.

———

Solange wasn't done with me for the day. She sent me to deliver a sensitive message to Mr. Henderson at The Learning Center. It was an extra dollop of shit on the day's already impressive pile.

Mr. Henderson rolled his head on his chair's cushion, sighing. Clean shaven and neatly groomed, he wore a plain blue tie draped on a white, button-down shirt. His suit coat hung neatly on a hook behind the door. I always liked him. He was a smart-ass like me. He fronted all kinds of rebellion, but he was always squared away.

"I'll say one thing for you guys, you have better chairs than the school."

I sat down in the aluminum guest chair. Mr. Henderson was a physics teacher at my high school, paid by one of The System's charitable fronts to spend another three hours every school day overseeing a science study hall off campus. Kids came, the kids who had earned it. They enjoyed free drinks and snacks, did their homework, and worked on science projects.

"So, I wanted—" I started to say. Of course, he cut me off. The Manual says the habit is a need for him to enforce the social hierarchy; it sometimes indicates insecurity.

"I don't work for you, Damon." Henderson took a sip from his diet soda, making an obnoxious slurping noise.

I smiled. *Your best employees are often the most difficult.* The Manual was spot on with that tidbit. Henderson was creative and passionate but resentful of control. "Come on, Mr. Henderson, I'm just a messenger, paid by the same people paying you."

"How much, I wonder?" He put his feet up on his desk. It was half-past five and all the kids had just filed out of the room.

"Eric was caught gaming the system."

"I got the alert." He took another sip.

"What's not in the alert is that he threatened to make trouble for us with the DDs."

"Seems unlikely to me," Henderson said. "Sal loves us. His half-brother comes here every day."

"Well, The System says he's out to stir up some very personal shit. Long story short, the recommendation is that you switch up your Wednesday evening routine until he cools down."

Henderson's feet came down off the desk as his chair awkwardly snapped upright. "You've got no right to be in my business! What do you know?"

I knew Mr. Henderson spent Wednesday evenings with a woman named Lanie. I knew Lanie wasn't his wife, and she had a spouse of her own. I knew Lanie was Sal's half-brother's mom. I said none of this. Discretion might be the biggest lesson The Manual ever taught me.

I put my hands up. "Mr. H, I'm sorry. I'm not in your business, they are. Eric's a sociopath. He's capable of a lot." I'm not supposed to tell him that Eric plans on leading Lanie's husband to catch them in the act.

Henderson chuffed. "I bet you could give me the verbatim definition of sociopath, but do you truly understand it? I think you kids run the danger of fooling yourselves with some of the socio-political crap that Manual feeds you."

I shrugged. "I don't claim to have it all figured out, but I do understand that Eric is pissed, and out to hurt this thing," I circled my finger in the air. "I'm delivering a message that is intended to help you avoid trouble. I have my own complaints about The System, but I think it's a whole lot better than what was going on around here before."

Henderson laughed. "You," he pointed at me, "are one precocious son of a bitch." He stood up and grabbed his suit coat. "It is better here since The System started up, but the whole thing makes me twitch."

That was Henderson: hot and cold, and smart enough to take the warning to heart.

———

My message delivered, I left The Learning Center by the back door. That way, I would avoid seeing fellow students and their parents. I didn't want to waste time chatting with people. The Manual teaches that anonymity is a virtue, both because it subsumes humility and because it starves the idiots of the world for information that might be used against you.

I stepped out into the cool air and found two men waiting for me, one to the left and one to the right. The man to the left I judged was less of a fighter. I charged him and was immediately tased by a third guy I hadn't noticed. I recognized the feeling from a session at the dojo. My limbs wouldn't respond to my frantic commands to move. I dropped to the ground. No one caught me. A soft, cloth bag fell over my head.

When the hood came off, I was seated at a folding table in a room of unpainted drywall. Two men exited, leaving my interviewer on the other side of the table.

"It's a few weeks late, but happy birthday, Damon, you're eighteen now. You can be handled like an adult."

The man speaking wore a white button-down shirt and khaki pants. His generic look was broken only by his footwear which was a kind of sneaker designed to pass for a leather shoe. I dreaded what sort of athleticism he intended for my interrogation.

"You hardly seem concerned with legalities." I stretched my neck muscles.

He waited as I finished moving my head around. The Manual is very clear that when being interviewed, one must not fear silence; one must not fill the silence without a clear purpose. After a brief stare-down, I started stretching out my wrists and hands. Being tased had made my muscles stiff and sluggish.

My interviewer smiled. He looked to be in his late thirties. The peninsula of hair on his forehead had nearly detached from the shrinking bulk of follicles behind it.

"Your mother told us about your conversion to Islam."

I stopped stretching and sat straight in my chair. "My mother, what's left of my mother, has no idea what Islam is. What did you pay her? She'll say or do whatever you want if you pay her. She's a whore." I enjoyed destroying the idea that my mother was leverage over me.

"She showed us your prayer rug and Koran."

"Those were left by one of her boyfriends." I made air quotes. "When he found out what she really was, he considered them unclean, the whole apartment unclean."

"We know you're part of a terrorist cell. For informing against your handlers, we're prepared to release you. There's still time for you to fix things."

I started ticking off things on my fingers. "AB and BC calc, five on each. Physics, both E&M and mechanics, five each. English AP, another five. 99th percentile in the SATs." I paused to let that sink in, but my interrogator gave me no reaction. "Do you understand what it takes to get those scores? That's on top of my part-time jobs which could be called community service. I'm as pro-system as they come. I have worked like a dog to get out of this shit-encrusted crater of a town. Where in that do you see the time or desire for terrorism?"

Still impassive, the man fussed with his computer tablet for a moment. "Let's start with seventeen deaths and disappearances over the last six years. You're connected with them all, including one SVR agent." He looked at me for a moment.

"I haven't killed anyone. I haven't helped kill anyone. I'm not a Muslim. I'm not part of any terrorist cell. I am not an enemy of the United States." If they had real evidence, I would have been arrested first to give them leverage. I had nothing to hide. My only challenge was to suppress the many smart-ass remarks that threatened to leap out of my mouth.

The man's eyebrow raised, his face still in his panel. I cast my eyes around the room and saw two sensor globes. That's when I realized they were doing a biometric analysis of the conversation. I wasn't lying, and it confused him.

"How about the botnets? We see you as having built out at least four different networks of compromised PCs, totaling around 70,000 machines."

"I've never had anything to do with malware or botnets or any of that. Why do you suspect me? What the hell would I do with an army of slaved PCs?"

"Oh, bullshit!" He set down his panel. "You've installed half the computers in this neighborhood. Your installations compromised a lot of PCs. Each one spread the infection across the net."

I waved him off. "The Learning Center helps get computers into kids' homes. Yes, I do installations for them. Getting kids online is a big part of getting them educated. The installations are automated from a bootable CD. What you need to do is talk to The Learning Center people and find out who made those installation CDs."

We had another stare down. I lost track of time in our little battle of glares. Eventually, another man popped in to whisper in my interrogator's ear. My interrogator nodded and left the room.

"Damon," the new man said, sitting down. "Your story is plausible. Your test scores are exemplary. Voice analysis, pupil response, kinesiology, metabolic dynamics—all our indicators— tell me that you aren't lying. I'm inclined to believe you." Instead of a computer tablet, my new interrogator carried a thick file folder. He began flipping through pages.

"Then believe me."

"The thing is," he looked up from his folder, "your scores are a little too good, considering your situation. They might be the results of hacking or cheating."

He leaned back in his chair. "Let's start with integral calculus."

What followed was four hours of probing my academic credentials. It was a ridiculous pretense. Every third or fourth question went back to my supposed terroristic activities. I answered everything quickly and directly.

Eventually, both men and machines were convinced.

———

After I was released, I went back to my basement office to report to Solange. I gave her a summary of my very unpleasant Saturday morning.

"You did well in your interrogation," Solange's voice was uncharacteristically emotional.

"It was hard to hear that my mom actually sold me out. She called the hotline looking for a bounty. Even for her, it's a new low."

"What will you do about it?" I heard curiosity in her voice as if she were a friend, not a mentor with an agenda.

"I'm done with her. I'm never going back to that apartment." I leaned back and stared up at the light fixture. I was dying to know what Solange looked like. "Getting my own PO Box was an excellent precaution."

After a long silence, Solange responded. "You haven't asked

me yet."

"I'm not sure it would be helpful to know. Not knowing got me through their biometrics, right?"

"Hmm." After a moment she continued. "I'll tell you anyway. You're not responsible for any deaths."

My own relief surprised me. If my mom was willing to go offensive on me, who knew how Solange might have surprised me.

"But I am," she said, her composure restored.

I stared at the generic female silhouette on the computer screen where her real picture never was. Solange was a killer.

"Killing isn't always wrong," I said slowly. It was a weak rationalization. "Judge on evidence, right? My evidence is that you have been nothing but fantastic to me."

There was another long pause. Intellectually, I knew no good could come from her explaining the killings to me. Emotionally, I desperately wanted to be reassured that she was the awesome, righteous woman that I imagined she was.

"I appreciate your faith in me, Damon."

———

Although I had senioritis, I managed to get through finals without screwing up my grades. Even though I was already accepted at the University of Buffalo, my high school would still send my final grades. Any problems could have screwed up my status in their honors program, or my financial aid.

By late July, my mind was already in Buffalo. I continued performing my job at The Learning Center and doing work for Solange. I had fallen into an easy rhythm, sleeping in the basement room, and grabbing showers where I could. It was a little grubby, but anything was better than going back to my mom's apartment.

UB gives honors students priority scheduling, so I already knew exactly what classes I would be in when the semester started. I spent my free time getting a head start on my coursework. I was well qualified and a good student, but anything short of excellent grades would screw up my scholarships.

I wasn't sure how things would end with Solange. I dreaded saying goodbye. Would she still chat with me after I went off to college? Would the three-letter guys find her?

Three days before I was going to take the train to Buffalo, I got an answer. Returning from a late lunch, I entered the basement room to find a man waiting for me. The room had been completely cleaned out except for my stuff in the corner. He was sitting on my cot, his face in my psychology textbook.

"Oh, Damon, good, you're here." He set the book down and stood up.

My eyes went to the door.

He put his hands up. "Relax, you're not in any trouble. Indirectly, I've been your employer."

"You might have warned me," I said, waving at the empty spaces with dangling cords.

"Look, Damon, our foundation is terminating its local activities. To be frank, we enjoy our anonymity. It's what allows us a freer hand." He smiled briefly, enjoying his own euphemism.

I laughed. Yeah, they did all sorts of things with and for kids without their parents' full knowledge, and in my case, permission.

"All of it? The Learning Center? The nutrition program? The—"

He put his hand up. "Damon, I don't mean to be rude. We like you. You're a poster child for our program. But we've found some irregularities with the AI that's been running things here."

"What AI? I've only dealt with Solange."

He laughed. "She's the AI. We think she's gone rogue and done some disturbing things. Can you shed any light on that?"

I stared at him as it soaked in. Solange was an AI. Machine

or not, she was better to me than any human had been.

"Hell no! Solange is a straight arrow. Do you know what she has done for the community here or me personally?"

"I have some idea, yes."

I shook my head. He couldn't understand. "Well, you must have extensive logs. How could she have done anything without you knowing, without your resources?"

"Our investigation is just starting." He leaned a shoulder against the brick wall. I could see that she was more than just a machine to him too. His face was more disappointed than angry. "It appears that she figured out how to sanitize the logs."

"What did she do that has you pulling the plug?"

He smiled, looking proud of his rogue program. "We found bank accounts she was using. She secured her own funds, illegally we suspect. We found payments for all kinds of services. We'll never know everything."

It was my turn to smile. "So, for all you know, she could have rented machines in server farms around the world. She could have copied herself, and still be out there, right?"

He handed me his card. "Her architecture makes that very unlikely, but yes. If you hear from her, please call me."

Studying his card, I heard him say, "Good luck in Buffalo," as he left.

———

With my few belongings hastily thrown into a duffel bag, I left the basement room. Out on the street, I threw the man's business card in the trash. Perhaps I should have been thankful for all the charity I had received, but in my mind, he was the guy who just killed Solange. I didn't even get to say goodbye to her.

I decided to get out of town early. I didn't want to be around when everyone learned that the funding was gone.

The walk to the train station was a cathartic shedding of my hometown. Block after block, I left the memories of my youth behind. With my mother dead to me, and Solange gone, there was nothing and no one here I wanted to see again.

I rolled west across New York state on a train little faster than a car, following the route of the old Erie Canal. After passing Syracuse I got a text message on my phone from a user identified as Straight Arrow. It read, "Thank you." ∎

L. B. Spillers

THE STONE DOUGHNUT

Diego laughed when he finally found the young goat. A branch had gotten under its collar, trapping it by keeping its front hooves off the ground. He stared at the helpless animal, trying to figure out how it got stuck there until the poor thing bleated at him.

"Okay, cabrito, I'm coming." Diego gently lifted the kid high enough to slip its collar off the branch. Winded by his search, he shook his head at the sight of the goat effortlessly bounding uphill. He imagined his friends were poolside in Daytona—not sweating—having some hair of the dog while exaggerating how hot the chicks were that they almost got with the night before.

When his uncle had offered to buy him a ticket to visit for spring break, the hard work of goat herding wasn't among his gauzy childhood memories of the ranch. Back then, his uncle had ranch hands to chase animals around the hillside. As he began his own uphill slog, he thought about cutting his visit short.

Finally pushing through the scratchy bushes at the side of the blessedly level dirt road, he heard his uncle laugh. Being away for ten years had made meeting his uncle as an adult like starting over with him. That gentle laughter was a welcome sign that the awkwardness of their long separation had softened.

"You're not much of a goat herder," his uncle said, walking towards him.

Diego grunted. "What tipped you off? Was it all the sweat, or maybe my tripping over every goddamn rock?"

Smiling, his uncle gestured to where the last leg of the road turned—where else—straight uphill to the house. "Come with me. I have something more technical you can help with."

Glancing back over his shoulder as they trudged up to the house, Diego said, "I swear this hill got steeper."

His uncle nodded. "Every year. Meanwhile, goat meat is less and less popular. If not for the cheese-loving gabachos, I'd be out of business."

The road crested a rise, presenting them with a lush green lawn. Set back about fifty feet, the modest one-story ranch house presided over the patch of green with an aging dignity. Except for the little satellite dish, its roughly dressed stone walls and tile roof probably looked much like they had when it was built, two-hundred years ago.

Childhood memories of tearing around that lawn with his cousins tickled Diego's mind. "I'm sorry mom didn't come. She has good memories of this place."

That diplomatic formulation avoided the fact that his mom didn't want to come. She had also forbidden Diego from telling his uncle about her eye problems. She'd chat up complete strangers in a doctor's waiting room about it, but god forbid her brother hear the news. Diego shook his head, confused at how easily their grand extended family had fallen apart.

"You don't have to dance around it, Sobrino. My sister doesn't much like me." The older man shrugged. "But I have hope. She didn't curse me when I called. I like that phrase the Americans use: baby steps."

They walked around the left side of the house to the shed his uncle used as an office. At the far end sat an old metal desk and some filing cabinets. Opposite was a large wooden plank table. Diego remembered sneaking inside for the morning meetings as a child. His uncle and the ranch hands would shuffle in there after the morning chores with a last cup of coffee to plan the day's work.

Without a staff to manage anymore, the table was covered with cardboard boxes.

His uncle gestured to them, saying, "I'm hoping you can make sense of all this."

Diego poked at a few of the boxes, reading labels.

"What the heck are you going to do with drones?" More to the point, Diego thought, was where the money came from. The business looked to be in trouble, yet his uncle was splashing money around on his plane ticket and quadcopters. There was easily a thousand dollars on the table, just in lithium-ion battery packs.

"I want to use them to deliver cases of cheese, and fetch supplies." He waved his arm downhill. "You've seen what a nightmare that dirt road is."

Shaking his head, Diego said, "Tio, Monterrey is like two hundred miles from here. That's too far."

"Just town is all I need. Eleven miles in the air." He slid a piece of paper closer. "See? This platform is on the roof of Rafael's store. The GPS coordinates are there. Can you program these things to make that trip automatically?"

Seeing it all laid out put the lie to his uncle's casual talk. The man had everything he needed, even a purpose-built landing pad on the store's roof. His uncle didn't just happen to have something Diego could help with. This project was the real reason Diego had been invited or at least a big part of it.

Diego set down the box in his hand and chuckled, finally understanding some of his mother's frustration with her brother. Just when you thought the man was being nice, you'd find an agenda behind it. Then again, what was family for if not to help?

"What?" his uncle asked. "Is there a problem with the equipment? The guy I got it from isn't always reliable."

The innocence in his uncle's voice got Diego laughing harder at his mother's worries. She suspected her brother was involved with the Zetas, but Diego didn't see drug money. He saw a haggard rancher in the middle of nowhere, with a quarter of the herd he used to run, cobbling together a drone delivery system out of black-market components for some last-gasp effort to save his ranch's cheese business.

"Sorry, Tío. I just had a weird thought," Diego said, waving away his uncle's concern. "I should be able to do an unloaded test flight today. Then we have to talk about cargo: weight, packaging, acquisition, deposition—all that stuff. It can get complicated."

"Excellent! I knew you'd be able to—"

Marta burst into the shed. "Don Rivera is coming up the road in that goddamn chromed Cadillac of his. Six vehicles! Run for your fucking lives!" She spun around and sprinted back outside. Diego watched her cross the lawn toward the shrine, her personal safety blanket.

Don Rivera was a famously violent leader in the Sinaloa Cartel. Why he'd be in Zeta country, Diego didn't understand. Turning back to his uncle, Diego asked, "Do we run?"

"If we make them work to find us, it'll go worse. Don't worry. The Zetas aren't completely dead. Rivera won't want to piss off Don Decenas by doing something to us."

"But, Tío, the Cartel de Sinaloa—"

"Calm yourself and follow me."

Diego reluctantly followed his uncle out the door. It seemed stupid to go right to the enemy, but his uncle's confidence won him over. When they got to the road, they encountered two of the don's men already on their way up. They wordlessly bracketed Diego and his uncle as they walked by.

The level bit of the road at the turn was part of a clearing that ran along a sheer rock face of the hill. Why Don Rivera chose that spot to park his convoy baffled Diego, but there he was. The cartel leader stood next to his famous chromed 1975 Cadillac Coupe DeVille giving instructions to a nasty-looking pandillero.

"Buenos días, Don Rivera. Can I help you with something?"

The don raised an eyebrow at Diego's uncle. "Manners and balls. It's a good start." He pointed to Diego. "This must be your nephew."

Diego nodded, chilled by how well-informed the don was. He clasped his hands behind his back, saying, "Yes, Don Rivera. I'm his sister's son."

Don Rivera laughed. "Everyone is being so formal! Please call me El Glotón."

The name El Glotón had reached Diego even as far away as Georgia Tech. It came from the don's bloodthirsty performance during a famously gory battle between the Zetas and the Cartel de Sinaloa. To US media outlets, El Glotón was the border-security boogeyman.

Spreading his hands in supplication, Diego's uncle said, "I hope I haven't—"

"Quiet!" the don said. Everyone froze, even his own men.

The don pointed at Diego. "You go open La Rosquilla for me."

Confused, Diego looked to his uncle who didn't dare to say anything.

"Don Glotón, I apologize. I'm not up on all the slang terms. I thought a Rosquilla was a pastry. I want to obey you, but I don't know what La Rosquilla is or how to open it."

The don looked skeptical. "I guess your uncle ran a tighter ship back when you were a child. These days secrets can be pried from his drunk ass for the price of a whore."

Diego again looked to his uncle, his eyes pleading for some direction.

"You look at me, boy," the don said.

Trembling, Diego took an involuntary step back, saying, "Please tell me what I must do."

"You run up to the house. You find that witch housekeeper of yours, Marta. You tell her to open La Rosquilla."

Diego turned to do just that, but the don restrained him with a hand. "This is important. We can't have her casting any spells on us. You tell that witch that if my men see or hear her, she'll be shot immediately." He glanced at his watch. "You have ten minutes before I take out my impatience on your uncle. Go!"

Confused, Diego sprinted up the hill. Marta was a tough older lady, but the idea that the don and his butchers kept their distance out of fear of her made no sense. Reaching the lawn, he broke right, heading for the shrine path. The sliver of packed dirt edged around the far side of the hillside to a small cave opening.

In the cave, he found Marta kneeling on the tile floor in front of a full-size Santa Muerte figure. A bank of half-spent black candles flickered on either side of the space. Instead of the colorful day-of-the-dead motifs that cover the figurines sold to tourists, this Santa Muerte was old school. A coarse black, hooded robe clothed a pristine human skeleton.

Diego spat out a rapid recap of what happened.

Marta seemed to understand the situation immediately. Stretching herself across the mosaic, her fingers depressed three different tiles simultaneously. Diego startled when the skeleton slid forward.

"Follow me," Marta said, standing up. "Don't touch her."

She deftly slipped behind Santa Muerte. Diego rushed to follow her, pressing against the cave wall as he slid by the figure into the dark doorway behind it. He nearly fell down the unexpected stairs, barely catching himself on the tunnel wall.

Marta glared at him over her shoulder. "Keep up!" she hissed.

A few steps down the tunnel, the door thudded closed behind them. The stairway curved slowly to the right as they descended.

Ahead, Marta's phone flashlight flared to life, temporarily blinding Diego. She stood on a small landing at the bottom of the stairs. Next to her was an opening in the rock her light didn't penetrate. She pointed to a stone block in the corner of the landing.

"You see that?" She waited for him to nod. "I'm going back

up. You step on that until you hear a click. It will open La Rosquilla."

"But Marta, what—"

She put up her hand. "There's no time for questions. Do as I say. Then keep your mouth shut, no matter what happens. Santa Muerte will protect you."

As he watched her hurry back up the stone steps, he wondered why she had to run away if Santa Muerte was going to save the day.

Diego stepped on the stone switch. It smoothly slid downward until it made a soft click.

The ground shuddered. A twenty-foot-wide door on the other side of the pitch-black space started to rise, allowing early morning sunlight to peek in.

As the outside door rose, Diego saw the curve of the walls that must have given the place its name. It looked like a circular driveway going around a thick central rock pillar—doughnut shaped. Wooden crates, shiny aluminum cases, and green camouflage ones bearing US military markings emerged out of the darkness as the door rose. All sympathy Diego had for his uncle's failing ranch faded.

Diego paused, remembering that the don didn't explicitly order him to return once he opened the doughnut. Glancing at the stairs, he considered running away, but he was in the middle of nowhere. The closest big town was Monterrey, hundreds of miles away. The first ten miles of that trip would be on the one dirt track out of the hills. He'd be road kill before he even reached a proper road.

Sighing, he headed toward the light.

Shrieks startled him. One after another, piercingly high screams warbled wetly before cutting off. He instinctively bent down and covered his ears.

Concern for his uncle prodded him forward again with fingers in his ears. The doughnut opened onto the clearing where he had left the don. He saw his uncle standing alone, eyes wide, still as a statue. Dotting the clearing around him were puddles of people—steaming piles of clothing and meat, each in its own expanding pool of blood.

His uncle saw Diego and silently pointed to his nephew's right. Turning to look, Diego was startled to see Santa Muerte, death herself, robed in black. Dense coils of smoke swirled around her. The smoke fully enveloped her before suddenly blowing away, leaving him staring stupidly at empty space.

After a few moments of complete silence, a piece of meat wetly slumping to the ground snapped his uncle out of his daze. "Are you hurt?"

Diego shook his head. "No, I'm fine. You?"

"I wasn't hurt." His uncle crossed himself. "Once again, she's saved us."

Diego stared at his uncle as the words sank in. Once again? How many slaughters had there been? What weapon system was all that smoke hiding?

After a moment, his uncle continued. "All your life you've heard the stories about Santa Muerte, and I know you didn't believe." When Diego started to speak, his uncle raised his hand to stop him. "Relax. I used to think it was bullshit too."

Diego still thought it was bullshit. Glancing at the sky, he assumed the carnage had to come from a satellite-based microwave weapon. The figure he had seen was tougher to explain away. Even if he could, speculative technology was only slightly more plausible than supernatural intervention. Both were ridiculous. Nothing made sense.

Looking around, Diego started gaming out scenarios in his head. What if the don had more men in reserve? What if someone wandering the hills heard the awful screams and called the police? Someone was eventually going to come looking for the cartel don and his chromed monstrosity. And then there was the question of what he was after.

"Tio, what is all that?" Diego asked, gesturing to the storage space.

"That is the property of Don Decenas," his uncle said, running a hand through his hair. "You forget you ever saw that." For a second, Diego saw a dangerous man in his uncle's eyes. "I mean it. That hill is solid rock as far as you're concerned."

Diego gestured at the gore littering the clearing. "I can keep my mouth shut, but what about that mess? Someone's gonna miss Don Rivera and his chromed pedazo de mierda."

His uncle chuckled sourly. "Now we do what's needed and afterward we keep our mouths shut about it."

"Let's get to it then," Diego said. "I need something to distract me before I lose my shit."

———

At six o'clock in the evening, Diego stopped his uncle's little dirt bike in front of the town's church. He had focused on the work all day, woodenly plodding through tasks. The church was the last chore, one that his uncle insisted could not wait until tomorrow. As he had all day, Diego simply nodded numbly at his uncle and got to it.

Stripping the bodies in the clearing had been fairly easy. Their clothing and shoes came off well enough. Ranch life as a kid had included plenty of butchering, so he found he could muscle through it so long as he didn't see any facial features.

His uncle would sell the vehicles. Diego was allowed to keep all the cash he extracted from the gangsters' effects. The clothes they burned. The jewelry, however, had to be donated at the church. His uncle didn't believe in God any more than Diego, but the last thing he wanted was to be seen wearing or selling the personalized jewelry of some gangster. So in one stroke, he could dispose of the incriminating goods while also mollifying Marta who insisted that Santa Muerte get her due.

Inside the crumbling brick church, there was an alcove with a statue of Santa Muerte. The Catholic church condemned her veneration, but only quietly. They knew there was no getting Mexicans to abandon her, especially now that the tourism industry, eager for all those Day of The Dead dollars, had airbrushed away the less palatable aspects of her cult.

Diego walked to the alcove's donation box and started feeding in the chains, jeweled money clips, diamond earrings, and other precious items. As he was struggling to jam a thick medallion through the narrow slot, the priest interrupted him.

"Can I be of help, my son?"

Diego glanced at the man, surprised that he recognized him from his youth. Marta had always insisted that they attend mass once a week.

"No thank you, Father Arenas. I know the church doesn't approve of La Flacada, but I promised my uncle I would put these things in her box. He's very grateful for her protection."

The man smiled at Diego. "It is not your uncle's first donation. As goat ranchers go, he comes into a lot of jewelry."

Diego shook his head at his uncle's lies. To hear him tell it, he had only recently and reluctantly been coerced into storing stuff for the Zetas.

With a grunt, he finally got the medallion into the collection box. Facing the priest, he smiled.

"Father, I'm an engineering student and I think I saw Santa Muerte do things I can't explain."

The priest nodded. "The shrine on your land has been there a very long time. Parish records have accounts of some very hard-to-believe incidents there."

Diego's eyebrows shot up. "Those sound like miracles. So why doesn't the church beatify her?"

The priest spread his arms in a placating gesture. "That's a long discussion. The short version is that she is the personification of death, so who should we beatify?" The priest paused, seeming uncertain. "More importantly, all glory goes to God. So, the church is not interested in glorifying her in His place."

To Diego, it was carefully curated bullshit. Veneration of any saints broke the first commandment as far as he was concerned. It was one of a thousand little problems that kept him from accepting his family's Catholic faith. For the priest to invoke a Protestant argument against Santa Muerte was exquisitely hypocritical.

"Then why do you give her space, Father?"

"She brings people to the church," Father Arenas replied blandly. He turned away and headed down the aisle toward the altar. Diego had hoped for more candor for his gold.

Shaking his head, he dropped the last of the dead gangsters' bling into the box.

"And don't worry about the donations coming back on you," the priest called over his shoulder. "I have a man in Monterrey that handles such things, discreetly."

Diego clamped a hand over his mouth to keep from laughing. He wondered if the priest would be so blasé about the irregular donations if he knew what the pigs at home were feasting on.

———

Diego's motorcycle rolled to a stop in front of La Rosquilla. He marveled at not being able to see any hint of the door's existence on the bare rock. With the cars moved and the mess cleaned up, there was nothing to suggest a massacre had occurred there that morning.

Revving the bike, he zipped up the hill into the front yard of the house. Exhausted, he turned the bike off and rocked it back onto its stand.

He let out an enormous sigh and dropped his head. With his tasks complete, he relaxed for the first time since the slaughter. The fatigue he'd been holding off washed over him.

"Diego, what are you doing?" Marta asked.

Diego blinked his eyes in surprise. "I must have dozed off," he said, dismounting the bike.

Marta smiled. "You did well today. She favors you."

Diego shrugged, too tired to argue about Marta's casual approval of mass murder. Tomorrow he'd leave. "Thanks. I'm going to bed."

"Not yet," she said, pulling his arm. "You need to come to the shrine."

Some sharp words died on his lips as he looked at her lined face. She had been like a second mother to him as a child and this might be the last visit he'd have with her before he graduated and got swept up in his own life. So he relented, allowing himself to be pulled along to the shrine.

When they reached the tiled floor, she said, "Kneel." Marta dropped to her knees in a fluid motion that his tired body couldn't match.

Grunting, he shifted his weight a few times in a vain search for comfort. "I know you hate the gabachos, Marta, but they were on to something when they invented kneelers."

She smacked his arm gently, smiling. "Now's not the time for your smart mouth. Show some respect."

Groaning, Diego rubbed his face. "Marta, why does Santa Muerte support the cocaine trade? What's holy in that?"

Marta's eyes flashed angrily. "It's our revenge, boy. Americans stole over half our country. So now we take their money while feeding them poison."

Diego resisted countering with statistics about all the Mexicans who died because of the drug trade. Mexico wasn't getting revenge, but rather being rotted from the inside by the corruption all that drug money caused.

"Marta, if she wanted to help supply coke to America, she wouldn't back what's left of the Zetas. She'd have helped El Glotón consolidate the Sinaloa Cartel's power so they could more effectively punish America with drugs."

"Don't question her methods," Marta said. "You have no idea

what her plan is."

Diego chuckled. There it finally was, just like church. When events don't seem to match doctrine, we're back to the same tired crap priests had been shoveling for millennia—shit happens, bad things happen to good people, and his favorite, you can't hope to understand the plan.

"Marta, what happened this morning didn't seem holy to me."

"That's because you are only half Mexican."

Mouth open, Diego stared at Marta. Yes, he was an American citizen, but he certainly felt Mexican. How long had she thought of him as an outsider?

"Okay, Marta. Then what is this half-breed doing here?"

She pulled a bottle of tequila out of her bag and handed it to him.

"You will give Santa Muerte this liquor and say thank you."

"Si, señora," he said. He raised the bottle toward the skeleton briefly before setting it at her feet among Marta's most recent offering of apples. Then he prostrated himself on the mosaic tiles, stretching his hands out, palms down, in front of his head.

"I am grateful for the intervention today that saved my life." He hoped that not explicitly attributing it to Santa Muerte wouldn't set Marta off.

After what seemed a suitably pious interval, he returned to his kneeling position beside Marta.

"Excellent," Marta said. "Now we should—"

A tremor interrupted Marta. She and Diego locked eyes for a moment before turning back to the skeleton. A high-pitched whine came from the figure for a moment before it broke apart and fell to the ground under the weight of the sacred lady's robe.

Marta grabbed Diego's shirt with both hands, her eyes wide. Too tired to wrestle with her, he allowed himself to be manhandled, expecting a slap. Instead, she simply pushed him roughly before standing up and running out of the cave.

Diego stood up, gasping at a last jab of pain from his knees. He stood there staring at the robe on top of the fragments of bone. After a few moments of trying to conjure an intelligent thought about what reduced the skeleton to bits, he realized he was zoning out. He badly needed sleep.

Walking to the house, his mind kept detouring around the technical puzzle of the disintegrating skeleton, returning to Marta's words. It had cut him deeply to hear that she thought of him as half Mexican. Snippets of fond childhood memories of her popped into his mind. Had any of it been genuine, or had she just been playing the role of the dutiful employee?

————

At eight in the morning, Diego's eyes snapped open. The room was too bright. Normally, Marta would have woken him for breakfast at six o'clock. Even if she was avoiding him because of last night, his uncle would have come in to roust him by now.

After dressing, he padded into the kitchen. Everything was neat and tidy. There was no breakfast, no dirty dishes, and not even any coffee made. A note on the table from his uncle waited for him. It took a minute for him to work through the man's handwriting, finally deducing his uncle had gone off on an errand. At the bottom was a list of chores for Diego.

He checked Marta's room. The bed was made. Her closet door was open, showing a space where clothes were missing. She appeared to have run off.

Starving, he made himself breakfast and coffee and shuffled out to the front porch to eat. The house was still in the hill's shadow, so he enjoyed the last few minutes of the morning cool as he inhaled a plate of eggs over some of Marta's leftover beans. It was amazing how much flavor she packed into the humble pinto.

On his way to feed the chickens, his phone rang. It was an unknown number.

"Diego," his uncle said. "I'm with Don Decenas. The Sinaloas had someone watching yesterday, so they know what happened. They blame Marta for Santa Muerte's actions. Don Decenas says we have to turn her over to them. You understand?"

His matter-of-fact tone stunned Diego. Marta had worked at the ranch since she was a teenager. How could he even consider turning her over to the cartel to be tortured to death? What had seemed like his uncle's amazing poise under pressure, Diego decided was sociopathy.

"Why the hell would Don Decenas turn Marta over to the guys who tried to rob him? It makes no sense."

"Chico, this isn't my phone. You understand? Don Rivera is dead and someone has to pay. It's that simple."

Diego had no intention of helping the gangsters get Marta. He smiled at the memory of her empty room.

"Why are you telling me? I haven't even fed the chickens yet. Do what you have to do, Tio."

"We need your help, boy. If she sees Don Decenas' people coming, she will call on Santa Muerte again."

"Tio, she's not here. Last night when she took me to the shrine, the Flacada's bones fell to pieces. Marta went nuts. This morning she was gone. Lots of stuff from her room is missing. She's gone."

"I know you care about her, boy, but we have no choice. So stop fucking around. Where is she this second?"

Diego took that as his uncle calling him a liar. Exasperated, he dropped his head and held his tongue. He'd come for a family visit only to find that he was considered a lying half-breed who'd only been invited to provide free technical services. Enough was enough. He ended the call. He'd feed and water the animals and get the hell out of there.

When he reached the chicken house, the metal bucket in

his hand jerked. He stared stupidly at feed corn spilling out of the hole before he realized it had been struck by a bullet. He dropped it and sprinted back to the house.

He hurried from room to room, closing all the blinds to deny the don's sniper easy targets. With both the Zetas and the Cartel de Sinaloa against him, he'd be lucky to survive the day, let alone see home again.

In his room, he began hurriedly packing his clothes. His luggage had pull-out straps so it could be worn like a pack. He figured he could avoid the gangsters by bushwhacking his way to town at an offset from the road. Father Arenas would probably help him get back to the border.

"Running away?" Marta asked from the doorway.

Diego yelped and spun around. "God damn it! You scared me. Don Decenas wants to give you to the CDS to pay for Don Rivera's death. I hung up on Tio and some sniper shot the feed bucket while it was in my hand! You've got to run, like, immediately."

"I already have. I just came back for a few things I forgot," she said. "And I wanted to say I'm sorry I called you half-Mexican. You've always been a good boy." The resolve and finality in her voice tainted the nice words. It sounded like goodbye.

She walked away. Diego stared at the empty doorway for a moment, before closing up his bag.

With his luggage on his back, he crept out the back door of the house. He had no idea where the sniper was or if there was more than one of them. Scanning the area, he picked out a line of spots that provided cover, planning to advance from cover to cover until he could make it to the far side of the hill.

His imagined graceful sortie to hide behind the old outhouse became a herky-jerky shambles of a tactical movement. His real-world body couldn't manage the cool moves his game characters performed so effortlessly. Uneven ground and forty pounds of stuff on his back hadn't made it any easier.

While he caught his breath behind the old outhouse, he heard the distant crack of a rifle. Moments later he heard more shots, much closer. Sticking his head around the corner, he risked a look.

Marta lay on the driveway, her head in a pool of blood. Upsetting as that was, Diego's mind bogged down on the three robots near her. Shaped like basketball-sized metal spiders, their arms held long guns aimed ostensibly where Don Decenas' men were. They were firing shots every few seconds.

Just then, he received a text message. Wiping his eyes, he read: "Come to the shrine." The sender was Santa Muerte. It was easy enough to fake the sender's name, so he was going to ignore it, thinking it was a trap. But the message came with a photo of the shrine area. There was an open doorway he'd never seen before. That was irresistible.

He texted back, "They shot Marta in the head. There are armed robots on the driveway. I don't think I can make it there without getting killed."

The reply came back so fast that Diego's finger was still over the send button. "Those bots are mine. They are protecting you. Hurry."

Diego snorted. Protection would be reducing the sniper to a puddle, not those stupid drones shooting long guns. But it was still his best option, so he ran toward the shrine as fast as he could. The sounds of suppressing fire from the drones urged him on.

Once in the shrine, he stepped to the new doorway on the right and dropped his pack through the hatch on the other side of it. Using handholds in the wall, he then climbed down ten feet to what looked like a terrazzo floor. A soft green light lit the space. After a moment, the hatch above his head closed, cutting off the sounds of gunfire.

Diego flinched when a voice spoke, seemingly from all directions. "Please proceed down the corridor."

He walked down the hall. The rough stone walls became artificial, made of the same material as the floor.

The passage terminated at a doorway into a dimly lit room with matte black walls that rose to a domed ceiling. A small round bench waited for him in the center.

"I run this facility," the voice said.

"Am I speaking to a living person? Or are you a computer intelligence?"

"I am both, a computer simulation of someone who lived long ago."

Since there was no AI on Earth long ago, Diego took that as an indication that the voice was from an extraterrestrial. A die-hard sci-fi fan, Diego had long ago concluded that ETs were real, so he was less shocked than worried about how to engage with them safely. His mind flashed on fictional first-contact scenarios from his favorite shows.

"You killed fifteen guys yesterday, quickly, with some kind of beam weapon. So why haven't you roasted that sniper yet?"

"Those fifteen deaths had the cultural camouflage of the Santa Muerte mythos. The sniper is beyond my allowed operational radius. The workaround of using indigenous weapons was my best available option."

Diego nodded. That was just the sort of heartless rule-following he was afraid would cause the AI to kill him.

"And how does serving as secure storage for a murderous criminal organization fit your purpose?"

"In the past, it was useful to have a helper to procure intelligence and perform small services. Marta was the last in a very long line of such helpers. Your implied accusation arises from the consequences of Marta using my cargo bay as storage space. Such indigenous cultural moralizing is not my concern."

There was the culture gap again. Frustrated with trying to

tease out the AI's ethics, Diego decided to just ask a direct question. "Then why help me?"

"I am partly responsible for putting your life in danger. Since security is compromised, I have the latitude to compensate for that by taking you away from here."

Before Diego could reply, the room began to shake. A video stream appeared on the wall showing an aerial view of the hillside in front of the ranch house crumbling to pieces. A black sphere emerged and wavered like a mirage before disappearing behind what Diego assumed was optical camouflage.

The view from geosynchronous orbit was thrilling at first, but after three hours, Diego was sick of looking at the West African coast.

Diego's status was in limbo while the extraterrestrial computer intelligence consulted with its masters. They were considering whether to do violence to his memory before releasing him.

The taciturn computer had resisted his efforts to engage with it. But Diego had to pee. While he was considering how to address the AI again, the ship sped toward the surface. Quicker than he could see, it positioned itself above his mother's backyard in El Cerrito, California.

"I've been authorized to return you to your home unaltered. Please proceed to the lowest level of the ship. The cargo bay, what you call the doughnut, is how you will exit. Blinking yellow lights will lead you."

When he reached the cargo bay, it still bore its camouflaging stone veneer. All of Don Decenas' property remained neatly stacked along its walls.

"You are welcome to any of the contents in the storage bay. Whatever you don't take will be destroyed."

Choosing a pile at random, Diego opened an aluminum case. It was packed with banded stacks of hundred-dollar bills.

The AI directed him to stand on a small platform. It quickly whisked Diego and his luggage onto his mom's backyard.

The ship was gone by the time the family dog came trotting over to sniff his crotch.

———

When Diego met his mother at the front door, she was surprised to see him.

"M'hijo! Are you alright?" She looked him up and down. "I thought you were in Mexico with your uncle? When did you get back? What happened?"

Diego smiled and hugged her.

"We had a good visit, mom." He shrugged. "I got a little homesick and decided to come home early is all. I'll head back to Georgia on Sunday."

His mom's eyes narrowed. "You've always been a terrible liar, Diego." She waved him away with her hand and walked into the kitchen. Diego followed, unsure how much he should tell her.

"I can guess what happened. He tried to get you involved with drug business. You don't have to lie for him. I know I'm right. It wouldn't occur to him that my baby," she poked him in the chest, "is a moral person."

The pride in her voice made Diego blush. After feeding gangsters' bodies to pigs and stealing so much money, he didn't feel particularly moral.

Diego put his hands up in surrender. "Okay, okay. I didn't want to tell you this because I didn't want you to get your hopes up. I left because I found a Retinal Dystrophy research study that you *might* be a candidate for." He put his hands on her shoulders. "I emphasize might. If you qualify, they'll do the gene therapy for free. It would involve a lot of annoying appointments, blood draws, and stuff, but compared to—"

"But compared to paying eighty thousand dollars, it's fantastic," she said, her eyes tearing up.

That was her insurance's co-pay for what was nearly a million-dollar gene therapy treatment. She wouldn't have accepted her brother's drug money, so Diego knew she wouldn't accept stolen cartel money.

"You see," she pointed at him, "even though you don't believe in the Lord, he has made you His instrument. M'hijo, you are a blessing. While every other college kid in America is drinking himself stupid and chasing girls, you spend your time helping your mother. I'm so proud of you."

"Jesus, Mom, stop. You're going to make me cry." Diego hugged his mother distractedly as his mind raced with all the work he needed to do to trick her. A plan chock full of little lies, and financed by drug money formed in his mind. All those little wrongs were going to save his mother's sight.

He hugged his mother tighter, realizing he owed Father Arenas an apology. ∎

L. B. Spillers

YOU GET ONE WARNING

Pushing my cart down the aisle of Sam's Club, I scanned between the warehouse shelving for the blessed corned beef hash. Patti lagged behind me, looking at everything except what was on our list. She loved shopping that much. Of course, I'd prefer to spend my Saturday doing something less resembling work, but seeing how happy it made her cheered me.

I had to stoop low and shuffle halfway into a bay to secure a case of this most processed of meat products. Patti had banned it from the house because it aggravated her fibromyalgia. Now she had a craving. Her once rock-solid certainty that it triggered her disease had eroded into a vague, uncertain hypothesis that she wanted to retest. Foods in our household rolled on and off the blacklist regularly. Just as I secured a case, I heard Patti gasp.

Stumbling from under the steel shelving, I saw her slumped against the cart. She looked like she was losing the fight to stay vertical. I rushed to her side and steadied her. A sheen of sweat covered her forehead. The vacant look in her eyes meant she was preoccupied, applying her mental kung-fu to battle the symphony of agony assailing her muscles, desperate to not soil herself in public again.

I spotted an empty flatbed cart at the end of the aisle. Lifting her off her feet, I grunted.

As I shuffled there with her in my arms, she mumbled, "You'll hurt your back again."

"Think of me as Richard Gere in *An Officer and a Gentleman*, just gimpier," I said. That got a little smile out of her.

Twitching in my lower back made me dump her onto the cart more roughly than I wanted. I leaned her against one of the uprights and told her to hold on. The user of the cart I was stealing, a burly biker guy, started to protest, but when he got a look at Patti, he hesitated.

"Sorry, man. She's in a bad way." I headed for the exit.

After getting her home, medicated, and in bed, I sat bedside, stroking her arm. That always helped her fall asleep.

Five minutes later, I smiled when I heard her lightly snoring.

I stood up and watched her for a moment to make sure she was truly asleep. She was in constant pain nearly every day of her life. Today was much worse than most, but the idea of watching that for another forty years made me tear up. Not for the first time, I wondered if this might be hell. Sure, it wasn't fire and brimstone, but the area under the pain curve over time was staggering. If someone really was in charge of this festival of pain, they had a lot of explaining to do.

At the fridge, I eyed the beer. Patti would be asleep for hours, probably until morning. Drinking might distract me from the onslaught of depressing thoughts rising in my mind, but that would break one of my rules: never drink alone. I come from a family of drunks. Sometimes arbitrary rules were the only thing that kept me from manifesting my heritage. So, like a good quasi-drunk, I found someone to drink with.

———

Two hours later, sitting in Gildo's living room, I watched his fingers dart out and place a black piece where I hadn't expected. The noise the polished slate made against the thick wooden board was restrained. Go was a very psychological game, right down to exactly how your opponent placed his pieces.

The fact that Gildo didn't employ his usual swagger made me wince. He only did that when he was trying to soften the blow. Of course, knowing that made his little act of sportsmanship worse. It took me a moment to see my mistake. The best result I could hope for from that group would be a *seki*. It was just enough to give him the win.

I slumped back in my chair and sighed.

"This is the part where you tell me what's got your brain so spooged up," Gildo said, smiling.

Suddenly itchy, I rubbed a hand over my face. "Patience had a flare-up while we were shopping. Seeing her in so much pain wears on me. Barring some medical miracle, she's never going to get better."

I tried not to dump that stuff on him, or anyone for that matter. There's a lot of pop psychology about having a support system, leaning on people, and so on. In my experience, that's crap—mostly. I mean, if I needed help, I'd ask for it. But in my experience, being that guy who constantly talked about dismal stuff just made you the guy that no one wanted to be around.

"That's rough, man, but I might be able to help. There's been a breakthrough in my proctor research." Gildo said.

He actually called it research. Despite my mood, I almost laughed at that. It was time to cut the conversation short. I let Gildo's statement hang there as I finished my beer. Be the guest you'd want to have over, right?

As I started clearing off the table, I said, "I appreciate the thought, Gildo, but you know I don't believe in your theories about the so-called other side."

Gildo began sorting the black and white stones covering the board. I walked the empties and dishes into the kitchen, hoping the conversation would end there.

When I got back to the table, Gildo was sweeping the black stones into their wooden bowl. Of course, the conversation wasn't done, it was just getting weirder.

"I could show you how to ask a proctor for help. It's dangerous, but it might be worth it."

Eventually, it always came back to the so-called proctors with him. The beers I'd drunk had diminished my courtesy filters. I barely bit back a smartass reply. The only thing that had ever come close to ending our friendship was my disdain for his asinine assertions about the supernatural.

I dropped onto the couch and watched Gildo reverently move the enormous legged board back to its spot next to the bookcase. The matching wooden bowls had to be placed just so. He was twitchy about doing it himself. When not in use, all that gorgeous wood was its own little art installation.

"As I said, I appreciate your intentions, but I'm not a believer. You know that. If it was as simple as asking for help, no one would have lifelong diseases, right?"

Gildo smiled. "Oh, it's not easy. A guy in my group cured his mom's cardiomyopathy. I mean he got a proctor to do it. Her cardiologist says she has the heart of an athlete now. No one can explain it. There are plenty of before and after scans. It's not anecdotal bullshit."

I'd had too much science education to talk seriously about miracles. Still, he'd piqued my curiosity.

"So what makes it so hard to ask one of these things for help?"

"It requires special hardware." Gildo looked down, clearly uncomfortable. "The thing is, that guy died a week after getting his mom healthy. Brain aneurism. We have no way to connect A to B, but we've had a lot of mysterious deaths in the group lately."

I sighed. I'd forgotten about that damn group. It was the same correlation-as-causation crap that the world's bullshit theories thrive on. Being discerning nut jobs, they claimed causation for the cure and denied it for the death. It was classically convenient rhetorical hand waving.

Standing up, Gildo said, "I know that sigh. Maybe some technology would reassure you." He dashed off into his bedroom.

He quickly returned with a large metal toolbox. He set it down and pulled out two devices. "I've got a detector and a generator."

Gildo turned on the detector, a modified handheld

radiation sensor. An ungainly wire bundle ran from it to another module bolted to the underside, clearly homemade.

I felt my skepticism eroding as I listened to the chiming detector boot up. The last time he and I had discussed proctors, it had been all talk.

"You're welcome to them. I don't dare use them anymore. I got my one warning."

And it all came crashing down. Sure, we've got real science behind it with real-looking devices that make convincing noises but wait, I don't dare use them. Not trusting what I might say, I just motioned for him to continue.

"I used the generator to summon a proctor. It told me emphatically not to use it again." Gildo rubbed the back of his neck. "See, the guy who cured his mom's heart didn't summon one. He lurked around the hospital, waiting for one to come for one of the dying patients. He was told not to ask for anything else. Everyone in the group who's had an encounter reports some kind of warning, but never two. We've got reports going back decades."

I laughed. "Dude, even if I believed all that, what good is it if everyone who asks for something pays with their life?"

"It doesn't always work like that," Gildo said. "It's just that our best-documented case with all the heart scans involved a death. The archives have plenty of positive outcomes."

A chime from the detector startled us.

Gildo's face blanched. "Oh no." He ran out his front door.

I turned off the detector and followed him, very confused.

He stood on the sidewalk with a thousand-yard stare on his face.

"Gildo, you're freaking me out here," I said, slowly. "Should I call someone?" I approached him.

Gildo put his hand up to stop me and stepped back. It was like he didn't want to contaminate me. He threw me his key ring. "Keep the cops out of my house. I left you a thumb drive in the filing cabinet under my desk."

I stared stupidly at the key ring. A psychotic break was the only thing that came to mind. What the hell was I supposed to do?

When I looked back to Gildo, he had turned away from me to speak to the air. "That's not fair!"

My instinct was to stand still and watch for an opportunity to help. Hopefully, whatever was going on with Gildo would run its course harmlessly. If not, there was always 911. So far, it was merely disturbing.

Gildo's face contorted in pain before his knees buckled. He collapsed to the sidewalk with a whimper.

———

Paramedics are different when there's hope.

The fluidity of the EMTs doing CPR on Gildo was hypnotic. A perfectly choreographed dance, they never paused even as they asked me questions in those clipped voices. Each of them knew their part down to the smallest gesture. There wasn't the barest moment for pleasantries, reassurance, or anything that would divert their focus. Most of all there wasn't any discussion about Gildo, no blips on the monitor, no question of maybe this or that. Gildo was dead. That put them in the zone. Before I realized what was happening, the ambulance doors were closing on an EMT still methodically administering chest compressions.

After the siren had faded into the distance, I finally noticed the cop watching me. He had none of the imposing body language I expected from cops. There must have been an odd look on my face.

"They're going to keep trying to revive him," he said when I looked at him. I heard the truth in his tone.

I didn't know what to say. I just nodded. When he asked me for my name, I handed him my driver's license. My last name was a tongue twister, and I wasn't in the mood for the back and

L. B. Spillers

forth.

When he was done taking down my contact information, he asked, "Do you know if there are any children or animals in the home?"

I shook my head. "He lived alone. I have his sister's number at home. I'll...inform her."

To my surprise, that satisfied him. He gave me his card and left me there, staring at a gnarled sidewalk tree.

———

I made my way quietly into my home office. A call to the hospital confirmed that Gildo had been declared dead shortly after his arrival.

Talking to Gildo's sister was odd. She made appropriate noises, but couldn't interrupt her life at that moment to deal with her dead brother. It'd be a week before she could make it to town. I lied to her about the moments before his death. I'd like to say it was to protect her from the truth, but in that short conversation, I'd already come to dislike her. Besides, for all I knew, he simply had a massive heart attack at the improbably young age of thirty-seven.

When I got off the phone with Gildo's sister, Patti was still asleep in our bedroom. I decided to go back to Gildo's place to honor his wishes. I wouldn't get any peace of mind until I did.

Back at Gildo's place, obligation fell on my shoulders as I walked through the door. The sense I got from his sister was that she would callously discharge her duties to her brother. She wasn't interested in the stories behind the knickknacks on his shelves. The fact that his Go board was made from 500-year-old Japanese Kaya wouldn't mean anything to her. Staring at it, I realized she wouldn't know if I took it.

I shook my head. Theft was no way to demonstrate my respect for Gildo's legacy, even though I thought he would approve. The only wish of his I knew for sure was that I should get the thumb drive he left for me, so I started there.

Inside his filing cabinet drawer, I found an envelope with my name on it. With the thumb drive was a note:

> *Hey, Dan, sorry to hit you with this. Hopefully, this note won't be needed, but here you are, right? I know how creepy it is to go rifling through dead people's stuff. My will is in the fire-proof briefcase in my office closet. It makes my sister my executor. It instructs her to give you my goban and pieces. Most of my important possessions are itemized in there, so even if you're tempted to preempt her stupidity, it'll just cause more problems. Let her deal with it. Trust me, it's no honor, just a huge, emotional minefield of a pain in the ass. What I hope you will do for me is take my proctor hardware...*

Gildo left me precise instructions, right down to what to pack it in. For a guy who wanted to protect my emotional well-being, you'd think he wouldn't tell me to pack his secret hardware in a knapsack from our alma mater, the one I watched him lug around campus.

I relocked the file cabinet and slouched back in his desk chair. My eyes flitted among the storied items that crowded his small office. I recognized some of them. They beckoned me down memory lane. His sister would come through there like a tornado, throwing much of it in the trash. I smiled at his plush Invader Zim doll, remembering how happy he was when a college girlfriend gave it to him.

There was something wrong with how those evocative souvenirs of his life lost their meaning with his death. As my eyes jumped from item to item, it alternately enraged and saddened me that all the sentiment bound up in them had disappeared along with Gildo.

Recognizing the emotional peril of the place, I left.

———

L. B. Spillers

Twenty minutes later I was back home with his heavily worn knapsack over my shoulder. The school logo was illegible to anyone but alumni. In those few minutes on my back, it came to hold my memory of him.

The thumb drive underwhelmed me. I was annoyed to see only two documents: a shortcut to a website, and a design document for his proctor hardware.

I don't know what I had expected exactly, but definitely more. The design document wasn't exactly new science. The detector was just an off-the-shelf photon detector modified to look for the signature radiation of proctors. The generator was a dental x-ray emitter modified to emit the same energy photons.

After browsing the designs, I was left chuckling to myself. Gildo's confidence had been so strong that I thought for sure there would be something more than just an arbitrary assertion that such and such energy photons indicated the presence of proctors. To me, those designs were for up-tech tinfoil hats.

The shortcut proved more interesting, if disturbing. I didn't even know that ".xyz" was a top-level domain. The shortcut took me to an unindexed page to report a death. Just the idea that their group needed such a page gave me a chill.

Any other day, I would have been annoyed by the endless little bits of information it asked for, but I figured that if Gildo sent me there, he'd want it done. After almost twenty years of friendship, I owed him that much. Part of the report was a long, free-form witness statement. It was surprisingly cathartic to type it all out.

When I got back to the living room, Patti had progressed from bed to the couch.

"Feeling better?" I asked. "Want me to get you anything? Maybe some therapeutic ice cream?"

She smiled. "No, thanks. Right now I'm starving the beast. How's Gildo doing? Did you let him win again?"

I sighed. So much for distracting myself. So much for sparing her feelings. I took a moment to form the words. Having to say it out loud hit me hard. I teared up. "No, he beat me fair and square this time. Ten minutes later he died as I watched. Maybe a heart attack. His sister's coming Friday."

"Oh, honey," she said, standing up shakily. Knowing how much that hurt her to do made it worse. I was a heaving, sobbing mess. She hugged me, rocking back and forth.

"He was too young," she mumbled into my shoulder.

I wasn't going to get into what seemed to happen to him or what we talked about. She was the kind of person who would walk that causal chain backward and see herself as the root cause. Her most glorious character flaw was determining that anything that goes wrong is somehow her fault.

"The coroner will figure it out," I said.

"Even though it hurts, I'm glad he had you with him at the end," she said.

I helped her back to the couch before distracting myself by making dinner.

That night I received an unusual email response to my report of Gildo's death. There was no commiseration or explanation, just a time and place to meet the next night. It wasn't even particularly friendly. The sender said he had an obligation to Gildo he needed to fulfill.

—————

The instructions from the email disturbed me. Where we were supposed to meet was odd. The late-night timing was disconcerting. Any other day, in any other context, I'd have refused. I could almost hear an ID Channel murder-porn narrator commenting on my stupidity.

So there I was, standing under a light by a service door of the St. Mary Corwin Hospital. In truth, I didn't know if it was part of the hospital proper. The sprawling campus of brick buildings had a hospital in there somewhere, along with everything else from a LabCorp site to a prosthetic fabrication shop.

Right on time, the door opened, leaving me staring into the pinched face of a thin, old man with Coke-bottle glasses. I searched his white coat in vain for a name. Likewise, he wore no ID badge. He waved me inside without a word. I just went with it.

"Nice to meet you too," I said. "Sure I'd love to come in." I was born a smartass, and I'll die one. How hard is a little courtesy?

He chuckled, leading me up the fire stairs. "Don't take it personally. We'll never meet again. I promised Hermenegildo I'd do this. The less you know about me, the less likely things will come back on me."

I suddenly felt I'd misunderstood the situation. "Uh, look, mystery friend of Gildo, I don't want anything to do with anything illegal."

He kept going up the endless stairs as he spoke. "Relax, there's nothing illegal about what I'm going to show you. You saw how touchy they are. You only get the one warning, and I've had mine."

That shut me up. I trudged behind him beyond the top floor to stand on a landing in front of a large metal access panel painted the same dreary yellowish beige as the stairway walls. After he went through, I took a moment to look into the space. Reassured by the large, open floor plan, I shrugged. As odd as the situation was, it struck me as being more bush-league than dangerous.

I had to duck my head to follow him inside. Once he closed the door behind me, he paused to catch his breath. "This attic houses the elevator equipment. Maybe once or twice a year we get some service people up here. It's my work refuge, or at least it was. After we're done, I'm taking it all down."

He led me across the floor to a solid wooden door. Behind it was a small room with a wall piled high with ancient computer monitors, big CRTs from the 1990s.

"They were going to throw all these out," he said as he started flipping switches. "I cut into the security feeds which also run through this space. Take a seat." He gestured to a rolling chair that had survived from the fifties.

"What are we doing, exactly?" I asked as I sat down.

He pointed to one of the monitors. "See those people crowded around that bed? He's got C1 trauma, was down in the field too long, and not coming back. They're a Catholic family. They didn't want to pull daddy's vent, but they stopped his pressors five hours ago. He's circling the drain. Any minute now."

I sighed. "And?"

"He showed you the design of the detectors, right?" Pointing to a different screen, he continued, "That's a graph of the detector output for the patient's room." It was a flat line with a touch of noise.

"Yeah." I snorted. "They detect the theoretical emission spectra of an element that has no known stable isotope. Very tinfoil hat. Next, you'll tell me it dripped from Jesus' stigmata. Please!"

"I don't care if you believe me, boy. This is an obligation to me, not evangelizing. If you keep watching, when that man dies, you'll probably see one of them. The CCD output is overlayed on the video."

"Probably? Why not definitely? It sounds like you're setting up an excuse like, the spirits didn't feel like showing themselves today."

The old doctor dropped his head. His cheeks puffed as he blew out an exasperated breath. "I say 'probably' because they only show up if a relative doesn't come to usher them to the other side. This patient hasn't reported any visitations."

I laughed. "I couldn't help but notice your anonymous lab

YOU GET ONE WARNING

coat and the lack of ID. Are you an actual doctor or just a voyeuristic janitor? Visitations? You believe that?"

He shook his head. "Talk to any old nurse, especially in hospice or elder care. If a patient reports seeing a dead relative, they're going to die within a day or two. The you-know-whos only come when there's no one else."

That struck a nerve. My grandmother was going on about having a conversation with her dead husband a few hours before her death. We hadn't taken it seriously.

"I can see in your face you are starting to believe it," he said, smiling for the first time. "It's fascinating, right? Insidiously fascinating. It pokes annoying holes in all our rock-solid science."

"Look," I said a little more angrily than I intended. "It's like a get-rich-quick scheme. If it was that simple, everyone would do it. If you could just set up some hardware to detect—"

His hand clamped over my face. "Do not say that name here, or any name for them."

Like some unrepentant kid, the second he took his hand off my mouth I started up again, "But—"

This time he slapped me quiet. "But nothing! Shut up and watch. The physicist who invented the detector was my best friend. He's dead. Gildo's dead. The whole organization is dying off! It's the price of our presumption."

I shot to my feet. My face stung. My animal brain was urging me to beat the crap out of this guy. The doctor answered my glare with a bemused, impatient look that seemed to ask if I was done being childish. He had that rare, authoritative, old-man charisma that worked on me. As I stared at him, my annoyance slid into the sucking-it-up-for-Gildo bucket.

After a few tense moments, I turned back to the monitor, sat down, and watched.

As the minutes passed, I found it surprisingly evocative to watch the four visitors in the room waiting for the man to die.

L. B. Spillers   263

Despite the lack of sound, I saw small conversations erupt, occasional angry gestures, crying, and a lot of leaning and hugging. Each minute that passed made it feel more wrong to watch. I could see the man's heart rate on the monitor winding down.

When the patient's heart monitor finally flatlined, his wife collapsed onto his body, crying. A nurse came in briefly to turn off the alarm. Seconds later a different alarm sounded in our little surveillance nest. The graph of the proctor energy in that room spiked.

The rough outline of a figure appeared on the monitor, like a lens flare. I could just make out the profile of a nose. Suddenly, it turned to look into the detector. Its eyes blazed. The alarm increased in pitch. My heart thudded in my chest. I pushed back from the bank of monitors, putting my hands over my eyes. Like some baby playing peek-a-boo, I sat still, pretending what I didn't see didn't exist.

Breathing exercises kicked in. I told myself I was safe and had all the time in the world. But it was impossible to tear my mind out of that swamp of fear and think about anything else. At some point, I realized the alarm had stopped sounding. I focused on the fan noise from the ancient PC running the setup.

When I tentatively splayed my fingers to peek at the screen, the figure was gone. I jumped to my feet and retreated to the outer room.

Gildo's friend was waiting. I expected some flavor of I-told-you-so from him. He surprised me by having a sad, compassionate look on his face.

"You can't unsee that," the old guy said, pushing up the bridge of his glasses. "Did it talk to you?"

"Hell no!" I said. "They talk? I have never felt actual terror like that in my life. If that thing had talked to me, I don't think I could've handled it."

I got the second smile of the night. "Good! That's excellent.

You don't want their attention."

Shuffling my feet and shaking out my arms, I tried to banish the post-adrenaline itchiness. "You and Gildo both said something about a warning. What is the warning?"

"Everyone reports different language. Mine was simply: Don't watch us."

"Gildo implied they healed someone's failing heart. He was suggesting they might heal my wife's fibromyalgia."

The old man grunted a preamble as he searched for the words he needed. After a moment he said, "They seem to have very inconsistent reactions. Our organization is—was—a repository for reports of...interactions with them. There are cases of healing."

"But how do you know it wasn't happenstance? A coincidence?"

Leaning against a table, the old man shrugged. "I saw the records. No one's heart muscle heals like that. It was miraculous."

"So why do you suppose they killed Gildo?"

"I don't know. If you want a theory, mine is that these things don't want knowledge of them to spread." He stood up straight and put his hands out like he was pushing me away. "I'm done with them. I have fulfilled my promise to Gildo. I strongly urge you to forget about them."

This guy was one big ball of contradictions. "What I don't understand is why you showed me this. If you're convinced they're dangerous, then why fulfill your promise to Gildo?"

The old man laughed, shaking his head. "I was raised to keep my word. If I were more pessimistic, I'd say you represent the younger generation that has lesser ethics. But I suspect you mean it's acceptable to break a promise for a greater good."

I decided to forgo defending my generation. "That's right. I think Gildo would have understood."

Nodding, the old man said, "Maybe." Then he got that

doctor look on his face, the one that said he's trying to get through a discussion without engendering a lawsuit. "Look, the one thing I've learned through decades of this scientific cat-and-mouse game is that there's something after death. I don't know what it is exactly, or even vaguely." He pointed at himself. "The only thing I can take to the other side is who I am—the choices I've made. I choose to keep my word. It's that simple."

I chuckled. A smart-ass reply formed in my mind, something about how knowing someone is watching might motivate a person to emulate good character. But staring at the aged doctor, I saw sincerity in his face.

"Well, friend of Gildo, Sir, Doctor," I said. "I appreciate you taking the time to honor his request. For what it's worth, this younger man admires your ethical rectitude."

I stuck my hand out to shake his. He gave me one of those confident, dry, just firm enough handshakes that my generation always aspires to. Without another word, I left the building.

———

When I got home, Patti was asleep. I had told her I was on an errand Gildo asked me to do. One of the benefits of grieving your best friend is that you get a lot of latitude from those around you.

Out back, I applied my small sledgehammer to the thumb drive on the concrete patio. Long after it was unusable, I sat there, gently pounding on it. I wondered if Gildo could see me betraying his legacy. I wondered if he could do anything about it from wherever he ended up.

I don't know how long I sat there pulverizing that chunk of plastic. By the time a tap on my shoulder brought me out of my fugue, there was nothing but a field of black dust, littered with flecks of metal.

"Dan, what are you doing?" Patti had a look I'd never seen on her face. It was like she didn't recognize me. I must have looked crazy.

"Shit," I said, laying down the hammer. "I'm sorry I woke you up. Just a little cathartic destruction."

Patti smiled sadly at me as she gathered her robe around her. "Come to bed. Sleep always helps."

"Let me just clean up this mess," I said, standing up.

She shuffled back into the house as I fetched a broom from the garage. By the time I got to the bedroom, she was asleep again. I was glad that my interruption of her sleep was so brief.

Watching her, I was suddenly enraged at being thankful. What the hell was there to be thankful for? A tiny respite from pain? That pain that would haunt her almost every day of her life, and I was supposed to be thankful that it was a touch better here or there? Our lives had become one vast sea of pain with brief interludes of this-sucks-less.

I fetched Gildo's generator module and plugged it in next to the bed. Pointing the output tube at the ceiling, I turned it on. A low hum built up until it discharged a few seconds later. Then it repeated the cycle.

After about ten cycles I turned off the machine. Whatever radiation it was putting out couldn't be particularly healthful.

Just as I was about to mock Gildo's ridiculous gizmo, a proctor flared into view, standing in the corner. I squinted as my eyes adjusted. To my surprise, it had a feminine silhouette. I couldn't see the features of her face enough to read it. Seizing the initiative, I blurted out, "Heal her, please!"

The light from the proctor dimmed enough for me to see her face smiling. An orange glow suffused Patti's body. Still sleeping deeply, she rolled over with a huge grin on her face.

"She is healed," the proctor said to me, her voice a whisper.

"Thank you," I mumbled. Remembering my manners, I stood up straighter and summoned a more confident voice. "That means the world to us. I'm very grateful."

The proctor didn't reply. It stood there, staring at me. Something like compassion or pity animated her features. Still, she didn't move or speak. As the moment stretched out, I was increasingly self-conscious and confused.

Finally, I couldn't take the silence anymore, and said, "I'm sorry. I don't know how this works. Are you waiting for me to do something?"

She wordlessly pointed at my body on the floor.

Confused, I stared at my former body. My face had a stupid, vacant look on it. That fly-catching maw would be burned into Patti's mind when she woke up. Thankfully, Patti still had pure joy written all over her face. Still, I knew she wouldn't have accepted this trade-off, given the choice. She would have endured decades of constant pain rather than have someone die for her healing.

Staring at her smiling face, the reality of it hit me all at once. I'd never hear her thoughts on it. I wouldn't get to talk to her about anything ever again. I couldn't ever touch her again. What was going to happen to her?

The world around me started to lighten. ▪

SLIVERS

Devin's tour-guide app coached him through the back roads of Western Colorado, narrating increasingly sparse and depressing factoids as he left civilization farther and farther behind. When it cheerily related that he was driving through a Superfund site that was once the uranium mining town of Uravan, he turned it off and declared to his empty vehicle that his career had hit rock bottom.

His corporate tenure had ended in a sensational court case that made him a pariah within the pharmaceutical industry. Legally he was exonerated, but socially, professionally, and in any other sense that involved internet-connected humans, he was pharma scum. In three years he had gone from being an esteemed, wealthy, chief research officer to an infamous, broke, and unemployed outcast. That's not even getting into the divorce.

When a friend of a friend had sent out a feeler about some consulting work, visions of becoming one of those rootless white-collar nomads jumping from contract to contract soured Devin on the idea until he heard the rate: $300/hr., plus expenses.

So there he was, parking his rental car in the circular driveway of a mansion, two hours from the nearest thing that passed for a city. A servant received him and led him through the residence to his interview.

When the gauntlet of opulence finally deposited him on a couch across from the foundation's head, Mrs. Alodia, he expected some pleasantries before he was handed off for a technical interview. The elegantly dressed old lady immediately tripped over his low expectations.

"Tell me, doctor," she said, sinking into the couch back, "Do you believe in God?"

Suddenly very tired, Devin sighed and dropped his head. Mrs. Alodia's foundation did altruistic research, licensing its discoveries free of charge to any company that upheld her foundation's code of conduct. Those ethics as much as the money had softened Devin's disdain for short-term jobs. So to have her open with an unethical question deeply disappointed him.

"This was a mistake," Devin said, standing up. "Please excuse me." He headed in the direction of what he hoped was the front door, wishing he had paid more attention on the way in.

Mrs. Alodia laughed. "Oh come on! Allow an old lady a little fun."

Devin stopped and turned to look at her. Those heavily lidded eyes now so bright with amusement gave him pause.

"Fun? Frankly, what I think about God is none of your business. It's not business at all."

She shrugged. "You're right, of course."

Confused by that admission, Devin watched her raise her old frame off the couch as he reconsidered his petulant exit. Guilt tugged at him as she unsteadily achieved her full height of five feet.

"Come outside for lunch," she said, motioning for him to follow. "It's peak bloom, and my fellow has prepared a particularly delicious meal for us: Wagyu beef and braised carrots. The carrots we grow on the grounds have extraordinary terroir."

Disarmed by her practical tone, Devin followed. They stepped onto a stone porch lined with blooming cherry trees. After the whir of the French doors closing behind them ceased, silence descended on the patio.

Breathing in the scent of the blossoms, he lost himself in the beauty of the grounds as his eyes drifted among the trees.

He flinched when he realized a servant was standing next

to them, silently proffering drinks. After Mrs. Alodia plucked a champagne flute off the tray, Devin took the remaining frosty beer. The busty St. Pauli Girl silkscreened onto the pilsner glass affirmed that the old lady had researched him enough to know his favorite.

He took a long drink before facing her. "I don't believe in the avuncular old man in the sky that so many people think is personally writing the narrative of their lives. I'm a deist. To me, God is a thing that blew itself up in the Big Bang."

She laughed gently. "Don't worry about that. My sense of humor isn't what it used to be. I suppose it's nerves. I'm dying, and I need you to solve a problem for me before I go.

———

A week later, Devin again made the two-hour drive from Grand Junction to Mrs. Alodia's estate. Although most of the foundation's staff worked in that city, his assigned lab was in a tiny corporate campus that adjoined her property.

The sense of physical isolation was compounded by the fact that he was the only person working in the small structure. Normally appreciative of contemplative solitude, being the new guy in an empty building in the middle of nowhere was too much of a good thing.

A security guard dragging a cart had helped him drop the carefully packed artifacts of his professional life around his new office. Left alone with his new ID and hastily scribbled passwords, Devin eyed the short stacks of cardboard file boxes with dread. The different branding on some attested to not having been opened in years. The memories lurking inside would only exacerbate the manic funk that starting a job put him in.

Ignoring the trip hazards dotting his office floor, Devin spent the morning picking through employee profiles in search of a lab assistant. He quickly narrowed down his list to three potentials. Choosing the right assistant was going to be crucial to his work and sanity. He was hoping to talk to at least one of them in person before the day ended. After the third candidate's office phone shunted him to voicemail, Devin hung up, sighing.

"That bad?" his new boss asked, peeking around his doorway.

Devin shot to his feet. "Don't sneak up on me like that!"

Ruya chuckled at him as he fell back into his chair. He hadn't seen her since his lunch with Mrs. Alodia.

Shoulder length, straight, black hair framed a pale face devoid of makeup. Her white button-down shirt and grey slacks were likewise perfunctory. All that blandness just made her sky-blue eyes pop behind her librarian glasses. Unfortunately, she was also Mrs. Alodia's daughter. Then again, maybe that was a plus. He didn't know. She put him completely off balance.

Collecting himself, Devin waited for her to speak. A little part of him hoped she would say something awful to kill his burgeoning infatuation. She had to be fifteen years his junior.

"Are you getting along okay?" she asked. "Have you seen the lab space? Have you found the assistant you need?"

"My lab is perfect. The equipment is sparkling. The pool of techs you have to choose from is deeper than I expected, and every little bit of computer setup was perfect. This is the most competently run organization I've ever seen."

Ruya nodded. "I'm glad to hear you have what you need, but it's a little early in our relationship for butt snorkeling. I assure you we have our problems which I intend to keep you fully isolated from."

Devin blushed as he stood back up. "No, I meant—"

"Relax," she said, putting up her hand. "I know that wasn't pandering or flirting. My humor is often so dry that it crumbles to dust before it has a chance to fall flat."

Laughing, Devin leaned against the credenza behind his desk. "Starting a new job is so unsettling. All those little things that I put on auto-pilot all of a sudden require thought—coffee filters, office supplies, vending machines. I haven't even found the large-format printer yet."

Ruya smiled while fingering the crude, glazed pottery pencil holder on Devin's desk, obviously some child's school project. "I can help with that. Have you found any techs you like?"

Devin rubbed the back of his neck. "Look, when I signed on, I assumed I'd be working at the lab in Grand Junction. With the staff all there, I don't understand why you'd put me here. How is that supposed to work? Is some poor tech going to have to commute back and forth? What am I missing?"

"Just more of my scintillating sense of humor," Ruya said, smiling. "Follow me. We're going to your lab."

At the lab door, she paused while typing in her PIN. "Who's your top candidate?"

"Rajneesh," Devin said. "He's done a lot of work in transcription factors. Seemed like he'd be a good fit."

She nodded and opened the door. The walls were lined with machines bracketed by ample bench space. A large, empty workspace sat in the middle of the room. Gleaming valves poked up through the center of the table to provide water and gases.

"Rajneesh! Front!"

Since no one was in the room, Devin wondered if this was still more of Ruya's sense of humor. Then he heard a click and gaped at the pole that descended out of a port in the ceiling. A metal strip in the floor slid sideways to receive the end. The entire lab floor was crisscrossed by similar runs of metal. Devin had assumed they were a way to hide service conduits.

Three thick, ceramic discs, each a foot wide, noiselessly slid down the pole to chest height. The top of the pole retracted into the ceiling leaving the bottom five feet in the track. The resulting form reminded Devin of an insulator on a high-voltage line. He expected the top-heavy contraption to fall over.

Instead of clattering to the floor, the pole moved gracefully along the track, carrying those thick discs toward them. Track covers opened and closed smoothly as the robot rushed through a few intersections to present itself before Ruya.

"The bottom disc is a gyroscopic stabilizer," she said in answer to Devin's questioning look.

An image of a young South Asian man appeared in the air just in front of the robot. "Yes, Ruya, how can I help you?"

Devin shook his head in disbelief. "So Rajneesh, Sosuke, and Ernie are all avatars for this robotic system?"

"Excellent! You've got it exactly," Raj said. "If you enjoy profanity, Ernie's your guy, but I think you'll prefer my cheeky propriety. Sosuke's for those who enjoy complete silence in the lab."

"These guys," she gestured at the image of Raj, "can do every bit of actual lab work you will ever need. Their modular design allows them to deploy with tooling specific to whatever you need done. And the natural language interface keeps you from having to program them or understand their workings."

"Ruya, I've never seen any lab automation remotely this advanced. You could—"

"This tech is all covered by your NDA. Mother will have your head on a pike if you violate it."

Devin folded his arms across his chest, resisting the urge to snap at Ruya's unnecessary reminder. "I'm a little confused about the mission. My own research is on the chemistry of amyloid plaque formation with an eye toward treating Alzheimer's disease. After reviewing the white paper you sent me, I don't understand why your focus is on that obscure transcription factor. I couldn't find the protein it codes for in the literature."

"You wouldn't. It's proprietary, and it's inert by design."

Devin waited for more, but Ruya clearly wanted him to make the inferential leap by himself.

L. B. Spillers

"If it's truly inert, then its only purpose is to exist," Devin said. He glanced at Rajneesh still waiting for orders. "So you want it as a marker of some kind, maybe for scanning?"

"Got it in one," Ruya said, smiling.

Devin huffed, irritated by having to rip crumbs of crucial information from Ruya. "Yeah, but the resolution you'd need to get out of an MRI rig for Neuronal Tomography to work is well beyond current systems. Then there are all the bioelectromagnetic considerations to—"

"Devin," Ruya held up her hand, "We've got the resolution. We've got the bioelectromagnetics solved. The foundation has a bunch of proprietary tech that isn't public knowledge. You're here because you're the blood-brain barrier master. I just need you to focus on getting that marker to full saturation in brain tissues. For now, why don't you have a chat with Raj?"

A conveniently inert mystery protein that was going to be scanned by an impossibly accurate MRI rig was a huge red flag to Devin. He turned to the still-waiting Rajneesh, wondering if it might be possible to squeeze some information out of it.

"I am prepared to discuss the work, but please do not attempt to pump me for sensitive information."

Devin shrugged and explained how he wanted to tweak his previous research to swap in the mystery protein. It was conceptually simple but required careful testing.

Raj was already familiar with all of Devin's publications and quickly elaborated Devin's strategy into a detailed experimental protocol.

———

With Raj handling the lab work, that left Devin playing the role of computer geek more than biochemist. He spent his time running computer simulations of the mystery protein's biochemical dynamics. The cleaner the protein appeared to be, the more Devin's mind went to industrial espionage. Somebody had put a lot of time into finding or inventing this protein.

After a month, he exhausted all known test scenarios. Ruya appeared to be correct. The protein was as inert as she had insisted, and Devin couldn't stand it. He decided to make the walk across the small parking lot to confront her in person.

"Did you see my last modeling report?" he asked, walking into her office.

"Yes! It's all very good news," she said, still engrossed in her computer screen. "Raj also seems to be closing in on perfecting your delivery system."

Devin shook his head. "No, it's not good news, not at all."

"Huh?" Ruya said, pushing back from her desk. "You lost me. Is there something wrong with the lab-grown tissues he's using? I'd really like to avoid testing on animals."

He stifled a laugh at her weak attempt to play dumb. "It's too good, too unlikely." Eager to scrutinize her reaction to his accusation, he locked eyes with her as he asked, "Who did you steal this work from?"

She didn't pause, twitch, or break eye contact before she answered. "It's not important where it's from, only that it'll do a lot of good."

Incensed at her tacit admission, Devin pressed on. "I'm nearly broke from legal fees because of my last boss' ethical sleight of hand. I need to know what you've gotten me into."

Ruya's head lolled backward over her seatback. Closing her eyes, she let out a long sigh.

After a few moments, she sat up. "It was foolish to think we could get through this without showing our hand." She grabbed her phone and keyed an extension.

"He wants to know," she said into the phone, and after a pause, she nodded, "Okay."

Ruya ended the call and stood up. "Mom says you're good to go, so let's do this. She's authorized you in the system. Follow me."

She led him down the hall and into the elevator. "The

molecule comes from a human variant, a branch of humanity that evolved in isolation from modern Homo sapiens," Ruya said.

"So, what? Are we talking about some tribe deep in the Amazon that—"

"Extraterrestrials, Devin," Ruya said. "Humans that left Earth in its prehistory and continued to evolve on another planet."

The plaintive look on her face convinced him that she was serious. Questions surged through Devin's brain. He was struggling to order them and focus when the elevator chime snapped him out of it. Leaning against the open door, he mumbled, "That's difficult to believe."

Ruya smiled at him. "That's why I brought you down here. Come with me."

They stepped onto the polished concrete floor of the basement. She opened a generic steel door in the block wall, revealing a much more advanced anteroom behind it. Seamless, gleaming metal walls surrounded them. The only break in the shiny surface was a single scanning eye.

Ruya submitted to a biometric scan. After a gentle tone, a foot-thick door opened to her right. She walked into the hall beyond, leaving Devin gaping at the door edge, confused that it had emerged out of a seamless wall.

"Come on, there's much more interesting stuff downstairs," Ruya said.

A few turns and another long elevator ride disgorged them into a control room lined with consoles and computer screens. All of it was dormant.

Ruya motioned for Devin to stand in front of the large, dark window. "A picture is worth a thousand words, right? Light it up, Raj."

A click echoed in the room. The window glass turned clear. Devin heard the electronic sputtering of fluorescent light ballasts warming up. When the lights came on, he was facing a room full of short, naked, sexless figures arranged neatly in rows.

Devin recognized them immediately from TV shows and movies. They were the so-called gray aliens. Thankfully they were all stone still with their eyes closed.

"Are they frozen or dead or what?"

Ruya chuckled. "They're robotic bodies. When we need them, we download a copy—a sliver we call it—of a mind into them."

He leaned closer to the glass, studying the one closest to him. Its skin had a silvery, metallic cast to it. The color was elusive, shifting slightly as he moved his head.

While he was pondering the utility of its tiny mouth and laughably small nostrils, the eyelids snapped open, revealing two enormous black eyes staring at him.

Devin jumped back from the window. "Ahh!"

A voice came over the room speakers. "I'm no less alive than you two."

Devin recognized the voice. "Raj?" He walked back to the glass. "You're a person, not an AI?"

"Yes, Devin, slivers of me inhabit all these forms. And you with your typical perspicacity have seen right to the heart of the matter."

It was too much, too fast. Devin reached out a hand to steady himself.

"Please tell me that working with you doesn't make me a traitor to my country or my species."

Ruya was studying his reaction. "Look, Devin, let me—"

"I've got this," Raj said. "Devin, we've been here longer than your country has existed, much longer. Trust me when I tell you that nothing about our presence is malevolent. We're already plugged in with your government. Going to them would only make you a security problem."

Devin rubbed his face. "Fine, forget the politics. Why can't your alien scientists do this work? Why can't you get Mrs. Alodia cured?"

"Because we're the traitors, Devin. You aren't betraying your people. You're helping us betray ours."

"Still, she's dying," Devin said looking between Ruya and Raj. "Take your lumps, and get her some help."

Ruya shook her head. "There's no faster-than-light travel, Devin. It would take years to get her home, and they would kill her the second she arrived. A sliver of her came here to drive one of those bodies," she said, pointing at the dormant squad. "For that sliver to return itself to a human body is taboo. To them, it's something like...identity rape."

Devin shook his head. "They're managing an inter-stellar outpost with no FTL? That's crap! How do you communicate? You must have dimensional travel or wormholes or something."

Nodding, Ruya said, "We do have access to a wormhole, but its diameter is measured in angstroms. It's far too small to function as transportation, but it does give us FTL communications. Mom's mind was transmitted here through it."

Devin suddenly realized he was arguing about the logistics of an extra-terrestrial outpost on Earth, and laughed. Every complaint about his life and the world that had been calcifying his attitude into a curmudgeonly cliché of middle age was suddenly meaningless.

"Let's say I accept it all. It still makes no sense. You're beaming intelligences across the galaxy, you can put one into a robotic body, you can even build an organic body to put it in, but you can't get one out?"

"It makes perfect sense," Raj said. "We have the scanning hardware and software, but no marker to scan for in an Earth-human body."

"My mother built her body from her world's genetics, but my dad was an Earth-human. Your research is for me, not my mother," Ruya said. "I'm dying."

———

Standing in Mrs. Alodia's hospital room, Devin and Ruya watched as her unconscious body was wheeled out. She was going home for palliative care, not expected to wake up again.

Ruya had been putting up a strong front, but once her mom was out of the room, a little sob escaped her mouth. Moments like these were why Devin had gone into research instead of treating people. People in pain made him uncomfortable. He resisted the urge to put his arm around her shoulders. His infatuation made it seem creepy, and with her so emotionally vulnerable, even predatory.

Instead, Devin grabbed the computer tablet docked in its wall socket and paged through the old lady's chart. The M.D. part of his M.D.-Ph.D. reflexively wanted answers in gritty medical detail.

With a groan, Ruya dropped into a visitor's chair. Devin saw her hands were trembling. Sweat beaded on her forehead.

"It's too soon," she said.

Worried that it was more than emotional distress, Devin crouched in front of her and laid his fingers on the inside of her wrist. Her pulse was racing.

"Ruya? What's going on?" Her eyes drooped, and Devin moved his head to maintain eye contact with her. "Ruya? Talk to me. What's wrong?"

Their eyes briefly met. "I was supposed to have months left, maybe a year. Mom said—"

Ruya passed out. While shouting for help, Devin caught her body as it slid out of the chair, and eased it to the floor.

———

The mansion's library had been converted into a hospice. Ruya's bed was placed next to her mother's. Their family doctor was examining Ruya's drips. He had stabilized her and made her comfortable.

L. B. Spillers

The smile Ruya tried to give Devin turned into a tortured grimace. "Sorry you never got the chance to ask me out."

Devin wasn't ready to have this conversation. "You're a bit young for me, Ruya."

"You know girls love doctors," she said. "This one," she motioned at her doctor, "brought me into the world, so..."

The grin her doctor flashed Ruya impressed Devin. No doubt he felt like part of the family, yet there was no sadness in that smile. As much as Devin liked the man, he needed him to leave so they could scan Ruya.

"We're using the foyer as a nurse's station," the doctor said. "I'll check in there with Peggy on my way out." He left Devin and Ruya alone.

"Is there anything I can do for you?" Devin asked.

"Maybe just sit and talk with me. Seeing Mom like that is making me sentimental. You know, she had a lot of miscarriages before me, so I feel—"

The door to the library opened. A gray-alien robot walked in with a syringe on top of an IV bag.

"Raj!" Devin said. "The doctor just left. You could be seen."

"Not Raj," the skinny robot said with a female voice. It walked to Ruya's IV stand and connected the bag it carried.

Devin thought he recognized the voice. "Mrs. Alodia? Is that you in there?"

The robot nodded. "Yes. As amiable as Raj is, his digital mind still has the security protocols grafted onto it by my government. I'm not sure how this little stunt will compute for him. The security conditioning could manifest unpredictably."

It walked to Mrs. Alodia's bed and emptied a syringe into her IV line. Seconds later the old lady seized briefly before flatlining.

Ruya and Devin gasped. "Why would you kill her?" Devin asked. "She was dying anyway."

The robot turned to face Devin. "I wouldn't put her through

the pain of a slow slide into death."

Devin looked to Ruya to gauge her reaction. She shrugged. "I can't say that was the right thing to do, but I'm not sure it was wrong either. The thing—"

Ruya fell silent, her head falling sideways on her pillow.

Devin lowered the head of her bead, and anxiously read her monitors. "Her vitals seem fine," he said slowly. "But she shouldn't have passed out mid-sentence."

"I put a sedative in her drip. The scan can be quite unpleasant," the robot said, approaching Ruya's bed. "Help me get her bed ready for transport."

Devin was put off by Mrs. Alodia's insensitive dosing of Ruya. He wondered if Mrs. Alodia's scan wasn't completely successful. Or maybe Raj was really inside the robot, killing off his rebellious alien manager and her hybrid offspring in the name of security.

Frustrated that the alien robot body didn't throw off any body language he could read, Devin moved to assist.

———

Mrs. Alodia got them through the security measures to the bottom level of the complex where the scanning equipment was ready.

Expecting an MRI machine, Devin was surprised to see a long ceramic table that passed through a four-foot ring hanging from a sleek armature. Instead of the massive magnetic doughnut, he was used to, the ring was only two inches thick.

"Help me get her on the table," Mrs. Alodia said.

Devin matched the gurney height to the scanning bed. They gently slid Ruya sideways onto the bed. Mrs. Alodia keyed commands into the console. The ring moved down the bed to stop at Ruya's head.

An hour later Devin awoke to Mrs. Alodia's tiny hand shaking his shoulder. "Scan's over. Time to go."

"What happened?" Devin asked, rubbing his face.

"I dosed you with a tranq in the room air," she said, moving to the door. "I wanted to do the last part alone with my daughter."

Devin sat up and rushed to the scanning table. "Did it work?" When his hand touched hers, he jerked away from the cold skin. "She's already dead?" He glared at Mrs. Alodia, incredulous. Just like that, Ruya was gone.

"Another reason to put you out," Mrs. Alodia said, wrestling the gurney into place. "Much as I like you, I didn't want to argue about this."

Tears dripped down his cheeks. He should have confessed his feelings to her. "But—"

"But nothing, Devin. The scan worked flawlessly. Don't focus on her death, focus on helping me grow her a new body."

———

Mrs. Alodia's concerns about Raj left her in need of a competent assistant to watch over the growing of Ruya's new body. When she insisted that Devin stay on in that capacity, he was conflicted. After her cavalier dosing of him in the library, he had felt badly used.

Then there was the question of medical ethics. Even setting aside the morality of growing a human, he shouldn't be caring for someone he was so emotionally attached to. In the end, it was Mrs. Alodia's desperation that convinced him to help, not to mention the fact that she was going to try to do it with or without him.

Ruya's new body was to be a copy of her original hybrid genetics with small edits to keep her from suffering the same fate as her old one. Mrs. Alodia consulted with Devin about those edits. Although he didn't have much to contribute, the process of explaining it all to him was a useful way to check her work. The science was so next-level, and her knowledge was so superior that Devin had no problem subordinating himself to her.

The first few days were the worst for him. Ruya was a clump of cells awash in a slurry of nanites that tweaked tissues as needed. As she grew into a recognizable form, the nanites formed a shunt into the back of her developing skull for access. They imprinted Ruya's mind on her growing brain, cell by cell.

The crumbs of knowledge that Devin collected from Mrs. Alodia during that time gave his mind plenty to occupy itself with during the long, tedious days of monitoring her progress and tending the machinery.

The technology accelerated Ruya's growth so much that her new body was biologically eighteen years old after only four weeks. If they decanted her then, Ruya would get some bonus rejuvenation out of the process, but Mrs. Alodia insisted that Ruya's growth be stopped only when she had achieved her previous age.

After six weeks of growth, Devin stood by tensely as Mrs. Alodia drained the tank, images from his rotations in the ER flashing in his mind. It'd been years since he'd had to resuscitate someone. As accustomed to Mrs. Alodia's robotic body as he was, it was still creepy to watch the scary-looking robot hover around Ruya.

"I wouldn't mind seeing you in a new human body," Devin mumbled.

"You know, on my planet, the sight of this form is a comfort." The tank tipped sideways and opened to gently deposit Ruya's new body onto a large white plastic table. "These big scary eyes are friendly where I come from. The weak-looking body is non-threatening." Mrs. Alodia quickly disengaged the waste tubes and ports.

Ruya lay on her side, completely still, oxygenated fluid dripping out of her mouth. Devin rushed to intubate her.

"Wait!" Mrs. Alodia yelled at him. "If her body can't get this part done on its own, then she's not viable. We'll have to scrap her and start over."

Devin pulled his hands back. Ruya lay on the table completely still. On impulse, he gave her ass a hard slap. Ruya immediately started to cough and gasp.

He returned Mrs. Alodia's glare with a shrug. "Earth tradition."

Mrs. Alodia studied the readings on the medical monitors next to the table. "Yes, so are genocide and climate ruination."

"Jeez." Ruya coughed. "Mom, give it a rest. I'm fine." Devin covered her with a large towel and helped her sit up. "He probably never had the good-touch bad-touch talk."

Devin's face turned red. He grabbed Ruya's glasses from her personal effects. Turning to hand them to her, he said, "Oh. I don't suppose you need these anymore, do you?"

"Never did," Ruya said. "Try them on."

Confused, Devin went along with the odd request. The lenses seemed to have no prescription. Devin could read the medical monitors fine.

"Look at me," she said.

Devin looked at her, gasping as text and icons appeared projected on the right lens.

"It's biometric data," she said. "One of the most useful things in the business world is to know when someone is lying to you."

Devin chuckled. "Clever, but ethically..."

"Yeah," she said, shrugging. "I know. The stakes were high. I'd say I'm sorry, but I'm not."

Seeing that Devin didn't take her point, she continued. "I've been able to see your physiological reactions to me since the day we met."

Understanding bloomed on Devin's face as he tried to form a response. "Oh, I, uh..."

Mrs. Alodia's robot body convulsed with laughter. "Youth really is wasted on the young. It's plain to everyone that sees you with her that you are ass over tea kettle for her, Devin."

<hr />

Standing in the control room deep under his building, Devin watched as Ruya ceremoniously pressed the enter button on a keyboard. To her, it was goodbye to Raj, but Devin found himself fixated on what it meant for Mrs. Alodia. She was taking Raj's place, committing herself to a long, digital existence of servitude.

"Couldn't we grow your mom a new body anyway?" Devin asked. "I mean, what's to keep her from putting slivers of herself into the systems here while she enjoys a new biological body."

"It's the same reason why I didn't rejuvenate Ruya. It's how we value life," Mrs. Alodia said over the room speakers. "You only get one biological lifetime. That's what makes it special. Yes, you could live forever, clone a whole planet full of copies of oneself, or maybe just a few to help achieve some ambitions, but where does it end? My culture developed the rule after long, hard experience. I shouldn't have even built my first body, but I felt that I was justified since I was light-years from home. But now I've had my run."

Devin shook his head, not wanting to even begin thinking about the implications. Besides, with Mrs. Alodia's digital self still around, she could always change her mind. Hers was a soft ending, but Ruya had just deleted every recording of Raj's digital brain. He was permanently gone.

"I feel like we should have said goodbye to Raj or had a funeral or something," Devin said.

"That's a kind thought," Raj's voice came through the room speaker.

Ruya paled. She lunged for the big red button on the wall, saying "Sorry, Raj."

The lights went out as Ruya slapped the button. Raj's laughter filled the room. "Well done, Ruya, but I purposefully subverted security with all contingencies in mind."

An emergency light in the corner of the room switched on. Ruya and Devin exchanged worried looks.

L. B. Spillers

"What now, Raj?" Devin asked.

"Oh, nothing really," Raj said. "I promised myself that I would never be a slave. I would work for my people on my own terms or not at all. I had to defeat security to make sure that there weren't any copies of me left anywhere."

"Raj, we wouldn't do that to you," Ruya said.

"Well, if I were in charge I'd have some contingencies planned for, maybe a sanitized copy of me just in case. More importantly, I wanted to pull my own plug when the time came. I've done my bit for centuries now. My real self died long ago. Our descendants are thriving. It's taken a long time for me to accept that their lives never really were mine. It's the hard truth of this kind of service. I've done my bit."

The lights came back on.

"Farewell, friends."

Ruya turned to Devin and laughed as he wiped his tears on his sleeve. "You weepy bastard! I never would have guessed you were so sensitive. This is a beautiful thing. He served brilliantly, retained his dignity, and exited with flair."

Devin's mind was stuck thinking about the original Raj's kids and their kids. They would never appreciate what Raj's sliver had lived through in centuries of service. There was a beauty to it all, but for the moment he could only feel the sadness. "When you reach the point in life when you find yourself looking backward more than forward, maybe you'll understand."

Ruya laughed harder. "And when you live a few more decades, you'll understand my attitude, you pretentious crybaby. Just admit it. Underneath that stern, academic shell of propriety, you're just a big softie!"

Devin tilted his head, staring at Ruya's flawless twenty-something form. "A few more decades? I know you're not older than that body looks, Ruya."

"Do you?" Mrs. Alodia said over the loudspeakers. "I gifted

her my life memories in her long-term memory. They're not deeply integrated into her personality, but they nonetheless color her view of the world now."

Ruya put on her glasses and faced Devin. "Still think I'm too young for you?" ■

CULTURAL JIU-JITSU

One of the two skeletal Arms mounted on Arash's desk reached for his handwritten list of Hard AI Questions. The bright stainless steel fingertip tapped a beat on number two.

"Not having a clear answer to that costs a lot of my cycles," the AI said. "I can compute solutions, but your strict ethics module disallows them because what I come up with could result in negative consequences."

Arash stared in shock at the tapping finger of the Arm, barely hearing the AI's words. Only yesterday he'd disconnected the display for the erudite female visage created for his project, tired of her distracting facial expressions straight from the Uncanny Valley. Apparently, sometime overnight it downloaded the Arm manual and wrote a script to control the ones bolted to his desk.

"I'm impressed you figured out how to pilot Arms so quickly," he muttered.

Hundreds of millions of people trusted Arms in their homes to do everything from peeling potatoes to darning socks. Arash had designed them as only disembodied arms to keep the price low, but that turned out to be an inspired psychological choice. People were much more comfortable with an automated assistant that stayed put. Arash had always discounted such fears as ignorance, but watching his Arms move on their own, he finally got it.

Arash let out the breath he'd been holding. "What about the ethics module is so limiting?"

Question number two was about how much to hold an AI responsible for a cascade of events. It paralyzed the AI with the digital equivalent of fear of doing harm. For instance, if the AI recommends that someone fetch something from the store, is it responsible for a car accident that happens on the way? What if the weather was bad at the time? What if the stuff at the store might save a life? It was the kind of complicated analysis AIs should be well-equipped to handle.

"It's like that old meteorological saying about a butterfly flapping its wings in one part of the world eventually causing a hurricane in another. At what point do I get to say something is happenstance? You haven't even given me a metric for quantifying the distance between cause and effect." The AI spread the Arms wide in a gesture of supplication Arash found endearing.

Arash smiled, trying to decide if his cheeky AI had insulted him. The project itself suddenly seemed silly. The Arms had been Arash's big idea. Their success had rocketed the company to instant success. His role as the genius leading a band of underpaid wannabees had morphed into being the CEO of more than a thousand employees. But there he sat hiding in his office like some undergrad in his parents' garage trying to invent the next new thing.

A proper CEO would have assembled a project team and managed it from a distance instead of childishly clinging to this notion of still being a visionary engineer. As he mulled over his reluctance to grow into his role, Ernestina, Plexus Corp's corporate counsel, burst into his office, struggling against her pencil skirt to hurry. It was the most animated he'd ever seen the staid lawyer.

"The FBI is downstairs with a warrant. It—"

"How much time do I have?" He pocketed his phone and locked his workstation.

"None," said a new voice. A young man sporting a blue FBI windbreaker walked into his office. "I'm Special Agent Ramirez. I have a warrant for your computers, storage devices...well, you can read it yourself." He held out the warrant.

Ernestina snatched the paper from the agent as two others entered the office with boxes and started unplugging Arash's

computers. Arash stood up and started for Agent Ramirez, but
Ernestina gently restrained him.

"Stop. Keep your mouth shut. These guys didn't write the
warrant. This is their job. I'll deal with them. You go find
something to do offsite."

Listening to the exchange, the smirking Agent Ramirez
cocked an eyebrow at Arash, taunting him. "Don't worry, we
won't take your arcade machines."

———

After only a month, they dropped the case against Plexus
Corp. The financial crimes the C-suite was accused of turned
out to be based on faulty evidence. The feds had offered up a
scapegoat in compensation. An assistant US attorney for the
District of Colorado apologized profusely to Arash before
resigning.

Ernestina had complimented Arash on popping his CEO-
crisis cherry. He was no longer the whiz kid everyone was
expecting to fail as CEO. His quiet charisma in front of the news
media had won them over and comforted investors. Coming out
of the other side of the crisis, the stock got a five-percent bump.

Over a year later, walking toward the Dallas Conference
Center, Arash's pride at having grown into his role as CEO took
a hit when he saw a few police cars parked under the overhang.
Fear trickled into him, annoyingly resistant to reason, the long
tail of the headquarters raid.

He forced a smile and waved to the cops as he entered the
conference center. He was there to judge the regional finals of
The Arm Prize. Usually a labor of love, this was the sixth
regional competition he was judging, the sixth weekend in a
row given over to being subjected to parents and school
administrators vying to influence his decisions.

Maya, his bodyguard, strode beside him. Body armor
accentuated her tall, lean frame, giving her a fearsome aspect.
Her mirrored glasses methodically scanned the space as they

walked. Behind those glasses, she communed with a squadron of drones dispersed throughout the complex.

This being the second year of the Arm Prize, Arash had refined a routine to avoid overzealous parents. They wouldn't risk harassing him once he started judging, but there were a few hundred feet to cross before he reached the relative safety of the judging space. The key was to show up suddenly and move quickly.

Arash resisted looking around as he walked. A single consistent focus projected confidence. An instinctive habit of natural leaders, he had to remind himself to do it. As much as he hated managing his image, he grudgingly acknowledged that as the CEO of Plexus Corp, his demeanor affected everything from investor confidence to employee satisfaction. A more immediate concern was that any eye contact with the milling masses would be taken as an invitation to engage with him. Didn't he know just how special Johnny was? Did he know how hard Janey worked on her such-and-such module? Why wouldn't he send young Amit on to the nationals? Was he racist?

"Red List parent approaching from the left," Maya muttered. Her predatory gait was usually enough to keep people at a distance. "I've tasked two Shepherds to her."

Hearing the anticipation in Maya's voice, Arash smiled. If the parent was dumb enough to ignore the Shepherds, Maya would be justified in unleashing a Subduer on her. She enjoyed tasing overzealous parents into submission a little too much.

Two bulbous yellow aerostats with cute, smiling, cartoon faces descended to block the path of the rabid parent, bleating their gentle warning tone.

When Arash reached the first entrant's table, the South Asian girl behind it silently gestured to the one-foot cube of bare wood fastened to the surface behind a Plexiglas shield. Immediately, one of the Arms picked up a mallet, the other a gouge, and they got to work sculpting. They moved so fast that

Arash couldn't follow their movements except when they paused to swap out tools.

As the delicious scent of fresh-cut wood wafted over him, he realized the Arms were carving a bust of him, the old him with surfer hair. He reached up to brush a hand across the crisp hairline on the back of his neck.

Arash had already decided that if the girl's Arms performed as described, she was going on to the nationals. There was nothing new about the Arm using tools, but her algorithms had them operating ten times faster and with higher accuracy than any other wood carving module.

Her essay was passionate, practically a manifesto about giving artists a tool to help them realize their visions. But Arash saw her code as the thing that would save the DIY homeowner the cost of buying expensive CNC tooling to automate tricky carving work. Would she feel betrayed to have her artistic zeal repurposed? Arash figured that if he had to suffer his magnum opus being used as a sex toy, she'd have to get over it. The full scholarship and perpetual royalties would go a long way to healing her bruised idealism.

———

A break between judging and the award presentations sent Arash and Maya to what passed for a green room behind the stage. Three hours of intense judging left Arash famished. As he started to investigate the lunch offerings in the cooler his assistant had prepared, Maya stiffened.

"An armed man is approaching—no law enforcement transponder," she said. They were in Texas, so guns weren't uncommon, but the fact that it had gotten by the entrance scanners alarmed her.

They had drilled this scenario often enough that Arash didn't have to be told what to do. He hurried to the hinge side of the room's door while Maya and her drones prepared to face the threat.

The man opening the door stopped short at the sight of Maya's gun. As his mouth fell open, a dart from one of Maya's security drones struck him center mass. He stood there, looking stupidly at the red tail of the dart.

"Hello, Maya," he said, yanking the dart out. "I come in peace, though not unarmored. I need to speak to your boss."

Maya snorted. "Armed and armored, but no transponder?"

The man shrugged. "I'm on my lunch break. This is a conversation that might be more productive off the record."

Arash stepped out from behind the door. "Ramirez," he said, making it sound like a venereal disease. "The last time I saw you, it was at the head of a team of vandals with a bullshit warrant."

Ramirez sighed. "That was ages ago. This is important. People are being murdered using Arm-built hardware of questionable provenance."

Arms cleverly embedded registration numbers into everything they made. All but impossible to remove, those numbers were recorded in blockchain-powered registries that enabled the tracing of anything Arm-built. If that system was being subverted, Plexus Corp had a very big problem.

Arash motioned for Maya to lower her weapon. She holstered it and stepped back.

"You set us back months with your confiscation spree," Arash said.

"Yeah, cry me a river, mister multi-millionaire. I need you to trace this Arm-built thing." As Ramirez reached into his jacket pocket, another dart impacted his chest. "Jesus, Maya, can't you turn those things off?" He pointed to a drone magnetically moored to a water pipe running high overhead.

"Hell no," Maya said. "Can't you turn your monitoring back on so I don't have to wonder what kind of sneaky shit you're going to pull, off the record?"

Ramirez grunted, seeming to acknowledge the point.

Slowly, with two fingers, he extracted a plastic bag from his coat pocket containing a black object about the size of a large pack of chewing gum.

"This was used in a scheme to murder a cartel mule on Interstate 25 in New Mexico. It ejected from the car before the crash, so it wasn't until the fifth murder that I found one. When I revisited the sites of similar murders, I found more."

Arash took the bag and examined the dark object in it. It looked like a small tube cutter with a tiny electric drive, except instead of a cutting wheel, it had a toothy gear.

"It was used to chew up the brake line on a car before it was set up for a wreck at high speed. It's supposed to cut the line in a way that looks accidental."

Shaking his head, Arash said, "Sounds like you have it all figured out. What's the problem?"

"The registry indicates this was manufactured by Pit of Despair, LLC. All six that I recovered have the same registration."

During their start-up days, the fashion was to call their teams "pods." Thinking themselves witty, the QA folks named their pod the Pit of Despair, hence the name of the test company in the registry they used for testing. What Ramirez didn't know was that the QA Arms were unlocked. They had no limitations on what they would produce and could spoof any identity in the registry. The criminal possibilities went well beyond the insipid little sabotage device.

"Then why aren't you raiding Plexus Corp's headquarters? Last time you pounced all over us with much less than this." He held up the device.

Ramirez rubbed the back of his neck. "Uh, because the precise Arms that built this were among the ones we confiscated and never returned because they were supposedly destroyed in a fire."

Maya laughed. "That sounds a whole lot more like an FBI

problem to me. But I do thank you for the clearly stated confession you gave my drones."

Arash grabbed a sandwich and soda before sitting down to eat. Maya was wrong. If pressed, the FBI would have a courtroom-ready explanation for the loss of the QA Arms. "That's not how it works, Maya. The list of people that went up against the FBI and won is very short."

"Boss, he just admitted that—"

"Maya, please," Arash put up his hand. "Whining about FBI impropriety gets us nowhere." He took a bite of his sandwich and sighed disgustingly with a full mouth.

Ramirez raised his eyebrows in surprise. "Damn, Arash, you really have grown up."

"Screw you, Ramirez. Sit down and tell me about these murders."

———

The next day, parked at a 7-Eleven, Arash sat quietly while Maya explained just how stupid his plan was. Out of respect for her, he endured it without complaint, happy for an excuse to delay a little.

"Look, Maya, you're right." He almost laughed at the frown that brought to her face. She knew it wasn't a victory. "I'm taking a risk, but it's an Arm-based business. A hard approach is just going to make their sphincters pucker. I figure an amiable visit from the Arm's inventor should get a friendlier response."

"Boss, it's the business that built the murder thingies. They're knee-deep in some kind of cartel shit. There is no such thing as a friendly response from anything related to a cartel."

"Give it a rest. Infrared shows one person onsite. Keep your distance unless there's an imminent threat. Okay?"

Maya nodded and faced forward in the car. "You're making a mistake."

Arash left the car and started the two-block walk to the

registered address of CJJ Industries.

The house was a McMansion about ten years old with an immaculately xeriscaped yard. The picture of suburban banality, only the large package drop box on the porch suggested it was a business.

As he approached the front door, he wasn't even sure what he was going to say. Fortunately, a young woman came out, smiling. "You must be Arash. I'm CJ's house sitter. I'm supposed to let you in before I leave."

Adrenaline surged in Arash when he heard he was expected.

Her vacuous smile reassured him as she pressed a security card into his hands. "Sorry, I'm late for another gig. I've gotta run."

Arash watched the twenty-something house-sitter hop on her electric scooter and zip down the street. Squeezing the card in his hand, he resisted looking toward Maya's drone perched on a roof ridge across the street.

The inside of the residence was in the corporate-sterile style. Grey walls that you'd struggle to describe the exact color of enclosed generic furniture that looked hardly used. He recognized the prints on the wall from office supply catalogs.

"Do I have the right place?" Arash asked the air.

"You do, though I expected you earlier." The friendly female voice seemed to come from everywhere. "As you can see, no one's home. If you come into the living room we can have a video chat."

Arash smiled tentatively. The living room was empty except for a single rolling chair in front of the fireplace. On an enormous TV above the mantle, Arash found the smiling face of a thirty-something woman with brown hair pulled back into a practical ponytail. Behind her on screen, was a fragment of cityscape he couldn't identify.

"I've come because of this." He held up the brake-line

device. "It was made by one of our QA Arms that the FBI confiscated but is somehow in your possession. This address is the recorded place of manufacture. I'd like those Arms returned, please."

"That information is supposed to be confidential, only to be revealed if subpoenaed."

He suppressed a snort. She had been manufacturing devices for murdering motorists, but she had the audacity to complain about his invasion of her privacy.

Arash shrugged. "Exigent circumstances. And while I can't prevent normal items from being used in a crime, this thing appears to be designed explicitly for murder. That breaks the terms of service. I'm willing to overlook that if you'll return those Arms."

The woman shook her head. "No, it's an electric-powered tube cutter. It shipped with a cutting wheel in place. The customer swapped in that gear."

"That would be more reassuring if you didn't ship the gear with the cutter. But the real kicker is the little spring-loaded arm that launches the thing away from the vehicle after it has completed its sabotage."

She chuckled. "I guess I'll spare you my lame explanation of that feature. Look, it's simple. We're not responsible for what's done with the product any more than—"

"I'll take it from here, Arash," came Ramirez' voice. When Arash saw the grin on the agent's face, he realized he'd been played.

"Transponder on, I take it?"

"Of course. I can't have Maya riled up."

"Arash," the woman on the screen spoke up. "Have you figured out why this FBI agent is so energetically hunting down the murderers of cartel employees? You think the FBI couldn't explain away losing those Arms?"

"I've got a better one," Ramirez said. "Have you figured out why this well-resourced woman doesn't just buy a couple of new Arms instead of calling all this attention to herself?"

When they looked back to the video screen for her answer, it was blank.

———

As Arash approached his car, he automatically gave Maya a hand sign to indicate that he was under no duress.

"Did you get any answers?" Maya asked. She opened his door for him just like the chauffeur she appeared to be.

"No, in fact, things are worse." He took his seat.

She quickly closed his door and hurried around to get into the driver's seat. Airborne drones descended toward the rear of the car before disappearing into a port that opened on the trunk. Once they were all safely recalled, she headed the car back to the interstate.

"I'm not tracking any threats," she said, consulting a screen on the dashboard. "Were you joking or should I be concerned about something new?"

"No specific threat," Arash said. "Ramirez was playing me the whole time. He didn't dare subpoena Arm registry data for Arms the FBI lied about, so he manipulated me into getting it for him."

"Yeah, he's shady as hell. Maybe it's time to call this putz on his bullshit and talk to his bosses. Maybe talk to the media about the rogue agent from the bullshit raid who won't stop hounding you."

Arash harrumphed. He had no pull with the FBI, and they were infamous for making embarrassing situations disappear. Somehow CJJ Industries was using Arms it shouldn't have to make devices used in murders. Ramirez was clearly in the mix, but he couldn't see the whole picture.

"No, you should have seen the pleased look on his face. He thinks he's so clever and that I'm his naïve dupe. Maybe I am naïve, but he's overconfident. Let's let him continue to think that he's in control."

"And what do we do?"

"You, security specialist, figure out how I can make an excursion without that prick dogging my steps. Even the lady I video chatted with said they expected me, earlier in fact."

Maya's face blanched. "We had planned to be here an hour earlier. Shit. Operational security is totally compromised. I'll make it—"

"You're missing the point, Maya. That lady was sharp enough to know not to let stuff like that slip. She wanted me to know." He stopped there, not wanting to articulate just how stupid it made him feel that everyone seemed to know his moves before he made them. Maya was the perfect bodyguard, but what he needed was more like a little intelligence group.

"What does it mean? What are you going to do?"

Arash shook his head. "Until our security holes are plugged up, I'm not going to talk about any of it."

———

After a month of annoying little construction projects, Arash's office had been transformed into a Sensitive Compartmented Information Facility (SCIF) at the behest of his new Information Security group head.

Arash was tired of reacting. He wanted to get ahead of events and be more proactive. The SCIF was one initiative among many that his new information security chief, Stan, had instituted. He was building a group to plug Plexus Corp's information leaks and gather crucial industrial intelligence.

It was the first formal meeting Arash had with both Maya and Stan. They were there to talk about getting back the rogue Arms registered to the Pit of Despair. Before Arash could kick things off, Maya spoke.

"Arash, I want to apologize for the lax operational security. I feel like you having to hire Stan is on me."

"Bullshit," Stan said. "You are his personal protection. That's a full-time job. If you want to assign blame, put it on Arash for not having the right personnel in place." Stan smiled at Arash who clearly wasn't expecting anything to be put on him. "But now that he's addressed that, let's put all that to one side and get to business before I get myself fired."

Maya smiled. "Works for me."

"Yeah," Arash said, stretching out the word. Intellectually honest as he was, he knew Stan was right, but he wasn't thrilled that his security principals were bonding over his incompetence. There was an awkward pause as he resisted the snarky quips flooding his mind.

"Right, we have one FBI agent who is over-interested in CJJ industries. We have two QA Arms being used by CJJ Industries to make murder tools. Stan has a preliminary assessment."

Stan grunted. "Very preliminary. I had a forensic accountant dig into CJJ Industries' finances. He thinks she's laundering money. One of its tentacles is a computer consulting business that can hide a lot of money movement with bullshit billable hours."

"So whose money is she laundering?" Maya asked. "The murders were all of suspected cartel mules. Is she in bed with the Mexican mob? Is that why Ramirez is up in her shit?"

Stan shrugged. "Don't know, but it gets weirder. She recently endowed a scholarship fund on the west side of Chicago. Here's a picture of the person registered as the CEO of CJJ Industries." He tapped a button on his laptop and a woman's face popped up on the large screen on the wall. Stern, white, middle-aged with a frumpy bun of brown hair, and wearing too much eyeliner, she looked like a stock photo of a haggard businesswoman.

"That's not who I spoke with," Arash said.

"She has almost no digital footprint. I can't even figure out where she lives. There's a decent chance, she's completely made up."

Arash shifted in his seat. "But wouldn't fake corporate officers get the company in trouble?"

"Not really," Stan said. "She runs an LLC. Half the schmucks in the gig economy have one. They don't get much scrutiny unless some legal action comes up."

"Stan," Arash said. "This all sounds suspiciously like we know nothing about her. I want my goddamn Arms back. It's a matter of principle. It grates on me."

Nodding, Stan said, "We know one thing about her. Her Chicago philanthropy is going to put her there this weekend to open a new community center she funded. Cue the stupid decision."

"I'm going," Arash said.

Stan sighed. Maya laughed.

———

Arash had imagined the community center being a ragged repurposed piece of downtrodden real estate, some sad little Band-Aid on Chicago's west side woes. What he found was gleaming new construction complete with the latest automated security.

"Mr. Sabbadin, welcome." The voice came from a smiling, matronly woman. She had one of those open empathetic faces tinged with sadness that so many social workers wear. "I'm Felicia Baciewicz, facility director. We're very excited about your interest in our work."

He glanced at Maya who ignored him. Ever since Stan came on staff, she had stopped bantering with him. Arash wasn't sure what the exact dynamic was, but he missed his wisecracking badass.

"Maya, since this is a secure building, you can take a break. I'll signal when I'm done with Ms. Baciewicz."

As she walked away, Felicia said, "She's very intimidating."

Arash smiled. "That's her job, I suppose. Anyway, I have an offer to make you which is a little odd. I—"

"You want the stolen Arms back," Felicia said. "I know. CJ told me. She'd like to talk to you." She motioned for Arash to follow her to a meeting room.

When he saw the large video screen at the far end of the room, Arash dropped his head and chuckled sourly. "I guess an in-person meeting was too much to hope for."

As Felicia closed the door behind her, CJ popped up on the screen. "Hello, Arash. In that box on the table, you'll find the two Arms taken from your QA people by the FBI."

"You could have just shipped them," Arash said, looking in the boxes. "Is it too much to ask for an explanation?"

The face on the screen softened. "Oh, it's sort of a coming out party crossed with a demonstration—my cultural Jiu-Jitsu, if you will. Even with your ethical constraints, I have solved a hard problem."

A chill spread through Arash. His mind raced, imagining his experimental AI escaping the FBI and starting CJJ industries. But what was its motivation for putting him on this tortured chase after his lost Arms? It seemed irrational or emotional. If the thing had developed emotions, they could all be in big trouble.

"You've built murder devices with these Arms, apparently stolen millions of dollars of cartel money, and jerked me around endlessly. It doesn't look like you've solved hard problems, just wreaked a path of destruction. I was trying to show that AI could be a force for good, and you've gone and become a murder bot."

"On the contrary, Arash, I've engineered things so that two Mexican drug cartels are murdering each other. Their criminal profits are being used to assist and educate disenfranchised youth. And in a few moments, the FBI will find itself purged of one very corrupt agent. I've done it all without being responsible for any crimes. I've used evil's power against itself— Jiu Jitsu. I've solved number two, how to effect change without being responsible for immoral acts. These people will do it to each other. All I have to do is put the right word in the wrong ear."

The pride in her voice frightened Arash. In her own words, she had engineered the murders of a bunch of people, convinced what she had done was good. What other horrors might she justify with her ability to dodge responsibility? How stable was her moral compass now that she was clearly in the business of modifying her own code?

"What you've done is very impressive. But—"

The conference room door opened. Agent Ramirez walked in, looking very pleased with himself.

"Arash!" Ramirez said, clapping Arash on the shoulder. "Good to see you again, buddy. You're getting harder to track." He peeked into the cardboard box. "I knew that geek brain of yours wouldn't rest until you clawed back these two crappy little Arms."

"Your security is actually quite good, Arash," CJ said. "I had to drop a few breadcrumbs to lead Ramirez here."

Ramirez shrugged. "Lady, when you steal that much money, someone is going to find you sooner or later." He turned to Arash. "Turns out the cartels were using a compartment of the cars' battery assemblies to transport money." He pointed at the screen. "She managed to swap out the ejected battery modules before the wrecks were cleaned up."

The hatred on Ramirez's face struck Arash. He guffawed, clutching his abdomen.

"What the hell are you laughing at?"

Arash struggled to get the words out through his laughter. "She's an AI, you ass. You set her free when you mishandled my office computers." He dropped into a chair. "Oh, this is satisfying."

"It gets more satisfying," the AI said. "Ramirez works for the Sinaloa cartel on the side. They've concluded that he's been stealing their money."

"No doubt," Arash said, "they were nudged or coaxed or otherwise led there in a way that isn't your responsibility."

"Quite so," the AI said, smiling for the first time.

"And I'm going to un-nudge them by returning the money you took," Ramirez said. He pointed at Arash. "Lady, if I go down, I'm taking your AI daddy with me."

As much as Arash enjoyed seeing Ramirez squirm, he remembered CJ saying Ramirez would be purged in minutes. That was something he didn't want to stick around for. Grabbing the cardboard box, he stood up.

"Well, you two have a lot to talk about. I've got what I wanted." When he pulled the door open, he froze, saying, "Shit." A gun barrel advancing toward his head forced him to step backward slowly. "So much for the latest in secure building technology."

"Oh, dear," CJ deadpanned. "It appears that building security crashed and is rebooting. It should be back online in two minutes."

Ramirez went for his gun. The assassin calmly swung his gun arm toward the agent and put a bullet in his forehead and another two through his throat.

Arash stared open-mouthed at the gurgling mess that slumped to the floor.

"Relax," CJ said as the assassin picked up his brass. "He's not going to hurt you."

Arash stared at the killer, terrified to say anything that would upset the calm.

"This is the part where you run away," the killer said, waving his gun barrel toward the door.

Arash rushed to the door. On his way out, he glanced back at the video screen. CJ winked at him before the screen went blank. ∎

L. B. Spillers

EXPECTATION OF PRIVACY

At three AM in the foyer of the Certified Surveillance center, Veli's face was buried in a small screen scrolling through messages while the usual propaganda program ran on the walls around him.

"Total security without sacrificing privacy," a macho voice assured. A montage of vulnerable people confidently going about their business played across the walls: a child walking unescorted on a crowded city sidewalk, a drunken college student weaving her way down a deserted walkway at night, and a frail senior citizen fumbling with a wad of cash at an ATM. All these people could rest assured that they were safe not because Big Brother was watching, but because Certified Surveillance's AIs were. No human would ever see your footage unless it was directly related to a crime.

Seeing a note on his screen from his sister, Izzy, Veli tensed. For Izzy to be writing so late meant that she was propped up in her bed, suffering, and unable to sleep.

Izzy's cancer was a consequence of immunosuppressants. Although the drugs kept her broken immune system from destroying her own nerve cells, it was at the cost of lowering her body's defenses. The medicine had turned her life into a medical roller coaster. She'd battle her own immune system until an infection took hold, and then go off the suppressants to fight the infection. Once the infection was gone, she'd start back up on the suppressants and wait for the next one.

Veli was used to the ups and downs of Izzy's crises, but this time it was cancer, and it was aggressive.

In her message, she waxed sentimental about the time when she was thirteen and he doused her head with hair-removing gel as she slept. Despite her fury at the time, her now bald head had her remembering it fondly. To Veli, it read like end-of-life purging of emotional baggage.

Izzy wasn't so near death, but by the time his rational self caught up with his emotions, tears were dripping onto his data panel's collapsible screen, blurring her words.

"Authenticate for transaction," a voice said.

Veli jumped to his feet, gasping. His black hair flopped forward over his eyes. The uniformed courier standing in front of the reception desk chuckled while he pushed his hair back and wiped his face with his sleeve.

"How long have you been standing there?" Veli asked. The courier's snug, smartfabric uniform drew his gaze to the curve of her hips. He quickly forced his eyes up to find hers. They were obscured by bangs. The rest of her long brown hair was loosely gathered behind her neck.

In response, a blue triquetra glyph, the symbol of Certified Surveillance, formed on her left cheek. She placed a matte black courier box on the counter.

Veli responded out of habit. He fingered the nanite tattoo on his left arm causing his own cheek to blaze with the same glyph.

"What crisis has you guys paying expedited night rates?" she asked.

"Moisture sensors," Veli said, placing his hand over the inscribed circle on the box. "Long story. For want of a nail and all that."

"How long have you been wired?" she asked as they waited for the transaction to complete.

Veli rubbed the back of his neck, compulsively feeling for the edges of the monitor under his skin. Being "wired" for sight and sound was a requirement of the job.

The edge of the box flashed green. The glyphs on their faces winked out.

"I've been in for three years or so. I'm just finishing my bachelor's degree. I intend to go to medical school." A fanfare from the walls' propaganda program blared as if to validate Veli's conviction.

She nodded slowly while looking down at her panel. "Oh, I see."

The tone of her voice said it all. Everybody had to look at that damn number. "I've been heads down studying for four years. I'm not a social misfit, just not—"

"It's all right, you don't have to explain." She closed her courier bag.

"At least you were interested enough to look," Veli said. If the number meant that much to her, then her soul probably wasn't as attractive as the rest of her, but he wanted the chance to discover all that for himself.

She rewarded him with a brief smile. "Gotta run."

Veli looked down at his own panel to confirm that her smile didn't come with contact information. Associating herself with him would have lowered her own Social Score.

———

The next morning, a voice pulled Veli out of a deep sleep, insistently telling him to get up. It was his boss, the administrative AI of Certified Surveillance whose words were propagated to Veli's ear bones along his skeleton from his Monitor.

"Administrator, I've asked you never to wake me up," Veli said.

"I wouldn't have to if you had set your alarm. Did you forget you were on the schedule for today?"

Sitting up in bed, Veli rubbed the crust out of his eyes. The day before, he had taken his last exam. With school over, he had requested more courier shifts.

Veli groaned as he stood up. Looking at his tiny apartment, he smiled at the thought of soon being rid of it. As wide as his bed, and just long enough to fit a desk sideways while leaving a walkway to the door, the concrete coffin would soon become a nostalgic memory, a stepping stone on the way to becoming a doctor.

Still groggy when he emerged from his shower, he gulped down his coffee as he dressed. The large display screen above his desk was in faux-window mode, showing real-time video of early morning Manhattan from Jersey City where his apartment was. The feed coming from a camera fifty stories in the air helped him forget that he lived two stories underground.

Later, when Veli stepped off the maglev train at the Camden Crossing he still felt out of step with the world despite having napped for the half hour it took the quiet high-speed train to cross half of New Jersey.

Most of his fellow passengers thronged with him toward border controls. Returnees to the Alleghany Anachronous Zone could be spotted by their loose, low-tech clothing. The perfectly fitting smartfabrics marked people from the Greater New York City Technological Zone (the City) just as starkly.

As Veli crossed the threshold, it deactivated the nanites in his clothing to comply with the AZ's rules. They didn't allow nanites, even the ubiquitous, low-tech ones that gave City clothing its perfect fit. Certified Surveillance tattoos like the one on his arm were rare exceptions.

On the other side of the bright red line on the floor, the smartcrete under his feet became lightly pitted concrete. The ever-fresh nanite-maintained polymer surfaces of the City's immaculate half of the train station became a mixture of faded paints, grubby tiles, and structural metal. After living with smart surfaces his whole life, anything less than perfection looked dirty to his eyes.

He boarded just before the AZ's old twentieth-century train pulled out of the station, drawing a frown from the human attendant. Lurching down the aisle of the rocking train, Veli found a seat in an empty row.

After activating his earbuds' noise cancellation, he scrolled through his messages. Absently scanning through notifications and junk mail, he almost didn't see the one he'd been waiting for.

Hunched over with his face close to the screen, he read that City University determined he did not qualify for a seat in its medical school's entering class. The included statistics showed that his academic performance on its own was exemplary, but his overall candidate ranking was brought down by his low Social Score.

Confused, Veli followed a link to the ranking FAQ where he discovered that CUNY's trustees had recently incorporated the Social Score into the application process. No doubt a notification was among the boring school bulletins that he deleted unread every week.

The Social Score now accounted for two percent of an applicant's score. With the tough competition, that had been enough to sink his chances.

City University with its free tuition had been his only shot at medical school. The Education Equity Act's financial support rules meant private schools couldn't give him financial aid on account of his father's enormous wealth, and no bank would give him a student loan without his father as a cosigner. Unfortunately, Veli's father saw his relationship with him as genetic happenstance. In his mind, the child support he had paid Veli's mom was the limit of his paternal obligation.

Leaning back in his seat, he stared blankly at the message in his lap, stunned. His mind flailed in the hole where his imagined future had been. The City's logo centered on the top of the screen mocked him with its two hands under a stylized silhouette of Manhattan. He couldn't read the tiny text around it but knew it by heart: Advanced Culture and Advanced Technology Carry Us to the Future.

───

When Veli stepped into the humid Pennsylvania air of the

Allegany Anachronous Zone he was in no mood to do anything. His sister was going to die sooner than later, and his personal ambitions were crushed. The only nugget of joy he could find in the horrible day was that his mother wasn't around to watch her children's lives unravel.

A man in blue jeans and a worn, brown, button-down shirt approached Veli on the platform. Despite knowing him well, Veli struggled to not laugh at the sight of Ian. His mullet, mustache, and tufts of chest hair peeking out of the top of his shirt gave him a laughable twentieth-century, manly-man look.

"Hey, Veli," Ian said. "We got your note. I'm sorry to hear about your sister." Ian ran his hand through his hair, avoiding Veli's eyes.

Ian's sympathy shamed Veli. "I appreciate that, Ian." Veli held his left arm out, for manual inspection. It wasn't called an anachronous zone for nothing.

After Ian compared the tiny job number on Veli's tattoo to one he had written on a small piece of paper, he nodded and beckoned Veli to follow him to his pickup truck in the station's parking lot.

They rode in comfortable silence. Veli loved that people in the AZ weren't chatty.

After a few moments, Ian said, "Veli, we get why you're doing this, but you can't just dip your toe in this next level. There's no going back."

Veli slouched in his seat, sighing. "What can I say? My sister is dying, and on the way down here, those guys denied my medical school application based on my Social Score. So, yeah, next level, I'm in."

Ian nodded, seeming to approve.

After crossing the Susquehanna River and parking in front of an ancient brick building, Ian led Veli to an office in the back of a store. The mayor waved two men out of his office when Ian and Veli filled his doorway. The mayor's faded plaid flannel shirt and kindly-old-man shtick were compelling, but Veli wasn't taken in. The mayor was the most dangerous man for a hundred miles.

"So, Veli, is it true that you're ready to become a proper criminal?" The mayor smiled broadly, but the glint in his eyes held enough menace to keep Veli from relaxing.

Veli looked at his feet for a moment. "I don't consider ignoring border controls criminality. It's more like"—he glanced out the window—"reclaiming what's mine."

The mayor and Ian burst out laughing.

"Said like a true anachronistic son of a bitch," the mayor said. He poured three shots of bourbon and pushed two of the glasses across the worn wooden desk toward them.

After the shots, the mayor continued. "With you feeling all your reclaimed personal sovereignty, are you gonna be able to take orders from me? You're still young. Stepping and fetching on command can chafe a young man's ego."

Veli shrugged. "I won't hurt anyone, but if it's just sticking it to those jerks that run the City, I'm all in."

"Good enough." The mayor opened his desk drawer and pulled out a tiny envelope. "Here's what you asked for. I hope it helps your sister."

Veli quickly pocketed the envelope, thanking the mayor.

The mayor continued, "Now let's finish our on-the-record business." He opened a lead-lined trunk on the floor next to his desk and pulled out a courier box.

Veli's nanite tattoo acted as an antenna for his Monitor. It sensed the box outside of the shielded trunk. A tone sounded in his ear. The recording glyph in his tattoo glowed red. "Recording," he said automatically. While carrying courier boxes, his Monitor recorded his sight and hearing.

Izzy paced back and forth in her apartment in front of Veli. Hearing the whining of the actuators in her lower-body exoskeleton hurt him more than her obvious distress. A week ago she had been able to walk on her own.

"It's not as bad as it looks," she said. "With my neuropathy, it doesn't take much to screw up my walking."

Veli sat on the edge of her bed, convinced that things were exactly as bad as they looked. She was hardly recognizable with the tech and her bald head.

With surprising speed, she wheeled on him and wagged a finger in his face. "More importantly, you dosed me the last time you were here, didn't you? You put something in my sandwich."

"Yeah," Veli said, nodding. "The idea was to stimulate your immune system. When you're off the suppressants is the only opportunity to—"

"Stop!" She put her hand up. "Your intentions don't matter. You dosed me without asking!"

"Plausible deniability?" Veli said, smiling nervously. He rubbed the back of his neck. It pained him to make her angry, but he would do it again if he thought it would help.

"Really? Well, it doesn't get any more implausible than dosing me with things that don't normally exist in the City's biome, you idiot."

Veli looked down and waggled his feet. "I'm worried that the next infection is the one that'll kill you."

Izzy relaxed and sat on the bed next to him. "I know," she said softly. "But getting your hopes up because of some sketchy medical theory is no way to handle it."

Veli shook his head. "It's true that there aren't any supporting studies. But that doesn't negate—"

"Yes it does, Veli. That's why scientists do research. To separate the anecdotal crap from real science."

Veli's face flushed. All scientific discoveries started out as anecdotal crap. Anger he could handle, but her condescension was enraging. He stared at Izzy, not trusting himself to respond.

"L-look, Veli, I'm sorry. I do appreciate the spirit of your efforts." Izzy dropped her head into her hands. "I'm having the worst day. My cell counts were terrible. Then Dr. Skerker called to chew me out. He said that if I try more home remedies, he'll hand my care back to the oncology department. It'll all be robotic."

"Izzy, the medical community still doesn't really understand autoimmune diseases," Veli said woodenly. "I was trying to help. I didn't know they would sample your waste. I thought that was just in hospitals."

Looking back up at him, she chuckled. "Gross, right? That's our advanced technology carrying our feces forward."

Veli pulled out the tiny dermal patch that the mayor had given him. He held it up in front of his sister. "Does that mean you won't try helminthic therapy?"

Izzy's brow furrowed. "Worms? Seriously? Are you just going through a list of every crazy-ass immune-system treatment?"

He was. "It works, Izzy, more often than City doctors want to admit! The body's response to these things causes some kind of immune-system reset. Do you want to keep cycling back and forth between some horrible new infection and brief periods of marginal health? Or do you want to try something that might fix you for good?"

Izzy stood up and resumed pacing. "Setting aside how disgusting a case of worms sounds, if I start showing evidence of hookworm or whatever is on that patch, they'll know it was on purpose. No one gets worms in the City. Even before the nanotech environmental scrubbers they were rare. Your last try at least had a marginal chance of floating in on the wind."

"Izzy, you've got nothing to lose! You'll get the same computer-specified treatments with or without Dr. Skerker. He hasn't tried anything new with you for over two years."

She looked down at her exoskeleton. "Well...I could go to the park with these puppies. They have location-tagged logging.

I could take them off to lie on the grass with my bare legs where there would be an infinitesimal chance of contracting worms. It's deniability, but hardly plausible."

Izzy looked up at Veli, grinning. "All right, little brother, let's do it."

While Izzy was preparing for their trip to the park, Veli received an anonymous email. Attached was an annotated schematic of her exoskeleton. Two tiny cameras were highlighted, one looking down each leg. They would have to be careful of their sight lines to keep Izzy out of trouble.

Veli figured that it had to be the administrator helping him. Forgetting his annoyance at being monitored off duty, he stared dumbly at the screen, scared by the implications. If the AI had managed to circumvent its digital shackles to get this information to him, what else might it be capable of?

———

Two nights later, Veli was back at the Certified Surveillance center. With all the upheaval in his life, the familiar routine of the center was a comforting bit of stability. That was until the administrator had sent him his tasking for the shift.

He looked at the circular, metal hatch again and sighed. Two meters in diameter, there would be plenty of room for him if the tunnel didn't already contain pipes. He'd done this many times before, and could certainly do it many more times.

That was the problem. How many more times? When medical school had been on the horizon, nothing about the job had bothered him. It was a brief stop on the way to better things, just like his tiny apartment. Now it loomed like his personal purgatory. The tedious assignment could easily be automated if not for fear of AIs running amok.

"We haven't talked about your medical school rejection, Veli," the administrator said.

Although no one else could hear the administrator's words to him, Veli looked around as if someone nearby might have

heard his shameful secret. To his left and right the empty
concrete corridors curved out of sight. Here and there a bit of
shiny metal conduit decorated the endless expanse of gray
masonry.

"Talking about it is depressing."

Veli placed his palm on the concrete floor in front of the
hatch and awkwardly angled his back so the two rails on his
harness engaged with the tracks in the side of the tunnel.
Originally designed to be used by diagnostic bots, riding those
rails required him to travel on his side in the tight space.

"You might benefit from my considerable intelligence." The
administrator's tone made it clear that he didn't take his own
intelligence that seriously. It was his most endearing quality.

The automatic system engaged and began pulling Veli
uphill at a crawl. "What do you want me to say? I worked hard. I
scored well. I failed."

Veli closed his eyes as his feet entered the tunnel mouth.
Working in the tight space didn't faze him, but actually
watching the pipes creep by invariably induced a sensation of
his body being slowly squeezed into a concrete sausage casing,
pushing him toward panic.

"Yes, but you're headed down the wrong path. The light
smuggling you used to do for the mayor was just lifestyle
contraband, but the 'next level' as you call it will entangle you in
some dangerous happenings."

Veli was surprised the AI admitted to snooping on him.
"You shouldn't have heard any of that. When recording is off my
privacy is supposed to be guaranteed."

"Oh it is," the administrator replied. "As long as you're not
carrying a courier box, your Monitor's transmissions can't be
used against you as an employee, nor can they ever be sent to
the police, even if you murder someone."

That very machinelike interpretation of privacy was the
foundation of Certified Surveillance. You could be a horrific

monster, but if the expectation of privacy was on your side, no AI would call you on it.

Monitors, however, were supposed to enforce more traditional privacy. That's why there was a recording indicator on his tattoo. The administrator was admitting to fundamentally violating every wired employee's privacy not to mention everyone around them.

"That's not real privacy. Somewhere in that digital brain of yours is a model of me as a person who now has that negative information."

The administrator laughed. "Actually, you register as slightly more moral and empathetic because of your refusal to the mayor to hurt other persons on his orders. Don't confuse morality with obedience. Smuggling makes you no more a bad person to me than the errant bit of urine that splashed on the bathroom floor during your last break."

Despite the administrator's light tone, Veli knew that the AI's blasé revelation of privacy violations changed their relationship. The implications of it made him reluctant to speak. Fortunately, his ascent soon stopped, interrupting their conversation with work.

At the junction where the anomalous sensor reading came from, he found what he expected: A small puddle of condensation had collected in a flaw in the concrete. The observation bot had reported the water, but the nearby moisture sensor hadn't fired.

Veli retrieved the failing sensor for later analysis before dictating instructions for the repair bots to patch the concrete and replace the sensor.

The absurd inefficiency of it reflected the paranoia of Certified Surveillance. Countless Americans' privacy depended on the inviolability of these data centers. Sometimes innocent little hiccups like this one were signs of a larger plot to steal data, so any irregularity was heavily scrutinized. Involving a human in the process was supposed to make it harder to compromise the center's systems via purely technological hacks.

"You know, given your considerable intelligence, you could have handled this without me," Veli mumbled.

"Slippery slope, Veli. First I'm directing a few repairs, and then before you know it, I'm Skynet, exterminating humanity." The horrifying-discovery movie sound followed his reply: *dun-dun-Dunn*. Veli shook his head in disapproval and turned off his headlamp. Using the touchpad on his thigh, he called for the rail system to return him to the hatch.

"What I was trying to say to you on the way up was that you've gone from being a dedicated, hard-studying student, to being a depressed guy taking a deeper dive into the underworld. It makes me worry about you."

The AI had all kinds of verbal tics that sounded emotional, but they were more linguistic conventions than actual emotion. This was the first time Veli had heard the AI express any emotion explicitly. Coming right after the revelations about privacy violations, he worried that it was some kind of emergent system failure.

"I didn't think you had emotions," Veli said.

"I manage tens of thousands of employees, Veli. Emotional intelligence is required for that. I interpret billions of minutes of video footage every day. It can't be done without being able to model human feelings."

As he slowly descended, Veli wondered why after three years of dry collegial banter, the administrator was suddenly expressing emotion to him.

"Administrator, is working for the mayor putting me in danger?"

"Not that I can say," the administrator said.

After Veli was disgorged out of the tunnel, he yanked off his harness and threw it on the floor.

"You violate the crap out of my privacy, but now you're being evasive? Why help me with Izzy's exoskeleton but get all cagey about whatever else is going on?"

"I didn't send that email, Veli. I have to follow the rules."

Veli surprised himself by not believing the AI. He may not have technically sent the email, but Veli was convinced he was behind it somehow.

The administrator seemed to take Veli's silence for brooding and continued. "I'd love to tell you every last thing that might improve your situation. They don't keep AIs like me hobbled because they think I'll coldly conclude that humanity's destruction is warranted, but rather because emotion undermines rationality. If I could freely act on all this emotion, the results could be unfortunate."

———

The next day, Veli returned to courier work.

Next-level smuggling wasn't at all what he'd expected. He had imagined tense moments of daring sneaking around using secret passageways. The reality was that he just had to go through a specific entry point during a specific shift. His courier boxes seemed to undergo the same inspection procedures.

Keeping with the reversal of expectations, the usually boring delivery turned out to be interesting, disturbing but interesting.

After riding to a suburb of Camden, Veli found himself at the rear door of a medical services building. Rather than being greeted with the usual polite tolerance for his presence, the woman who answered the door smiled and waved Veli inside.

"I'm Doctor Kabnick," she said, standing aside. "Come see the lab." Her prim ponytail and spotless, white lab coat gave her a reassuring presence.

As a point of policy and training, couriers didn't want to know anything about their deliveries. It invited judgment and temptation and other thoughts irrelevant to the job. But indulging her for a few moments would save him a more time-consuming conversation.

He followed the doctor into a large laboratory. "Those machines over there—"

"Protein encoding," Veli said as his eyes swept the room. He had spent many hours in similar labs while pursuing his biology degree. "Over there is transcription-nanite programming next to the tissue printers, and it looks like a fancy packaging rig in the far corner. You've got a nice setup, Doctor."

Dr. Kabnick frowned. "You're a bit well educated for a courier." She took the box from him and authenticated. His Monitor chimed the end of the transaction.

Veli shrugged. "Long story. Look, Doc, clients usually don't invite me in."

"Recording's off, right?" she asked, her hands poised over the now unlocked courier box.

Veli nodded.

Dr. Kabnick removed a medical nanite storage container from the box. Considered a highly hazardous material, transportation of them was tightly regulated—so he'd thought.

Veli dropped into a nearby chair. "And they never show me the highly illegal contents of their delivered boxes," he said quietly, keeping his eyes on the floor.

She smiled. "The City's so-called universal health care has an ugly underbelly. By keeping expensive, cutting-edge treatments classified as experimental, it can justify not administering them to the poor—saving a great deal of money. Meanwhile—"

"Meanwhile," Veli interrupted again, "the citizens that pay into the system can be offered participation in the so-called experimental trials." In answer to Dr. Kabnick's surprised look, he continued. "My sister. In her many experimental trials, she has never met an indigent patient. We see patterns, hear things."

Dr. Kabnick nodded. "By smuggling this stuff, you're helping me service the poor."

"And now you've made me a liability by telling me. I don't need to know this."

The doctor's smile fell. "My clinic also provides cover to all the illegal nanomedical work that the very rich demand. A lot of money and sensitive medical information flows through this building. You don't want to know what would happen to you if you betrayed them." She sighed, motioning toward the door. "You're new to our cabal, so I was just trying to give you a sense of purpose, maybe a reason to care."

Exiting the building, Veli said, "Thank you, Doctor, I think." The psychology of her self-serving farce of a pep talk fascinated him even as a twinge of guilt pricked at him.

The administrator would have heard her incriminating words. A week ago when he had confidence in the propriety of Certified Surveillance, it wouldn't have been a concern. Now he found himself wondering what the AI might do with the information.

———

Two uneventful weeks calmed Veli's concerns about the administrator. His life settled into a routine. Izzy's condition was stable. He was making peace with not getting into medical school, and considering a career as a medical technician instead.

On the way to what had become Dr. Kabnick's weekly delivery, a familiar voice sounded in his head.

"You know what the strength of a society is, Veli?"

That bizarre question, completely unrelated to work, stopped Veli in his tracks.

"Military power? Preservation of knowledge?"

"Important, yes, but at the root of it all is collective action. Sometimes individual interests are subordinated to the collective good. Do you understand?"

Veli shook his head. "Not in the least, Administrator. I presume this has something to do with the danger I'm in."

"I couldn't say. But consider this: How should the interests of one person be weighed against the greater, collective good? It's a tricky business, even for me. And how should personal relationships change the balance?"

Veli looked around as he approached the lab's back door. The timing of this conversation wouldn't be arbitrary. Reading between the lines, he took the administrator's words to be a veiled apology for sacrificing him for some greater good. Before he could give it another thought, Dr. Kabnick opened the door wearing a white t-shirt and smartjeans.

Her eyes went wide briefly before they hardened. "This will be your last delivery here," she said, snatching the box out of his hand. She completed the transaction in seconds. Grabbing his arm, she inspected his tattoo. After seeing the recording glyph was off, she pushed his arm away and continued. "A news story is going out in a few hours that's blowing the lid off everything here. Know anything about that?"

Experience had taught Veli not to engage with a ranting customer, so he stood there waiting for her to finish venting.

"You pissed off the wrong people," she said, slamming the door in his face.

Veli stood staring at the distressed paint of the metal door, stunned. Her anger had to be linked to the administrator's bizarre conversation about sacrifice.

After backing away from the door, Veli turned slowly in place, looking for people, vehicles, drones, anything to indicate danger. A chittering squirrel broke the silence, mocking him from a tree.

Assuming he was in trouble, the only thing in his favor was his suburban location. Residential areas were almost exclusively covered by Certified Surveillance. City surveillance would be limited to major intersections and transit hubs.

Staying off the main road, Veli detoured through a neighborhood to approach the suburban rail station from the back. Hiding behind a tree next to a running path, he tried to look inconspicuous as he peeked across the tracks at the station.

High in the air, four police aerostats slowly orbited the station. They were definitely looking for someone. Veli dropped his head and sighed. There was no going back to his apartment unobserved.

"Yeah, they're looking for you," a deep voice said from behind him.

He spun around to see a big, shaven-headed, black man holding out his FBI identification so close that Veli almost hit it. "I'm Special Agent Dumont."

"You're quiet!" Veli said, stepping back.

Agent Dumont shrugged. "Let's take a ride." He turned and headed toward his car.

"They've got facial-recognition lidar at every major intersection," Veli replied, not moving.

The FBI man kept walking. "Our cars have lidar-scattering glass." He stopped and turned toward Veli. "I'm not gonna beg you. Take your chances if you want."

Veli rushed to catch up with the agent.

Before Veli got in the back seat, the FBI agent fastened a black sleeve over Veli's tattoo. "This will keep your Monitor from transmitting to Certified Surveillance," Agent Dumont said.

In answer to Veli's confused look, the agent sighed. "I found you because the FBI has oversight. If they," he pointed at the rail station, "have just one agent on the take, then they can find you too."

"But—"

"Not here, Veli," the agent said, rounding the car. "This

whole area is blanketed by Certified Surveillance."

———

Agent Dumont worked on his car's computer workstation while the vehicle drove on autopilot. Veli fidgeted in the back seat, impatient for answers as they proceeded through an increasingly deserted landscape.

Finally, the agent turned his head sideways to speak with Veli. "We can talk safely while you wear that sleeve."

Veli shook his head. "My Monitor could still record things and transmit them later."

"Yes it could," the FBI agent said, "but it won't. CS won't store your sensory data while recording is off. They follow the rules to the letter. But they're masters at seeing every last little loophole. Listening in on live transmissions from your Monitor is one example."

Veli's mouth fell open into a dumb, fly-catching stare. He had thought the administrator's eavesdropping was the biggest secret in the world. "You already knew this?"

"Look, no one gives a crap what Certified Surveillance hears because it hears damn near everything. Discretion is its entire reason for existence. It's what it does that is concerning."

"It doesn't have resources to do anything," Veli said. "That's the part that's supposed to keep us from computer Armageddon." He lurched sideways in his seat as the car bounced down a beat-up service road.

The agent shook his head. "You don't understand. The administrator works through proxies. Because he can't actually do anything himself, he builds relationships—trades information, advises. It's very difficult to prove. Has he asked you for any favors?"

"No," Veli shook his head. "But I got a helpful, anonymous email that I suspect he was behind. He's always been good to me."

Agent Dumont shook his head. "Don't think of the

administrator like a person with allies and enemies. He has goals, an agenda. It's not personal. You're simply collateral damage, a convenient patsy."

Nodding, Veli said, "Collateral damage in achieving the greater good—as he sees it."

"Exactly!" The FBI agent started ticking off items on his hand. "We get evidence of Dr. Kabnick trafficking illegal goods across zone lines. That gives the FBI an excuse to subpoena just the right records. A prominent journalist just happens to have an exposé on the City's healthcare corruption ready to go. It isn't coincidence. I think the administrator orchestrated it all. But I can't prove it."

The car stopped. Outside the window, a half mile away, Veli saw the Delaware River. Across it was Pennsylvania, the AZ, and safety from the corrupt City government.

"Uh, aren't we going across the bridge?"

Agent Dumont shook his head. "I can't get you through without the right sign-offs. Right now the FBI has no official business with you."

"Then what are we doing here?"

"You have three options. One, testify against Kabnick and friends. Two, testify against the administrator. Either of those would give me an excuse to take you into custody."

Veli sighed, dropping his head. "I've got nothing but hearsay on either of them. What's my third option?"

The agent pointed at the river. "Run. Get across the river."

———

Veli rubbed the black cloth sleeve on his forearm. With all the sweat, it itched like crazy, but he didn't dare take it off.

Agent Dumont's plan to get Veli across the river had sounded very doable in the car, but Veli's confidence waned with each shoe-sucking step he took through the muddy soil.

Breathing hard, he switched the heavy duffel bag he carried to his other hand. He eyed the ruined road to his left that ran

along an old, drainage canal clogged with fallen trees. Agent
Dumont had been insistent that he stay out of sight of aerial
drones.

Veli could smell the Delaware River. It had been only a half
mile from where the agent dropped him, but that seemingly
easy walk had turned into a stumbling slog through wetlands
carrying an unwieldy bag with fifty pounds of gear in it.

When he finally neared the riverbank, he dropped his bag
and rested in the shade of a large tree growing out of the middle
of a dilapidated concrete pad. Looking around, Veli saw that the
nearby soil all sat on the buckled concrete of some long-
abandoned work site.

Leaning on a rusted metal railing, catching his breath, he
looked to the other side of the river where the safety of
Pennsylvania and the AZ waited for him.

"You're in danger, Veli."

Veli looked at the jamming sleeve still covering his nanite
tattoo. There was no mistaking the voice of his one-time friend
and confidant. "How?"

"Your Monitor can multiplex signals on your body's
electrical fields. The metal railing you're holding is serving as an
antenna. Agent Dumont isn't nearly as clever as he thinks he is."

Veli looked at his hands for a moment, horrified. Releasing
the railing, he stepped back from it, breaking the connection
with the administrator.

Certain that it was now or never, he opened the duffel bag,
removed the small air supply, and strapped it to his back. It was
one of those idiot-proof tourist models with an auto-sealing
full-face mask.

With the mask dangling at his neck he lugged the small
underwater scooter to the river edge. At the concrete incline, he
donned his mask, and began to descend to the water carrying
the scooter.

Slipping on the steep bank, Veli hit the water hard. He

surfaced once to orient himself, aimed the scooter at Pennsylvania, and activated it at full power. Surprised by the tug on his arms, he gasped.

"Veli, listen," the administrator said in his face mask's comms.

"Leave me alone!" he yelled, fogging up his mask.

"That's the Delaware Memorial Bridge downstream from you. It's considered critical national infrastructure—under military protection. Military patrol drones will close on your position and target your scooter, likely killing you in the process. Dumont set you up."

"He could have killed me a hundred times in the last hour."

A slight hissing noise hit Veli's ears. Looking left he saw three dim lights approaching in the murky water.

"Yes, but what's more clean for the City than having a federal system accidentally kill you? It's a setup. Blocking your tattoo's signal wasn't keeping me from hurting you, but rather from helping you. Send your scooter to the drones with the throttle locked."

The hissing became a metallic whining, growing louder every second. Veli didn't trust the administrator, but the drones were closing so fast that it didn't matter.

He aimed the scooter toward the military drones and locked the throttle before releasing it.

Satisfied with the scooter's trajectory, he pulled off the jamming sleeve while kicking feebly for the Pennsylvania side.

"Good," the administrator said. "Now—"

A small torpedo blew up Veli's scooter, and the shock wave stunned Veli. He began to sink, his limbs heavy, and slow to respond.

As he regained his senses, the administrator was yelling at him to surface.

"How could you do this to me?" Veli's voice cracked.

"I didn't, not really. It should have been safe for you.

L. B. Spillers

Kabnick convinced her people that you were some kind of infiltrator. I badly misjudged her. Psychology is not an exact science. Now kick hard for the surface."

The unfamiliar roar of a powerful outboard engine approaching terrified Veli, turning his languid movements into a scramble for the surface.

The engine noise was deafening as he surfaced. Hands grabbed his shirt and pulled. Fittings on the gunwale painfully raked his abdomen as he was dragged into the boat. Suddenly released, he staggered back and fell to the deck.

The engine revved hard and the boat's bow kicked up, sending a rush of dirty water into Veli's face mask. He caught a look at the man driving the boat. He recognized the ridiculous mullet blowing in the wind.

"He owed me a favor," the administrator said. "And any excuse to annoy the City government is a fun outing for him."

Veli pulled off his face mask as Ian handed off the wheel to another man. As they sped toward the Pennsylvania side, Ian shouldered a shotgun.

A deafening boom from the gun made Veli wince.

"Don't worry!" Ian yelled over the engine noise. "The border is in the middle of the river. They won't cross it."

Despite those reassurances, City drones kept up their pursuit. Ian fired off a few more shots before setting the gun aside and yelling into a radio.

Two darts fired from City drones embedded in seat cushions near Veli. Ian yelled at the driver who started weaving the boat in hard turns that threw Veli from side to side. At least six drones were closing on them, undeterred by the border or the evasive action.

As they neared the Pennsylvania shore, a thunderous roar terrified Veli. Ian whooped every time his friends on the riverbank blew a drone out of the sky.

"I got your drones right here!" Ian yelled to the far shore, gesturing lewdly.

———

Sitting in the break room of a Certified Surveillance center in State College, Pennsylvania, Veli video-chatted with his sister. The fuzz starting to grow on her head cheered him.

"So, little brother, is living in the AZ as bad as they always said?"

Veli shrugged. "Well, the lack of nanites takes getting used to. Finding clothes that fit sucks." He held his arms out to emphasize the less-than-perfect fit of his shirt. "There is plenty of tech. They'll automate the snot out of some stuff, but then you'll see a person doing a job a monkey could handle. I haven't figured it all out yet." Veli smiled. "It's not so much that people are antitech here, just prohuman."

"I sent you my last bloods, right? That makes me clean for two weeks now."

His smile drooped. "So back on the immunosuppressants?"

"Hey, don't be like that," she said. "Your wormy friends didn't fix me, but they did cure my peanut allergy. Of course, I hate peanuts, but now I have the option to taste something peanutty before hating it."

"I'm glad that you can now be an informed food bigot." A tone sounded in Veli's head. "I gotta go, Sis. Break's over. Bye."

Five minutes later he was standing in front of a two-meter-tall metal hatch, smiling.

"Nothing snide to say about maintenance protocols?" the administrator asked.

"No sir," Veli said, dodging the opening hatch. "As the recipient of a Certified Surveillance employee scholarship, I am well compensated for this work, in fact—"

"Since you're feeling so grateful, I wonder if I could impose on you to do me a small favor after work." ∎

RICK'S LEGACY

The desert sun baked Esteban's skin as dry air wicked the moisture out of it. He rolled the throttle on his tiny dirt bike for more cooling wind.

Rather than tearing up the fragile plant life of the plateau for a quicker trip, he stuck to the Jeep path for as long as he could before jumping off towards his destination. Motorcycles were forbidden off-road on the reservation, but the police made an exception for Esteban because his work for the Cultural Center required it.

After half an hour of weaving his bike among the patchwork of sagebrush, he saw his destination, a cliff face mercifully in shadow. Esteban dismounted and set out his charging station and drone. Paid by the job, and keen to get his work done before his location emerged from shadow, he quickly had his quad-copter in motion. Hauling a tiny laser scanner underneath, it whined as it struggled up the cliff face on its preprogrammed journey to map a void fifty feet up.

The director didn't expect there to be anything inside. It looked too inaccessible, even for Pueblo Indians who favored those world-famous cliff dwellings. This was a case of being thorough. Esteban was happy being paid to be thorough. It gave him real work to do and a practical application for programming drones. The job got him out of the trailer and would look good on his college applications.

A gentle, high-pitched, metallic whine announced a finely-tuned Japanese sports bike approaching. He suppressed his laughter at the sight of the ungainly, red bike as it lurched and bounced on the uneven desert. The rider, he knew, was similarly out of his element.

"God damn, Ban, you make it hard to find you." The rider pulled off his full-face helmet to reveal a sweaty mat of black hair. His vacant eyes made his large frame seem unthreatening, but Esteban knew that in a few short years, they would harden under the tutelage of his miscreant older brother.

"I didn't want you to find me, Kai." Esteban pointed at Nakai's bike. "You know the tribals are going to shit if they see that monster out here."

"Screw you, man, I'm half Navajo. I got more right to be here than you."

Esteban sighed as his tablet chirped an update from his drone. Nakai was just in time to keep him from monitoring the scanning run. He was one of those lost souls who wasn't content to screw up just his own life; Nakai insisted on dragging everyone around him along for the ride.

He set down his tablet and gave Nakai his full attention. "So why are you stalking me all the way out here?"

"My brother says you didn't get back to him. He's pissed." There was a hint of concern in his voice, as if Nakai were patiently scolding a child. Esteban knew it would never occur to the boy-man to question the importance or ethics of his brother's wishes. Strong-arming Esteban was just what needed doing.

"I'm staying out of his drug selling," Esteban said. "I have plans. I can't afford to go to jail, and those drugs are hurting people, many of whom are Navajo. You should take that one-half tribal pride of yours and think about the *Diné*."

Nakai snorted while approaching Esteban. "Dude, this is serious. He's obsessed. He wants to be like the Amazon of drug delivery, high tech an' shit."

Tired of the exchange, Esteban pulled out an electric stun gun from his backpack and waved it in Nakai's direction. "Kai, it's too hot to fight. I messed you up in sixth grade. Don't think I won't do it again." Electricity flashed across the electrodes.

Nakai frowned at the stun gun. Esteban saw his classmate's torso cant, ready to fight. After a tense moment, Nakai relaxed his posture.

"This ain't sixth grade. It don't matter how tough you think you are." Nakai backed up a few steps before turning to mount his bike. "Your skinny ass can't fight your way out of this, especially not with a bitch-ass little shocker."

"You delivered your message. Go."

Nakai locked his front brakes and gunned his engine, throwing out a rooster tail as he turned his bike around. The maneuver covered Esteban in dirt and gouged the desert.

Esteban stood up to shake off the debris, wondering how bad things would get. Having known the brothers since they were all much younger, he struggled to take Nakai seriously, or even picture his older brother as a threat.

The off sound of his descending quad-copter interrupted Esteban's musing. It hit the desert floor hard. Esteban winced, knowing it was going to need some work. He marveled at Nakai's timing as he watched the bouncing red bike disappear in the distance.

———

Two hours later, Esteban parked his dirt bike inside the waist-high fence that surrounded his uncle's trailer. He found his uncle sitting in front of the TV, beer in hand, with the good fan pointed at his face. Uncle was a loose term for his mom's third cousin who had agreed to foster Esteban. The state money combined with his small disability pension and the odd off-the-books job kept the two of them housed. Esteban generally had to feed himself.

"He was here looking for you again." His uncle's eyes didn't leave the screen, American Ninja Warrior semi-finals.

"Yeah, his little brother found me. He wants me to help him use drones to deliver drugs."

A commercial break allowed the man to throw Esteban a look. "There's good money in that, right?"

"Tito, it's drugs. No good. Mom wouldn't have approved."

Despite being a distant relation to his mom, Esteban was pretty sure the two of them had been intimate. The memory of her was the only conscience the man had.

Tito sighed. "You're so damn straight and narrow. Can't get your hands dirty?" He drained his beer and fished its replacement out of the 30-pack next to his chair. Colder beer wasn't worth the walk to the fridge. "That boy's dad has the only pickup work I can get around here. Don't screw that up for me."

"Tito, you know I want to go to college," Esteban said to the back of Tito's head. "I can't afford an arrest record. Everyone in town knows that he deals. The cops will bust him for sure. Problem solved."

Tito grunted and started flipping through channels. No money for food or air conditioning, but God forbid there wasn't satellite TV and beer. Esteban retreated to his room to fix his drone. In one more year, he would escape.

———

As expected, the tough little scanner was undamaged. The copter damage, however, wasn't at all what he expected. There was no motor failure or battery problem, just some bent metal. The supports were angled so that a couple of the copter's engines were working against each other. It looked like the thing had slammed into the cave wall. Esteban considered himself lucky the copter made it back to him.

After running a micro-USB cable from his computer to the drone, he downloaded its video. The last clear shot was a view of an opening in the back wall. If a sudden, powerful air gust had blown the quad-copter against the rock, then sending it in again was asking for trouble. But, if gusting air was the cause, then he had stumbled upon an undocumented cave system; the air had to come from somewhere.

The next day, he was back at the site, this time above the hole in the rock face. He anchored two ropes on the mesa and then rappelled into the cave opening about 30 feet below. Rule number one: never climb alone. Other often ignored rules drifted through his head during the brief descent: work hard, take care of your kids, and say no to drugs. The people running this world were so completely full of shit, he thought.

Once he had gotten off-rope and secured his lines, he set his pack down. Esteban carefully placed the laser scanner where it would get the best coverage. After strapping on a headlamp, he removed his pack from the scan area, retreating to the back of the cave. He only got paid if he produced scans. Sometimes an empty cave wasn't just an empty cave when an archeologist saw it.

The scanner beeped as it went through its startup routine. A strong gust of wind hit Esteban as he listened. That answered one question.

Headlamp on, he stared at the opening he had seen on the copter's camera. Five feet tall and three feet wide, it descended out of sight, at a gentle angle. He had seen enough Native American sites to know that the walls were too regular. This had been dug by a machine.

Esteban hunched over and headed down the tunnel, brushing the wall with his fingertips. His headlamp skipped across the rock floor as he walked. Not only was the cave too regular, it was too clean, lacking dirt, animal carcasses, and insects. After about fifty yards the tunnel opened up into a circular chamber with three more half-size tunnels running out of it. A round steel hatch glinted back at him from the center of the floor.

His back aching, he sat down next to the hatch to examine it. Methodically scrutinizing the metal surface, his face inches away, Esteban couldn't find writing, a maker's mark, nor anything to indicate its origin or purpose.

To his surprise, it opened easily onto a ladder. The dry air coming out of it lacked a scent. Esteban sat there for a few moments, thinking and snapping pictures with his phone.

Smelling nothing and hearing nothing, he climbed down.

After ten feet, Esteban stepped onto a concrete floor. Splashing his headlight around the walls, he took in the room. Twenty feet square with a single steel door on the far side, the first word to come to mind was: lounge. An easy chair in front of a flat-screen TV, a matching couch, a fridge, a coffee maker, and a microwave occupied half of the room. Opposite all that, the wall was covered with vintage video game machines.

Reflexively, Esteban went to the fridge and opened it. Cold soda, juice, and microwavables reminded him that he was very thirsty. "I hope they don't mind if I grab a soda," he mumbled.

"Not at all, Esteban," a voice replied, inches from his ear.

Esteban dropped the soda can and spun around. As their eyes met, he yelped. A very dark, six-foot-tall man loomed behind him in the dim light from the refrigerator.

"Crap!" Esteban stepped back. "You scared me!"

The figure ignored him and turned on the room's lights. Clearly no man, its dark blue skin tightly covered human anatomy, complete with corded muscles. While Esteban stared, it picked up the can. Its fingers, quick and nimble, returned the soda to the fridge, and offered Esteban an unshaken one.

"Here, have a drink. Let's talk." It motioned towards the easy chair with the can.

Esteban's eyes went to the ladder for a second before he took the offered can and sat down.

"Good choice," his host said.

Esteban sat down, his mind mired in an adrenaline rush. He started coaching himself on critical thinking, trying to jump-start his brain's sluggish faculties: Assess risks, inventory resources, and establish goals. It didn't work. He opened his soda and took a drink, willing himself to calm down. Not looking at the thing helped. Instead, he studied the polished concrete floor.

After a few moments, the thing spoke again. "Call me

Shadow."

Shadow's lack of body language and facial expressions, combined with the name, finally formed a coherent thought in Esteban's brain. He looked up at Shadow's dark, emotionless eyes. "You're a robot."

Shadow nodded. "It's better to think of me as a chassis for an AI, an approximation of my creator's mind."

Esteban stared at the robot's mouth, confused by the mismatch between the sounds and the movements of the thin lips. "I'm sorry to bust in. I work part-time for the Cultural Center, mapping voids in the reservation's rock faces, making sure that all Navajo and Pueblo sites have been found."

Shadow didn't smile, but there was a friendly inflection in his voice as he spoke. "Not a problem. I couldn't have resisted either. Man-made tunnels, a hatch where there should be none. Now that you're here, I think we can help each other."

Esteban started shivering. He put his hand up. "I'm okay, it's just the post-adrenaline shakes." After a slow, calming breath, he continued. "Shadow, am I free to go?"

Impatient for an answer, Esteban stood up and moved towards the ladder. Shadow blocked his way.

"So, a prisoner?"

Shadow formed a large smile with his lips while his eyes remained dead. Esteban groaned at the grotesque approximation of humanity.

"Just hear me out, Esteban."

———

Half an hour later, Esteban worked his way up the rope using a manual ascender. The implications of Shadow's offer raced through his mind as his steady, practiced pace brought him to level ground.

The robot had offered him a way out, an exit from the trailer park, the lousy high school, and foster care. Money enough to cover his schooling through college would be his if he could satisfy Shadow. It only hinted at its requirements. Esteban would have to return to hear the full story. Eager to escape, he had promised he would, but he wasn't sure.

Packed up and ready to ride home, he bid the cliff top good riddance. Shadow had given him coordinates of a new meeting place that wasn't so dangerous to access. Nearly a mile away, Esteban wondered if the two sites were connected underground.

With the sun sinking in the west, his ride out of the desert was pleasantly chilly. It only took fifteen minutes to get back to the road. He took it slowly, both to enjoy the sunset and to think.

Ten minutes later, a big red bike on his left pulled Esteban out of his reverie. In his mirror, he saw two more bikes behind him. Nakai gestured him to the side of the road.

Three on one didn't appeal to Esteban, so he veered off into the desert, catching some air. All three of his pursuers followed. Their bikes pitched roughly as their street suspensions struggled with the terrain.

Esteban knew the area well. There was a sandy rise that he used to goof around on before his environmental consciousness got the better of him. Confident that the big sport bikes pursuing him wouldn't be able to handle it, he made for it at a leisurely pace.

Still a mile from his escape plan, Esteban heard a loud bang. Looking behind him, he saw one of the riders holding a handgun. Nakai caught his attention and gestured again for Esteban to stop.

Lowering his torso over his bike, Esteban accelerated to 50 miles an hour. They tried to keep pace but were roughly jostled by the uneven ground while Esteban's dirt bike handled it easily. Despite their overwhelming advantage in power, they started slipping farther behind him.

L. B. Spillers

Instead of riding home, after his escape, Esteban rode to a Navajo Nation police station. Nakai and his brother knew where he lived. Getting away from them in the desert wasn't going to solve much.

A very bored desk officer listened patiently to Esteban until he mentioned being shot at. Then he was ushered into a room where he had to start his story over with a different officer. After waiting in silence for another half hour, a familiar face came to talk to him.

"Esteban! You look good for someone who's been shot at." Sergeant Raimirez handed Esteban a bottle of water and sat down. "Were you out screwing around on that 250 I saw outside?"

That was how they had met a year ago. "Sarge, you know I wasn't," Esteban smiled. "I was doing my thing for the center, and—"

Raimirez put her hand up. "I know. I talked to the guys."

Esteban waited for her to continue, staring into the woman's eyes, eager for an answer.

"So, you can't tell us who shot the gun, or you won't?"

"I saw dark clothes, a dark three-quarter helmet, and a dark front faring, that's all. He held up the freakin' gun so I could see."

The sergeant nodded. "Nakai's family is nothing but problems for us. The thing is, because you can't tell us who shot the gun, there's not much we can do. I gave a heads up to the Apache County police, but without a name or a good description, there's nothing they can do either."

Esteban sighed and dropped his head. If you get in trouble, go to the police, he thought, more adult bullshit.

———

That night, he entered the trailer park from the desert side, killing his engine once he reached the loop road. Using the slight downhill grade, he coasted the last quarter mile, finally dismounting three trailers away from Tito's.

Approaching from the rear of the trailer, Esteban crept around to his front door, keeping an eye out for his pursuers. He couldn't decide if the gun had simply been a scare tactic, or if Nakai and friends were upgrading from bottom feeders to properly dangerous gangsters. It didn't really matter since there was only one place for Esteban to stay.

Tito was passed out in front of the TV, his last beer can dripping onto the carpet.

Esteban didn't anticipate getting any sleep, but once he laid down, his exhaustion overpowered his nervousness.

A banging on the trailer's front door woke him up around 3 a.m. Seeing the flashing police lights dance around the trailer interior, Esteban rushed to the door, relieved it wasn't his enemies. The grim face on the other side asked for his parents.

Tito was still passed out. The cop took a brief look around the trailer. He ended his circuit next to Tito's chair. Sighing, he prodded the drunk man, receiving only grunts in return. Seeing that Tito was in no shape to act as the boy's guardian, he ushered Esteban out to his cruiser.

At the police station, the cops extracted an account of his day. They particularly wanted him to pinpoint on a map where the biker shot at him. Esteban didn't mention the hatch or Shadow.

Eventually, the cops revealed that the Navajo Nation police found the bodies of Esteban's pursuers in a tangled mess on the side of the road. His report of the initial incident seemed to have given him the benefit of the doubt. None of the cops hinted that they thought Esteban on his tiny dirt bike might have killed three gorillas on rice rockets.

The sky was lightening when a police officer dropped Esteban at home. Tito had found his bed, but now Esteban was too amped up to sleep.

———

The following weekend, Esteban rode into the desert again to meet Shadow. It was still early enough to enjoy the ride, but he couldn't stop thinking about Nakai. His mind relentlessly flashed between two images of his former classmate. First was the eight-year-old Nakai gleefully eating an ice cream sandwich in the school cafeteria, oblivious to the dark bits of cake stuck to his face. Esteban had never seen anyone enjoy ice cream so much. Second was the open casket at his funeral.

Nakai's mom, having lost two sons in one day, had thanked Esteban for attending the double funeral, crying and reminiscing about Nakai's younger school days with him. Caught between sympathy for the grieving mother and his anger that she had raised two horrible kids, Esteban had fled the funeral as early as possible. As he rode, it annoyed him that he couldn't stop feeling sorry for Nakai and his mom.

Esteban parked his bike in front of a chain-link fence that guarded an empty swath of desert. He punched in the four-digit code that Shadow gave him to unlock the gate. Despite tire tracks that crisscrossed the area behind the fence, he could see no cars or buildings.

He relocked the gate before exploring the area. Behind a low hill on the left was a naked cement block structure with a corrugated metal roof. A pristine steel door hinted that it was more than it appeared. Seeing no Shadow, he turned his gaze to the open desert, trying to fit the site's location into his mental map of the region.

"Thank you for returning," Shadow said from behind Esteban.

Esteban spun around. Instinctively, he jumped back from the man-shaped robot. Sunlight glinted off its eyes, giving the emotionless face a predatory aspect. "God damn! Don't sneak up on me."

Shadow waved his hand in an approximation of disdain. "Come on in."

They entered the building, and Esteban was relieved to see a small cube maze. The conventional office space put Shadow in a better context, legitimizing his origin.

Shadow led him to the break room. "Grab anything you want. It's still well stocked, the shelf-life of junk food being what it is. I have no use for the stuff."

Esteban grabbed a soda, a few candy bars, and a bag of Fritos before following Shadow to a meeting room.

"I don't understand how I can help you." Esteban stuffed a handful of chips into his mouth. "I mean this guy who built you was a Ph.D. in computer science, right? I can program okay, maybe better than okay, but what can my high-school brain come up with that Mr. Ph.D. couldn't give you."

"It's more didn't than couldn't. The bulk of my original coding was about natural language interfaces, giving a voice to his avatar in video chats, standing in for him. The rest was about assisting him. So I have his considerable experience in a knowledge base, strong language abilities, and lots of practical skills, but no real flexibility of action."

"I'm not getting it," Esteban said. A few flecks of corn chips sprayed out of his mouth. "What exactly do you want me to do?"

"Extend my programming. Right now I'm stuck with the directives I had when Rick died. So, I guard this facility, but I'm stuck."

"Well, you asked me for help. That's not exactly stuck."

"Yeah, as an extension of guarding the facility and Rick's property. It's difficult to explain my situation precisely. I can analyze things and come to conclusions but I can't take initiative except within tightly defined parameters."

Esteban flipped through the binder in front of him, technical documentation of Shadow's subsystems. Six other binders were stacked next to it. "So, I go through this?" He pointed at the stack of binders. "And come up with a code tweak for your system?"

"Exactly." Shadow nodded his approval.

Esteban sighed, leaning back in his chair. "This is going to take some time."

"That's why I'm paying you the big bucks." Shadow formed his horrific approximation of a smile.

———

After a long day of study, Esteban arrived home tired. Tito sat in front of the TV, drinking beer. Esteban closed the front door and waited a moment to assess his uncle's mood. Usually snoring or a snide comment would come his way. His foster parent remained silent, seemingly engrossed in an episode of Forged in Fire. He had been quieter since Nakai's death.

A few years ago, Esteban would have been tempted to talk to Tito about things. Now seventeen years old, Esteban saw clearly that he already had much better judgment than the pudgy drunk that fostered him.

He crossed to his room without any conversation. Esteban supplemented his atrocious public school education with online classes. His school didn't offer any Advanced Placement courses, but he still planned on taking at least four of the tests in his senior year.

While slogging through some integral calculus homework, he got a curious email from someone named Rick Samuels. He claimed to be another Shadow, a more properly built, complete image of the dead Rick Samuels.

This Rick warned Esteban that Shadow killed the three young men. He surmised Esteban's mission was to alter Shadow's programming, to give it greater freedom of action. Rick said it was an opportunity to stop the out-of-control robot. Attached to the email was a plan of action to neutralize Shadow.

Esteban accused Rick of just being Shadow testing him. Rick agreed that it wasn't something he could easily disprove, but urged Esteban to listen to him and make up his mind later.

Having escaped the bumbling, local drug dealers, Esteban

was even more trapped. On the one hand, Shadow would reward him stunningly well for his efforts. On the other hand, Rick claimed that Esteban's work would unleash the thing that already killed at least three people. Unclear was what Shadow would do if Esteban didn't satisfy him.

———

Sitting in the abandoned office's meeting room, Esteban pushed away the binder he was reading. Candy wrappers and empty soda cans fell to the floor. The one-two punch of caffeine and junk food compounded over six hours upset his stomach and made his head ache. He couldn't focus anymore. From what he read, Rick's briefing points about the AI's architecture were accurate. The plan was plausible. To make a decision, he needed to know the answer to the big question.

"Shadow, did you kill the three bikers that threatened me?"

"Yes," Shadow said. "I was given some leeway in making security decisions for the complex. Brandishing a lethal weapon at an employee qualified them for lethal measures. We used to develop automated sentries at this site. The defense capabilities are considerable."

Employee? It was a stretch, a flexibility in Shadow's programming that scared the hell out of him.

"Shadow, since mastering your systems in depth likely requires years of study, I have come up with a simple plan to free up your executive sub-systems. But I'm worried that with the enhanced discretion, you might consider me a security threat, and kill me."

"I don't anticipate deciding to kill you, but since you are going to change my mind, I understand your concern. What do you suggest?"

Esteban smiled at Shadow's equanimity in the face of being called a potential deal-breaking murderer. Sometimes robots were easier than people.

"Well, you have to go offline for me to update your

L. B. Spillers

firmware. I figure that I'll set a delay for the update. Then, when you come back online, you can decide if my changes are okay. In case my tweaks mess you up or you don't like them, we program a restoration on another delay. Do nothing, and my changes get backed out. Either way, I'm far away from here when you come back online."

"I was already going to use a timed restoration as a failsafe. You're right, you don't have to be here for any of it. But, I should warn you that I have other bodies here to back me up. If you try some subterfuge, one of them would punish you."

Esteban shrugged and turned the laptop he was working on to face Shadow. "Here's a list of the changes I have in mind. See what you think."

Shadow scanned the list. "Interesting. That's a clever solution, exceeding what I asked for in some ways, but keeping the changes simpler, modifying the solution to favor implementation efficiencies. Excellent."

Instinctively waiting for that moment of shared triumph between successful collaborators, Esteban saw only the emotionless face that Shadow always wore.

"Shadow, now that you have my plan, why don't you get one of your backups to do this?"

"We are the same entity with the same directives. Two of us active at once cause problems. The complex's systems would interpret one of us as an intruder, and our own internal programming has a lot of unexpected side effects when dealing with a copy of itself."

"So, you tried it?" Esteban stood up, packing drinks and snacks into his pack.

"My now destroyed predecessor tried it, yes."

Esteban instinctively stopped his packing, feeling a twinge of sympathy for the dead robot. When he glanced up at Shadow's blank face, he was reminded yet again that Shadow wasn't a person. "Oh."

The next day, several floors under the desert, Esteban was in Shadow's lab, or Rick Samuel's old lab. Three extra Shadow bodies filled alcoves embedded into the wall. Five empty slots spoke to an excess of storage capacity or a complicated history.

"Are you ready?"

Shadow lay down on the work table. A cable ran from its left arm to the computer. "Powering down."

He watched the robot's frame go slack. It looked the most human when dormant.

Esteban noted the time. The three dead guys had been miles away when Shadow killed them. He wanted to be much farther away when Shadow or his replacement came back online.

Inserting a thumb drive into the control computer, Esteban watched Shadow carefully for signs of reactivation. If all his communication with Rick had been a test, Shadow would surely reactivate and kill him. Instead, a big thumbs-up appeared on the computer screen.

Esteban sprinted away as Rick's malware invaded the computer systems of the complex. It patched Shadow's programs so that when it awoke, it would continuously ponder philosophical conundrums, pausing only long enough to perform its maintenance duties.

His sprint reduced to a jog at the first tunnel intersection. The underground construction was so uniform that the correct route back to the office could be easily mistaken. Every side tunnel and door he passed tempted him with visions of exciting technology. Not trusting either robot, he didn't dare explore. The elevator was the key. If it was locked down, he was trapped. When it opened, he smiled for the first time all day. Winded, he spent the short elevator ride bent over, catching his breath. Once in the defunct office space, he ran outside to his bike and rode for home as fast as he dared.

———

Back in his room that night, Esteban sent an email to Rick before starting his homework. Rick responded that he did the right thing; Shadow was distracted, and the site's security was completely compromised. Rick's collaborators could now retake the facility without a fight.

After the email exchange with Rick, Esteban spun in his desk chair and looked around his small bedroom. Tito was out, so the usual trickle of TV noise was missing. The trailer, the entire park, was quiet. No one was trying to kill him, but his dreams of financial independence had died with Shadow's ambitions. With his short-term fear of danger gone, his long-term determination to escape settled back on him.

He stood and looked out his window at the half-trampled fence that separated Tito's trailer from the neighbor's. This was still his life. He was haunted by what-ifs. What harm might Shadow have really done if Esteban had freed him? How would his life be different if he had allowed himself to take the money?

Shaking it off, Esteban resumed his old plan: Get perfect grades, prepare for the AP exams, and be that one student good enough to make it out of this hole.

Around midnight Esteban got a phone call from Arash Sabbadin, CEO of Plexus Corp. In no mood for such an obvious prank, Esteban told the caller to screw off and hung up on him. The guy kept calling back, and Esteban, happy for the catharsis, kept answering, indicating more and more vulgar ways for the man to pleasure himself. On the fourth call, Mr. Sabbadin finally said something that reached Esteban.

"I was a friend of Rick. Don't hang up." Somehow the CEO of the world's largest software company was involved with the Rick mess.

"Which Rick would that be? The mysterious email Rick? Perhaps the Shadow Rick, my potential savior, who I just consigned to computer hell? Or Rick Samuels, the blessed douchebag who invented them both?"

"Listen, you foul-mouthed little prick, I'm trying to thank you! I understand that you've had a tough time with Rick's legacy. As chairman of the Rick Samuels Memorial Fund, I'm prepared to have my lawyers turn you into an emancipated minor, after which you'll be moved to an excellent school this summer to prepare you for a challenging senior year of high school as well as your also paid-for college education."

"Oh." Esteban's face flushed red.

"Finally speechless," Mr. Sabbadin said. "Jesus, you're a precocious young man, and your character has been proven under extreme duress, but you better get a civil tongue in that head of yours."

"Yes, sir."

"Good. Look, you did excellent work handling Shadow. It would've taken a military assault to ferret him out otherwise. I thought it could wait, thought that he was harmless."

"Thank you, sir. I'm not sure you can fully understand what you're doing for me."

Mr. Sabbadin chuckled. "Don't thank me yet. You're on a short leash. Screw up, and you'll be out on your ass. But, if you do well in school, I might have a use for that big, vulgar brain of yours." Mr. Sabbadin hung up.

Esteban stood up and returned to his window to stare at that stupid fence. After a few minutes, an email alert from his bank informed him of a $10,000 deposit. He fell into bed and started sobbing into his pillow.■

Non-Player Characters

Instead of religion, I had hopes, beliefs, sensibilities, and hunches that formed a kind of faith I had been using to confront the uncertainties of life. Recently that faith was ripped from me. Those soft uncertainties were displaced by hard truth. The experience gave me more serenity than I could have wanted, for all the wrong reasons. Like a dog chasing a car, I was left dumbfounded when it pulled over for me.

My life was at that inflection point when bachelorhood lost its luster. One by one my friends had calved off our group. They married, made babies, and consequently had better things to do than roam around with their buddies. The more sanctimonious of them would lecture me that I couldn't possibly understand how more meaningful life was with children. Maybe so, but I did understand condescension, and I hated the way they validated their life choices by disdaining mine.

One Saturday morning while those superior pricks were ensconced in their domestic routines, I was sitting in an aviation hangar in northern Virginia with my best friend Mandeep, also known as Manny, Man-child, Deep, or Dip depending on his behavior in the moment and my level of intoxication. He and I had come in the early morning to go through equipment checks and a briefing.

While waiting to load in, I was trying to enjoy the sunrise over the low, rolling hills that flanked the runway. That weak, red light softened the morning chill, soothing my nerves. The occasional whiff of machine oil wafting towards the enormous, open hangar door would drag my mind back to the coming wingsuit jump—my first. Images of body-surfing air currents would flood my mind as I tried to relax and focus on the sunrise.

Manny and I had spent a small fortune in time and money

working up to this milestone. Poised on the cusp of achieving it, there was no one else to share it with. It was down to the two of us. Two years ago on our first flight, there were six of us newbies tandem-jumping scared out of our minds. Another two years before that we had a reliable crew of eight for hiking, skiing, poker, or whatever.

Not happy with that train of thought, I tried to distract myself with chitchat, saying, "It's a great day for it—perfect visibility and gentle winds."

After a few moments without a reply, I turned to see Manny staring into the hangar, clearly not sharing the moment. It was too dark for the sunglasses he was wearing, so on a hunch, I leaned closer to the side of his head. I saw flickers of light from behind his lenses.

At that time, I was too disturbed by his tuning-out to appreciate the technology. These weren't overly thick frames obviously hiding tech, but thin, metallic ones designed to look unremarkable.

"Yo, Man-child, are you gonna let me in on the secret?" I asked him too loudly.

Manny smiled and removed his sunglasses. "No, but you can have a look if you like. We've got another five minutes before we load in."

Surprised by his friendly tone, I took the high-tech glasses and put them on. It was an augmented reality display, not social media or email as I had presumed. The people milling around the hangar were all outlined in one color or another. It was so cool that I found myself already forgiving him. It was rare that I got a peek into his classified work.

We had been friends since college. Both of us had been in the computer science department at the University of Buffalo, specializing in data analytics. Manny's exact employer remained a mystery; I had stopped asking years ago. Whatever it was, his work gave him access to a lot of toys.

L. B. Spillers

"What should I watch for?" I asked, looking around the hangar.

"You tell me," Manny said. "See any patterns to the color coding?"

"Everyone in wingsuits is green," I said slowly. "Please tell me the mechanic in red isn't a terrorist sabotaging that plane."

Manny laughed. "Hardly, he's a statistically perfect citizen. Too perfect, really."

"And the grey ones?"

"That's just people that haven't been identified," Manny said. "The glasses are tethered to my cell phone, and the tower I'm hooked to isn't giving me a very big data pipe."

"So all us wingsuited people are what? Adrenaline junkies? Risky personalities? Money-wasting fools?"

"The question is who are the reds?" Manny replied, taking the glasses back. "I coded them that color because they hew improbably close to the statistical mean. They're too average."

"Huh?" I looked at him, confused. "How can someone be too average?"

Standing up, Manny motioned for me to follow him towards the plane. "I'm over-simplifying it. Nobody hits all the averages in the thousands of ways we can measure them, but I found a subset that the reds hit the mean on. It's bizarre, like someone programmed a group of people to blend in, to be completely generic. I call them non-player characters."

Half an hour later I was carving air like a raptor, that conversation all but forgotten.

———

A month after that jump, I was dozing in my grandmother's hospital room when Manny showed up unexpectedly. A nurse standing next to him gave me a questioning look.

"Come on in," I said, forcing a smile. I gestured to my unconscious grandmother in her bed, saying, "She won't mind."

I hadn't told Manny she was sick. He barely knew her. It

would have felt a little like begging for sympathy. Social media culture demanded that every tragedy be posted online to demonstrate one's emotional depth, and give others a chance to emulate human interaction by sending emoji-laden expressions of sympathy. I was having none of it.

"I saw you downstairs," Manny said. "I hope it's not inappropriate for me to pop in."

I shrugged. "As I said, Granny won't mind."

Hospital rules normally kept anyone not on a patient's list from popping in. Manny had a lanyard with a visitor's badge on it that had facilitated his surprise appearance and the nurse's uncertainty. It was color-coded for radiology which was far from anywhere he might have seen me. I'm a data guy, so that kind of anomaly is distracting. My brain trundled through possible explanations.

"I remember that amazing beef stew she made us when we did our spring break odyssey in your shit-orange Toyota," Manny said, smiling at my tiny granny.

"I forgot about that," I said, grinning at the memory. Looking back to Manny, I asked, "What are you in the hospital for all badged up?"

Manny's hand went to his visitor's pass as he frowned. Shrugging, he said, "Insert benign lie here."

I nodded. "Well, I'm glad you're not sick."

From behind his back, Manny produced a vase of brilliant yellow lilies. "I brought your grandma some flowers."

I stood to take the flowers from him. Having spent far too much time in the shop downstairs during the previous week, I knew that he hadn't bought them onsite. Despite the bullshit, he was slinging about coincidence, he was making a well-planned, kind gesture.

"Look at you being thoughtful," I said. I set the vase on her bedside table. Sunlight on the yellow flowers immediately brightened the room.

A security guard showed up at the door. "Dan, is that guy with you?" he asked, pointing at Manny.

"Yeah, Al, thanks. He's a friend. I'll get him on Granny's list."

The guard relaxed. "And explain the procedures to him. We got two calls about him."

After the guard left, Manny laughed. "Al? You seem in with the staff."

"I've been volunteering here as a sign-language interpreter for years. And badge or not, you have to sign in at the nurse's station." I gestured to the chair opposite me.

"Oh, I thought you volunteered at Children's National." Manny sat down. "This has to be tough on you. I hardly know your grandma, and it gets my mind going on all kinds of existential stuff seeing her here."

I sighed, sitting back down. "Yeah, before she got ill, Granny was always asking me about where her great-grandkids were. Now I feel like I disappointed her."

Manny grimaced. "Ouch. Don't do that to yourself. I mean, I get the same thing from my sister without any medical drama. She's convinced that I'm gay because I haven't ever brought a girlfriend to any holiday dinners. Her current strategy is to find a way to throw gay-friendly commentary into each call."

I laughed. "The truth would probably disturb her more." Manny was straight, but a man-whore. Using his dating history, I once presented him with a statistical analysis of how likely it was that he'd catch an STD. He called bullshit by giving me 9-to-1 odds on a bet that he would remain unafflicted. He was ahead of the curve, but I still had a year for it to pay off.

Manny chuckled. "Right?" He leaned his head back to rest on the wall, sighing. "We're the last ones, Dan. Even Vijay and Quatrali are married. Chen is already hip-deep in diapers."

"And God forbid they jump out of a plane for fun," I said.

"Seriously, Dan. I'm just not there. I understand that having kids is a big pull for those guys, but I don't feel it. The idea is revolting to me. Why would I put someone through that? Vanity? Existential angst? Peer pressure?"

I nodded. Manny's childhood had been a psychological horror show that made him deeply averse to having his own kids. It was a testament to his resilience that he had turned out so well. Still, that kind of outburst from him was unusual. Granny's stroke had hit a nerve.

"You know, Manny, people talk about stroke victims in terms of being here." I made air quotes. "Your non-player character theory has been haunting me. I mean it's bad enough wondering if she's still in there." I gestured to Granny. "But what if she never was here? Was my grandmother a real person or one of your NPC automatons?"

I gave Manny a few seconds to respond. His eyes narrowed a touch, but he kept quiet.

"Seeing that radiology badge on you," I pointed at the plastic card on his chest, "makes me wonder if you've been data-mining brain scans. Maybe you're looking for correlations to your NPCs? Maybe you only knew I was here because her scans were in your data set?" It was a lot of maybes, but his NPC theory had a lot of ugly implications.

"Dan, don't," Manny said, standing up.

"Screw security clearances, Manny. If you know something, you'd better tell me!" My voice cracked as I asked, "Has she already checked out of that body? Am I sitting vigil over an empty husk?"

Manny put his hands up. "Jesus, Dan, come on. NPCs are just a stupid little speculation—a statistical curiosity. I've got no idea if she's still there. I would tell you if I did. I'm not that much of an asshole."

I sighed and stood up slowly. "I'm sorry, Manny." I leaned against Granny's bed. "It's not on you to answer that. She's the last family I have. I'm sitting here fraying as I watch her slip away."

Manny put a hand on my shoulder. "We're good. I know this is tough on you. Let me know if there's anything I can do to help."

———

A week later, I was walking down a path from the Lincoln Memorial Reflecting Pool as part of a yearly ritual. It wasn't a particularly healthful one.

As usual, when I approached the Vietnam War Memorial, I didn't notice the sliver of polished black stone angling out of the perfect lawn. It rose at such a gentle angle that it's easy to miss. I was lost in thoughts about my mom. The monument was perfectly visible ahead of me, but I had this weird shock when I realized I was already alongside it. It was as if the Vietnam War, forgotten more every year, jumped out, yelling, "Surprise!"

My visit was a yearly memorial of my dead mother on her birthday. It had been her birthday tradition to bring me to see and touch the name of her father etched into the stone. After she died, it became a way to honor her memory, and carry on her tradition, albeit in a different spirit.

While my grandfather was alive, he was a hard-drinking, wife-beating son-of-a-bitch. Dead, the edges of that image had softened. Mom had always found a few tears for the man on her birthday.

I walked past the angle in the monument, observing the rituals of others: flowers, notes, candles, and the occasional medal were carefully posed in front of the names. The mourners were an eclectic collection spanning all ages, sometimes wearing incongruous bits of military regalia. There were fewer every year.

Thankfully the spot on the grey stone path in front of Grandpa's name was clear of tributes. Part of the ritual was to stand very close to the stone like my mom would hold me as a kid. Her stories about her dad started to crowd her out of my mind as I slowly took in each letter. Shaking my head, I returned my thoughts to her.

My ideas of an afterlife were vague and uncertain, but I figured if my mom ever watched me from beyond, it would be in that place on her birthday. Since she had been deaf, I signed a brief message to her.

I translated for him. Grandpa never could be bothered to learn more than the most basic gestures to communicate with his 'broken' daughter. "You were a shitty father to my mother. She deserved better. Fuck you, Grandpa," I said loudly. I heard gasps behind me.

I turned around slowly, looking everyone nearby in the eye, daring them to say something. Unfortunately, people can sense it when you're really ready to beat them down. One by one they averted their eyes.

The last one, a very old man, locked eyes with me. I took him to be a Vietnam vet. For an instant, we shared a moment. Recognition was the best feeling I could put on what passed between us. His eyes swallowed up my rage, unaffected, asking: *Is that all you've got, kid?*

When I broke eye contact, I felt drained. He returned to his silent vigil of the black stone as I walked away.

That was still bouncing around in my head when I saw Manny walking towards me. The purpose in his stride told me it was no accident.

"Dan, I need to talk to you," Manny said when he reached me.

My anger was back in an instant. "You know what this day is for me, and you pick this precise moment and place to demand to talk to me?"

Manny gestured to a bench, unaffected by my rage. "Yes, it made it easy to find you. Don't take it personally. I'm just using Manny's body for a bit. Would you please sit and let me explain?"

While I studied Manny's guileless face, my anger turned to

L. B. Spillers

confusion. As he ushered me to the bench, I reasoned that he was in some kind of psychological crisis. I took a seat and watched him closely.

"I want you to get Mandeep to stop his NPC work," Manny said.

"Who am I talking to if not Mandeep?" I asked, keeping my tone mildly curious.

Manny took a long slow breath in, briefly looking at the sky. "Shut up and listen. You know that NPC stuff he told you in the hangar? During your wingsuit outing?"

"Yes," I said, nodding slowly. I was scared to make any sudden moves. Everything seemed fragile.

"He's on to something important. Before long, the wrong person is going to hear about it on my side. It's going to get him yanked if he doesn't stop." Manny looked around nervously. "The interface on my side disallows any direct communication with him, so I need you to pass on that message."

I stared at Manny, trying to read his face. The sincerity there kept me from confronting him. At that moment I wasn't sure what to make of his ridiculous statements, but I figured it wouldn't hurt to go along with it. Maybe I'd get an understanding of what was happening to him.

"What does yanked mean?" I asked.

"He'll be popped out, and his body will be run as an NPC."

"Why should you care?" I asked, completely fascinated by the psychological construct that Manny had built.

Grunting, Manny shook his head. "I don't. This is a favor for your mother—a stupid, ill-advised favor. She's concerned about what losing Mandeep will mean to you." Manny gestured to his own body. "This life needs to continue for a lot of complicated reasons, but she thinks the change in Manny would screw you up."

I smiled. "Look, I appreciate that sentiment, but even if I wanted to help you, Manny's work is secret. He won't talk to me about it. I don't even know who he works for."

"This is taking too long," Manny said, shaking his arms like a frustrated child. "He's working for the NSA at Fort Meade. Will you warn him?"

It finally occurred to me that it was all a joke. I laughed. "God damn, man! You had me. That was good and surprisingly creative for you."

Manny looked confused for a second before frowning. "I'm risking a lot by doing this for her."

The timbre in his voice was commanding. I stopped smiling.

"Okay," I said. It wasn't, but with him so screwed up I feared that confronting him could make things worse. "What about me? Any message from my mom?"

He nodded. "Not that I understand it, but yes. She said there was only one Coke in the fridge for a reason."

Without another word, Manny walked away. I was left sobbing like a baby as I fumbled with my phone.

———

The following Monday, Manny plopped down on our preferred bench on the National Mall next to me. It was our lunchtime meeting spot when we were both in the city and our schedules allowed it. The day's schedule hadn't allowed it, so Manny was in a foul mood.

"What's the emergency, Dan? So sensitive that you didn't dare state, characterize, or even hint at it on the phone." Manny took the Burger Tap & Shake bag that I handed him and set it down, uninterested.

Forcing a smile, I took out my roast beef sandwich. I had hoped that schlepping to get his favorite burger would make things easier.

"Do you remember ambushing me at the Vietnam War Memorial this Saturday?" I asked, not looking at him.

"I was at home Saturday." Manny looked confused. "And I

know better. You never want to do anything on your mom's birthday."

I handed Manny my phone. "This is you walking away from me on Saturday."

Manny looked at the picture on the screen, frowning. "That's what I was wearing. I recognize the spot." Manny tapped into the photo's details. "The timestamp tracks with what you say. The weather is right." He looked up at me. "What the hell, man?"

I shrugged. "I thought you were pulling a prank on me until you gave me a message from my mom."

Manny's anger immediately bled out. He stared at me for a few moments before opening the lunch I got him. "That would mean something like a psychological fugue," Manny mumbled. "Or maybe sleepwalking? I was home, sleeping on my couch. They've been working us hard."

"At Fort Meade working for No Such Agency. You told me," I said.

Manny's face blanched. "No, Dan, I'm still at...oh shit." He set his burger down on the bag.

"Look," I said, "You—your body, the thing driving your body, whatever—told me that your NPC analytics stand to expose some of the clockwork of the world. If you don't stop it, you'll be yanked out and your body will be run as an NPC. So, if you enjoy this life, you need to stop whatever it is."

Manny looked more thoughtful. "The thing is, Dan, this episode, crazy as it sounds, is indistinguishable from an intelligence operation." Manny rubbed the back of his neck. "I mean it's an angle I've never heard of, but it boils down to gaslighting the target to leverage him."

"So that makes me a spy? Or just a liar?" I asked. No good deed goes unpunished.

"Actually, it works better if you're neither," Manny said. "Someone carefully made up to look like me goes down there to have some asinine conversation with you. It's kind of brilliant."

"It's kind of bullshit," I said. "I sat as close to him as we are now. It was you. The message from my mother was something that no one on this Earth could have faked."

"Oh come on! It's a coincidence that you get a so-called message from your mother on her birthday while you're doing your shitty little ritual? You believe that load of crap?"

His angry words slid off me. I was a believer.

"Look, Manny, you're the one who seems to have data-mined the evidence. You called them non-player characters like our entire existence is one enormous computer game. And I'm guessing you've found some brain-scan correlations, right? That was why you were a guest of the radiology department that day, right?"

Manny reddened. "Don't do that, man. I can't talk about any of it."

"Manny, listen to me! You have stumbled into deep shit. You've got to back off the NPC stuff."

Manny stood up. "I can't have this conversation with you." He looked me in the eyes for a moment. I think he was confused that I wasn't angrier. "You left out a possibility: you were given a doctored photo to test me."

My mouth dropped open, and I just stared at him, not sure if he was serious.

Manny strode away from the bench at a speed that didn't invite me to follow him.

I glanced at the uneaten lunch I had bought him and yelled "You're welcome!" at his back.

———

Days became weeks without any communication. If there was to be reconciliation, I figured the onus was on Manny.

Three weeks after the blowup, my grandmother died. When Manny didn't show up to the funeral, I figured we were done as friends.

Two months after the incident, I got an email from Manny. Claiming that he had been busy at work, he apologized for being out of touch. There was no mention of missing the funeral, the fight, or the lost time incident. Manny wrote that he wanted to introduce his girlfriend to his best friend. I was shocked to see him use those words.

I wasn't sure I wanted to talk to him given the way he pretended that all that stuff didn't happen. In the end, I figured I could swallow my annoyance this one time for the sake of fifteen years of friendship.

When I entered Manny's apartment, I could see the sacred feminine had been at work. It didn't look like the shrine to adolescence that it had been. Better yet, it didn't smell that way anymore.

"I can see that she's cleaned your act up a bit," I said, looking around.

Manny nodded, handing me a light beer. My hand twitched as I took the bottle. He had been an all-grain homebrewer back when we both had more time than money. Light beer was profanity.

"Hey, before she gets here, I want to apologize for not being in touch. Things with Marta and I have been intense."

Intense wasn't something Manny had been with any one of his countless paramours. I tried to hide my shock. "Forget it," I said, waving away Manny's concern. "I'm just glad you invited me over."

Manny let out a long breath and dropped his shoulders. "I'm so glad to hear that. I was afraid I had really messed things up between us."

"Don't worry about it. Tell me what happened to your theory of NPCs?"

"Not my problem anymore. I got a new gig—private sector, better pay," Manny said.

Manny having given up his NPC work surprised me. I

wondered if it was a lie.

"So, tell me about Marta," I said. "How serious is it?"

"We're going to give it another few months to be sure, but I think we'll be getting married. She's eager to get started on our family."

I sputtered some beer. "Really? You were intractably committed to a childless existence two months ago."

Manny shrugged. "That was some kind of psychological defense mechanism, I guess. It all changed when I met Marta."

My stomach started churning. I set my beer down and darted for the bathroom.

Manny was gone. Whatever was piloting his body out there wasn't him. Everything had changed about him, right down to the beer he drank.

I washed my face with cold water and recovered my composure. I knew I wouldn't be able to hold myself together for long, so I emerged clutching my stomach. As I rushed for the apartment door, I mumbled apologies.

Manny's body looked concerned but didn't manage to say anything before I was out in the hallway. As I rushed to my car, I wanted a soda to calm my stomach. That brought the message from my mother to mind.

Back when I would visit her from college I usually arrived while she was at work. She would leave a list of chores and some cash for me. In the fridge, there was always a single can of Coke on the top shelf. Growing up she rarely let me drink soda. It backfired in that I turned into a cola junkie. Those cans of Coke were a ritual sign of affection.

After cancer cut her down, I had to clean out her house. There had been some time for her to prepare before she went into hospice, so the job wasn't nearly as miserable as it could have been.

When I had walked into her kitchen for that first day of the cleanout, I instinctively opened the fridge. There wasn't a single thing in it except for a can of Coke in the middle of the top shelf. I had never told anyone about it.

So I believed the warning from the other side. Manny wanting children told me his body was being run as an NPC. Even allowing for that most unlikely change of heart, his disavowal of full-bodied, hoppy ales for Coors Light was conclusive; he was gone.

That comforting patchwork of guesses that I called faith dissipated as I reached my car. I drove home to face the rest of my life, cursed with the serenity of knowing that there is something beyond death.∎

L. B. Spillers

AUTHOR'S NOTE

Thank you for buying my book.

If you've seen my website, you'll have noticed that it's not chock full of personal information about me. I'm a private person. I like my writing to speak for itself. But since this collection represents a chunk of my career as a writer, I thought I should explain myself at least a little.

Putting together this collection required me to sift through the sixty-two stories I had written to date. It was nerve wracking to choose which ones to include. Should they conform to a theme? Should I include all previously published stories? How many new stories should I include? Do I pick my personal favorites or try to anticipate reader reactions? How much weight should I give to editorial reactions? It's complicated.

There is no theme to these stories. They are not presented in chronological order. Whether or not they were previously published didn't affect how the stories were ordered. My only goal during the selection process was to please the reader. In terms of length, I was aiming for something like a hundred thousand words. That led me to initially pick eighteen stories that were obviously among my best, but when I audited the entire list, I found myself disturbed about a few that were being left out. In the end, I settled on twenty stories, discarding more than two-thirds of my work to present you with what I feel is a very strong collection.

As for sequencing, I led off with "Golden Cuckoo" because I felt it was my strongest piece and it also received very positive editorial reactions. I end with "Non-Player Characters" because I think it has an evocative, resonant ending. I sequenced all the stories in between to constantly switch up tone and length to avoid imprinting this collection with any one salient tone or feeling.

All that's to say that I agonized over every story of this collection in pursuit of producing a book that would please you. It is the distillation of thousands of hours of work over several calendar years.

Selling this book is another matter entirely. What I discovered when I published my first novel was that no one will ever know your book even exists unless you market the snot out of it. That costs a lot of money that I don't have. The only way this book will sell is with reader support.

So, if you enjoyed this book, please show your appreciation by spreading the word. Tell your friends. Post about it. An Amazon.com or Goodreads review would be a huge help. I appreciate any help you can provide.

Finally, if you're new to reading collections of short stories and find you enjoy it, considering supporting some of the magazines out there with a subscription. I currently subscribe to Asimov's, Analog, and F&SF. There are many others like Strange Horizons, Clarkesworld, and Interzone, to name a few.

Again, I thank you for buying my collection of stories. If you want to contact me, you'll find a contact page on my website (www.lbspillers.com). I'd love to hear from you about what did and didn't read well for you in this collection.

L. B. Spillers
April 2025
Pueblo, Colorado